Six Days in June

ISBN: 978-1-935356-40-0

Cover photo: "Solitary Stroll" taken on Lake Michigan by Andrew Soundarajan—Vision & Light Photography

First edition, published by Joker's Conundrum LLC

Chris Zimmerman

P.O. Box 180

Shepherd, MI 48883

E-mail: setterindebtor@yahoo.com

Website: www.authorchriszimmerman.com

Printed in the United States of America

Six Days in June

CHRIS ZIMMERMAN

Also by Chris Zimmerman:

INTENTIONAL ACTS

THE SECRET-KEEPER

THE COVENANT FIELD

FORTY MILE POINT

JUROR 55

One

Whack!

I looked up from a sip of coffee just in time to see a deer blast off the hood of my truck, carom off the windshield, and catapult into the stratosphere. The noise, and the sudden, split-second thud of the collision nearly took my breath away.

Most traffic accidents come with a little warning, don't they? I'm thinking screeching tires, a slippery road, or a blown stop sign. In those instances, it makes it easy to brace yourself for impact.

When I plowed into the deer, however, there was no warning.

All I know is that I was driving sixty-five miles an hour—feeling the warm coffee please my taste buds—when the animal bashed into the front of the Suburban.

I was trying to see where the deer might come down, while at the same time concentrating on driving the truck to the side of the road. The deer was somewhere out of view, eventually surrendering to the laws of gravity.

I caught myself thinking, *not in my brand new boat.*

Of course, I couldn't have been that lucky.

In the rearview mirror, I saw the deer land on the boat's windshield, then bash each seat on its way to the stern.

"Oh, no!" I cried.

The noise from the collision—mixed with the gush of adrenalin from such an impact—jump-started my morning, and ruined my fishing plans for the day.

I guided the old Suburban limping to the side of the expressway, near the grassy base of an overpass. The emergency flashers were engaged, and I stepped out of the truck to assess the damage. My windshield was splintered and broken, which matched the feelings in my heart. White smoke erupted from beneath the crinkled hood that had hair wedged into every crack and crevice.

My old truck was hurting.

What a bummer.

I looked behind me to where the incident took place.

It looked like the deer might have charged out of the cattails on the edge of US-10 and made a mad dash across the gauntlet of vehicles.

Was it a doe or last year's fawn that made the fatal error, or could it have been a buck? I suppose it was all irrelevant now; the point is that my fishing trip was over, my truck was going to be totaled, and my boat would have to wait till another day to see its first action on the water.

My wife, Colleen, was disappointed when I called her; not so much in the deer development, but that she had to give up her sleeping-in day to rescue me.

"Accidents happen," she sighed. "We'll be there in a bit."

"I'll be on the overpass, just east of the Valley Plaza Motel, east of Midland on US-10."

"See you soon."

My next call was to a towing company who said that they would be there right away.

And what about my new boat?

I walked behind the truck, stepped on the tongue of the trailer, and peered over the fiberglass nose. Inside was a mess. The deer didn't land on the windshield but rather the bow. It caromed off every fixture on its way to the stern. The darn thing smashed the pedestal seat in the front, the console, bent the rear seat, and part of the rigging for the canopy. It lay near the outboard motor—cracked limbs and all—deader than a doornail.

I went back to the stern, hoisted the corpse with two hands, and flung it onto the grassy shoulder of the expressway. Its bodily fluids and fur were everywhere—in spatters and spurts, wedged into cracks and crevices from stem to stern.

Deer are unique creatures. They have that tallow, musky flavor that sticks to the roof of my mouth when I'm eating it, and the odor clung to my hands after disposing of the body.

I opened the back of the truck, and pulled a water bottle from the cooler. A few minutes later, my hands were relatively free of the mess, but not necessarily the smell.

The sun was peeking out of the horizon; the sky, the wispy clouds, and even a passing flock of mallards were basked in the tangerine-colored glow of sunrise. In relative terms, all was right with the world on the breath of dawn, in the heart of mid-Michigan.

The roar of a diesel pickup truck interrupted my musing. I was in a bit of peril there, on the edge of the expressway, so I decided to climb the embankment and wait for my posse to arrive.

When I made it to the summit, slightly out of breath, I saw a woman standing on the overpass, thirty yards away. It seemed rather odd, so I ambled in her direction.

"Morning," I said.

She hardly acknowledged my greeting. I looked at her wardrobe and figured that she wasn't a jogger. We could have been twins, with our sweatshirts and blue jeans. All she did was lean over the guardrail and stare at the oncoming traffic.

"I saw you hit that deer," she said, at last. "It died instantly. No more suffering."

"How long have you been standing here?"

"I don't know, maybe half hour."

She rubbed the side of her face with her left hand. No wedding ring. She had a nose that made her look a little like a puffer snake: slightly up-turned, and nostrils carved out of the sides. No makeup and her hair was an absolute mess.

"What's your deal?" I asked.

"What do you mean?"

"What are you doing here?" I asked. "What's your story?"

"You sure are nosey. What are you some kind of reporter?" she asked.

"As a matter of fact I am a reporter for the *Gratiot County Recorder*. My name is Derrick Twitchell." I extended my hand for her to shake it. She turned me down.

I looked down at the traffic as it sailed by at a hefty pace. A logging truck rumbled past, loaded with tree trunks. For a half second I wondered what type of cargo was being hauled—cedars from the swamp edges, oaks from the highlands, or the pulpwood favorite: aspen.

"This is my last day on earth, so smell my breath."

Smell your breath? Why would I do that?

"What do you mean, 'smell your breath?'" I asked.

She looked at me like I was some sort of lame brain. "I said, 'this is my last day on earth, the hour of my death!'"

"Gee whiz, I'm sorry."

She sniffled, then reached into her pocket for a coin.

I wasn't sure what to say, or what to do. The coin had little relevance, at least that I could tell.

"They're hassling me at my job. I lost my house. My husband ran away with some floozy."

"The bank foreclosed?"

"Yes. I had no way to pay them without my husband's

income. I gave them everything I could afford. The bank didn't understand when the money ran out, and they wouldn't accept a short sale from a buyer." She seemed like a nice person, desperate for a solution to the pain coursing through her head.

A second semi truck captured her attention. Casually, she dropped the coin from her hand and together we watched it free fall until it was intercepted by the speeding tractor trailer.

All at once, I realized that she was serious about the "hour of my death" comment. The coin was her attempt to time her own fall, I assume, to get the biggest bang for her buck when she decided to take the plunge.

"You don't have to do this," I said.

"Oh, yes, I do. They're coming to get me."

"Who is? Come on, let's talk this through."

"The company. The government."

The woman never looked in my direction.

"What company? What government?"

She kept looking over the horizon with faraway eyes, like the woman in the Old Spice commercial, who was waiting for her man to return from the sea.

"Let's talk this through. You don't want to jump, do you?" I pleaded, taking another step her way.

Off in the distance, I noticed two more semis headed our way. I moved closer to the woman, and asked "Don't you have any friends to talk to? Maybe a priest or a counselor?"

"Just back off, will you? I'm done with this world. They're not going to get me."

"Who's not going to get you? At least tell me your name..." I urged her.

She was silent. Seconds passed as I thought of something to ask.

"Ma'am, how am I going to tell the police who you are?"

I took another step towards her when the semis were an eighth of a mile away.

"Back off, man," she snarled, flashing her left palm.

"Don't do this," I yelled, not sure what to say next. "Those truck drivers don't deserve this!"

The mystery woman broke her macabre concentration, and glanced in my direction.

"They're nice people," I said softly. "They have families and pets, a job to do." It seemed like a dumb thing to say, but I never was any good at thinking on my feet.

Instead of stepping away from the edge, the woman glanced at the oncoming traffic, and bent at the waist. The guard rail seemed to fold her in half as she began her descent, head first. I reached for her knees, her ankles, her feet, anything, but it was too late. She was gone.

"No!" I screamed, but it only seemed to hasten her fall.

It didn't take long until I heard the screeching brakes of the semi, and the thud of metal and windshield smashing flesh and bones. It was the second time in twenty minutes that I had heard the grisly *whack* of vehicular slaughter.

I ran across both lanes of the overpass, and looked down upon the faint trail of blood on the pavement. The semi slowed to a stop some distance away and southerly winds carried the stench of burning rubber. I watched the truck's emergency lights engage, then the driver get out of the cab. She was talking on her cell phone, I assume to the authorities.

It was a terrible scene. The driver looked up at the cab of her rig at what had to be a ghastly spectacle. I could only imagine the mess that the body had made, in and outside of the cab. No wonder the driver lit up a smoke. In the morning glow, she sat against the wheel of her truck, knees bent, one hand feeding her mouth the cigarette, the other hand kneading the skin on her forehead.

The cops would be along at any moment, I was certain. After taking photographs of the body, they'd cover it with a yellow plastic blanket. They'd close the left lanes of traffic and conduct their investigation, little by little. Of course, they would want to speak to me; I was the last person to see the victim alive.

Even though I didn't know the woman who had jumped, I was shaken up to see her die. I was upset and mad at the same time. There must have been something I could have done to prevent it from happening. It's not every day that you get so close to a suicide and all the nastiness that goes with it. I felt bad for her, and her family, whoever that was. The poor truck driver; I bet that she never goes beneath another overpass again without looking for a mad jumper.

All of a sudden, my day of fishing had gone from bad to worse. On the emotional roller coaster of life, I had my share of ups and downs for one day. Trouble was, the day was only a few hours old.

I tuned my back to the truck driver and rested against the guardrail of the overpass. The situation behind me was a terrible mess. It was just awful.

I focused my attention to where the woman leapt. My mind speculated to what I could have done to prevent it. Maybe I should have tackled her, been more adamant in my intervention, or called the police when I realized the severity of the situation. Hindsight is always twenty-twenty.

As I leaned against the guardrail of the overpass, listening to the sirens wailing in the distance, my eyes drifted to the place where the woman had made her fateful decision. There, on the concrete walkway near the guardrail, was an envelope. The woman must have been standing on it all along, and when she took the plunge, it was left behind.

I skipped across four lanes of traffic, opened the envelope, and pulled out the sheets of paper:

To Helen,

Surely the suddenness of my passing will come as quite a shock to you. For that, I am sorry. We had a lot of good times together, and I always thought of you as my best friend.

Daddy always said we should leave our mark on this world. Lord only knows I tried my best.

You should know that all my stuff is out of my apartment and my belongings moved into a storage facility on Wilder Road in Bay City. Locker number 224. The combination to the lock is 19.10.24. There's a small life insurance policy, car title, and papers in the bureau drawer. Take everything. It's all yours.

I cannot deal with the company's continuous hassling. I've told you about it before, but now it's unbearable. The government is just as bad.

I wish you well, Godspeed, and good tidings and my endless love.

Your devoted sister, Becky.

The letter fit on a single page, and was hand written. Things became even more interesting, however, when I read Becky's post script on the second page:

I should tell you that I believe I know who killed those people up north, the Garl family. I've written a letter to the Detroit Free Press, *who offered a $100,000 reward. All you have to do is tear off the corner of the page that has six numbers written on it. The* Free Press *wanted to keep the tipsters' identity a secret so they said to write six numbers on the letter and in the corner of the paper. They said to tear off the corner of the paper, so that we could remain unanimous in case my tip led to the* *conviction of the peeps who did it. If the paper says I won the reward money, take the corner piece of paper, and collect the prize. The money is yours to keep. The letter to the* Free Press *and a zip drive with all the evidence is located in Grandma's bureau drawer inside the storage locker.*

I was still a bit confused about what Becky might have meant by the whole "unanimous" details. The longer I thought about it, however, the more I realized that this was the *Free Press'* way of keeping leads pouring into their newsroom, while preserving the tipster's identity a secret.

It seemed as if she had something to live for; I thought. *The reward money itself was worth the price of existence.*

By then, a state police cruiser had pulled behind the idling semi. The truck driver was chatting with the trooper through the trooper's driver's side window. She was pointing up in my direction, recanting the visceral events that had just taken place. The trooper got out of his cruiser, placed his hat atop his head, and marched towards the front of the semi. After securing the area, and preserving the scene, he'd be wanting to talk to me.

With the letter still in my hand, I had to think about the Garl case from "up north." It was a mystery all right. Unsolved. Unheard of. The whole family of five wiped out. Mom and pop and the two sisters were shot in the chest, in double-tap fashion. The little boy killed with a hatchet or a small axe, police theorized.

I was vaguely aware of the *Free Press'* reward money and the Garl's case in general, but it never really captured my attention until now.

Since these circumstances landed in my lap, I felt a little compelled to pursue the truth.

Before the state troopers could take my statement, the tow truck had hauled away my Suburban, and Colleen had showed up on the scene. Traffic was snarled, bumper to bumper. Instead of trying to weave my way through three lanes of traffic to meet with the trooper, I attached the boat to her van, eased down the shoulder of the expressway, and drove away.

I'm always in a rush, a hurry, a major yank to get things done. There really wasn't much for me to say to the cops, anyway. She wanted to kill herself, and I couldn't stop her.

The contents of Becky's letter, and the notion that it might solve the mystery "up north" were the seeds that were sown in the garden of my imagination. Sometimes, newspaper stories start out small and evolve into something big. Occasionally, they don't amount to anything at all. This case—Becky the mad jumper, and Garls' grisly murder—had my journalistic juices flowing.

I am Derrick Twitchell: reporter, chief, cook and bottle washer at my very own newspaper, the *Gratiot County Recorder*. On that remarkable day in early summer, I never knew that those journalistic juices would lead me across the heart and soul of Michigan's peninsulas and involve more danger than anything I had ever experienced.

It all began simply enough—a fishing trip to Saginaw Bay—where it would end, I never knew.

Two

Colleen wasn't in the best of moods when she realized that her early morning trip to Midland was only half of her rescue detail. She loved to stay up late on Friday nights and sleep in on Saturday mornings. If anything interrupted her eight hours of rest, it had better be a good reason.

"What do you mean, we have to take the boat to the dealership?" she asked.

I looked at her as if it wasn't an especially smart thing to ask. After all, the boat, motor, and trailer were attached to her van's bumper and we were racing along with traffic on US-10. She read my body language—raised eyebrows and all—and took the last swallow of her diet Coke.

"Where is the dealership?" she asked.

"Bay City."

"Oh great."

Instead of thumping Colleen with the grisly details of Becky's suicide, I eased into the topic with a question about breakfast.

"Come on, Baby, let's go out for breakfast. How about a nice, big farmer's omelet?"

She curled a lip halfheartedly.

"Aren't you curious about why there were so many cops?" I asked her.

"Well, yeah," she countered, "seems a little extreme for just hitting a deer."

"There's a lot more to the story, Colleen. It's really, really sad, too."

Colleen sensed the conflict in my voice, the exhilaration in my actions. And when I whipped out Becky's letter, and handed it across the console, she was confused.

"What is this?"she asked.

"Sweetheart, I just witnessed a suicide. A woman just jumped off the overpass and left these papers behind."

After a moment of sifting through the papers and reading each word of the note, she looked at me and asked, "Derrick Twitchell, we need to turn around and give this to the cops!"

"If I give it to the cops we'll lose our chance at the reward."

"I know, but this is crazy, Derrick," she said, while running her fingers through her blonde mane. "Think the cops might be interested in this?"

"There really wasn't a crime that was committed, so I don't understand what's the big yank."

Her eyes quit glaring in my direction, and she focused on the road ahead. "I still think this is crazy. Don't tell me that you're going to break into that poor woman's storage locker after we take the boat to the dealership?"

I wasn't quite that far along in my train of thought. Leave it up to Colleen to be two steps ahead of me.

"I don't know about that," I hesitated. "Don't you think that's crossing the line?"

Colleen nodded. "A little."

"Then again, it might be a great way to find out who this Becky person really is."

She sat there, stoic as a cigar store Indian as we neared the intersection of I-75.

I had to think of something—an incentive of some sort. "Wouldn't it be great to cash in on the reward money?"

Colleen barely flinched so I prodded her gently.

"Sweetheart," I said, "the six numbers on the letter are like our very own lottery ticket. All we have to do is watch the news and follow the *Free Press*. If the Garl's murderers are convicted, and the *Free Press* announces these six numbers lead to their arrest, we'll be rich."

"Sure," she waxed sarcastic. "Like that'll really happen."

"What do you mean?"

"Derrick, let's just say that the cops solve the case and credit Becky's tip for the information...don't you think the *Free Press* will want you to validate the facts contained in the letter?"

She had me reeling.

"They won't just hand over the money and say, 'Here ya go' without making sure you're the one who wrote it."

By then, we were in Bay City headed east on M-25 amongst the mansions that were built more than a century ago. Some of them had been refurbished into funeral homes or law offices, with cement, gargoyle-like lions or dragons near the front porches.

"You don't even know if this Becky signed her name to the thing, or if her death nullifies the reward."

I grimaced.

"Derrick, you know I love you, but the newspaper business is as bad as ever. I doubt if the *Free Press* will fork over the cash if there's any doubt in their mind about the letter's authenticity. Can't you be a little more sensible?"

I sat there, somewhat deflated. She had, indeed, taken the wind out of my sails, especially with the comment about being sensible. My multi-tasking delusions of cracking the Garl case, and collecting the reward money, had slipped between my fingers.

Still, though, Colleen was a journalist at heart, and despite her busy schedule, I knew that she still had an occasional craving to cover a good old-fashioned mystery.

"So, what do you want to do, quit covering this thing before we even start?" I asked.

Colleen sighed. "Don't you remember what happened the last time you got involved in a major Michigan story?"

"Don't remind me."

"We lost twenty-five grand, that's what."

"Thanks for the reminder."

As we passed the Michigan Sportsman bait shop on the outskirts of Bay City, Colleen apologized. "I just don't want to get involved with this. It's just not a good idea."

I acknowledged her hesitation, and wheeled into the marina. The salesman was there to greet me, and was just as disappointed as I was with what had happened. I handed him my insurance agent's business card, and asked that he fax an estimate for the damage. Five minutes later, I was back in Colleen's vehicle and we were headed west, towards home, responsibility, and the daily grind.

"You know, Derrick, there's a Meijer on Wilder Road."

I smiled at Colleen. "Oh, really?"

"We need paper products and some cleaning supplies. It's not far from the storage place, I bet."

I nodded my head. Her message was loud and clear, "I'll be flying solo on this one."

"That's right. Just leave me out of it. Can you think of anything else on our grocery list?"

"Nope," I said, scratching my chin. "Maybe some massage oil?"

"You jackass," she frowned.

"Candles?" I prodded her. "We need red, scented candles. Maybe Barry White's greatest hits, a baby-sitter, and…"

"Walleye," she interrupted, "walleye for dinner. I'll see if it's on sale."

"Lovely. See if they'll trade the filets for a few dozen night-crawlers. That was my offer to the fish gods…"

"Yeah, dream on."

"I'll be back in a bit," I smiled.

"Just leave me out of it, okay?" she barked, "and don't be long."

I gave her a kiss on the cheek as she opened the car door. Instead of driving away, I watched her be-bop towards the entryway. Charming. Simply charming.

Now it was up to me and my conscience. The storage facility was only a half mile away, and as much as I wanted to explore Becky's storage locker, the thought of rummaging through her belongings seemed a little strange.

But I persevered.

The storage facility had a long, gravel drive between the rows of cubicles. Security cameras hung suspiciously on poles at every corner and for a moment, I regretted not covering Colleen's license plate with a paper bag or a tackle box bungeed to her bumper.

By then it was mid morning, and the world was starting to bustle. The noise from the traffic on Wilder Road carried into the metal and pebble-stone enclave.

I tried my best to act casually as I spun the lock's tumbler and found each number on the dial. A look to the south and north; the coast was clear. The wide, metal door was easy enough to hoist into the ceiling, and when I did, it revealed a ten by twenty foot area jammed with a lifetime of belongings.

Becky liked her antiques, it appeared. She had a chest of drawers, headboards, and an old wooden desk that looked like it could have been Abe Lincoln's. Almost every one of the pieces had an old-fashioned ice cream maker resting on it, complete with the crank. The paint was worn off some of those old gems; others had *Sonny Boy* or *The Alaskan* inscribed on them, plain as day. There were other fixtures too that were covered in ratty looking sheets, or canvas, oil-smelling drop cloths.

I stepped out of the door quickly and scanned the gangway for anybody who might ruin my investigation. Someone ten or fifteen bays away was loading cardboard boxes onto a flatbed trailer. He acted like he was in a hurry, just like me.

Trouble was I had no idea what a "bureau" was. As I looked around the cubicle, it could have been anything. There was a wooden desk, a two-drawer metal filing cabinet, and two small coffee tables; boxy, standing dressers with ornate, metal handles, and heavy, wooden chests stacked one on top of the other. Ice cream makers were everywhere.

Upon closer inspection, Becky's furniture pieces all had price tags on them. It's like she wanted to make sure that her sister got a fair price for her treasures at a memorial-style garage sale.

With that, I started opening and shutting drawer after drawer.

After fifteen or twenty guesses, I found the prize.

She had a whole stack of items. Her car title was there, signed and ready to be processed. A coupon book for her car loan. Becky's life insurance policy too, in its faux leather folder. Raymond James and Charles Schwab were present. They each had account statements and year-end information. Report cards from St. Cecilia, wherever that was. An eight by ten glossy of some freckle faced girl in pigtails. It seemed cluttered and unorganized. The further I dug in the stack of documents, however, the more newspaper clippings I saw towards the bottom.

I set all her personal stuff aside and dove into the meat and potatoes.

About three more photos down, I found a plain envelope with the words, *Detroit Free Press* typed across the face. Bingo.

This was what I was after. I took one last look around to make sure nobody was watching me. Even though I couldn't see far, the coast was clear.

I opened the envelope and took a quick inventory of what was inside: a zip drive and a letter, typewritten, plain paper. It had to be a copy of the letter she sent the *Free Press*, the buried treasure. I stuffed the letter and the zip drive back into the envelope and rammed both into my back pocket.

My attention turned to the remaining stack of clutter, which looked like memos and copies of emails. Damning evidence, no doubt, and worthy of a closer inspection once I buttoned up the locker and made my getaway.

Some of the newspaper clippings weren't clippings at all, but rather, entire pages of the *Charlevoix Courier, Petoskey News*, the *Saginaw News* or the *Free Press*. They were folded and tattered at the edges; a smoke-yellow color. I only caught a headline or two: *Massacre on the lake. Six months later, still no arrests.* For this journalist, it was red meat to a Bengal tiger.

I opened the dresser drawer, and put Becky's belongings back inside. The memos, emails and the papers were coming home with me. Never mind the walleyes; this was a fine catch.

I couldn't wait to show Colleen.

It was a wonderful find, a splendid haul, and we did it before the next of kin even knew Becky was departed.

I felt a little sorry for Helen as I covered the dresser with a drop cloth. It reminded me of a flag draped over a casket.

I spun to the open door, precious cargo in hand.

Blocking my escape was a man armed with a chemical sprayer shaped like a miniature beer barrel. The sprayer was long and eel-like, dripping chemical saliva from its pointy mouth. "I need a word with you."

Three

"Morning," I said, nonchalantly.

The man with the sprayer barely flinched, so I came at him again with the same meek greeting.

"I think you owe me something," he finally said.

"What's that?"

"Don't play smart with me." The goon never moved.

"Hey, hey," I tried to appease him, "I'm just a neighbor of Becky's. I don't know what you're talking about."

"The money. Becky never dropped off her security deposit."

"Oh, oh," I said reaching into my pocket, "how much is it?"

"Hundred."

"Oh sure, that's fair."

The twenties inside my wallet were mixed with a fifty, and a ten, and a few ones. I peeled four or five bills from the wad, stuffed them into his hand, and slid past. Without hesitation, I grabbed the overhead door handle, gave it a yank, and sent the door sliding down its tracks. The man with the sprayer folded the currency twice, and tucked it neatly into his breast pocket. No receipt, no thank you, or "have a nice day." He returned to his chore of spraying the tiny weed shoots amongst the gravel and stone. If he scribbled down my license plate, I didn't see him do it.

I buttoned up Becky's locker, jumped in Colleen's vehicle and was on my way. Colleen had sent me a text that said she was ready to be picked up in front of the store. Her timing was perfect, and the treasure in Becky's locker was just what the doctor ordered. It occurred to me that whacking that deer wasn't such a bad thing after all. If I hadn't hit the deer I wouldn't have met Becky, and if I hadn't met Becky, I wouldn't have this juicy story thrown in my lap.

I knew that I could talk Colleen into pursuing the story with me. Her reticence could only last so long.

And what a story it was.

Colleen tried to organize the information as we retraced our tracks through the streets of Bay City and west into the sprawling, rich farmland near Auburn and Freeland.

"Looks like she has all kinds of stories here, Derrick."

"Let's just cut to the chase, shall we?" I pleaded, "Read the letter she wrote to the *Free Press.*"

Colleen didn't have to be asked twice. She unfolded the envelope, pulled out the papers inside and used her phone to take pictures of everything.

> *Dear Free Press,*
>
> *For the past seventeen years I was Robert Luxton's personal assistant at the Drake Media Group in Grand Blanc, Michigan. They handled some of the government's printing obligations for Healthcare.gov as well as private companies throughout the state.*
>
> *My baby sister had a similar position at Cecil Garl's company Ener-X in Bay City . I say that she had a position there, because she quit several months before he was murdered. That Cecil Garl was a real jerk. More than once, he tried to take advantage of my sister in inappropriate ways.*

She told me that Cecil invited her into his office one day after work. He locked the door and asked her to sit down.

Colleen's head turned from the letter towards me. I rolled my eyes in mock disgust, how could anyone be so insensitive as to ask an employee to sit down?

My sister said that Cecil started saying things to her about 'what a great job she had done,' and 'what's in store for you and the company' and stuff like that. The next thing she knew, he started commenting on her dress and what nice legs she had."

Colleen glared in my direction

"Keep reading," I urged her.

The next thing she tells me is that Mr. Garl asked her to raise her skirt so he could see her legs. My sister didn't want to make the boss mad, so she did what she was told."

"Derrick, this is kind of foolish, don't you think?"

"Not yet. Let's just see what happens."

Colleen kept reading, *"Nothing sexual ever happened, but she did say that he told her 'he'd like to paint a nude portrait of her.' He was an art lover. The situation gave her the creeps and she eventually quit her job."*

"It really doesn't say much about who committed the murder, does it?" I asked.

"There's more to it," she added. *"Mr. Luxton, my boss, and Mr. Garl were business associates in that Mr. Luxton was a shareholder in Ener-X. Cecil Garl was a shareholder too and was one of the most vocal critics at the shareholder's meeting, which was held on the campus of Saginaw Valley State University. It's not like Luxton just pulled Mr. Garl aside, and had a few words with him. Nope, he used to take the microphone during the question and answer time and speak for five or ten minutes. I think he thought he was Gordon Gecko or something."*

Colleen and I were near the overpass where Becky had jumped. Instead of going east towards the bay, we were headed west towards our home in Mt. Pleasant. No cops. No trucker. No sign of death. The people driving by never knew what had taken place. It was just another late Saturday morning in mid-Michigan.

"When will she get to the point?" I asked.

Colleen held up a finger. *"What Mr. Luxton said at the board meeting before his death was what made me believe that Robert Luxton had a part in his murder."*

"Finally," I grimaced, "the crux of the story."

> *Watch the video of the board meeting. It's on the zip drive. Luxton took the microphone and said, 'it's time to take the company in a new direction. A vote of confidence for Cecil Garl will sink this organization. You want proof of his incompetence; look no further than this video.' With that, he played a video of Ener-X's design flaw with their solar panels. In fact, they're not panels at all, but tubes that are designed to catch more light. 'That design would work' he said, 'as long as the price for the raw materials remains low. As soon as the Chinese get involved it won't make financial sense. Ener-X is a ticking time bomb of failure.'*

Colleen flipped a page, *"Luxton didn't get enough votes to become chairman, and he was subsequently thrown out of the meeting. The company was getting financed through the Department of Energy. The mismanagement by Garl created the motive for Mr. Luxton to murder him. As for the weapon, I know that the Garl family was killed with a .25 caliber. Mr. Luxton had a .25 caliber handgun in his safe, which was mounted into the bathroom wall adjacent to his office. I seen it in there many times."*

I cringed when I heard "seen" it. Whatever happened to "saw"?

Look at the zip drive. Cecil Garl was a really good fundraiser for the president and his political party. He and his buddies donated thousands and thousands of dollars to his re-election campaign. In return, they received no-bid contracts from the Department of Energy.

Becky had made an excellent discovery. It was a sickening revelation about how the politically connected get their way before and after an election. That notion—of you scratch mine and I'll scratch yours—has been going on in politics for generations; much of it out of view of the public. I couldn't blame Cecil Garl for doing what he did. It seemed like a smart risk to take: bundle a bunch of money together and give it to the movers and shakers within the party. A wink and a nod later, and the unsavory understanding of a business windfall after the election was cast in stone. Even though I really didn't know much about Cecil Garl, it seemed like he was a ruthless, yet smart, businessman.

"Look at the zip drive," Colleen continued to read, *"It's all on there: The bank statements and secret slush funds, the gifts they bought her, the telephone conversations, texts and emails. Pay close attention to the folder titled Kelly Mathers. She's the top dog at the Department of Energy. We paid for lots of things for her. She loved to stay at the Grand Hotel and golf at Arcadia Bluffs north of Ludington, Oakland Hills downstate, and Egypt Valley over in Grand Rapids. Mr. Luxton thought they were schmoozing, but they were all bribes."*

Colleen shook her head. "Look at this, she has plane tickets and hotel receipts from Antigua. This is awful. I don't want you to do anything with this case. You're liable to get killed."

"What the heck, Colleen, this is what reporters do. We get into mischief. We search for the truth. We're the ones who expose what's going on behind closed doors. If it wasn't for us, the government could get away with whatever they wanted."

Colleen shook her head. I could tell that she was weighing the gravity of the situation before she started reading again.

> *Drake Media called the plane fare to and from Antigua as business travel on their taxes, but I know better. The accountants helped them cook the books. Drake Media overcharged the government and Ener-X for their printing, and had the money sent to Caribbean. They sent it back to the company lawyers, who distributed it as proceeds from trusts. I heard Mr. Luxton call it 'round tripping,' but I think he was a crook.*

Colleen put the letter down for a second. "This is awful, Derrick. I don't want to keep reading."

I shrugged my shoulders. "Come on, Colleen. You know I love this kind of thing."

Colleen turned back to the letter, *"There are three things in every murder: motivation, opportunity and the means to carry it out, Mr. Luxton had all three. It had to be Robert Luxton who did it. Sincerely, Becky Tocca."*

The letter ended rather abruptly, we thought. Colleen and I sat there for a moment or two in silence, trying to make heads or tails of the developing information.

Finally, I asked her, "What was the date of that letter?"

"About a month ago."

"And the murder happened..."

"Last summer. Almost a year. I wonder why she waited so long to come forward with the info?" Colleen pondered. "You would think that she would have spilled the beans right after his murder."

I let her languish in her thoughts. It seemed like a good idea if I was ever going to have her join me on the investigation.

"Maybe the reward wasn't posted until recently," I wondered, "either that, or she didn't want to come forward on her murder theory until she was in the clear on her allegation about the company."

The miles flew by. I was mesmerized by the details swimming in my head. "This thing makes me wonder who she was referring to: Drake Media or Ener-X."

"It had to be Drake," she said, folding the letter and tucking it into the envelope. "Don't you think we ought to take a peek at the newspapers or see what's on the zip drive?" Her voice was calm and deliberate. She could have been reading the news.

"I guess this really sums it up: *Downstate family slain in Good Hart.*"

"Where's that?"

"Looks like it's up north, maybe Charlevoix County, on Lake Michigan."

I waited for the Paul Harvey. Colleen delivered.

"A Saginaw family was found dead in their lake-front cottage early Saturday morning. Cecil Garl, his wife, Winifred, and three children were discovered shot to death by a small caliber firearm.

"Beverly Johnson, 76, a neighbor of the Garls said 'The smell coming from their house was so bad, I thought that maybe they left the freezer door open and the contents were spoiled. That's when I went over there and discovered a massacre.'"

"Sheriff Peter Jackson said that the bodies had been dead for 'almost a week' and that 'whoever did this heinous act had turned the heat up to 80 degrees, which helped speed up the decomposition process.'"

"Derrick, I'm not so sure I want to keep reading," Colleen said as we exited the highway on the south edge of Midland. "This is really sickening. Look at the picture."

I glanced in her direction. The photograph showed a deputy clad in a gas mask, holding a hatchet in his hand.

"The Garl family was supposed to be in Antigua for a ten-day vacation but they never made it to the airport."

"Good heavens," I mumbled.

"No, Derrick, good deal," Colleen said, pointing to a sign in front of a butcher shop on the south edge of Midland.

"What?"

"Pot roast: three-twenty a pound. Jack's Market. Can we stop and get some?"

"Sure."

Jack's is notorious for their homemade sausage, great cuts of meat, and wonderful produce. Colleen hardly ever buys meat from Meijer, even though it may come from the same farm. A minute or so later, I pulled into the parking lot and Colleen jumped out. "I'll fill up your van with gas. Meet you right here."

She didn't say "thanks" or "you're so sweet." It's almost as if she expected it.

It didn't take long to get fuel, or to get a handle on the remainder of the newspaper articles. The Garls had been killed the previous summer inside a little cottage on the edge of a huge lake. Authorities were greeted inside by a stench so putrid it would make the most grizzled veterans on the force say it was one of the worst days of their careers. And the flies: a snarling mass that was a thousand times worse than any barnyard.

The cabin itself was a horrendous mix of evidence and decomposition. Three of the five Garls had been clumped together on the hallway's furnace register, warm air blasting them in the face. The little boy was found in the attic, amongst the seldom-used hardware, Christmas decorations, and a half dozen duck decoys that were stuffed into a burlap sack. Mrs. Garl, was discovered near the front door, her underwear around her ankles, sundress bunched at the waist.

She had to endure the same demeaning ordeal that Cecil Garl's victims had.

The newspaper articles made me think that Becky's story was beginning to be substantiated. It appeared as if she was close enough to the case to have some relevant details, but then again, the story I was looking at was written the previous summer, way, way before Becky penned her letter to the *Free Press.*

The police surely had their work cut out for them. Almost a year and still no arrests.

The Garl murders had taken hold of me, but I wasn't exactly sure what to do next. Even though I had just found out about it, there seemed to be many angles that needed to be investigated. We could go to Becky's funeral and introduce ourselves to her sister. I could visit the crime scene up north and talk to the local police departments. The reporters up there might talk to me too. Ideas were swimming inside my head, swirling with the realization that, for the time being, I had the inside track on who might have committed the murders.

"So, what do you think we ought to do?" I asked Colleen as she opened the car door and hoisted three plastic bags into the back seat. I saw traces of celery and packages wrapped in white butcher's paper. Colleen buckled her seatbelt, sighed slightly, and said, "I think we ought to have pork chops for dinner, although, I did pick up some swordfish steaks that looked simply marvelous…"

She rambled on for a minute or two about the provisions she had scored, and how they would fit into the coming day's menu. I didn't interrupt her, or change her train of thought. It occurred to me that I loved this woman and her quirky, wholesome ways more than anything else in the world.

Try as I might to show her my love every day, I wasn't so sure the reverse was true. I had the feeling that I had become an inconvenience, a necessary evil, a ball and chain around the ankle of her life.

Four

The following morning, I woke up early, packed my fly rod, camera, and reporter's bag in my Impala and headed north, up the spine of Michigan's Lower Peninsula. On the way, I listened to a new age program on public radio. Its dreamy, fluid tracks were the perfect serenade for the developing season. Summer was nearly upon us, and the forests, fields and marshes of northern Michigan were lush and green. Mosquito season was in full bloom, and they peppered the front of my car as I raced past the gigantic swamp west of Houghton Lake.

A bundle of teal wheeled over the highway in the shadows of the great blue heron rookery on the north side of the huge marsh. The herons were already on their nests, and taking their toll on the local frog population. For a moment or two, I was with the herons and feeling how much fun it would be to pluck dinner with my nose, then haul it back to the lair, fifty feet above the cattails.

Near the confluence of US-27 and I-75, I spotted a pair of crows playing tug-of-war with a freshly killed possum.

When I passed over the Au Sable River, I had a sudden urge to stop and flail the water with a woolly bugger, a muddler minnow, or some other concoction of fur and feather that imitates a tasty meal for a hungry trout. But I couldn't fish; I never can when there's work to be done. The Garl case was luring me up north as if it was some sort of primal spawning run. There would be other times to fish—perhaps after dinner—if I felt like I had gotten in a full day's work.

By the time I climbed the undulating hills north of Gaylord

and made the left turn near Wolverine, I was tired of driving. A pit stop, and a coffee later, I was seventy-five dollars lighter in the pocket.

It seemed hopeless to think about the cost of filling up a car with gasoline. There are winners and losers in every economy. I wasn't sure if I was a winner or a loser for paying that price for gas. Good Hart was a long way to drive on a whim, a hunch, a reporter's folly.

Aside from the cost, nothing bad could come from my travels, I was certain.

It felt good to take hold of a story, and have the means to see it through.

Even though a host of other newspapers had taken a whack at the case, Becky Tocca's letter gave me the inside track. The more I repeated her name in my head, the more "Becky Tocca" sounded like "Tapioca."

My day couldn't have been more organized. The first stop would be the cabin where the Garls were murdered. I'd take some photos, maybe talk to the neighbors and get a feel for the scene, the setting, the reality of what had taken place. From there, I'd visit the local police station and shake down the police chief. If I had enough time, I'd visit the local paper and invite myself into the newsroom. Maybe I'd flaunt a little info about Cecil Garl's contention at the board meeting and the design flaw in Ener-X's solar panels, in exchange for some morsels about the status of the case.

Then I thought about dinner, and the possibility of shrimp etouffee and cornbread at Pearl's Cajun Restaurant near Elk Rapids. I could almost taste the warmth of the sauces in my mouth; hear the music, the bustling, chatty crowd, and the clink of silverware on oval shaped plates. I love that place.

If time allowed, I'd drop farther south into the Jordan River valley and introduce myself to the local population of brown trout. With any luck, the mayflies would be hatching in the lengthening evening shadows, the trout would be feeding and

I'd have a drive home filled with the memories of a great night of relaxation and concentration rolled into one. Murder, dinner, music and people watching aside, I like quiet. Trout fishing is all about being silent and tactful. It's a constant conversation between mind and body: "nice cast, pick up the slack, mend the line, careful now." Peel back the layers of any trout fishermen, and they'll tell you that they enjoy the solitude on the river serenaded by the rhythmic song of fly line cast in the evening still.

I'm an eternal optimist when it comes to a new dawn and what's in store for the day ahead. The uncertainty of life is what makes it so interesting. My trip north was filled with unbridled possibilities and a feeling that something great was going to take place.

When I finally rolled into Good Hart, the town looked as if it had been hit hard by Michigan's never-ending recession. Building after building along Main Street had "for lease" written on its store-front windows, or an orange sign taped to the doors. A couple of gas stations at either end of town were old and rundown. The new clock in the center of town may have brought the Rotarians a sense of pride, but it was the only bright spot in a one-horse town that was down on its luck.

The rent was due on my coffee, so I stopped at the only bakery in town. A table full of old timers were solving the world's problems near the front door. They were nursing their Styrofoam cups, milking the bakery owners for as much coffee as they could get. I heard chuckling, and harmless, verbal harpoons that brought more and more laughter. By their wardrobes I surmised that they were locals who had spent the long Michigan winter in the same flannel shirts and Dickie work pants.

Out of towners don't have time to sit and chew the fat. They only want a taste of northern Michigan, and then they leave. I was guilty of exactly that.

The woman behind the counter was more than happy to warm up my pecan roll in the microwave, but she was less than thrilled when she gave me directions to the Garl cabin.

"Not you, too!" she gasped.

I nodded affirmatively.

"Stay on this road out of town about four miles. Look for the church and the cemetery. The Garl cabin is the next drive on the right. There's not much around, other than forest and trees. Look for the sign E-I-E-I-O."

I looked at her, confused.

"It's kinda dumb, I know," she said. "They bought the cabin from the McDonalds and you know how the song goes about old McDonald had a farm."

"Gotcha."

"The Garls never took the sign down when they bought the place, and they can't take it down now, obviously."

"Do you get a lot of requests for directions?"

"All the time. Especially to the Garl Place."

"That's what I meant."

"I don't understand what the big yank is," she huffed, handing me my plastic plate and silverware. I handed her the money, and as she rammed the keys on her cash register she said, "People were killed there. I think it's a tragedy."

"What about the reward?" I asked.

"What reward?"

"The *Free Press. Detroit Free Press.* They offered a hundred thousand."

"Well no wonder we got so many people up here sniffin' round. You go on up to the cabin and have your little fun. I'm sick of it. Just plain sick of it. So are the police. They've got to patrol that place just to make sure everything is okay." Her voice was beginning to rise, her pace quickened. "These people, the damn reporters and cops snooping around. I just wish it would all go away and people would quit comin' in here."

The gentlemen at the table fifteen feet away raised their cups and laughed gleefully. "We heard that."

Five

The woman at the bakery never said what kind of church I should expect as a landmark, but it seemed unlikely that it would be something grand; after all, we were in the boonies of northern Michigan, "above" the most popular cities, tourist traps and destinations. My hunch proved correct in that it was more like a one-room monument to the perseverance of the people who built it hundreds of years ago. It had a tall steeple and six or eight wide concrete stairs that lead to a set of double doors. The roof was covered in bizarre-shaped shingles that looked like giant carp scales.

E-I-E-I-O was easy enough to find. The sign looked like it could have been made by an Amish woodworker with its scrolled, beveled top. A pair of solar-powered lights were aimed in its direction, making prime hunting grounds for spiders. Each letter of the sign was engulfed in a gauzy film of dead bugs.

The driveway was long and twisty, cloaked in beech and maple that shaded the smooth blacktop. A chipmunk dashed across the drive, tail on high. If my windows were rolled down, I would have heard its chirpy little squeal.

I followed the drive left, then down a steep incline bordered by rocks, stones and pines that clung to craggy life on the edge of a big lake. At last, the Garl family's murder scene, on the part of a lake the mariners call "Devil's Elbow."

Aside from the police barrier of yellow tape, it had oodles of charm and a setting that would have made Norman Rockwell or Terry Redlin proud. Instead of being built on the precipice above, Devil's Elbow was constructed on a five-acre outcropping on the edge of Lake Michigan. The bottom third of the cabin was field stone, or more likely, lake stone; its top stacked with logs stained a buttery yellow. Hardly any lawn. Plenty of sand and driftwood and splashy waves. The cedars—scattered here and there—must have framed the sun as it set every evening in the pastures and dairy farms of Wisconsin.

I parked the car in front of the wooden garage door, got out, and peeked inside the window. Two stall. One bay was filled with some sort of convertible, which was covered by a canvas tarp. The second bay had an assortment of workout equipment. I noticed a set of waders on the wall and a host of camouflage and blaze orange colored clothing. Cecil Garl was a sportsman.

I took a photo of the detached garage, then turned my sights on the cabin. The view almost took my breath away. Lake Michigan lay before me like an enormous blue tabletop, sprinkled with sport fishermen and sailboat enthusiasts. I pictured the Garl five: swimming in last summer's warmth, roasting marshmallows on the evening bonfire, and enjoying barbecued chicken round the picnic table. It was easy to understand why nobody may have heard the gunshots: the closest neighbor was two hundred yards to the south. To the north, more lake and forest and wilderness.

I snapped photo after photo, still staying outside the police's perimeter.

An on-shore breeze captured the cedar bows overhead. They whistled a haunting song of loneliness.

I stood there for a few seconds, listening to the north woods and the waves crashing on the shore. It seemed strange to imagine myself with psychic powers, but that's exactly what I was hoping for. Maybe I didn't give the spirits long enough to percolate. My mind was still buried in the realities of the moment and the hustle of figuring out what might have taken place the previous summer. If I was to find out who killed the Garls, I'd have to do it with hard work and a stroke of good luck.

What could I possibly discover that the police had missed?

Probably nothing.

I circled the cabin, taking shot after shot. Everything seemed to be in order. No broken windows or racial epitaphs spray painted on the front door. Even the horseshoes were leaning against a metal post inside a makeshift pit, ready for play.

My drive to northern Michigan had come down to this: If I was to move ahead on the investigation, I'd have to lift the police barrier and get inside. In a lot of ways, I've never had any problem bending the rules. I was already trespassing, if I took another step inside the barrier it wouldn't have been a big deal. I'd be quick and nimble. Snap a few photos and get the heck out of there. The long drive home would give me time to process my investigation—for now I just need to get it done.

Nobody was watching. Even a white-throated sparrow at the top of a cedar couldn't have cared less; he was preoccupied with his chorus of "poor Canada, Canada, Canada."

I lifted the yellow tape, stepped on the lawn and the wide, flat rocks inlaid on the grass. The lake-side door handle was locked, but I could see through its window to the hardwood floor and the nasty tattoo of Mrs. Garl's rotting bodily fluids. Three steps to my left, and I was at the kitchen window. I cupped my hands around my eyes, pressed them against the glass, and took a look inside. The hallway wasn't especially long, but it hid the mysteries of the Garls' final breaths.

I pressed up on the window, and miraculously it slid.

This was my big break. Without a second thought, I pulled some medical rubber gloves from my pocket, put them on, and opened the window. The sill was nothing more than a speed bump as I hopped inside and took notice of the rancid environs. Instead of smelling like knotty pine or cedar furniture, it had a putrid, slaughterhouse kind of odor. Maybe it was the stale confines mixed with the grim setting that made the air smell so peculiar. Either way, I didn't dally. Picture, picture, picture. First I captured the wife, outlined in white tape at the cabin's threshold. One of her legs was wildly splayed, her wrists behind her head. The kitchen was stunning, with its granite countertops and modern appliances. So much for a rustic flair. Then it was Cecil and his two daughters bunched together on the hallway floor register. Strange, how I wanted to "step over" the corpses as if they were still piled up in a lifeless blob.

A rather plain down comforter was wrapped neatly around the queen bed inside the master bedroom. Baby blue pillow cases. A small stack of magazines on the nightstand had collected dust and a smorgasbord of dead flies. Some of the magazines were rather familiar; others had to do with the energy business. I found one copy of *Pursuit* magazine that seemed out of place. Beneath the word *Pursuit,* were the words *The Magazine Devoted to Private Investigators.* I picked it up and thumbed through the pages. There was a story about body armor being an essential tool for bounty hunters, and one about "pink collar crime" as more and more women rise to positions of power in today's business world. Near the back of the magazine was a catalog of everything that a private investigator might need: tiny lenses and motion-sensing, remote cameras.

One of the magazines, three or four down in the stack had a piece of paper wedged between two pages. I figured it would have been one of those postcards from AARP, Time-Life magazine, or a company selling its brand of mechanized weed whackers. It proved to be bigger than a postcard, but it was a solicitation just the same.

It is with great pleasure that we offer you and your spouse membership into the Fatima Cultural Society with all its privileges and advantages.

The font was smooth and elaborate; the paper heavier than card stock. Reminded me of a wedding invitation.

Applications available on line at Fatima, dear Fatima.com.

The invite seemed rather strange, so I stuffed it into my back pocket. The magazine was a copy of *Men's Health*. On the cover was a thirty-something, shirtless specimen with a towel wrapped around his neck and another around his hips. Not a hair on his body, plenty on his head. The featured stories were all about the benefits of green vegetables, and working out your pectoral muscles to create your very own "bulletproof vest." It was ironic. Morbidly so.

I whipped out my pencil and scribbled down the mailing address in my reporter's pad. It looked like Cecil Garl's company could have maintained the subscription.

I opened the nightstand drawer and took an inventory of the contents. It wasn't really a collection of matchbooks, but there were more than a few from restaurants across the North Country represented. Spike's Keg O Nails in Grayling. Audie's in Mackinaw City. Whitecaps in Petoskey. Pearl's had a funky-looking presence with a blood-red crawdad on the cover. Everyone knew about Pearl's.

Cecil had a small, red candle in his stash, a pencil-thin flashlight, a tube of Noxema hand lotion, a set of car keys labeled "Vette," and a fingernail clipper.

If he had anything incriminating—like a handgun, a box of bullets, a folder with important documents—the police must have confiscated it.

The framed photographs on the wall behind the bed were covered in dust. Cecil and his wife, in happy times. The children were pictured on Santa's lap, in crazy Halloween costumes, and holding bronze-clad trophies after sweaty tennis tournaments. I'm not sure why I wanted to snap their photos, but I did. Maybe it was my own sense of getting to know them that made me want to take their picture.

One of the family photos on the opposite wall was quite large, the size of an impressive flat screen television. It looked like it was taken several years ago. Cecil and his wife, the children, and a plump, golden retriever captured on the banks of a dreamy autumn river. Except for the dog, they all wore matching argyle sweaters. Everyone seemed so happy, so perfect and content.

I snapped a photo, which seemed a little crooked when I looked at it in the camera's display. Was it the way I looked through the viewfinder, or was the portrait crooked? I stepped toward the picture, and the chest of drawers beneath. The portrait was anchored to the log wall by two grommets and a pair of wood screws. An equally impressive set of grommets at the bottom made sure that nobody would steal it.

Weird. I mean, why would someone care so much about a family photo?

If someone stole mine, I'd go back to the studio and order another one.

I stood there for a second or two, deep in thought.

My eyes drifted to the driveway, and my sleeping Impala. What a dopey name for a car in northern Michigan. In the land where white-tail deer hunting is king, I would have thought that "Whitetail" might be more appropriate.

Then again, some Al Sharpton type would say that General Motors was racist.

The subtle *tick-tock* of the bird clock on the wall brought me back to reality. It was deadly quiet. Just the way I like it.

The state police detectives would have donned their sterile clothing and combed every inch of the cabin, I was sure of it.

Even the twenty acre Garl property would have been subjected to a metal detector, if not a pack of bloodhounds.

There was nothing left to find, I was certain.

On a whim, however, I pulled my Swiss army knife out of my pocket and found the little Phillips head screwdriver. Two minutes later, I had the top of the portrait free. It bowed towards me, heavily.

Behind it, logs and more logs.

Had there been a safe, the cops would have found it.

Everybody hides a safe behind the family portrait, I thought. *Cecil Garl was different.*

He would leave his Corvette keys in the nightstand drawer because he had nothing to hide. The convertible was beneath its cover in the garage.

His office inside his downstate home was probably a better place to snoop. There, the police would find a stash of clues regarding his finances and dealings.

Here, at the cabin, there would be nothing.

Or would there?

It would be the perfect place to hide something if he really wanted to.

Heck, I didn't even know what I was looking for. I never do. I just put my nose to the wind and hunt for the truth little by little.

Cecil's closet wasn't exceptionally large, but the metal rod six feet long was filled with his and her corduroy trousers and an assortment of shirts from L.L. Bean, Woolrich and Orvis. I paid no attention to the golf shirts, but patted down the shirt pockets of Mr. Garl's side of the closet. When I reached his sport coats, I stuffed a hand in each one of his breast pockets. Nothing in the blue blazer. A spare button and flecks of lint in the olive tweed. In the gray herringbone I found a business card: *Kelly Mathers, Executive Director US Department of Energy.*

Interesting. This is the second time Kelly Mathers' name has come to my attention. I stuffed the card in my back pocket and continued my search.

On the floor, I sorted through the slippers and loafers, hiking boots and sneakers. A shoe box was stuffed with an assortment of polish, mottled cloths, and horse mane brushes. It smelled like chemicals, dye, and petroleum, rolled into one. I tried to peel back the corners of the closet carpet in hopes that it would reveal a false floor to a secret hiding compartment. Nothing.

Next, I turned my attention to the chest of drawers. Mr. Garl kept his camera lenses in a purple, Crown Royal bags and stored them with his socks. The lenses were rather squat-looking and must have been wide angle. They appeared to be quite old and well worn.

His underwear and white t-shirts were neatly folded. His blue jeans, khaki pants were just as tidy. I pulled out each drawer and looked behind it. Nothing.

I looked at my watch. Almost noon. I don't know how long I had been snooping around, but time seemed to have gone by fast. The clock radios on the Garls' nightstand were off, naturally, but the wind-up clock on top of the dresser drawers had the right time. It looked rather odd, that clock, so I picked it up and checked it out. Seemed like it should have had a wind-up propeller to engage, but it didn't.

What it did have was a pea-sized hole just below the twelve. The more I looked at it, the more I thought it looked like a tiny lens.

Son of a gun, I thought. *It is a friggin lens.*

Cecil Garl kept a motion activated, spy camera in his bedroom. It looked a lot like the unit I saw in the pages of his spy magazine.

I couldn't wait to see the photos from inside.

My treasure was adding up, but I still wasn't done yet. There had to be something more, so I looked under the bed.

Slippers, and dust bunnies. I pulled the mattress from the box frame. Nothing.

I went back to Mr. Garl's side of the bed and pulled the nightstand away from the wall. The flimsy particle- board backing revealed no secrets. The magazines, the little lamp, and the clock radio were placed on the floor, so I could look at the bottom of the nightstand. Nothing.

My reporter's instincts kept urging me on, so I pulled the top drawer from the nightstand. Nothing. The bottom drawer came out just as easily. Nothing again. When I peeked into the cavity of the nightstand, however, I noticed a something small taped to the ceiling of the nightstand's undercarriage. It was black electrical tape, and it looked like it was hiding a set of car keys. Without a second thought, I ripped the tape from the wood, which revealed a plain, black zip drive. Bingo.

Damn, I was having a great day, but I didn't want to get caught.

I threw the drawers back in the nightstand and put everything back on top. Nobody would know I was there.

I left the bedroom and stepped over the corpses again. The kitchen had canisters of tea, sugar and flour. The lazy Susan had a supply of diced tomatoes, kidney beans and Bartlett pears in heavy syrup. The refrigerator was unplugged, and except for a box of baking soda, was completely empty. No spy clocks anywhere in sight.

I drifted into the living room again. The sunshine poured through the giant bay window. Cecil went first class when it came to furniture. Leather all around. Hickory end tables. Stained glass lamps. I noticed an ashtray on one of the end tables. A pipe rested inside; and a bag of stale Captain Black tobacco not far away. The walls were covered in dramatic images from northern Michigan—freighters plowing through rough seas, ice covered piers and lonesome lighthouses, of course, the Mackinac Bridge during a summer storm.

My attention turned to the coffee table between the sofa and the matching set of recliners. Half furniture, half display, the coffee table featured a male grouse perched on a freshly cut stump. The grouse was all puffed up as if it was the spring mating season. Two hens looked up at him as if he was a preacher in the pulpit.

Instead of leaving with the treasure I had obtained, I decided to find out where the Garl boy had perished. Down the hallway I went, to the trap door in the ceiling. I pulled the flimsy attic stairs from the hideaway and skipped into the warm air, the aroma of rough hewn cedar. The rafters down the center of the attic were covered in two-by-fours, creating a gangway that lead into the attic bowels. Giant plastic bins flanked each side and were labeled with masking tape: *camping, skiing, Christmas, photo albums etc.* Black garbage bags could have been filled with extra blankets, sleeping bags or pillows.

Four paces later, I found the boy's outline. One arm was draped across the gangway, a foot diagonally on a rafter. It was easy to imagine the villains flushing him out of cover like a hare, and killing him without an ounce of remorse. Seemed rather odd that he was up there. It was hardly a cool place for a boy to hang out. He was trapped. Easy pickings. And probably the last to join the family in their heavenly reward.

After taking several photos, I realized that I was trapped, too.

And in the stillness of the cabin's attic, I heard voices. At first, I thought maybe it was one of those bird-clocks that whistles a different bird call on the hour. Not even close. It was people voices.

Oh, fudge, I thought. My heart rate jumped another octave, if that's possible.

Down the stairs I scampered. When I made it to the hallway, I looked out the master bedroom window to the driveway. A giant passenger van was parked next to my Impala. It looked like one of those vans that the cops use to transport prisoners from one jail to another.

In this case, I figured it was the deputies themselves, surrounding the cabin. At any moment they'd demand that I come out the front door with my hands in the air.

I tried to make myself small, by hiding against the bathroom door. All of a sudden I heard the tick-tock of the clock inside the master bedroom and a raised voice muffled by the cabin walls.

"For years this spit of land has been called the Devil's Elbow by sailors on the Great Lakes. There are seventeen shipwrecks in this area, most of them from before the invention of sonar and radar. Long before the mariners sailed these waters, though, the Odawa Indian tribe thought this area was haunted by evil spirits that roamed after dark during a harvest moon. Police don't know who killed the Garl family, but they suspect that Mr. Garl's business dealings had something to do with it."

Confused, I poked my head into the girls' bedroom.

There were eight or ten people in the entourage. Most were walking forward, but the woman in front was skating backwards, a green banker's visor on her forehead.

"Cecil Garl was a player in the solar panel industry, but he also was a publisher of *Fatima Magazine*, an upscale periodical devoted to the arts, the sporting life, and environmental issues in the Midwest."

She extended her palm the cabin's way.

"The Garl daughters were stars on their high school tennis team. One had signed a letter of intent to play at Western Michigan, the younger sister was being courted by the University of Michigan and Syracuse."

As they rounded the corner of the cabin, I slipped into the master bedroom, disengaged the window locks, and jumped outside.

I ran. Across the modest lawn, the shrubbery, the giant rocks adorned with painted seagulls and white-throated sparrows. My keys were easy to find. I unlocked the Impala doors, started the engine and prepared for a speedy takeaway.

Before roaring away, I noticed the white van and the words etched across its flanks: *Michigan Mystery Tours…touring "up north's" murder scenes since 2001.*

Six

The Charlevoix County sheriff's office wasn't exactly a blur of activity when I rolled in at a few minutes before one. A rather elderly woman behind the counter was banging away on her keyboard and chewing gum like a Guernsey cow in a field of clover. When she looked up at me over the top of her glasses, I knew what was coming next: "Can I help you?"

"I'm here for the Garls' police report."

"You'll have to speak up, sir."

"I'm here to pick up the Garls' police report," I yelled through the bulletproof glass.

The poor woman could hardly lift her head. She seemed to have a medical condition that kept her chin glued to the top of her chest.

"They've gone to a powwow," she said, matter of fact.

A powwow, I thought. *That doesn't make any sense at all. The Garls aren't Native American.*

The woman behind the counter bailed me out: "I said, 'What have they done now?'"

"Oh, nothing," I said defensively. "Why do you ask?"

"Oh never mind. If you're after the police report, we can't give that out. It's still an ongoing investigation."

"Is Sheriff Jackson in?"

"No, it's Saturday. I think he's at the funeral."

"Whose funeral?"

The nice lady with the crunched up neck took off her glasses. They dangled around her neck on a rosary-looking string of beads. She stopped chewing her cud. I was getting on her nerves, no doubt about it. "Was there anything else you needed?"

I backed off. Backed away.

"No, I guess not."

A few steps later, I was outside again. A patrol car was parked on the curb in front of the station, engine running. It sounded like the air conditioning was running too. What a waste. It seems that everyone but the government is concerned with saving money.

For a few seconds, I thought about writing a story about government waste, but I had bigger fish to fry.

I walked back to my car and pulled out the stories from Becky's stash of newspaper articles. The *Charlevoix Currier* had three stories: The first was from the day after the bodies were recovered, and the next two were a month and six months, respectively. I had to admit, the reporter knew what she was doing. Her stories were thorough, steeped in facts, sources, and well chosen words.

If anyone knew what was going on with the Garl case, it would be reporter Dorothy Kalakay.

The trouble was, it was Saturday afternoon, and I knew that the front door of the Charlevoix Currier would be closed. I had a hunch that Kalakay and the other reporters would be in the newsroom, banging out their stories for Sunday's edition. If I was to get in to see her, I'd either have to wait her out in the parking lot, or rap on the employee entrance and talk my way inside. Either way, it would take some time.

The *Charlevoix News* was housed in a two-story brick

building a block off the main drag. Six or eight vehicles were in the parking lot—most of them were older, and not especially clean. A smallish pickup had a wooden frame in the bed and a pair of kayaks resting on top. Kayaking looked like something fun to do on a beautiful day in northern Michigan.

I backed into a parking place and imagined Kalakay strolling out of the employee entrance, and into a vehicle next door. I'd engage her with a little ice breaker, then get into the meat and potatoes of the Garl matter.

Instead, I waited impatiently. Colleen had emailed and said that everything was okay on the home front. She said we would have the swordfish steaks for dinner tomorrow. I turned on the radio; Justin Verlander was on the mound for the Detroit Tigers in a matinee with the Boston Red Sox.

Everything seemed right with the world.

I was dying to see what was on Cecil Garl's zip drive, but I had neglected to bring my laptop with me. The public library was no place to take a peek what was on it.

Instead of forcing the issue, I reached into my little cooler and pulled out a bottle of flavored water. When it hit the back of my throat, I realized that the whole stake-out situation made me feel a little like Jim Rockford from the Rockford Files. I always admired his smooth style and his ability to get in and out of jams with diplomacy and charm. All I needed for this stakeout was a hound's tooth sportcoat and a gold-colored Firebird to be the perfect private investigator.

There was one thing wrong with a stakeout: Waiting around isn't exactly my strong suit. In other words, patience isn't a virtue I possess.

After about five minutes of waiting, I became restless.

Verlander hit a batter with a wild pitch, then walked another. Perhaps ol' Justin was in the mood for a little drama.

So was I.

Without a second thought, I marched across the parking

lot to the employee entrance. The door was locked, so I rapped on it three or four times. I waited for a minute or so, then knocked again.

Finally, footsteps. The door flung open and a rather portly woman with a sweaty upper lip looked up at me. She didn't say "hi" or "hello" or "what do you want?"

Jim Rockford took hold of me. "Dorothy?" I asked, smiling.

"No, she's come and gone."

"Oh, shoot," I said, holding a folded piece of paper. "I had something really important for her…" I curled my lip, and scratched my chin pensively.

The woman relaxed slightly. I think she took an interest in what her co-worker might have coming her way.

"I really don't want to say too much," I swaggered. "She's not in any trouble, I can assure you." If I were Rockford, I'd have some business cards in my breast pocket with "lottery commission" printed on them.

The chubby woman seemed to buy my story, and said that Dorothy was working her other job down the street.

"Where?"

"The Town House. She's a bartender."

"Thank you," I smiled.

The woman slammed the door shut, and I was on my way down the street.

Instead of driving the few blocks, I decided to walk.

When I stepped inside the dark confines of the Town House Bar, it took a moment or two for my eyes to adjust. Three or four locals looked up from their suds at the bar. They didn't nod or say hello, but I wasn't surprised; there are lots of people who just want to be left alone.

I walked past them all, and made my way to the last stool at the end. Dorothy Kalakay was wiping down the beer mugs with a miniature white towel. She held each mug to the glow of the television before placing it in the overhead bin.

We didn't need any introductions. I recognized her charming smile, the curve of her face and the funny way she laughed.

She was my old flame from yesteryear, and I must admit that my heart skipped a beat. It's not every day that you see a person with whom you shared a bed. Oh, heck, we shared more than a bed. We had a lot of great times together.

Quickly, I tried to do my best Humphrey Bogart imitation, "What's a nice girl like you doing in a place like this?"

Dorothy looked up from her glassware and smiled the smiles of familiarity. "Well, well, if it isn't Derrick Twitchell in the flesh…"

"How you doing, Dottie?" I found myself smiling ear to ear.

"Oh. My. Gosh," she sputtered. "I'm doing great," she said with a smile, hands over her heart. "This is so exciting!" She patted my hand on the bar like she used to pat the skull of her pet schnauzer, Dixie.

"You look well, Derrick. How are things?"

"Great. How about you?"

"Couldn't be better. I'm living a dream up here," she said sarcastically, "tending bar and doing a little writing on the side."

"That's what I hear."

"How long has it been, fifteen or twenty years?" she asked.

"Probably."

"This is so exciting. Got any kids?"

"One, Elizabeth. She's nine."

"Aw, that's great, Derrick…Single?"

"No-no," I stammered, "I'm still married." I don't know what made me say "still" married. Seemed foolish to say it that way. It's not like I was planning on getting divorced anytime soon.

"How about you?"

"I'm single and enjoying my freedom." I looked at her neck. Her skin had reddened in places, starting from somewhere beneath her tank top and blouse. Dottie never was a good liar, nor could she hide her arousal in the heat of passion.

The quickening pulse and surge of endorphins went straight to the skin on her neck.

"I notice that you have a different last name."

"Yep. I was married for fourteen years, but my husband died in a plane crash. Got a son at Hope College. He wants to be an engineer."

"Nice. Aren't you proud?"

"Sure am, but college is killing me."

I made a concerned face.

"That's why I have to make the hundred grand."

"From the *Free Press*?" I asked.

"Yes. How did you know about it?"

I nodded. "I'm a professional, remember?"

She raised her eyebrows, "It's totally right there for the taking."

Dottie talked a bit like a valley girl.

"Is there a lot of buzz up here about the Garl murders?"

"People are curious, that's for sure. No one can believe it's still unsolved." She laughed and smiled at the circumstance. I was half expecting that she might post something on Facebook right then and there about our little reunion. "What sounds good today?"

"Do you have a menu?"

"No, but we make really good popcorn."

"Sounds great, Dottie, and a bottle of O'Doul's."

"You want a glass with that, Hun?"

"Sure." Back in the day she called everybody *Hun* or *Love,* which I couldn't stand. It diluted the meaning of the words.

I glanced over the edge of the bar when she stooped to get my beer. She still had beautiful cleavage, and a long dark mane that hung to her shoulders.

"Derrick Twitchell in the flesh," she smiled. "How exciting!"

I laughed. It had been a long time since we had seen each other. I'm glad she wasn't pissed.

"You still wear a rubber band around your wrist, don't you?"

"Of course," I said, "you never know when you might need it."

She laughed. "Have you ever needed it?"

"Once in a while," I defended myself.

"What brings you to town?"

"The Garl matter, of course."

"Yeah. It's a crazy situation."

"I've read your stories about the murders. They're excellent."

"Thanks."

"I would have never known it was you who had written those stories, since you have a different last name."

"I'm glad you tracked me down."

"Why?"

She shrugged her shoulders. "Every once in a while, I think about you."

"Yeah?"

"Yeah, I do."

I didn't know what to say, so I changed gears, "Who do you think killed the Garl family?"

"I don't know. Nobody does. Will you excuse me?"

"Sure."

Dottie waltzed to the other end of the bar, and dropped off two cans of beer to the old timers sitting there. I wondered if she still had a small birthmark on the inside of her left thigh that was shaped like a pear and the size of a dime. Dottie brought a basket of freshly popped popcorn, then grabbed a couple of limes from a small plastic bin beneath the counter.

"He sure is a good pitcher," I said, gesturing up at Verlander.

Dorothy cut the limes in half, then half again. "I like it that he doesn't take all day on the mound. He gets the ball and hums it at the plate."

"Makes the game go by faster," I said.

"Remember that time in eighty-seven…" she waxed, "when the Tigers won the division title? Where did we watch that last game against the Toronto Blue Jays at the very end of the year? Tom's Oyster Bar, wasn't it?"

"I don't think so. Tom's wasn't opened yet. I'm pretty sure it was Maxie's on Main Street in Royal Oak. It was a happening place, back in the day."

"That was fun."

"We had a lot of fun back then, don't you think, Dottie?"

She giggled, then sighed. "Time flies. You blink once or twice and your life is half over."

I smiled.

"Have any regrets, Derrick?"

I smirked. "Not yet. The popcorn is excellent. The beer is everything I dreamed of and the conversation with an old..." My mind didn't know how to describe her… "lover is top notch."

"You still have a way of dodging serious topics, don't you?"

I smiled. "What makes you say that?"

"I don't know," she smiled at me. "It's fun to think about our good times together."

I found myself smiling because of the memory in the front of my mind. On a hot, July evening, we went to see Journey at the DTE Music Theater. Back then it was called Pine Knob. We tailgated, danced, and sang the lyrics to *The Wheel in the Sky*, *Faithfully*, and *Any Way You Want It.* Just as the concert ended, the skies opened up in a torrential thunderstorm. We were drenched….in fun, romance, good times, and of course the rain.

When we arrived back at the car, and tried to nose our way free of the traffic, Dottie took her shirt and pants off. I remember asking her, "What the heck are you doing, girl?"

"I saw that blanket in the back seat. I'm going to cover up."

She was a wild woman: frisky as a feline and uninhibited as a five year old on a beach full of skipping stones, seashells and driftwood.

I didn't dare remind her about the concert, or the way we made out in a rest area along I-75. The cops who interrupted our little rendezvous were nice enough to let us go with just a warning. They could have written us up for lewd and lascivious conduct if they wanted to, and then we'd be the ones to sing *Who's Crying Now*.

She probably had a few great memories of her own.

"You still have fun now; it's just grown up fun, right?" I asked her.

"Oh shoot, hang on a second."

Her attention turned to a leather-clad man and woman in Harley outfits who stepped inside the front door. A sliver of light bounced off the mirrored beer signs hanging on the wall as the woman fluffed and raked the insects from her hair. They were bikers.

Dottie stepped around the far edge of the bar and took their drink order. She was as chipper as I remember, and in the perfect profession for someone who loves to drink.

On her return trip to her post, she put her arm around me.

"Come here, Derrick. Give me a hug for old time's sake."

I stepped off the stool and obliged her request. She gave me an enormous squeeze. I returned the favor, taking in the wonderful scent of her perfume and the wholesome goodness of what was beneath her blouse.

I took another sip, while Dottie filled a pitcher with Killian's.

"Any idea about the main suspects?" I asked.

Dorothy didn't hesitate. "I still think it's his business connections downstate."

"Robert Luxton?"

"That's him. He's a bad, bad dude, Derrick."

"Why do you say that?"

"He just is. I have some stories about him that would make your hair curl."

"What about Mr. Garl?"

"Oh," she smiled, "he doesn't sound that bad. One of his college roommates comes in here all the time. Blind guy. Claims that he and Cecil were best friends back at Ferris State."

"Oh yeah?" I egged her on.

"He says that Cecil used to whistle *He's Got the Whole World in His Hands* every time he went to the men's room."

I chuckled, naturally. "The roommate must have been upset when Cecil was murdered," I said.

"Of course, even though they really hadn't seen much of each other since college," she smirked.

"Did you ask him about who might have killed Cecil and his family?"

Dottie shook her head, no, then wheeled around the bar again. I watched her go to the motorcyclists, Killians in her hand.

When she returned to the bar, I dangled a carrot in front of her nose. "I have some inside information about the murders."

Dottie's ears perked up.

"What kind of inside information?"

I huffed slightly. "Hmmm, well, I think the cops may have missed a few clues out at the cabin."

"The Devil's Elbow?"

I nodded, as cool as James Rockford on a block of ice.

"Well, they'd better find those clues quickly, because tomorrow morning they're tearing it down," she said, eyebrows lifted.

"The Devil's Elbow?" I asked.

"Yup. The police are having an auction. They're going to get rid of all their belongings."

My heart sank. "Then what?"

"They're going to bulldoze it into a big pile and light it on fire."

"Why?"

Dottie looked to her right, then left. "The Garls never paid their summer or winter taxes."

"Why wouldn't the family pay them?"

Dottie shook her head. "It wasn't paid—by their family or anybody else. The county repossessed the property about a month ago for back taxes. The proceeds from the auction go towards improvements at the township hall."

"Why didn't they tear it down last month?"

"In April? Fire danger," she said. "Spring is the worst time for wildfires. Besides, the fire department is totally volunteer."

"Why don't they just sell the cabin as it is?"

"The Corp of Engineers say it's a navigation hazard. The cabin has been there so long that it had been granted grandfather status. Now that no family members have come forth, the authorities figured it was their chance to have it destroyed."

I raised my eyebrows and pulled on the last of the fake beer.

"The forecast is for light, offshore winds tomorrow. They figured that on Memorial Day weekend they'd have a bunch of volunteers available to help."

"Hmmm." My mind was back at the Garl cabin and the treasure I had procured.

Dottie rounded the bar and flitted from table to table like a butterfly in a field of wildflowers. She was a wealth of information when it came to the Garl matter, and it made me sad to think that she couldn't make a living just by being a reporter. Then again, maybe it was her choice to have two or three jobs.

Regardless, she seemed happy and content.

Same for me.

Dottie interrupted my train of thought, "Want another beer?"

I glanced her way, "No thank you. The check would be fine."

She spun to the computer beneath the television, tapped the cash register's screen a few times, and a piece of paper ratcheted into view. I watched her spin my way, "Here you are, Luv."

I grimaced.

Instead of waiting for me to figure out if I was going to pay with a credit card or cash, Dottie picked up her cell phone and gave it a quick check. She thumbed the keys momentarily, and then peered at me with a crooked, raised eyebrow.

"Is everything okay?" I asked.

"You tell me," she said, aggressively.

"What?"

"One of my coworkers texted me and said that you were looking for me."

"Oh, yeah?" I tried to play dumb.

"She said you had something important."

All of a sudden, I wasn't her Luv any longer.

She had given me all the info I wanted but I really didn't have anything important. *What would Jim Rockford do?*

I opened my wallet, pulled out a smiling twenty dollar bill, and slid it across the bar top.

"This is for you, Dottie. Thanks for your help. Keep the change."

Dottie clung to the twenty but it really didn't make her smile. It was hard to tell if she felt used. A twinge of guilt poured over me.

We were trapped in a bit of purgatory it seemed. I felt like she wanted to say something and I wanted to tell her what I had found at the Garl place.

Without a laptop, I needed her help. I hated to ask for a favor because I was the one who ended our relationship many moons ago.

"Would you like to help me?" I asked.

She laughed. "Just a minute."

Dottie pushed the buttons on the computer screen and the cash drawer snapped open. I watched her tuck the twenty in the drawer, then take the change and stuff it into her pants pocket.

"Don't go anywhere," she demanded. "Hell, yeah, I want to help. I'm done in a little while," she said, a white dishrag in her hand. "A block south of here there's a marina. Meet me on the *Fortitude*."

"What's that?"

"You can't miss it," she said. "There are three docks in the harbor. Take the middle dock to the end. I'll be there in a bit."

Seven

I could have been mistaken for a tourist as I strolled along Main Street in downtown Charlevoix, munching on a waffle ice cream cone in the bright afternoon sunshine. All I needed was a pair of madras plaid shorts, a pink polo, and an Airedale named "Buffy" and I would have fit the template to a T. I caught a silky whiff of chocolate fudge in the moist afternoon air. It was the smell of summer, of prosperity, of sweet, carefree times "up north."

I made my way to the marina and glanced over the break-wall. Mr. and Mrs. Mallard looked up at me with crooked necks, seemingly waiting for a free lunch. If I'd have thought of it, I could have stuffed my pockets with popcorn and shared it with the ducks. Instead, I peered into the crystal-clear waters at the moss-covered pilings that framed the boundary of every boat slip. The underwater world seemed to be void of life until a herd of carp galloped into view. The lead specimen must have been a hen; her four suitors weren't carrying flowers, or wearing bow ties, but for all I know they could have been humming a romantic ballad, carp style. Courtship takes all forms.

Laughter filled the air. I spotted two or three couples in the cockpit of a cruiser, fifty feet away. They were getting a head start on happy hour, it appeared. For a second, I wished I was part of their group. They were having a ball on the first holiday weekend of the season.

This was no time for fun, however. The images of the Garl family kept flashing before my eyes. It was a ghastly scene and one that had haunted the community for almost an entire year. I bet whoever killed the Garls went to The Devil's Elbow via the water. That way there would be no witnesses on the road, or tire tracks on the driveway. I wondered if the killers showed up at seven in the morning, or eleven at night, when they knew that the Garls would all be there.

Seemed like a shame to destroy their beautiful cabin. It was a bit of a landmark, after all, and a setting that was Pure Michigan.

The pictures I had taken may be the last ones ever captured. For years people would talk about the unsolved Garl murders and the setting along the shoreline.

Between the photographs, the clues, the camera-clock, and the zip drive, I had made a nice little haul. For a second or two I thought about heading home, where I could spend the remainder of the weekend with the family. Then again, if Dottie was right about the auction the following day, it might not be a bad idea to attend. I'm sure the Sheriff would be in attendance, if not the State Police investigators. I marveled at all they had missed inside the cabin of clues.

If the *Free Press* hadn't assigned a reporter to the destruction of the cabin, and the auction that preceded it, I could probably sell the photographs to them for a decent price.

And then it occurred to me that the *Free Press* wouldn't pay the reward to me or Becky's sister. Becky was dead, and I'm sure that the paper would use her death as a reason for denial. That didn't mean that I couldn't submit my own letter and set of "unanimous" six numbers in the corner.

Of course, I didn't have a theory about the murders yet.

Nobody did. I had opened a can of worms and now the worms were oozing into the crevices of my head. An hour ago, Dorothy Kalakay was just another reporter; now we had formed an unofficial partnership in the quest for the truth.

As I walked past the party people, and looked to the end of the dock, I expected to see a ramshackle structure adorned with faux palm trees, a pink flamingo, and tiki torches. "*Fortitude*" may not have been the most appropriate name for a harborside bar, but in my head, that's what I expected. It was the perfect spot for a lakeside watering hole, where thirsty patrons might sip strawberry daiquiris and nibble on whitefish pate in the lengthening shadows of the day.

Instead, a powerboat at least eighty feet long and three yards wide was resting against the dock, moored to giant metal cleats with a set of ropes the thickness of a fire hose. I walked to the stern to make sure I had the right craft. When I did, a turtle the size of a saucer plopped off the swim platform and paddled into the depths.

It was the *Fortitude* all right, from Charlevoix.

Why would Dottie be involved with this?

I skipped over the gunwale and was aboard. The craft hardly budged. It was a floating goliath made of fiberglass, teak, and polished brass hardware. Somewhere beneath the floor was a pair of engines that had more horsepower than a stable full of Clydesdales. I couldn't imagine why someone would want to own something so extreme, so flamboyant, and so impractical. After all, there wasn't a fishing pole in sight.

I climbed up the stairs and unzipped the white canvas cover that protected the cockpit from the elements. Once inside, a musty smell reminded me of an old fashioned tent or a camper. My eyes drifted past three or four mayfly husks on the windshield to the spread of marine life in the harbor. The party people were doing their thing. A variety of boats motored around the harbor with the same carefree urgency as the passing seagulls. It was a neat perspective—way up top—but I had to wonder what it would have been like in the tossing waves of Lake Michigan.

Standing there, I couldn't help but explore. I wanted to know more about the boat, its owner and how he or she made their fortune. No doubt about it—this beast cost a boatload to buy, an arm and a leg to operate.

I didn't get far. Before I opened the plastic envelope stuffed with important-looking papers, I saw Dottie ambling down the boardwalk. She was pulling a small wagon that had several boxes in it. For a second or two I thought about what the boxes were for.

I scampered down the ladder just in time to hear her say, "Howdy."

"Doody," I smiled.

"Can you take these?" She asked, handing me a copy-paper box filled with provisions.

"Sure can. Are we going on a trip?"

"Hardly," she rolled her eyes and sent a five-gallon bucket over the gunwale. It was filled with cleaning supplies, brushes and a can of air freshener. "I' have some work to do."

"I thought we were going to go over the Garl matter?"

"We will," she said, calmly. "Don't you believe in multi-tasking?"

She extended her hand. I took it in mine and she came aboard.

"Well, yeah, doesn't everyone?" I confessed. "Is this your boat?"

She laughed. "Hardly, Derrick. It belongs to Shafeek Heanley."

"Who's he?"

"He's a fat-cat from down below." Down below meant *downstate.*

Dottie reached into her pocket and pulled out a set of keys. They jingled slightly as she rammed one into the underbelly of a lock that hung on a set of bi-fold doors. The door swung open and she skipped down the stairs into the cushioned plenty of the cabin. "Come on down," she said, Price-is-Right style.

I followed her down the stairs and she directed me to have a seat at the galley table.

"Want something to drink?" she asked politely.

"No, thanks."

She stooped near the stairway and plucked a brass ring from the wooden floor. When she did, a square section of teakwood came up with the ring. I watched her fiddle with the knobs beneath the floor.

"What are you doing?" I asked.

"It's the pilot light…for the refrigerator, the hot-water heater, and the stove."

"Gotcha. Did you bring your laptop?"

"No, but there's one on board."

"Dottie!"

"What?"

"Maybe this wasn't a good idea after all. I don't want to get someone else's laptop involved."

"Chill out, Derrick. Mr. Heanley won't mind. He won't even know about it."

Dottie closed the little madras curtains that framed the galley. It wasn't exactly dark inside that floating goliath, but it wasn't light, either. "Let's get down to brass tacks, shall we?"

Sounded painful, I thought. "What do you mean?"

"Here," she said, handing me a petite, cloth briefcase. "There's a plug behind you."

I tugged at the zipper and removed the laptop from its padded nest. A second later the computer came to life.

Dottie opened the galley's refrigerator and was stuffing the contents with can after can of soft drinks, Sam Adams and Heineken. When that was through, she set her sights on bottles in her stash. Tonic water, club soda, and Canada Dry ginger ale. Then she delivered the alcohol in mini bottles: Grey Goose, the Captain, Jack Daniels, and Grand Marnier. I don't know how many bottles there were, but it was a bunch.

I hated to ask her what she was doing, but it wouldn't be out of the ordinary for me to inquire.

"You're probably wondering what's going on, aren't you?"

"Well, yeah."

"I have my own concierge service."

"What's that?"

"Think of me as a glorified gopher," she snickered. "I'm going to have a little drink. You sure you don't want one?"

"Positive."

"I do all the things that a boat owner hates to do," she said, as she twisted the cap off a mini bottle of Captain.

"Like stuff the fridge?"

"Exactly," she said, closing the refrigerator door. The liquor made tiny gulping sounds as it drizzled over the ice. "If Mr. Heanley wants to entertain, I'll be his bartender and roll out the *hors d'oeuvres*. If he needs to be picked up at the airport, or wants the boat moved to Mackinac Island or Beaver Island, all he has to do is call. He doesn't want to deal with cleaning the boat, or filling it up with gas. He wants all the enjoyment and none of the hassle."

"Must be nice."

"The man's a genius and has done very well for himself. He'll be up here on Friday for the weekend."

Dottie opened a little cubby near the engine well, and pulled out a miniature vacuum. She plugged it in and started doing her thing at the opposite end of the galley.

For a fleeting instant, I remembered the time we took one of those tour boats from Grand Marais to the Pictured Rocks National Lakeshore on Lake Superior. She had packed a few of those mini bottles of liquor in her purse, but they didn't set well with her when the big lake kicked up her heels and the boat started rocking. I was never really sure what made her sick—the liquor or the rough seas. It doesn't really matter now. All I remember are the vile, gut wrenching sounds she made off the railing in the back of the boat.

And the guide's timing couldn't have been worse: "Ladies and gentlemen, welcome to Lake Superior, which poet Henry Wadsworth Longfellow and musician Gordon Lightfoot called 'Gitche Gumee.' But long before Lake Superior got its name, the Ojibwe paddled these waters in search of game to eat and fish to catch. If you listen quietly some say you can hear the echoes of their music and their haunting, lonesome wails."

Dottie, "Huuuuurl!"

Of course, I didn't know what to do while she was draped over the back railing, turning green behind the gills. I felt like a midwife, patting her back, grimacing along with her at every painful, delirious contraction.

Instead of dwelling on the distant past, I dove headfirst into the thumb drive and its scores of files. Looked like some of the files were Word documents. Others in Excel. Some of the icons I didn't recognize, but I just clicked away.

When I did, the computer screen was filled with a woman's thighs, knees and ankles. It looked like maybe the picture was taken from beneath a desk. I clicked the button and the next image was just like the first, only this time the person wore a different colored skirt or a dress of some sort. Another click, another day. There were dozens of images and each one revealed the same set of legs in varying degrees of exposure.

What the heck?

I backed out of the file and went on to the next. It was the same thing, only this time the woman had much skinnier legs. Her knees were rather bony –almost like a pair of broomsticks that glowed in the ultraviolet light. Occasionally, woman number two would scratch her knee or calf. When she uncrossed her legs I caught the glimpse of her white underwear. I felt like I shouldn't be looking at something so bizarre.

What the hell?

"What's going on?" Dottie asked.

"This is sick," I told her.

"What is it?"

"Check this out," I said. "I found this zip drive out at the Garl place. I knew that Cecil Garl was a bit of a leg man, but this is weird."

Dottie coiled the cord around the mini-vacuum, and sat down next to me.

"O-M-G," Dottie muttered after the first dozen images.

"This is the second file I opened," I said. "There are lots more."

I closed the file and opened a third. Instead of a pair of legs, this time the point of view was from the ceiling of a women's restroom. The stalls, the sinks, the flooring were trimmed in granite. Woman after woman disappeared into the stall—then washed their hands in the sink. Almost all of them bent over the sink and looked in the mirror as if they were looking for a dab of spinach or a huckleberry between an incisor and a bicuspid.

"This is frickin' weird, Derrick," Dottie gasped.

"Cecil Garl was a pervert."

I kept clicking and tried to get an idea of how many different women visited the washroom. Seemed like ten or fifteen. Maybe twenty. Blondes and brunettes. Redheads.

"Is it just me, or does it seem like there are an inordinate number of women who wear dresses?" Dottie wondered. "I haven't seen one yet who hasn't."

"Maybe it was Cecil's dress code..."

Five or six clicks later, the computer screen showed two women, one looked rather tall and in her late twenties, the other middle aged and plump. They were at the sink, but I could tell that they were talking to each other.

When they finished washing their hands the skinny one touched up her lipstick in the mirror. The chubby woman watched, hand on hip.

I clicked again and the two women were hugging.

"Oh geez," Dottie said. "I don't like the looks of this."

"Maybe they're friends," I lamented. "Friends hug all the time."

I clicked again.

"Lez-be-friends," Dottie jeered.

The women were kissing each other passionately.

"Looks like the chubby one is the aggressor," I observed. "The skinny girl isn't resisting."

I clicked again and the chubby one's lips were on the skinny one's neck, a hand firmly on her partner's caboose.

"This is getting a little out of hand, don't you think, Derrick?"

I clicked one more time and the chubby woman's head was between the skinny person's cleavage.

"You're right," I said. "Those two might need some privacy."

I exited.

"What does FS0612 mean?" she asked, pointing to the screen.

One click later and the screen came to life with a magazine cover of the Fatima Cultural Society. The image on the cover looked like some kind of vase that belonged in a museum.

"Oh yeah," I said. "Fatima, dear Fatima."

"What the hell, Derrick. How did you find this?"

I laughed. "What can I say, Dottie. There are sleuths, and there are sleuth slayers."

"Cecil was the publisher, you knew that, didn't you?"

"Sure I did," I smiled.

The subtitle explained everything: *The magazine devoted to societal evolution.*

"I've never heard of it," Dottie said.

"Me, either," I said, as the cursor motored past a double-page advertisement for a sleek countertop of granite. "Does that mean we have no culture?"

"Wait!" Dottie said, index finger pointed at the screen. "I want to see what the stories are. Go back to the table of contents."

I scrolled to the top of the content page: The editor had a column on page six, titled *Who was Lady Fatima?* A movie maker from Royal Oak was featured on page seventeen. On page thirty-seven, Cecil Garl himself wrote a piece titled: 'Fun in the sun: pure Antigua style.' Following Cecil's story, was a piece about the Detroit Institute of Art's concerns about the plans to auction their treasure to combat the city's bankruptcy. The picture on the content page was the same as the cover.

Poor Detroit, I thought.

"Poor Detroit," Dottie sighed. "It seems like our professional sports teams are the only bright spot in the city. If it wasn't for the Tigers, Red Wings, and Lions that place would be a ghost town."

I kept the cursor on the content page—Michigan's wines, gay marriage, and the "stand your ground" situation in Florida—were featured. There was a health section, a technology segment and a judge's profile, titled: *Candace Dunleavy, changing Michigan's mores, one decision at a time.*

"She must be one of those judges who make their decisions based on how they think the law ought to be, not what it says," Dottie said. "Can you email me the file?"

She had me wondering. *Did she mean the whole zip drive or just the file that contained the issue of the magazine?*

"Sure," I agreed, thinking that she wanted just the magazine. "I'd like to read the magazine myself. Maybe then I'd have more culture."

"How many other files are there?" She asked.

I left the magazine, and returned to the index page of the zip drive. It looked like there were plenty of other magazine issues to be reviewed.

"*Fantasy's One*. What's that?" Dottie asked, pointing to a file on the screen.

I followed her instructions. When I did, the computer screen came to life with the video of a woman dressed in a skimpy, sequined bikini. Our perspective was dark, but not too dark to see what was going on. We heard music in the background, and the blink and flash of disco lights when the camera panned a certain direction.

"Looks like a strip club," Dottie suggested.

Whoever the woman was, she spun in tiny circles. Her hips swayed seductively in the same pulsating way that a belly dancer might. The music kept time, thumping a rhythmic beat. The view panned up to her face—blonde bangs and a heavy layer of eye shadow. The view then went south—past her bikini bottom and a nasty little tattoo sprawled across the small of her back —to the foreground, and a set of legs inside a pair of trousers.

"I think she's giving him a lap dance," I confessed. "Can you turn up the volume? I want to see if she says anything."

Dottie pressed a button and the music became louder. It sounded like Burt Bacharach singing "Wives and Lovers." A bald-headed bouncer passed directly behind the woman, just as she reached for the clasp on her bikini top.

"C'mon baby, let me see those puppies," the voice said.

"You got it bad, don't ya, Mr. G?"

Our view nodded up and down.

"Mr. G must have the camera mounted on a hat or something," Dottie said.

"It has to be Cecil Garl."

Five seconds later, the dancer removed her top, revealing her much-anticipated puppies. They didn't whimper, or toddle around the floor, pooping and peeing on old newspaper. Instead, the dancer brought them in for closer inspection.

"They're so adorable," the voice on the video said. "I want to cuddle your puppies."

The woman's face struck a weird expression.

"I want to slurp them up one side and down the other."

Whoever was behind the camera wanted to bury his face in the woman's chest. The woman would have none of it. She slapped the man across the face, which made a *crack* sound on the video. An instant later the camera view panned on the ceiling, then went completely blank.

"Well now," Dottie sighed, "so much for a happy ending."

"Why would he save something like that?" I asked.

"And why would he call them puppies?"

Dottie and I were both stumped, but finally she asked: "Where did you find this, Derrick?"

"At the Devil's Elbow."

"I know but *where* at the Devil's Elbow?"

"Now, now, Dottie. A gentleman never tells."

"I bet the police would like to see it."

I shrugged my shoulders, pressed the keys on the laptop and said, "Eventually, I'll show them. I've set my sights on the reward money."

"That's what I'm after too."

Dottie made a strange face when I clicked on *Fantasy's Two.* It was another point-of-view-style video. It started with a voice and a picture of a stage. The voice was loud and clear: *"Only from Fantasy's and ready to rock your world.....gentlemen, how about a nice, warm Traverse City welcome for Gen-e-sis?"*

"Sounds like a chapter in the Bible," I said.

"Old Testament," Dottie agreed with me.

A woman slid from behind the curtain like a cheetah on the prowl. Eyes straight ahead, every muscle and tendon fixated on some faraway prey. She slithered toward the camera, wearing a red boa, high heels and a matching teddy. Of course, we heard the slobbering whistles from the "gentlemen" and the overbearing music, thumping in the background.

"Are you into strip clubs, Derrick?"

"Not really."

"I don't remember you having an interest in them. What does 'not really' mean?"

"It means that I seldom go, and it's usually only when someone else drags me there."

Genesis had her back to one of the brass poles. She used it to support herself as she stood from crouched position. I must admit that she had a captivating style and the body of a goddess.

"Derrick, you're drooling."

I laughed.

"That's the same girl who slapped Mr. G," she said. "At least they have the same tattoo."

"I think you're right. She's beautiful."

Genesis had spun against the brass pole and it slid between her thighs and breasts. She had some girth, some muscle wrapped around a feminine physique.

"No wonder the guys are howling," Dottie observed.

"She's what you'd call a tall drink of water," I confessed.

"Metaphorically speaking, right Derrick?"

"Yep."

The view suddenly changed to an equally attractive woman, standing over the camera. "Here's your cocktail, Mr. G. Grand Marnier, on the rocks." She removed the glass from her tray and placed it on a napkin, next to a small bowl of nuts.

"Thanks, Cookie." The camera panned across a wad of currency. A left hand peeled a twenty and a five out of the bundle. "I'll need another one in a bit. Keep the change."

"Thank you." The waitress slid the money under another glass on her tray and the screen went blank. The show was over.

Dottie and I were wondering what had happened.

"Why would you ever save that video?" Dottie asked. "I mean, there's nothing to it."

"Maybe he was obsessed with Genesis."

"What do you mean?"

"It's that whole *conquering male* mentality," I suggested. "Some men are like that. They want to rule the world, but if they can't, they just want a piece of the pie. Seems like Cecil couldn't get enough of her."

Dottie wiggled around the edge of the galley table, held the salt and pepper shakers to the light, and put away the vacuum.

I asked her if Cecil Garl was a leftie.

"I don't know," she said. "I can find out. Wouldn't it be easier if we went to Fantasy's and talked to Genesis?"

"Who's *we*?"

"You and me, Derrick."

"Us?"

"Yes," she smirked. "Couples go all the time.....at least that's what I've heard."

I felt my chin crinkle with doubt.

"I'm going to check it out," Dottie said, pulling her phone out of her pocket.

While she did that, I opened the Excel spreadsheets from the zip drive. Cecil Garl had several lists: for the membership in the Society; for the advertisers in the magazine; and the country clubs throughout Michigan.

"Yes, what time does Genesis perform?" Dottie asked, telephone stuck to her ear. "Seven thirty? That would be fine." She held her hand over her mouth as if she was surprised. "Oh really. Sounds delightful. Thank you. Thank you so much."

She hung up the phone and turned in my direction. "Derrick, we're in luck," she cooed.

"Genesis performs at seven thirty." I stole some of her thunder.

"You're right. And ten thirty," Dottie frowned. "In between, they're having amateur hour. First prize is five hundred dollars."

"Hmm," I thought aloud, "there's no way I'm getting up on stage."

"Well, me neither," she said. "If we hurry, we'll only have to sit through two other dancers before she performs."

I closed Shafeek Heanley's laptop, pulled the zip drive from its port and tucked it into my shirt pocket. The thought of watching beautiful ladies take off their clothes seemed like a pleasant way to spend the evening. Never mind trout fishing or dinner at Pearl's, there was work to be done, "If we hurry."

Eight

"Do you like penis?"

I looked up at the waitress who was smiling politely in my direction. The music was rather loud and the chit-chat from the other patrons inside the club made it hard to understand what she was asking.

What do you mean, 'do I like penis?' That's kind of a bizarre question, isn't it?

After three or four seconds of waiting, the waitress lost her patience. "I tell ya what…I'll leave the *peanuts* right here, ok? Feel free to munch away."

"Oh, sure, that would be fine," I said, glancing at the salted peanuts in a small glass bowl.

"Are you hard of hearing, Luv?" Dottie asked.

I looked at her rather incredulously. What do you mean, '*am I God fearing?*'

"Of course I am, Dottie, why do you ask?"

"That's good that you can admit it. Lots of people wouldn't."

Her question seemed a little off the wall, but I wanted to remain polite. "I'm not going to let it stand in the way of a fun time. There's nothing wrong with admiring all God's creatures, know what I mean?"

"Yep," she nodded, somewhat graciously, "I'm glad we're on the same page."

Dottie had her hand on a rum and Coke; her index finger pinched the straw against the edge of the glass.

"I'm not surprised they have a two-drink minimum," Dottie yelled, "in addition to the cover charge you paid."

"How do you know so much about it?" I yelled.

"I used to be one."

"A stripper?"

Dottie smirked. "A dancer…it was a long time ago. After we split. Helped me finish my degree."

"Where was that?"

"Michigan State. I worked at Cheetah's, downtown. It was only a few blocks from the Capitol and a few more from campus." She raised the drink to her mouth and poured the liquid into the back of her throat. She was a gulper, not a sipper. "When all my friends were taking out student loans and scrimping to get by, I was pulling down seven hundred a week, cash."

"That's good money for a college kid."

Dottie smiled. "For a grown kid it's good money too. Those were the days."

"So what's the plan?"

Dottie didn't hesitate. "We'll ask her for a lap dance when she's finished on stage. Once we get her back there we'll start asking questions." She gestured to a bank of cubicles shrouded in purple and black buntings. "Did you bring money?"

"Yeah…did you?"

"No," she smirked.

"Sounds like I'm going to be the one financing this endeavor. What should I pay her for the lap dance?"

"Fifty, and she'll sing like a canary."

I looked at the stage, twenty yards away. Genesis was in her own little world, performing for an imaginary lover with the same care-free innocence as an adolescent dancing to her favorite song. She was spinning and crouching, throwing her head back, and thrusting her hips seductively. Aside from a pair of fluffy, feathered wings in her hands, and dark pink polish on her nails, she was completely nude. Her choice of music was old fashioned, but it seemed to compliment her style, her physique, her flair for the esoteric: *"Volare, whoa-oh-oh-oh. Compari. Nel blu dipinto di blu."*

"Try not to drool, ok, Luv?" Dottie prodded.

"Is that what it means?" I asked.

"What?"

"*Nel blu dipinto di blu.*"

"Hardly. *In the sky, painted blue.*"

"Serious?"

"Seriously, Luv. It's Italian."

The bouncer passed in front of us. He looked like the same bald-headed bloke from the Garl video and a much larger version than what I remembered. Dottie realized it, too. She looked up from her empty cocktail glass and nudged my elbow. "I bet he'd have some info for us," she cooed.

"How's that going to work, Dottie? You can't just go racing up to him and start drilling him to go on the record."

"Oh, no?" she asked, taking the ice chunks in her mouth. "Do you have any better ideas?"

"Well, yeah. You have to ease into it sometimes. I try to build a little rapport with people before asking questions. Let's just play it cool and see where this leads us."

Dottie poked the ice with her straw. She scanned the patrons who appeared to be a mix of locals and out-of-towners. There were plenty of men and more than a few women; the vast majority less than forty years old.

"Of course, I'll have another," Dottie blurted to the waitress. "Make it a tall, will you?"

"And for you, sir?" she asked, pointing in my direction.

"I'm doing just fine, thank you."

The waitress whisked away, and I asked Dottie if we were working or having fun.

"Of course, we're working," she scoffed. "I just want to have fun while we're at it."

The announcer's voice came over the public address system: "Guys and gals. Ladies and gentlemen, how about a nice round of applause for Genesis?"

The crowd didn't exactly erupt with raucous applause, but rather, a polite, nonchalant approval.

Genesis picked up the dollars spread across the stage as if they were her children's dirty laundry. She scooped up her assorted garments and disappeared behind a velour curtain at the back of the stage.

"I'll be right back," I told Dottie.

One of the two goons at the front door stamped the back of my hand when I told him I was going outdoors to have a smoke. Instead of lighting up within a few feet of the entrance, I ambled around the back to where I figured most of the talent would do the same.

It was dusk in northern Michigan. Seagulls passed overhead and I heard the lonesome wail of a killdeer off in the distance. They were all headed north—to the hallowed breeding grounds—and the perfect summertime destination.

I noticed the coffee can at the back door. It had an inch or two of butts in the bottom; most were smeared with lipstick.

Instead of waiting just outside the door—which might be threatening—I decided to stand ten or fifteen feet away. Regardless, I heard female voices inside and the clip-clop of high heels on a tile floor.

Finally, the door burst open and two ladies stepped outside. They were complaining about a patron or one of the managers, I was certain. Foul language and an angry tone preceded them.

Genesis was one of the women. She was wrapped in a white, terrycloth robe and matching pair of house slippers. Their conversation ended when they realized that their smoking lounge had been infested by an outsider.

"You're not supposed to be out here," a redheaded woman barked.

"Oh?" I acted dumb.

"This is our place to smoke. If you don't get outta here, I'm gonna get Hal out here. He'll crack your skull."

"That won't be necessary," I pleaded. "I just need a few minutes with Genesis."

Genesis pinched a long, thin cigarette between her fingers. She seemed to weigh my request, a hand on her hip. "Don't get Hal. It'll be okay," she said.

Genesis ambled towards me, clutching her robe under her neck. Its collar was smeared with the orangey residue of make-up. "What is it?"

"I want to ask you about a man named Cecil Garl."

"What about him?"

"You know he was murdered, don't you?"

She didn't say a thing.

"You know that his family was killed too, and that the police haven't made any arrests."

She stood there, arms crossed. One hand stuffing the smoke into her mouth, the other flicking fake nails attached to her long, feminine fingers.

"Are you a cop or something?"

"No."

"Well, who are you?"

"Derrick Twitchell. I'm a down-stater."

After several seconds, she softened her stance. I must have passed her unofficial litmus test.

"Look," I said, "I know that you've had some dealings with him. Was he in love with you?"

"No, heck no," she said softly. "He was married. All he ever wanted was a good time."

"What was he like?"

She glanced over her shoulder to her co-worker who was

fiddling with her phone. Both women looked to be in their late twenties, tall and fit. Museum-grade female specimens.

"He was a peculiar kind of cat," she said. "The guy liked literature and the humanities. Cultural stuff."

"Like what?"

Genesis didn't hesitate. "Edgar Allen Poe. He loved that guy. Used to quote passages from *The Raven* all the time."

"Do you remember some verses?"

She pulled on her smoke and I could tell that she was sifting through the files in her memory bank. The more I admired her silky blonde hair, and fine features, the more she looked like a Scandinavian. "It was something about forgotten lore, as a way to forget about his love, Lenore."

"That's good. I'm surprised that you remember."

"Why?"

"I don't know. He's been gone for almost a year."

"Maybe I'm a bit eccentric myself," she mused.

It would have been easy to ask her why, but I knew that she'd say more. She took one last puff on her cigarette, scraped the end against the brick wall of the building, and gave the butt a fling into the hedges' green plenty. So much for the coffee can. "Yeah, it was forgotten lore, the love Lenore, and the raven's name, Nevermore," she confessed.

"Have the police talked to you?"

"No, why?"

"You may have been one of the last people to see him alive."

She huffed. "Mr. Twitchell, do I need an attorney?"

"No, not now. And besides, it sounds like you have nothing to worry about."

The redhead opened the door and went inside. It was just Genesis and me in the evening still.

"What can you tell me about the Fatima Cultural Society?" I asked.

She took the invitation I had found at the cabin and made a sour face. "It was some hoity-toity club that he came up with.

Since he was the founder, he wanted me to write a story for the magazine. He thought it would be great for me to become a writer, so somehow I could quit being a dancer."

"What did he want you to write?"

She shook her head and handed the invitation back to me, "Something about Washington Irving."

"What about him?"

"He wrote the Legend of Sleepy Hollow. You know, it's about a Dutch town and its quirky customs. Mr. G thought Sleepy Hollow was a lot like Holland because of all the Dutch people who live there."

"Yeah, but the Legend is about the Headless Horseman and Ichabod Crane."

She shook her head and rolled her eyes. "That guy had a lot of messed up ideas."

"How much time did you spend with him?"

"Not a whole lot."

"What does that mean?"

"I met him a long time ago, and I cared for him. He used to help me with my rent," she sighed. "My car insurance, too."

"I see. Where do you live?"

"The Arbors in Traverse."

"Nice."

"When he came to town, we'd meet at the apartment and then go out to eat."

"Like where?" I asked.

"Dinner and drinks at Fischer's Happy Hour up in Northport. He loved their perch sandwiches and strawberry pie."

"What else?"

"They had sweet potato fries—"

"No, no. What other places did you go?"

Her eyebrows rose. "His cabin up in Good Hart. Sometimes he had business in Paradise and we'd go up together."

"Paradise in the Upper Peninsula?"

"Yep. Cecil had an old Corvette that he liked to drive when

the weather was decent. He always made me feel special when he asked me to go with him."

"Why did he go up there?"

"He had an important client, and I think Cecil had a post office box too."

"So he lived in the Saginaw area, had a cabin in Good Hart, but spent some time in Paradise?"

"Yep. We spent some time in Antigua, too."

"Nice. Anything else?"

"All I remember him saying is that 'if anything ever happens to me, they'll find me handcuffed and drowned somewhere out in Whitefish Bay.'"

"Who said that?"

"Mr. G," she sighed. "He never would tell me why he felt threatened."

"Did he ever mention a Mr. Luxton, or a company called Ener-X?"

She paused for a second or two. "The guy was constantly on the phone. I'm trying to remember who he may have spoken to."

She seemed to know more than what she was leading on. It begged the question: "Were you sleeping with him?"

I seem to have struck a nerve with her. She clasped her robe under her chin and shook her head.

Just then the back door opened and Hal the Bouncer appeared. "Everything okay, Jenna?"

"Yeah," she said out of the side of her mouth.

"Boss Man wants you in here. Three tables need a dance."

"Right," she mumbled, "I'll be right in."

Hal didn't leave. Instead, he tapped the edge of the door with a massive index finger.

"Jenna," I begged, "take my business card. Call me if you can think of anything else."

She stuffed my card in the pocket of her robe and calmly nodded, "Happy trails."

Nine

Dottie was still nursing her cocktail when I finally made it back to the table. Her eyes seemed to have a bit of a glaze on them so I figured that she was well on her way to inebriation.

Even though I felt like the stop at Fantasy's was worthwhile—after speaking to Genesis—I believed Dottie had more to share with me than what we had discussed.

What better way to pry the facts from someone than with the truth serum of alcohol?

"What are you drinking, Dottie?"

"Captain and Coke."

"Have you had enough booze to strike the Captain's pose on a barrel of rum?"

She laughed. "Not yet."

I gathered a handful of nuts in my hand and tossed them into the back of my mouth. A second later, she started asking questions, in rat-a-tat fashion. "Did you tell her about the secret videos of her?"

"No"

"Did you tell her that you know Mr. G liked to drink Grand Marnier?"

"No."

"Did you ask her about 'the puppies'?"

"No. Heck no."

She grimaced. "Did she deny knowing Cecil?"

"Not at all."

"So she knew him?"

"Sounded like Cecil was a really good customer and paid for some of her bills."

"Really?"

"Yeah. She also said that he spent some time up in Paradise." Dottie slugged her drink, so I mentioned the warning. "He told her 'if anything ever happens to me, I'll be handcuffed and drowned in Whitefish Bay.'"

"Nasty. How about Luxton?" she demanded.

"She didn't remember Cecil saying that name, but she did say that Cecil was on his cell phone constantly."

"Do you believe her?"

"Sure. She seemed sincere. Let's just say that I had no reason to doubt her."

Dottie's attention turned to a table near the stage. Genesis was sifting through the patrons, trolling for whoever wanted her attention.

"I don't think we need a lap dance anymore," I told Dottie. "I have all the information I needed."

"By the sounds of things, it wasn't much."

"You're correct."

"Then what are we doing here?" Dottie asked.

"I don't know," I shrugged. "Did you want to talk about the case?"

"What about it?"

"What do the police have for evidence?"

"They know that the family was killed at close range by a

twenty-five caliber handgun. They know that there was only one set of bloody footprints at the crime scene."

"What size?"

"Ten."

"What kind of shoe?" I asked.

"It was a boot. They think it was a work boot. The tread was worn."

"So they know that whoever killed the Garls might have been in the trades? Maybe a farmer, fruit grower, a handyman?"

"True and correct."

"Keep going," I said.

"They know that Garl and Luxton had some bad blood between them. They had a beef at a board meeting."

"And that Garl was a bit quirky, wouldn't you say?"

"No doubt about it," she opined.

"Did Luxton have a twenty-five caliber?" I asked.

"Yep. The cops found it when they conducted the search warrant, but ballistics tests proved it wasn't the murder weapon."

"You think Luxton was leading them on?" I asked.

Dottie watched Genesis lead a man in a blue polo to a more private setting. The redhead was on stage, fawning all over herself to Prince's *Red Corvette.*

"I don't know if he was or he wasn't. All I know is that he had an alibi, and he passed a polygraph."

Dottie raised her glass and the waitress scooped up the empty.

"Now it's your turn, Luv." She nudged me on the elbow. "Tell me what you know."

I wasn't exactly sure how to answer, so I dodged the question. "I know that this case is almost a year old, and still no arrests."

Dottie picked at the peanuts. She pivoted in the booth so that we were much closer to one another. I caught the hint of her perfume and it smelled great.

"What I can't understand is that everybody keeps pointing to Luxton as the culprit, but it appears as if he's not the man."

"What do you mean?" she asked.

"I mean, the cops must not have anything on him to issue an arrest."

"What size shoe did he wear?"

"Ten," she laughed, playfully.

"Hmm."

"Are you going to buy me another drink, Derrick?"

"I can," I said with a smile. "So why did it take so long for the bodies to be discovered?"

"The Garls were going on vacation," she said.

"Didn't anyone call them? They didn't have cell service?"

"Not on Lake Michigan. Have you ever been on the Great Lakes? You'd think the cell service would be terrific without any clutter, but the opposite is true."

"Where were they going?" I asked.

"Antigua, eventually, but first Beaver Island. The whole family was the guest of Mr. Heanley."

"You mean the boat we were on?"

"Yep."

"What was their relationship?"

"They did some business."

"Like what?" I asked.

"Well now, aren't you Mr. Inquisitive." The waitress brought another drink. Dottie made the first obvious signal that she was drunk: "Did I tell you that the footprints were a size ten?"

"Sure did," I grimaced. "Boots, too."

"You're so smart, Derrick." She placed her hand on my bicep. "Aren't you going to have a drink?"

"No," I smirked. "I have a long drive ahead of me."

"Lighten up, Luv," she said, as he took another swallow. "Let's have some fun now that the work is over."

The redhead finished her performance and sauntered off stage. A buzz of conversation circulated amongst the crowd before another song drowned the din.

"How do you do it, Derrick?"

"Do what?" I asked.

"Make a living as a writer."

I laughed.

Dottie wasn't laughing. "I mean people still read newspapers. They want to know what's going on, but I can't get the paper to give me a raise. I have twenty years of experience and yet, I really struggle to make ends meet."

I felt sorry for Dottie and her financial plight. Something about her situation reminded me of just how tenuous our careers can be. Her shoulder was barely an arm's length away. I placed my hand on her back and gave it a friendly pat. "You know how to console a grammar Nazi, don't you?"

"No," she smiled.

"There, they're, their."

"Ha," she laughed, "very clever, Derrick."

The waitress brought the check. I just about fell out of my chair when I saw the tally: fifty-five dollars for four drinks. *No wonder I don't go to strip joints.*

"That's the difference between you and me," she said. "You'd figure out a way to get around the bosses at the paper and make your way in life. You're clever and creative, good looking and…"

"Keep going," I cracked.

"Witty," she smacked me on the thigh. "I'm stuck in a rut. I'm a reporter, a bartender and take care of rich people's boats." Her hand didn't leave my thigh. It made me squirm in my seat.

Perhaps my strategy of getting her a little tipsy was backfiring. Dottie seemed to be after a little more than impromptu undercover work. Her words were drawn out and somewhat slurred. Five fingers on my thigh brought back so many erotic encounters with her. She didn't miss a beat, even though twenty-five years had passed.

Dottie was holding something back. She never did say what the relationship was between Shafeek Heanley and Cecil Garl.

"I just have to win that prize money from the *Free Press*," she lamented. "It would mean so much to me and my family, and my family too. Heck, it would be a major boost to my career. I could tell the bosses and their bosses where to go."

She was repeating herself, *ad nauseam*.

The more she waxed poetic about the hundred grand and how she would spend it, the more I thought about how we arrived at the south end of Traverse City. After putting gas in Shafeek Heanley's yacht and changing the oil in the dinghy's outboard, Dottie followed me from Charlevoix down Highway 31, past the little hamlets of Atwood, Eastport, and Elk Rapids. Eventually, we made our way around the picturesque waters of East Bay, which looked as pretty as a postcard. Dottie and I passed the sprawling shopping centers near Chum's Corners, south of town. The rationale for driving separate vehicles was that I'd be going south from there, while Dottie would return to the North Country.

Now that she was teetering on the edge of inebriation, I felt a twinge of guilt for wanting to leave. At the risk of sounding schizophrenic, an angel on one shoulder whispered in my ear: "Buy her a cab….get something to eat and a cup of coffee… give her a ride." On the other shoulder was the devil: "It's not your problem that she had too much to drink. Don't spend the money for dinner. Head for the hills, man."

Dottie seemed to have read my mind: "I think I've had enough, Derrick."

"Ya think?"

She nodded.

"Come on." I stuffed three twenties and a pair of ones in the check holder, took Dottie's hand and helped her slide out of the booth. We ambled past big Hal at the door to the parking lot outside. As we approached my Impala and her Subaru, adorned with a kayak rack, I asked her to walk a white line on the pavement.

"You're crazy, Derrick. That will be no problem at all." She stepped to the line and held out her arms. "I used to be a gymnast," she slurred.

"If the cops were here, they'd tell you to walk heel to toe."

Dottie mounted the imaginary balance beam, but didn't get far. She yelped in delight when she lost her footing and nearly fell. "I guess that'll be a two-point deduction."

"Come on," I said, "let's try another one. Put your head back and your arms out to the side. Close your eyes and try to touch your nose."

Dottie giggled when one finger poked her ear, the other, her eye. She almost fell into my arms.

"You okay, Dottie?" I asked. Her head was squarely on my shoulder. She nodded, halfheartedly, but I had the strangest sensation that maybe she wanted me to sweep her off her feet. "Hate to tell you this, but you've failed the field sobriety test. Since Captain Morgan isn't here to drive, I will. Come on," I said, holding the Impala's passenger side door open, "jump in."

"Let me get my phone," she said, crouching inside her door. "Where are we going, anyway?"

"Across the street."

Her head snapped to the surroundings. There, in the twilight of northern Michigan, the illuminated signage beckoned weary, and penny-wise travelers from near and far: Econo-lodge.

"Oh, Derrick," she purred, "aren't you counting your chickens before they hatch?"

"What do you mean?"

"I'm not that kind of girl."

"What kind of girl?"

"The kind you take to a motel on the first date."

"This isn't our first date, Dottie. We've just taken twenty years off in between."

Instead of holding my feet to the fire, Dottie pushed the buttons on her phone. She scrolled through her emails and texts while I drove across the street. "Give me a minute," I said as I hopped from the car and headed for the motel office.

I was half expecting to be overwhelmed with the odor of curry chicken and incense when I opened the office door to the motel. Instead, I was greeted with fresh air and a smiling woman who only charged me sixty-seven dollars for a room with a king-sized bed. Seemed like a really good rate for a holiday weekend in northern Michigan. "Check out is at eleven. Continental breakfast is six to ten-thirty."

"Perfect."

Dottie was still flipping through her phone when I returned to the car. "Everything ok?" I asked.

"Yep. Nothing I can't handle in the morning."

A minute later I found the correct room and slid the key through the waiting lips on the lock. The light blinked green and I swung the door wide. Dottie went in first, and placed a hand on the wall. She reached for a shoe and gave it a fling. The second met the same fate.

"Derrick," she pleaded, "can you do me a huge favor and bring me my purse? I left it in the car across the street."

"Why don't you give me the keys to the car and I'll bring both?"

"You're so smart, Derrick," she laughed. "Here ya go. The clutch is a little touchy. You'll figure it out."

I caught the keys, and started walking. With no one to talk to—or a phone to occupy my attention—I was alone with my thoughts, my conscience, my forty-something years of existence. It was rather difficult to banish the scenarios that were banging around my head; the angels and demons barking in my ears made it a hundred times worse. "Run, Forest Run," the voices said. I swatted them away as if they were birdies in a game of badminton. I felt like a jerk for putting myself in this position, while at the same time I knew that I really hadn't done anything wrong. My wife, my child, the nice little life we have in Mid-Michigan are a million miles away. I'm not really a cheater, but I'm not opposed to capitalizing on a situation, either. The walk across the street might as well have been the five-mile walk across the Mackinac Bridge. It took forever.

My actions may have been justified, but it certainly didn't appear to be all that kosher. *Even though my wife would slit my throat if she knew what I was doing, I had the best intentions of being home before midnight.*

Five or ten minutes later I was back at the room, a black leather bag over my wrist. The only light was from the bathroom. No television or bedside lamp. Dottie was sprawled out on the comforter—facing me, wearing a matching set of flesh-colored bra and panties. Middle age had caught up to us. Gone were the days of skimpy undergarments tied together with spaghetti strings and lace; Dottie's granny panties and bra—at least three inches wide across her back—looked comfortable and downright sexy in a steel-belted kind of way.

"Nice bag, Derrick," she giggled. "Thank you so much."

"You're welcome, Dottie." I placed her purse and keys near the TV stand. "I think you were going to tell me about the relationship between Shafeek Heanley and Mr. G."

"Oh, Derrick, do we *have* to talk business?"

"Well…"

"Wouldn't you rather come over here and play with me, just for old time's sake?" She rolled on her back, one leg stroking the other leg's shin. Her arms were over her head, fingers kneading an imaginary baguette.

I hesitated for the longest time, admiring the view, toying with the possibilities, relishing the incandescent fire that was boiling madly in front of me.

"Sleep well, Dorothy Kalakay," I sighed, "it's been real...."

"But not real fun," she confessed.

"See ya round."

"Hey, Derrick," she said, as I stepped one foot across the threshold.

"Yeah?"

"Thanks."

I closed the door behind me, mounted my trusty Impala, and drove home.

Ten

Two hours later, I turned back the covers on our bed and slid quietly between the sheets. They smelled fresh and clean—like they had been washed in the spring rain and dried with a box of potpourri. It had been a long day. A very long day.

Try as I might not to wake my bedmate, she rolled on her side, and placed her arm across my chest.

"Welcome home, baby."

"Thanks," I sighed.

"Everything okay?" she asked.

"Yep," I whispered, "it's good to be home."

Colleen's hand moved from my chest to the side of my face. It was good to be home, in her loving arms.

My eyelids were getting heavy. I could feel my lungs fill up with air, then gradually let go. Sleep was carrying me away on the current of a gentle breeze. Try as I might to forget about it, the image of Dottie sprawled out on the bed stated on my mind. It was a pleasant mental picture and one that I couldn't banish.

"Baby…" Colleen purred.

"Yes," I uttered, clinging to the last crumb of consciousness.

"Do you want me to wait till morning to tell you what happened?"

Colleen's words splashed me in the face. She made me think about all the good things around the house that possibly could have gone wrong. Before she spoke, I remembered seeing the dog inside the front door. Her van didn't have any dents in it, and my daughter was sound asleep in her bed. No urgent mail on the counter, and when I brushed my teeth, cold water poured from the faucet the way it should.

It was a terrible question to ask. *Of course, I wanted to know what happened.*

"Tell me, Colleen."

"We had a visitor this afternoon. Two of them, actually. Right after you called. They left a card on the kitchen counter."

"Who?"

"The state police."

"What?" My heart was racing again.

"A couple of detectives from the state police post in Midland: Jerry VanWyk and Richard Nutting."

"Oh, jeez," I gasped. Now I was wide awake. "What did they want?"

"It's about the case, Derrick. The jumper lady. They said that they have to investigate every death as a murder until they can prove otherwise."

I didn't know what to say. It was really bad news.

"They said that the jumper was a person of interest in the Garl murders up north. Since you were the last person to see her alive, they're investigating you, too."

My mind was racing.

"You had a really good plan, by avoiding the cops at the bridge in Midland, and going to the storage facility before anyone knew she was gone, but now it looks like you're not going to get away with it."

"They knew about the storage thing too?"

"Oh yeah."

"What did they say?"

"They said a witness at the storage place had written down my van's license plate, and found out that it belonged to me."

"That nosey—"

"Don't be mad, Derrick. The detectives told me that the

truck driver said there was another person on the bridge with the jumper."

"For heaven's sake, what should I do?" I asked. The question seemed to linger in the evening air like the plume from the rear end of a skunk.

"Tell the truth," she said.

I sighed.

"The truth never hurts," she said.

"What? Show them the suicide note?"

"Yes."

"What about the part where she had the combination to her storage locker?"

"Yes."

"But I didn't have permission to access it."

"Probably, but you gotta face the music."

"Colleen!"

"What? Don't look at me. I didn't do anything wrong."

Our voices were getting loud. We were having an old-fashioned argument. It was the last thing I wanted to do after such a long day.

"Just tell the truth," she said again. "The truth will set you free."

"Maybe I should call a lawyer."

"It wouldn't hurt."

"Just a second. What did *you* tell the detectives?"

"I denied knowing anything about the suicide," she said. "You borrowed my van to go fishing and that was all I knew."

I looked at her in disbelief. "Whatever happened to telling the truth?"

She huffed.

"Come on, Colleen."

"I couldn't tell them the truth and at the same time throw you under the bus."

"Thanks, I think. Did they ask where I was?"

"No," she shook her head.

"Anything about the Garl murder?"

"No."

"Are you sure?" I asked.

"Derrick!"

I hopped out of bed, steaming mad that I might have gotten caught. It seemed like the perfect plan—hatched on a whim, and executed without a glitch. My timing was impeccable, or so it seemed.

"Where you going?"

"I'm getting up."

"Why?"

"I'm going to re-write Becky Tocca's suicide note."

"What?"

"You heard me."

"Derrick!"

"What?" I demanded. "If she gave me permission to be in her locker, the cops can't charge me with anything."

Colleen grunted. "You…you…" She grunted again. "Just tell the truth!"

It seemed like the tenth time she had mentioned telling the truth. After hearing it so many times, it gave me pause. I disappeared into the walk-in closet and pulled out another plain, gray sweatshirt and a Tigers cap.

"On second thought, Derrick, I think you should just leave."

"Leave?" I barked, incredulously.

"Yeah," she backhanded. "Get out of here. Go fishing. Go up north. Tomorrow is Memorial Day and the detectives won't be working."

"Why the change of heart?"

"When you come home smelling like perfume with no explanation, I have to wonder what's going on."

"Colleen…"

"Go!"

Eleven

The following morning I woke up early and drove up north all over again. Instead of taking my time and enjoying the solitude, I felt a pang of remorse for hurting Colleen's feelings. Instead of sleeping on the couch, and getting up early in the morning, I should have told her all about the information I had gleaned from my trip to the Tip of the Mitt. She would have appreciated the predicament I was in, and believed me when I told her that the encounter with Genesis and Dorothy was completely innocent. Since I had departed without saying a word, a note on the counter, or a kiss goodbye, her agitation with me made things a thousand times worse.

I had a horrible sense of regret for not being smarter when it came to the storage facility. Jim Rockford would have parked some distance away, and walked to Becky's locker. That way, the guy with the weed sprayer may never have known I was there. If I was quicker, he wouldn't have caught me. If I was friendlier, he might not have written down my license plate. The regrets and anger piled up faster than the miles on my Impala.

The cops who came to our house were just doing their job. If I had to do it all over again, I would have given Becky's note to the trooper, given the cops my statement, and went on my way. It would have taken an hour out of my day, but at least I wouldn't have this heartache and lament hanging over my head.

Since I really wasn't involved in the Garl murders before meeting Becky Tocca, it really shouldn't have been a big deal to surrender the letter. There are lots of murders in Michigan, and plenty of missing people, too. I should have turned a blind eye to the information Becky provided, and gone about my business of fixing the boat and repairing the old Suburban.

Now that I was in the middle of this mess, I had to do something.

I could tell the truth and face the music, as Colleen suggested. The most the cops could charge me with would be breaking and entering—a felony—or a misdemeanor charge of illegal entry. Either way, I was in big trouble. I'd have to hire a lawyer to help me get out of this, and that was an expense I really didn't want to incur.

Of course, without Becky's note and testimony, the state police would have no evidence to suggest that I was in Becky's storage locker illegally. Becky was dead, and without a star witness, the cops wouldn't have much to go on.

The wheels in my head kept spinning as I passed the exits for Frederic, Gaylord, Indian River, and Cheboygan. I kept driving north—up I-75—the main artery for tourists bent on a northern Michigan getaway. When I reached the Straits of Mackinac, I called in a food order to Clyde's Drive In in St. Ignace. After crossing the Mighty Mac, and paying the toll, breakfast was waiting for me on the counter: three eggs over easy, hash browns, bacon, wheat toast, and hot coffee. I made nice with an elderly couple from Plymouth who were on their way to the Porcupine Mountains. They couldn't help but smile at the novelty of eating breakfast a long ways from home. Twenty minutes later, and ten dollars lighter in the pocketbook, I was back on the road, up Highway 123 and through the little outpost of Trout Lake. Seems like such a cozy place; an afterthought of a villa that once must have been a train depot. Above the general store is a sign that reads: Rooms $40 a night. Seemed like a peculiar place to crash, but if I had too much to drink at Yogi's Bar or the Village Inn down the street, it would be a cheap option to hole up for the evening.

Before I reached the intersection of 123 and Highway 28, I had all but decided to rewrite Becky's suicide note.

It would be simple enough.

> *To whom it may concern,*
>
> *I am sorry about the damage to your vehicle. Feel free to file a lien against what little possessions I have left in this world. All my belongings are in a storage facility on Wilder Road in Bay City. The combination is 19-10-24, locker 224. Whoever finds this note can have access. My sister will handle the estate sale.*

I'd type the note on an old fashioned typewriter, burn the ribbon, and replace it with a new one. To make the letters on my typewriter look differently from the letters on Becky's suicide note, I'd take a tiny rasp, or a chain saw file, to several letters on the keyboard. The "e" might have a cleft tail; the "F" a pockmark on its back. It was a brilliant plan, and one that I thought was foolproof.

If the cops took the letter and examined it for Becky's fingerprints, I didn't have to explain why they weren't there. They would have the burden of proof. My fingerprints on the paper were easy to explain; I found the note fair and square.

If the detectives wanted to know what we talked about, I'd tell most of the truth. Maybe not the whole truth, but a lot of it.

How would they know any different? Becky Tocca was dead. What was left of her body would still be resting in the morgue. Becky's sister, her associates at work, her friends and relatives would all be shocked and saddened by the news of her departure. They'd be calling each other and sending flowers, or handwritten, sorrow-filled notes. There would be hugs and tears and heartfelt mourning. Becky's sister might not have known about the storage locker; she may not even know that her apartment was vacated. Either way, it was none of my concern.

North I drove, past the abandoned Bear Butt Inn in Eckerman and the turnoff for the Curly Lewis Highway, along the edge of Lake Superior. The maple and aspen forests had melted into a balsam and tag alder swamp. Gone were the subtle, charismatic undulations in the geography south of M-28; Paradise is nestled on the edge of the Tahquamenon River valley; a chip shot away from an unsalted sea.

I hadn't been to Paradise in quite some time. When I rolled into town and saw the robins parading across the lawns of the cabins, the library, the deputy's house, and the community center, it made me realize that things hadn't changed much. The tourists and residents still needed a place to stay, places to eat, and things to do. Beneath the hardened, weather-worn façade of the business fronts, were the residents who made the community a home.

My first stop was at the hardware store. A rather frail woman behind the counter was on the internet when I walked inside. She greeted me with a wholesome smile although I could tell that whatever she was doing on her laptop held quite an attraction. The hardwood floor creaked and groaned as I made my way past the paint department, the plumbing supplies, and the pots and pans. A modest selection of fishing tackle caught my eye. Tiny spinners, adorned with colorful blades and wisps of squirrel tail, made me realize that we were in trout fishing country. Then again, there were several pictures of giant-sized muskellunge and pike taped to the particleboard partition. Whoever took the photos seemed to relish in the fish's dental attributes. They were toothy and dripping with slobber, all of which gave me the creeps.

"Can I help you find something?"

"I'm sorry," I panted, "you startled me."

She smiled. "Didn't mean to do that."

I looked at her feet. A pair of white sneakers helped muffle her approach. Everything in the UP serves a purpose: the musky's dental lair and the woman's choice in footwear.

"Have any canning supplies?" I asked.

"Right this way."

I followed her past the trapping equipment, roofing nails, and the gun cleaning kits, to a small shelf stacked with jars and lids. The boxes of pectin were covered in a fine layer of dust.

"The sugar is across the street at the grocery store. You're a bit early for blueberry picking."

I smiled. "Should I come back later today?"

"Ha, ha. No, I meant—"

"Later in the summer. Couple months, wouldn't you say?"

"Maybe two and a half. The first or second week of August is prime time, if we get the right amount of rain."

I picked up a dozen jelly jars and a gallon of roof cement and placed them on the counter. The woman banged at the keys on the register, and told me the total. If I was going to get her to open up about the Garl murders, the exchange of currency would be an excellent way to loosen up her vocal cords.

The woman took my credit card and I moved into high gear: "Who's the postmaster, anyway?"

"Here?" she asked, somewhat baffled by the abnormal query. "It's Ben Whitepigeon, but they're closed today."

I nodded. Of course they're closed. It's Memorial Day.

"Where does he live?" I asked.

The woman behind the counter lost her friendliness. "I…I…don't know."

I knew what she was thinking: *Why do you want to know?*

"He's not in any trouble, is he?"

"No, no. I wonder if he might have known Cecil Garl."

A pause settled between us. The woman blinked the blinks of insecurity as she ran my credit card through the little machine. "Why do you want to know that?"

Her question was more like an answer. Not only did she know who Cecil Garl was, but she seemed to have a vested interest in following his plight. I gave her the benefit of the doubt when I casually mentioned, "You might not know it, but he and his family were murdered last summer."

"Oh, we know all about it. If you're all set here, why don't you be on your way?"

I was stunned by her comment. It had been quite a few years since I had been thrown out of any establishment.

"Alrighty," I said, sarcastically.

I grabbed my supplies and stepped outside. The door slammed shut at about the same time it struck a small bell mounted to the frame. Instead of moving quickly away, I lingered on the stoop for several seconds. When I glanced inside, the woman was already on the phone. It could have been anybody she was talking to, but I suspected it was Mr. Whitepigeon himself.

That didn't take long, I thought. *The word is out...a stranger's in town.*

Several seconds later, the internet on my phone didn't have any records of Mr. Whitepigeon's home address. I was out of luck.

It was too early for lunch; way too early to go to the bar. I could have gone to Tahquamenon Falls, but that wouldn't have accomplished much. The tourists there wouldn't have any information. I was convinced that the meat and potatoes of the Garl situation were right here in downtown Paradise.

I stuffed my supplies in the Impala, and drove to the auspicious giant hotel near the edge of Whitefish Bay. It had more than a couple signs posted about "No Dogs" or "No Parking," which seemed rather unwelcoming. The young man behind the counter offered no help regarding Cecil Garl. Of course, management wasn't there either.

I set my sights on the hotel just north of the blinking light on the left. They didn't know Mr. Garl, and said it's not their policy to reveal their guests' names. Unless I posed as an FBI agent or some fictitious licensing person from Lansing, nobody was going to help me. In reality, I wouldn't help me out either; my request for information was way out of line.

I was getting frustrated.

This trip to the UP was turning into a wild goose chase; the odds of recovery worse than finding a needle in a haystack.

My hunch was a bust.

I went back to a diner and ordered a coffee and a piece of homemade blueberry pie. The place was bustling with people and conversation. When the waitress presented a plate of giant buttermilk pancakes to my neighbor at the counter, he said with a laugh, "Why, they're as big as saddle blankets!"

The waitress smiled and said "You're lucky they're not pale faces."

They laughed. It must have been a line from a movie, a play, or a church production that had them snickering.

As much as I wanted to join in on the frivolity, I couldn't shake the images of what must have been taking place at the Devil's Elbow. The organizers would have a sandwich board posted at the end of the driveway that read: Auction Today. The church parking lot would be full of cars and pickups, not to mention the mystery tour bus. Volunteers in their golf carts and six wheeled vehicles would shuttle folks up and down the long, winding driveway to the cozy gravel area between the Garls' garage and the cabin itself. I'm sure the auctioneer would be on a wooden hay wagon of some sort, surrounded by the Garls' belongings that were light enough to be transported from inside the cabin. *"Who'll give me twenty-five bucks for this bag of stuff? Spatulas, knives and forks; great for chicken, fish and pork."* Away he'd go, with the rambly-scrambly way auctioneers up the ante.

"Anybody sitting here?"

I snapped out of my daydream, just in time to see a brown pant leg swing over the stool next to me. "No, suit yourself.... deputy."

"Thank you."

"The usual, Gordie?" the waitress asked.

"Just a coffee today, Sherry. I'm on official business and don't have much time to eat."

"What's that?" she asked.

"Got some down-stater up here sniffing around where he doesn't belong."

"Oh?" she asked, placing a mug of coffee in front of the deputy. "What does he look like?"

"Gray sweatshirt." When he picked up his mug, it left a brown ring on the paper placemat adorned with advertisements for saw mills, insurance agencies, and funeral homes. "And a tan Tigers' cap."

"No kidding."

I pushed my plate and fork towards the waitress and tipped my Tigers cap on my head.

She picked up my plate and the deputy's discarded creamer container, oblivious to the ruse that was taking place.

"When you find this person, what are you going to say to him?"

"That we don't need any down-staters up here sniffing around."

I was starting to get a little hot under the collar. Maybe it was the jolt of coffee coursing through my veins that made me want to speak up.

"What do you have to hide?" I asked with a smirk.

The deputy barely acknowledged my question. He kept the mug pressed to his upper lip, as if he was inhaling the coffee beans themselves. I glanced down at the hardware clipped to his belt: the handgun, the cuffs, a giant ring for a baton. It was all right there, an arm length's away.

His face was rather long; a flap of skin beneath his chin looked like a miniature waddle a chicken or a turkey would be proud of. It drooped over his cream-colored necktie and the button-down collar adorned with miniature pins from career achievements past.

My question seemed to fester in the bustling commotion. The waitress had moved on to other patrons while I reached in to my pocket and pulled out my money clip. The bill came to four seventy-five, but I left seven on the counter.

"My daddy always told me to leave a nice tip for the wait staff," I mentioned to the deputy. "He said 'It's like good karma. What goes around comes around.'"

The deputy ignored me.

"I'm going to give you a tip," I whispered loudly in his ear. "This down-stater isn't the least bit intimidated by your nonsense. If you're going to try to throw your weight around, you might want to have something to back it up."

Twelve

Instead of staying in Paradise and risking more conflict with Mr. Deputy, I decided to slide up the coast—through the sad-faced ghost town of Shelldrake—to the very tip of Whitefish Point. The parking lot at the lighthouse was full of vehicles from all over the Midwest and Canada. A pair of Greyhound-style tour buses idled some distance away, spewing their foul diesel odor into the North Woods' playground.

It took me several laps around the parking lot before I finally found a place with a view of the water. I unzipped the computer case, plugged in the inverter to the car's cigarette lighter, and got down to business.

It was a nice day in Northern Michigan. Seagulls soared overhead, and children whipped rocks into the frothy surf while their parents held onto hands or wicker picnic baskets. If ever there was a perfect day to do things in God's Country, this was it.

I had forgotten all about the point's significance to bird watchers until a pair of young men ambled up the sidewalk, carrying a tripod, cameras and binoculars. They wore khaki-colored photographer's vests, adorned with little gauges and clips, zippers and snaps. As they loaded their gear into the car, and remarked about what "special" birds they had spotted, I couldn't help but think that perhaps they were gay. Maybe it was the way they spoke, their tight, skinny jeans, or their peculiar mannerisms that made me think that. It was only when they mashed lips over the console that I realized that there was no "maybe" about it.

I looked away and said nothing.

A gentleman doesn't stare.

The Garl murders had a bizarre flavor to them. An entire family wiped off the face of the earth. There were plenty of clues, but no motives; lots of suspects, but no arrests. And the people…they seemed so out of the ordinary. Men kissing men. Women kissing women. The hidden cameras and strip joints. Can't anyone murder their lover in a wild rage? Why does it have to be so complicated?

The two bird watchers in the car next to me drove off.

I found the camera-clock from the Garl cabin and removed the little chip from its trap door on the back. It fit perfectly into the side of my laptop and took a second or two to load, which seemed rather encouraging. If there was nothing there on the chip, the computer wouldn't have done a thing.

A woman of about sixty years pulled into the parking place next to me. Even though there was a lot going on there with the sounds of the lake, the children, and the gathering breeze, I could hear every word she spoke. She was talking on the phone, and rambled on and on about her family's trust and the wicker furniture at a cabin. "The lawyers will handle it all. I'm telling you. You can have the damn furniture, the eighty acres, my life insurance, and the china, just as soon as I'm gone."

She climbed out of her VW Beetle and strolled up to one of the park benches. I watched her hang up the phone and dig into her sleeve for a tissue. It looked like she was doing some heavy thinking about her life, her children, and how everything would be handled when she was gone.

My laptop came to life. There were one hundred ninety seven images to review. The first one was dated the end of May, almost a year ago. It was a close up of Mr. Garl himself. His head. His hand. Looked like maybe he was testing the camera to see if it worked. In the background, his bed, and the three-drawer nightstand where I found the zip drive.

The second image was his belt buckle.

The third image had to have been Mrs. Garl. It looked like a woman's midsection.

I clicked and clicked. The kids. Then Cecil. Mrs. Garl. Over and over their images flashed before the screen.

It looked like they spent a week at the cabin in May, then a long weekend in June.

Cecil must not have cared that his wife's fluffy, strawberry-blonde private parts were revealed on camera. It looked like she was putting on her bathing suit, twelve inches in front of the lens. Mr. Garl never was exposed in an inappropriate way; after all, he knew that the camera was there.

By the time I made it to the Garls' fateful week's vacation in July, I had already zipped through one hundred twenty-five images.

The woman on the park bench climbed back in her car and drove away.

It was just me and a key piece of evidence. I clicked the forward button. Cecil Garl was wearing an olive tweed sports-jacket that I remember seeing in his closet.

Mrs. Garl was pictured in her underwear, a dingy-white apron, a gingham button-down blouse.

I kept clicking. Closer and closer I neared the end of the show. If I was going to get a glimpse into who may have killed the Garl family, it would show up in the next few images.

At image one hundred thirty-five, the date jumped from July—the Garls' fateful vacation—to August. That's when the cops became involved. The sheriff's department was first, then a state trooper. I could tell the difference between the two by the color of their shirts and trousers. They all wore blue rubber gloves.

The detectives and forensic investigators were next. I saw cameras dangling around their necks. One of the detectives actually picked up the camera-clock and looked at the lens. It took a photo of the man's nose and eye. His mustache was thick and peppered with gray. He looked a little like the Pink Panther. It made me want to do an impression of chief inspector, Jacques Clouseau, but since I didn't have an audience, it wouldn't be any fun.

The second to last image was of me, with the same quirky look on my face as the detective. While the detective dismissed the clock as legitimate, I realized that there was a little treasure buried inside.

The last image was completely blank. That's when I stuffed the zip drive into the pocket of my hooded sweatshirt.

Regrettably, it appeared as if the evidence on the camera-clock was a dead end. Nevertheless, I saved all the photos under one file, and emailed them to myself.

There was no smoking gun, per se; no horrific image of the murderer pointing a twenty-five caliber at Mr. Garl's temple. I was glad I discovered the clock and inventoried its contents, but in this instance, it really didn't offer much in the way of evidence. Sometimes I get lucky as a reporter; other times, the clues of a good story are as cold as the winters in Northern Michigan.

My cell phone blinked a text from Colleen: *So, are you spending the day with your mistress?*

I rolled my eyes.

Of course not, I answered.

Instead of getting a response from Colleen right away, it was Dottie who answered the call: *I'm at the auction. Plenty of bargain hunters.*

I typed: *Sounds intriguing.*

Dottie answered: *The cops are staking it out, looks like.*

A smallish Lincoln pulled into the parking space next to me. It was bright and shiny, a moistened-dirt color. Its occupants were three men: middle aged and wearing sunglasses. The driver had a thick, dark beard and his skin was the color of rye bread. The man closest to me had a giant clove cigarette in his hand, and the smoke drifted obnoxiously in my direction.

I answered Dottie: *The cops probably think that the murderer will come back to the scene because he's a sick puppy. I bet the detectives write down every license plate in the church parking lot across the street.*

Dottie: *Count on that.*

Colleen: *If you come home smelling like perfume again, your belongings will be on the front lawn, doused with lighter fluid.*

I had a lot going on there: the texts, the view of Lake Superior, and the conversation next door. It was easy enough to hear bits and pieces of my neighbor's dialogue that was mixed with spicy, rank smoke from Indonesia. "We don't really care about that."

"I think you should."

"I don't think so, Vern. We're the ones paying you to do a job."

They could have been talking about almost anything: a contract, a new swimming pool, paving the cabin's driveway.

I texted Colleen: *I'm sorry.*

I texted Dottie: *I'm in Paradise, actually up at Whitefish Point at the museum.*

Colleen: *For what?*

Dottie: *Send me a postcard.*

To Colleen: *For smelling like perfume. For leaving early this morning.*

To Dottie: *Would an electronic postcard work?*

The men next to me continued their dialogue. "If you can't do the job, we'll find someone who can."

"No, no. I'm game."

Dottie: *Electronic postcards are my favorite kind. See if Luxton has a place up there.*

In the phone book? I typed.

Naw, she countered. *Go to Chippewa County's website. Click on their 'parcel search' and follow the links.*

Good idea.

I had no reason to rush, no reason to get confused, but I did. In all the hubbub, I thought I was texting Colleen, but instead it went to Dottie: *I should have been more assertive last night and made love to you like a madman.*

As soon as I hit the send button, I knew what a horrible mistake I had made. With baited breath, I waited for Dottie's response.

The men started in again: "We don't have all kinds of time, you know."

"I know, I know."

"You got our money, our deposit. I'd hate to think that maybe you were taking advantage of the situation."

"Let's not go there."

"We have a lot of information on you and your family. Did you want me to review all that?"

Dottie: *I've never made love to a madman before, but I'm cool with role playing so maybe I could be your nurse in a mental institution.*

I rolled my eyes again. *This girl is crazy….and she hasn't changed a bit.*

Colleen: *We are going to the park to have a picnic. Your daughter wants to do some sparklers tonight. It'd be nice if you could make it.*

I didn't have time to reply. The man with the cigarette flung the butt out his car window oblivious to the fact that there was someone parked three feet away. It fired into my Impala at a high rate of speed, banking off my headrest, and landing who knows where.

"Hey!" I yelled in a fit of rage, opening the car door.

The cloth headrest was burned, so was the seat bottom.

I shooed the butt from the seat and onto the sand-covered concrete.

I'm not sure what possessed me, but something did. Like an idiot, I grabbed hold of the Lincoln's car door and flung it open. The man wasn't wearing a seatbelt, and I pulled him outside. His partners in the car yelled at me. "Hey, hey. What the hell is wrong with you?"

I didn't listen to what they were saying. Instead, I slammed the rude smoker into the door frame of the Impala, twisting his arm behind his back. "You want to take a look at my seat, tough guy?"

The man squirmed, but didn't get far. "Who's going to pay for that?" I grunted in his ear.

I had leverage, momentum, and fury on my side, temporarily.

Very temporarily.

Even though I'm a rather hefty fellow, I felt a little like a rag doll as the men overpowered me.

I felt a twinge of regret for making such a big deal out of the butt in my car. I should have politely asked the smoker to glance at the singe marks in my seat, and inquired who was going to pay for it. In retrospect, I should have mentioned that it was quite rude of him to fling his butt into my vehicle.

Strange, what your mind thinks about when your arms are unavailable.

Even though the parking lot was crowded with tourists, I never thought to scream for help.

When fists are coming at you, you want to get out of their way.

I avoided one fist that sailed past my ear.

The bearded man reloaded, but I introduced him to my size-ten Nike. When the crown of my foot met the underbelly of his genitals, it made a satisfying thud. Down he went. To his knees. To the clove-smelling pavement.

Instead of letting him wince in his private hell, I let him have it again. This time, it was on the side of his face. *Whack!*

His head bore the brunt of that collision. Had it been a football, it would have sailed into the frothy surf of Lake Superior, thirty yards away.

His buddies didn't take kindly to my punting prowess.

They shoved me backwards, taking my feet from under me.

I fell.

My descent seemed like an eternity.

I'm not sure what made a more sinister sound—the bearded man's package getting pummeled by my foot, or my own head hitting the pavement at a high rate of speed.

Either way, everything went incredibly still.

All at once, I was looking skyward into the puffy white clouds over Whitefish Point. The sky was as blue and inviting as the water itself. It had been forever since I had taken the time to relax and enjoy the serenity of northern Michigan. I couldn't remember the last time I laid on my back and tried to concoct familiar shapes from the formations within the clouds. It was an innocent daydream, a peaceful kind of sensation.

All I ever do is go, go, go—sunup to sundown—day after day.

I chase my tail.

Raise my daughter.

Love my wife.

Go, man, go.

Until now.

My limbs, my mind, my will went blank.

Very, very, blank.

Thirteen

When I finally opened my eyes, I was greeted by the subtle light from a small lamp ten or fifteen feet away. I tried to roll out of bed, but didn't get far. My right hand was in cuffs, and the cuffs were attached to a wooden bed post. The entire bed looked like it had been made out of logs—rustic and sturdy—a buttery yellow color.

My head was aching like I had been clubbed with a frying pan.

I reached behind me and felt the dried blood matted to my hair. It was smeared all over the white pillowcase too.

"Ugh," I groaned.

I looked up at the ceiling. A thousand pine knots looked down at me from the tongue and groove paneling. As far as I could tell I was in a fairly nice place. The ceiling had a nice steep pitch, and the duvet cover depicted an abstruse mix of beach, seagulls and sky.

A clock radio on the nightstand flipped from five-thirty to five-thirty-one. I had slept—or been knocked out—for sixteen hours straight.

When it came to relieving myself, I laid there for a moment or two and weighed my options. Whoever kidnapped me didn't care about my full bladder, my pounding headache or my parched throat. I was a captured animal, a prisoner of war, awaiting euthanasia or a trial of some sort.

The pair of windows next to the bed presented the best option for a bathroom. There was no mini trash can near the bed; no plaster vase overflowing with potpourri and miniature pine cones.

Without a second thought, I climbed out of bed, unlocked the window and took a look outside. I was on the second floor, shrouded in a forest. A full moon cast shadows through the aspens, the balsams, the cedar boughs swirling with scent. The cabin was on a bit of a hill that evaporated into a body of water a hundred yards away. I didn't see any other cabins, or hear any traffic. It was deathly quiet, except for a robin somewhere off in the distance greeting the new day with a lovesick warble.

Slowly, and carefully, I slid the screen up through its track. Next, I swung my legs over the window sill, unzipped my fly and let loose. I felt really weird doing what I was doing, but desperate times call for desperate measures. My urine stream wasn't exactly Tahquamenon Falls, but I certainly tried my best to hose down the grill, the flower box and a patio chair in a glorious golden shower.

It felt great to relieve myself and enact a little revenge at the same time. I take pride in doing multiple things at once. Colleen says that I'm passive aggressive. I think she's probably right.

Of course my phone was gone. Who knows about my car, the laptop, my canning supplies and the other goodies I had bought at the hardware store.

I guess Colleen figured out that I wasn't home for the swordfish steaks and the sparkler show.

She must have left a dozen messages on my phone.

I wondered if the cops were involved yet, or if she hesitated calling them because she figured that I had spent the night with a mystery lover. Either way, I knew that she'd be worried. Really, really worried.

Of course, she'd have to hide her anxiety from our daughter, who was a lot like her dad when it came to ferreting out the truth. "Where's Daddy, Mommy? Why you crying, Mommy? Are you worried?" Over and over Elizabeth would needle her.

I felt like screaming, like sounding the alarm, if that was at all possible.

A stack of magazines on the nightstand distracted my attention. *Outdoor Living. Popular Mechanic. AARP.* The kind of stuff that you'd only read if you were handcuffed to a bed, at five in the morning, with nothing better to do.

All of the magazines were several years old. The address labels were sliced from the covers.

I was stuck.

There was no spare screwdriver lying around so I could dismantle the hardware from the frame. No handcuff key, either.

I decided to say a little prayer. Maybe a lot of little prayers.

By seven o'clock I heard voices and footsteps downstairs. The smell of coffee and bacon filled my little bedroom cell and made me wish I were free again. The things I take for granted overwhelmed me. Breakfast and hot coffee. Trout fishing and projects around the house. I wanted to be free. Free as a bird. Free as a kite.

Then I started to think about who would do this to me.

Who were the three men in the car?

Did they have anything to do with the deputy?

I backtracked. The three men, the deputy, the woman at the hardware store were the most recent contacts. The day before, it was Dottie, Genesis, and the bouncer at the strip joint. On Saturday it was the man at the storage facility and the mad jumper herself, Becky Tocca. The three men seemed to be the most capable of violence, obviously, but I did provoke them after all. Was it just coincidence they were there, or did the lady at the hardware store tip off the deputy, who in turn told the three men? If that was the case, they must have something to hide that was entirely dreadful.

The footsteps and conversation downstairs were rather muffled, although I could tell there was at least one female.

They weren't arguing or bickering.

It seemed like an ordinary day at the cabin up north.

After about an hour of breakfast making, dishes doing, and toilets flushing, I heard the door downstairs slam two or three times. It was at the opposite end of the cabin, so I couldn't tell how many people were there.

What the hell? I thought. *I want to be executed, not left to starve.*

I sat there for an hour. Every moment that slid by felt like an eternity. It was terrible.

Hour two wasn't any better. I made paper airplanes from the pages of the magazines and sent them flying out the bedroom window. My hope was that someone—anyone—would see the trash and think that there was something amiss.

I stared out the cabin window. The water at the end of the lawn looked completely inviting. I think it was some sort of river, but there was very little boat traffic.

And why would there be boat traffic? It was the Tuesday after Memorial Day, and everybody should have been back to work.

It seemed like I was up a creek without a paddle.

Just as my hopes couldn't sink any deeper, magically, she appeared.

It was Dottie, dressed in a sleek, black wet suit.

"Hey!" I yelled.

She stopped dead in her tracks.

"Derrick?" she asked, head cocked like a captivated dog.

"Yes. Come help me."

She raced up the remaining lawn, and hopped on the deck.

"What are you doing?" she asked.

"I'm handcuffed. Come help me."

"What?" she yelled.

"Please help me, Dottie. Come on."

Dottie didn't know how to react. "Is anybody home?"

"I don't think so. They left a little while ago."

She peered in the windows off the deck. "They must have a cat or a dog, because it smells like piss down here."

I rolled my eyes.

"They must have troublesome little boys, too. These paper airplanes are all over the place."

"Dottie please!"

"What?" she huffed. "Did you piss out the window? How am I going to get up there?"

"I don't know. There must be a window open. Heck, look for a key."

Dottie pulled on the sliding glass doors that separated the deck from the house. They were locked. "Just a minute," she said, "I'll check."

Dottie rounded the corner of the house, and out of sight.

My spirits had been lifted. My prayers answered.

At any second, she'd come prancing up the stairs, a hacksaw in her hand, a smile stretched between her cheekbones. In no more than ten minutes, we'd be on our way to safety.

Instead, she came back to the deck, exhausted by the exercise.

"Did you check for a key under the welcome mat?" I asked.

"Yep. The overhang for the woodpile too."

"Damn. How close are the neighbors?"

"There aren't any."

"None at all?" I asked.

"None. I tried to drive in the driveway early this morning, but it was gated."

"Where are we?" I asked.

"In Paradise. That's the Tahquamenon River behind me."

I felt a little relieved.

"Are we above, or below, the falls?"

She propped a hand on her hip, as if was a dumb question. "Of course, we're downstream. It would be kind a hard to paddle up the falls, don't you think?"

"Cut me some slack, will you?" I said groggily. "I've been knocked out since yesterday afternoon. How did you find me?" I asked.

"The website I was telling you about, Chippewa County dot org. You can find any property owner. All you need is their name."

"How did you know that I was in trouble?"

Dottie looked up at me and shrugged her shoulders. "You never answered my texts. It was just like you fell off the face of the earth."

"Well I guess I owe you a debt of gratitude."

Dottie laughed. "Not yet, you don't. We gotta get you out of there."

"How? Should we call the police?"

"I could, but I don't have cell service. Besides, my phone is back at the Subaru."

My mind was racing again. *How could she get me out of here?*

"Did you see an axe or a hatchet?"

"No."

"What if you threw a log or a stone through a window?"

"I don't think that will work."

"Do you have a rope?"

"I do, back at the kayak."

"I'll pull you up."

She looked up at me doubtfully.

"Have any better ideas?" I asked.

She grimaced, "No."

"It's not that far up here. Come on, Dottie."

Dottie skipped off the deck, and disappeared towards the water.

It seemed like forever until she returned, a coiled mass of rope in her hands.

"Ready?" she yelled.

"Ready!" I replied.

She fired the rope my way, and I caught it. A second later, I had the rope tied around the bed post. Dottie gave me the "thumbs up" sign and I gave a mighty left-handed heave. Up she came, six inches. Another heave-hoe and we had gained a foot. Although I dared not look over the sill, I bet that Dottie was half repelling, half climbing. With every hoist, I wrapped the rope around the bed post with a quick half-hitch.

Dottie is not as petite as she used to be. It took everything I had to heave her up the side of the cabin wall, but it was working.

After eight or ten heaves, Dottie gasped, "I'm almost there."

Our plan was working in more ways than one. The bed frame was beginning to buckle from the stress of so much weight on its post. Dottie was only a few inches away from being able to grasp the sill. I tugged with all my might, and after ten intense seconds, I saw her hand come aboard.

A second hand reached the sill, and she gasped mightily for assistance. I didn't know where to grab her, so I just started mauling her wetsuit. I grabbed a handful on her back and yanked. I reached for her ass, and did the same. Little-by-little she crested the threshold of my little jail cell.

When she finally plopped inside, both of us gasped.

"Oh, Derrick," she sighed, "I'm getting too old for this kind of crap."

"Me too," I sighed, breathlessly.

"I have to keep my eyes on the prize," she sighed.

"What prize is that?"

"The hundred grand."

"Oh yeah. Can't forget about that."

Dottie rolled on her back, and I saw that she had a giant gash on her wetsuit. She placed her hand inside the rip that stretched from the top of her freckled thigh to her knee.

"I guess I owe you a bit of gratitude and a new wetsuit," I said.

Dottie looked down and cursed. "Yes, you do, Mr. Twitchell."

"Just get me out of here, okay, Dottie, and I'll take really good care of you."

Dottie rose to her feet, opened the bedroom door, and disappeared down the hall.

"Look for an axe or a chainsaw."

"Yeah, yeah," she said.

Minutes passed. I clung to the end of my restraint like a chained dog just before feeding time. Yeah, I was hungry and thirsty and anxious to be rid of the bondage that kept me there. I uncoiled the rope from the bedpost and thought about tossing it to the deck below. On second thought, we might need the rope for a quick departure.

"Hurry!" I barked.

Dottie didn't say a thing. She was already gone. My mind kept working, and there was no governor on the things that blurted from my mouth: "Get a screwdriver or a crowbar if you can't find a saw," I yelled.

Two minutes later, Dottie made her way upstairs. She was carrying a chainsaw and a hatchet. A scene from a horror movie came to mind.

"Look what I found," she said.

"Great. I'll start chopping; see if you can figure out how to start it."

It felt a little weird. I'm right handed, but I could only use my left. Undaunted, the first blow to the bedpost glanced off the wood and caromed into the side of the handcuff.

"Damn," I muttered, "that could have been ugly."

Another whack, and the hatchet slammed into the post. "That's it," I said.

It was a shame to ruin such a nice piece of furniture. The owners of the cabin were going to have a fit once they got home.

"Looks like the saw has gas," Dottie said. "What are you supposed to do, just pull on the cord?"

"You have to prime it, first."

"How?"

"Push the bulb, and pull out the choke. Let me show you." She brought the saw closer to me and together we managed to get it started. It was crazy-loud and bigger than any saw I had ever used. The bar part was at least thirty inches long and filled with snarling little teeth.

Dottie gasped. "Oh, Derrick, it's so big."

I smiled at the suggestion. "I know," I yelled. "Use two hands and squeeze tight. Have you used one before?"

She shook her head.

"Just start at the far end of the bed and practice."

Tentatively, she mowed through the foot board. In the process, she managed to destroy the duvet. It ripped and flailed with every passing saw tooth.

"Ok, good, now move up here," I yelled. Dottie hopped on the bed next to me. The saw roared to life, sending bits of wood over the duvet. "You got it."

"This is fun," she yelled.

We switched places and Dottie finished off the bed post and the cross beam.

I was free. Free at last.

Thank God almighty.

"Thank you, Dottie," I gasped, "thank you so much!"

I didn't know how to react, so I gave her a giant bear hug. Emotion overwhelmed me. The bear hug turned into a kiss on the cheek. Dottie smiled.

"Let's get out of here, Derrick," she prodded me.

Dottie started toward the bedroom door, but had to ask, "Don't you want to repel down the side of the cabin?"

"Not me. But you go right ahead."

When Dottie waltzed down the hallway, I re-tied the rope to the partition between the two windows. Instead of leaving right then and there, I had a golden opportunity to enact a little revenge. Colleen would have been disappointed with me.

I started the saw again, hopped on the bed and looked up at the ceiling. The eyes of pine looked down at me. They were a blank canvas, a painter's playground.

The saw motor revved, sending a plume of toxic blue smoke billowing from its tailpipe. I was boiling mad, too. Thoughts of revenge were overflowing.

I raised the saw and carved a giant "F" into the paneling. The chips of wood and bits of finishing nails showered my head. It felt great.

Beneath it three little letters: "Y-O-U."

Fourteen

Dottie and I paddled down the Tahquamenon River, past scores of cabins, and families of Canada geese that were enjoying the sunshine. I half expected that someone would have taken a few potshots at us, considering our hasty getaway and the damage we had done to the cabin. Instead, we slid peacefully through the eerie, stained water to where the river dumped into Lake Superior.

Dottie must have had a decent workout on the way upstream. Then again, kayaks have a way of sliding over the current, instead of getting bogged down like a canoe.

In no time at all we had the rope stowed in the kayak, and the kayak on top of her Subaru.

"Where to?" she asked.

"I guess we should see if my Impala's still up at Whitefish Point, don't you think?"

"Makes sense to me."

"Just take it easy going through town. I don't want the deputy to see me."

"Why not?" she asked.

I shrugged my shoulders. "I had a little run-in with him earlier in the day…I mean yesterday."

"Derrick, you can't go around burning bridges like that."

"I know, but haven't you heard the old saying about a burning bridge never burns brighter?"

As we inched into town, the deputy's patrol car wasn't in his driveway. It wasn't at the diner either.

I didn't need to ask Dottie to stop at the gas station. She pulled right in, and parked around the back, near the discarded milk crates and vacant pallets.

"Can you give me a moment, Derrick? I'd like to change my clothes."

"Of course," I said.

Instead of going inside to the ladies' washroom, Dottie explained that she wanted me to go inside so she'd have some privacy.

"Got ya. That would be no problem. Could I borrow a couple dollars for a bottle of water and a candy bar? They stole my wallet, my car keys, everything."

"Sure thing."

She reached into the ashtray and pulled out a wad of crumpled up currency.

"Here you go," she said, handing me a five-dollar bill.

"Thank you. Put it on my tab."

As I walked into the gas station, it occurred to me that I might run into one of the three men who accosted me. I didn't care. There were enough people around as witnesses to keep me from being kidnapped all over again. What I did care about were the handcuffs tucked beneath the sleeve of my sweatshirt. They made a rather ominous clunk when I whipped out Dottie's five dollar bill and placed it on the counter. The woman at the register didn't ask, and I didn't want to tell what was going on beneath my shirt.

Before leaving the store, I took the change from Dottie's

five dollars and called home. It cost me a dollar twenty-five to leave a message on the machine: "Hello Twitchell family. Everything is okay now. I'm in the UP, and hope to be home later today. Love you both, bunches and bunches. Bye."

Tentatively, I walked back to the Subaru, just as Dottie was sliding a striped shirt over her head. She removed her ball cap, and fluffed her thick, black locks. With mild amusement, I watched her paint her lips with gloss. In just a few minutes, Dottie had transformed herself from something seen on Jacques Cousteau, to a completely normal-looking tourist.

"I don't suppose you have a handcuff key in your vehicle, do you?" I asked, mouthful of bottled water.

"No, I don't."

"I'd like to get out of these darn things."

"I bet," Dottie said, as she turned north out of the parking lot. "Why did you start the chainsaw again?"

I hemmed and hawed for a moment as we passed the Yukon Bar at the north edge of town. "I…I…didn't have a pen, and I really wanted to leave them a thank you note."

Dottie smiled.

"Only thing, is, my 'thank' in 'thank you' looked like an 'F.'"

Dottie laughed nervously. "There you go again, burning bridges."

"I couldn't just get out of there without rubbing their noses in it."

"Why did you do that? Those guys are the lead suspects in the Garl murders."

"Who is?"

"Luxton. That was his cabin you just vandalized."

My heart sank. "Seriously."

"Yes, Derrick. You don't want to mess around with them. You're liable to end up the same way as Cecil and his family."

"I don't want that. At least not before we go to Clyde's Drive In on the way home."

"You should have thought of that earlier, don't you think?"

"Ah, yeah," I said sarcastically.

"How did you know to look for me at the Luxton place?"

"I had a hunch, but when Genesis told you that he had business up here, that hunch turned into action." Dottie never took her foot off the gas as we passed through Shelldrake. I glanced at the dashboard: we were doing sixty in a forty-five, her gas tank only a quarter full. From there, I reeled in the view of her freckled thigh beneath the hem of her shorts; no funky tattoos, or scrapes from the collapse over the window sill. It was a pleasant view, but I didn't want to stare. Dottie interrupted me: "Why did you come up here?"

I swallowed the pretzel bite and spoke the truth. "I really wasn't sure, other than Cecil's Cultural Society has a post office box."

"What were you going to do, just waltz right in there and talk to the postmaster?"

"Yeah, I was. Now that they're open, we could probably do that as soon as we get my car."

"What if it's not?" she asked.

"It's Tuesday, they have to be open."

"No, no, silly," she smirked. "What if your car's not there?"

"Oh…" My heart sank. "You had to mention that, didn't you?"

Dottie didn't answer. She didn't have to. It seemed more and more likely that it wouldn't be there; the closer we were to the Point.

Dottie fiddled with the buttons on her car stereo and Fleetwood Mac came to life. *Gold Dust Woman* strummed and wailed as we bounced along the bumpy, paved road, lined with scraggly jack pines and ferns that looked to be belt loop high. *Lousy lovers pick their prey but they never cry out loud. Did she make you cry, make you break down, shatter your illusions of love?*

When the forest finally parted and the road entered the

parking lot for the lighthouse and museum, my heart sank. The Impala wasn't there.

"Turn in right here, will you?" I pointed to a parking place next door to a truck with Indiana plates. "That's where I was."

"Look, Derrick," she said, "there's a baseball cap. Is that yours?"

I laughed. "Sure is."

Dottie put the Subaru in park, and I reached under the truck next door. "It's as good as new."

I placed the cap back on my head. The strap on the back covered most of the scab.

"What do you want to do?" she asked.

"I don't know."

Dottie and I sat there for several minutes as Stevie Nicks jabbed me in the ribs: *Is it over now, do you know how to pick up the pieces and go home.*

"We could leave," Dottie suggested. "I'll give you a ride as far as I can."

"We can't really call the police. At least, I can't."

"Nobody ever said that the hundred grand would come easy," she sighed.

"You know, Dottie, they have my laptop, and all my stuff related to the case."

"Really?"

"Yeah, all your stories were in there."

"Ugh."

I didn't tell her about Becky's suicide note, and how I was lead to the Garls' cabin in the first place.

"You probably made copies of everything, didn't you?"

"Well…"

"You didn't?"

"No, I didn't, but I still have the zip drive. Left it in the bedroom dresser at home. They'll never think to look for it in my sock drawer."

"That's good."

Dottie's attention turned from me to the view of Lake Superior. She tapped her temple with an index finger. I wasn't sure if that was her way of thinking or if she did it for some other reason.

It appeared as if we were out of aces.

With no car, no wallet, no phone or money, I was stuck with Dottie. As long as she was willing to help me, I was going to let her.

"I don't know if it's a good idea to talk to the postmaster," she lamented.

"No?" I asked.

"What's he going to tell you?"

"I don't know. Probably where Luxton's cabin is."

"And we already know that," she admitted.

"What about the post office box for the society?"

"What about it?" she asked.

"Maybe there's some mail? Where was their physical location? Who was it that picked up the mail?"

"Derrick, Cecil Garl has been gone for almost a year. The guy probably didn't pay his rent for the box and the postmaster assigned it to somebody else."

She was right. Undaunted, though, I asked: "Maybe this would be a good time to tell me about Shafeek Heanley and Cecil Garl?"

Dottie bit her lip and raised an eyebrow. "It's really hard for me to talk about because Mr. Heanley has been so good to me."

"I understand. The only thing you said is that they had some business dealings."

"That's right."

"Doesn't that make him a person of interest?"

"Yes. He's talked to the cops already, I'm pretty sure."

"Mr. Heanley?"

"That's right."

"And..."

"You know...nothing. There haven't been any arrests."

"What about Luxton?" I asked.

"That's the sixty-four-thousand dollar question," Dottie said as she backed out of the parking space. "You didn't see the rest of his cabin. It's spectacular."

Dottie had a way of leading me off course. I think she was waiting for me to ask her what was so special about it, but I didn't really care. The three men were responsible for my kidnapping, not to mention the theft of my Impala. Who knows if one of the three guys was Luxton himself, or if they were all hired goons.

Dottie couldn't contain herself. She had to tell me all about the kitchen, and its marvelous countertop. I tried to act mildly enthused.

"Did you happen to see my Impala while you were there?"

"No, I didn't. There was an older Ford Escape in the garage, but that was it for vehicles."

"Well shoot, Dottie."

"I know, right? It's like we're out of leads."

"We can't hang out here," I said. "Maybe we should get out of here."

"And do what?"

"I don't care. Aside from eating fresh whitefish, trail riding, trout fishing, or blueberry picking, there's nothing good that can come from spending more time in Paradise."

Fifteen

About thirty minutes later, Dottie parked her vehicle near the railroad tracks of Highway 123 in downtown Trout Lake. An idling locomotive hissed and farted in the afternoon sunshine as an engineer stepped out of the cockpit and climbed down the metal gangway.

Dottie and I walked inside Toby's Buckhorn Inn, which drew the attention of a couple of old-timers at the bar. The waitress rounded up a beer for Dottie and a glass of water for me. For a fleering moment, it occurred to me that for being a non-drinker, I sure had spent a lot of time in establishments that serve alcohol.

Toby's is a lot like the other bars in northern Michigan. The deer mounts and sports paraphernalia on the walls belie a rustic mix of outdoor adventure and competitive athleticism. It isn't the place to get French onion soup and a side order of oysters, but rather a large chunk of dead cow, and potatoes fried in scalding-hot grease.

"Thanks for stopping, Dottie. I'm starving."

"No big deal, Derrick," she said, winking. "I know you'll pay me back."

"With interest, and I know you'll love the wetsuit."

"I don't know about that."

"What do you mean?"

"You don't even know what size I wear, or what brand it was."

"True. How about I send you enough money to buy the nicest suit around?"

"Works for me."

The waitress waltzed toward our table and took our food order.

"So, you say that the auction wasn't too exciting?" I asked her.

"No, it wasn't. I'm pretty sure they made a bunch of money, though."

"Why's that?""

"There were tons of people there. Everybody wanted to buy something because of the novelty of it all."

"I suppose you're right."

"Anything with the Garl name on it brought really big bucks."

"Like what?"

"The welcome mat had their name on it. So did some coffee mugs with a photo of their cabin on it. Mr. Garl had his name stitched into the breast pocket of a sport coat and some guy from Adrian paid four hundred dollars for it."

"That's crazy."

"Yeah, but what are you going to do? It's still a great country. People buy things for bizarre reasons," she said.

"What about the Corvette? How much did it go for?"

"I think it was close to thirty thousand. One of the people I spoke to said it was only worth half that even if it was in fine shape."

"Was the place crawling with cops?"

"Not too bad," she said, wiping the suds from her upper lip. "I think I know half the guys on the force."

The waitress brought our food and the check. I dove head first into the meal. French fries and a cheeseburger never tasted so good.

"Do you think the guys at the Luxton place figured out that you aren't there?" Dottie asked.

"I don't know. I don't want to know," I said, mouthful.

"Seeing you handcuffed to the bed up there was kind of weird. Reminded me of old times."

I munched and drank the water that tasted like UP minerals. "I'm not sure weird is the right word."

Dottie snickered.

"If you hadn't have rescued me, I'm sure I'd be dead by now."

Dottie bobbed her head, as if to say, "It was nothing."

"Seriously, I think I told you what Genesis said about Cecil Garl. 'They'll find me handcuffed and drowned in Whitefish Bay.'"

Dottie opened her purse and slid fifteen dollars under the salt and pepper shakers. "You wore the cuffs, all you needed was a ride off shore."

"Scary," I said, "I don't know how I can ever repay you."

I felt compelled to do something more than just say a few words. Talk is cheap, after all. For that reason alone, I put my hand on Dottie's wrist.

I couldn't really blame her for thinking that my gesture was steeped in something more than innocence. She was a beautiful woman and if she could read minds, she'd know that more than once I thought about making out with her for old time's sake.

And it wasn't just a physical attraction that sparked between us. We had great conversation, a mutual interest in solving the Garl matter, plenty of history together, and at the moment were a long, long way from home.

Of course, there was the "madman" text I sent her the day before. Dottie didn't know that it was a mistake. She was the victim of my error, and I'm sure it was front and center on her mind.

"Derrick, I have an idea about the repayment," she said, somewhat nonchalant. Instead of my hand on her wrist, it was her hand on mine. She slid forward in her chair and stared into my eyes as if I should be looking for signs of glaucoma or cataracts. Her painted lips alluded to my misplaced text, "I think you're a wonderful man, Derrick. You're fun to hang out with and I find myself enjoying your company just like I did twenty-five years ago."

Her comment brought on a smile. "Oh, Dottie. There has been a huge mistake."

"Just wait. I'm not finished."

"What is it?" I asked.

"I want to unleash that inner madman. What do you say

we go back to my place, and have a little barbecue? Maybe a bonfire. You can take a shower, and I'll look at that nasty gash on your head."

"I can't."

"It's that whole marriage thing, isn't it?"

"Yeah."

"Are you sure?"

"Of course I'm sure," I said emphatically. "I'm unavailable. That's what it means to be married."

She raised her voice and asked, "You're not gay are you?"

The men at the bar looked up from their suds.

"Will you quit that?" I hushed.

She jumped up from the table and stormed to the back of the restaurant.

I didn't know what else to do. It would have been rude to follow her into the ladies' room and yell apologies through the door.

Time seemed to stand still. The locals at the bar swiveled on their stools to take in the drama. Apparently, *The Young and the Restless* on the television didn't have as much allure as a mid-afternoon quarrel between two down-staters.

After several minutes the waitress ambled in my direction. "Don't let the guys at the bar get on your nerves," she said. "They mean well, but they're a bit nosey, that's all."

"Oh, I won't," I said, smiling. "Who needs a soap opera when you have real life drama."

She laughed slightly and picked up the currency. "Thanks for the tip. Looks like you're going to be here a while. Do you want another glass of water?"

I felt my heart sink. "What do you mean, 'I'm going to be here a while?'"

She gestured out the front window. I stood, just in time to see Dottie buckle her seatbelt and drive away.

"Looks like your woman slipped out the back door."

"Oh, no."

"Maybe you'd rather have whiskey…"

Sixteen

I didn't bother to race out of the bar, and wave my arms, or cry out Dottie's name. She's a big girl; I'm a big boy. We can both take care of ourselves. Apparently she decided to renege on that ride downstate. She had no interest in how I was going to get home when it meant that her affections had been spurned. What mattered is that she put her cards on the table, and I quashed them silly.

She was gone.

I was stranded.

Life goes on.

I got myself into this mess; I could surely find a way out of it.

Instead of drinking whiskey, I decided to amble across M-123 to a pay phone in the parking lot of the General Store. Once there, I placed a collect call to home, but nobody answered. That was twice in one day that Colleen wasn't there. I was beginning to think that maybe something was awry.

The train across the road blasted its horn, and a billow of heady black smoke gushed from its stack. Seemed like a confounding contrast—that horn—when compared to the relative silence of a small UP town.

I called work, the *Gratiot Country Recorder*, who accepted

the charges for the collect call. Walter Claety was the best employee at the paper, not to mention a good friend. I told him a little bit about the jam I was in, but I didn't get far.

"Derrick, you don't have to tell me all about it."

"Why?"

"I just picked something off the wire. Let me grab it."

Walter never used the *hold* button on the telephone, which drove me nuts. I heard our other phone lines ring, and the chatter from the folks in the office. One of the voices was a customer, and it sounded like she had just moved back to mid-Michigan from her winter home in Florida. I listened to her say that she wanted to re-activate her subscription to the paper.

"My credit card number is..."

"Are you still there, Derrick?" Walter asked.

"Yes," I said. "I was overhearing the woman at the counter give her credit card information."

"Ha, ha. Good one. You ready to listen now?"

"Yes, I'm ready."

"Police in Midland County have issued a warrant for Derrick Twitchell, the publisher of the *Gratiot County Recorder*."

"What? You're pulling my leg," I interrupted him.

"Twitchell is wanted for questioning in the death of Becky Tocca, who fell—or was pushed—from an overpass on US-10, Saturday morning."

"Oh brother..."

"Want me to keep going?"

"No, that's okay." I stated the obvious, "What a mess. I guess I have to call my lawyer when I get home." An enormous sigh poured out of me. "Will you do me a favor, Walter?"

"Sure."

"Can you stop by the house and talk to Colleen? Tell her that I'm stranded in the UP, and I might need a ride home. I left a message earlier in the day, but she can't call me back because my phone was stolen?"

"You got it. What else?"

"The car was stolen too."

"Oh boy."

"Yeah, no kidding," I sighed. "Can you call the credit card company and tell them that my wallet was stolen?"

I turned my head so that I was looking toward the bar, the gas station, and a mom and pop style motel. A brown and white patrol car was pulling into the bar.

My heart sank, *oh no.*

"You've had yourself a stroke of bad luck, haven't you, Derrick."

"You could say that."

The cop parked the car only sixty or seventy yards away. I watched him step out and head for the door, carrying several papers in his hand. Something told me he wasn't looking to serve a subpoena or an eviction notice.

"Walter, I want to thank you very much for your help, but I have to go."

I hung up the phone and without a second thought, scampered south, past the Trout Lake Hall towards the railroad tracks. Fifty yards later, I met up with the train that had grunted and groaned its way free of inertia. It was crawling east, I thought, toward St. Ignace, which was on my way home.

Perfect.

When I finally caught up to the train, there didn't seem to be a good place to jump aboard. Most of the cars were loaded with logs held in place with giant metal stanchions stuck to the sides of the cars. Steadily, the train gained momentum and speed. Ten cars from the caboose, the logs ended and the boxcars began. The first two boxcars had their doors closed, but the third was wide open. I trotted along, spotting a metal handle on the edge of the door. A hand on the handle and an awkward gymnastic move later and I was aboard. It wasn't a pretty ascension into my temporary berth, but that was okay;

nobody saw me roll into the boxcar, breathless from the sudden surge of adrenalin.

As I passed behind the Buckhorn, the cop car was still there. Maybe he had other business to attend. Perhaps he was just grabbing a cheeseburger of his own. Either way, I barreled slowly along the tracks, feeling every little bump along the way.

An eighth of a mile later, I saw Dottie at the gas station standing next to her Subaru.

I stood up and grabbed hold of the door. The only thing separating us was a hundred yards of cluttered gravel on the edge of the tracks, a grassy shoulder and a thin row of trees.

I don't know what possessed me, but I yelled her name.

She looked up from her chore, just in time to see me wave.

I laughed.

There are lots of things that I could have yelled back at her, but I decided not to. She waved in my direction, and that's all that matters. If she was mad at me, she wouldn't have waved at all. Had she wanted to give me a ride, she would have waved me over.

Maybe it was just as well that I cut her off the way I did. She knew that I was grateful, but not interested in what she had to offer.

I would just as soon not burn bridges where Dottie was concerned. She did me a huge favor when she saved my life, and I had every intention of re-paying her debt.

For now, though, I bumbled along the tracks, slightly faster than a cantering horse. At this pace, I'd get to St. Ignace by dinnertime, and if Walter spoke to Colleen, she'd already be on her way up north. Maybe, just maybe, I could take her out to eat, and spend the night in a comfy motel, with clean sheets and a hot shower. I didn't care what it cost or how much time we were missing from our routines; it seemed like a good time to take my foot off the gas pedal and explain to her everything that had happened. It wasn't the first time I had gotten myself into trouble, and undoubtedly not the last. We'd have plenty to talk about, that's for sure.

The train tracks didn't exactly parallel Highway 123, but I figured it was just beyond the tree line. I don't know if Dottie was keeping pace with the train, or if she went on her merry way back to civilization downstate. She may not have even known who yelled her name. Then again, she was perceptive and paid attention to detail.

I was safe, well-fed, and headed for home.

I didn't need any money.

I had no stress.

As the forests and farmsteads and faraway hunting camps passed in and out of view, I couldn't help but pick up an imaginary harmonica, and hum the ballad of vagabonds everywhere:

Third boxcar, midnight train
Destination…Bangor, Maine
Old worn out suits and shoes,
I don't pay no union dues,

I smoke old stogies I have found
Short, but not too big around
I'm a man of means, by no means
King of the Road.

Seventeen

About three or four hours into my train ride, I realized that I had made a terrible mistake. The eastbound train from Trout Lake had made a northbound turn, and somehow I ended up in Sault Ste Marie, Ontario, instead of St. Ignace.

The train didn't stop or slow down when we crossed the St. Mary's River, nor did it announce the names of the towns we had passed. I probably should have paid more attention to the signs on the storefronts as we made our way through Rudyard and Dafter. Heck, I thought they could have been the towns of Ozark or Moran that were on the way to St. Ignace.

Either way, the train chugged past customs and made a sweeping right turn through town, a bit too fast for me to jump off. When the train crossed the intersections of the streets, the people in their cars looked up at me from behind their windshields. Some of them pointed in my direction, as if to tell their children, "Look, kids, there's a hobo, eh?"

I didn't care what they thought: I was in a tight spot and had to get out of it.

When I stuck my head out of the boxcar, I saw fences, and lights, and heavy equipment up ahead. The tracks we were on had split into several others, which split again. Our two iron tracks had become five or six others just like it. There were boxcars and locomotives everywhere, all of which were in various stages of hibernation. It must have been some sort of spur for the train company, which made the conductor take his foot off the gas. We gradually slowed our pace; it was my time for departure.

Just as we entered the main part of the spur, I jumped off without spraining an ankle or ripping an Achilles.

Before I could scuff the dirt from my jeans, someone in the caboose yelled in my direction. "Hey, get back here!"

I didn't answer. Instead, I ran as fast as I could from the train.

Trouble was…I was trapped. The railroad tracks were fenced and lined with barbed wire that separated them from the surrounding neighborhoods. The only way to get out of the train company's little enclave was to make it to a crossing at the previous street. For a second or two, I beat myself up for not planning my jump a little better. Then again, I never would have thought that there would be someone in the caboose. Regardless, the man sounded a dreadful alarm that had me high-tailing it to the first available crossing.

When I finally made it to an intersection, I realized that I was far from safe. If the guy on the caboose called the cops, they would be along at any moment. I scurried as fast as I could, keeping one eye out for a pay phone, the other eye for the cops.

The town was bustling. People were on the sidewalks, enjoying the pleasant weather after a brutally long winter. I tried to fit in—calm and cool as Jim Rockford—and hope that the cops wouldn't recognize me.

I felt like a stranger in a foreign land. All the vehicles had white "licence" plates with little crowns in their "centre." The houses were old and tall, and for the most part, stacked on top of one another. They all had steep roofs and aged, weathered siding. I saw Toronto Maple Leafs banners hanging in bedroom windows, and on the closest street corner: Tim Horton's and an Esso gas station.

Where was I going? I had no money, no car, no identification, and no resources, but, I did have my senses.

Quickly, I picked up the receiver of the payphone at the Esso station and placed it to my ear. At first, I couldn't hear a dial tone so I pressed the handle firmly against my head. When I did, I felt something soft and gooey on the lobe of my ear. Someone had left a piece of softened chewing gum on the receiver. When I pulled it away from my head, it oozed between my head and the handle.

They scribbled *tough luck Chuck* on the metal frame for the phone, which seemed like a peculiar way to say "this isn't your day."

I hung up the phone, collected myself, and walked down the street to look for another phone. A white pickup truck with a gigantic CP on its flanks whizzed past. The driver was going quite swiftly, I thought, and he was headed for the train crossing. Maybe it was the train's own security detail who was after the man with the gray sweatshirt. If I had been more observant I would have realized that CP was on the train that brought me here. After all, CP means Canadian Pacific.

Across the street, I spotted a coffee shop, and a "free wi-fi" sign in the window. I skipped across three lanes of one-way traffic, and ducked inside, somewhat breathless from the exercise. The woman behind the counter wanted to sell me a cup of coffee, but I had to turn her down. Instead, I asked her where the nearest Western Union might be located.

She scratched her chin and pointed farther down the street. "About three blocks down Queen Street you'll see Cash-n-Dash." Her "about" sounded like "a boat," but I was thankful for the information.

"Sounds like you're in a bit of a pickle," she said.

"I am."

"I thought maybe you were going to have a wobbler when you set foot in here."

"What's a 'wobbler'?"

"You're not from around here, are ya?"

"No, I'm not, but I really have to make a collect call."

The girl behind the counter passed me her IPhone. "Make it quick, eh?"

"I will. Thank you."

Colleen didn't answer. My mom didn't answer either. The newspaper was closed. That was it for phone numbers committed to memory.

Discouraged, I pulled up the internet on her phone. Walter Claety's home number was easy enough to find. He accepted the charges for the call.

"Thank you Walter," I said. "This call will cost you a fortune. I'm up in Sault Ste Marie, Ontario."

"You're what?"

"Yeah. It's a long story. I'm in a heck of a bind up here."

"Sounds like it."

"Did you get a hold of Colleen?"

"Well, I swung by the house, but there was nobody home. "

My heart sank. "Shoot."

Just as my mind started contemplating all the horrible scenarios of where Colleen could be, Walter piped up with a troubling announcement: "I have to tell you that there was a bouquet of flowers on the front porch."

"Really?"

"Yeah. The note with it, said 'To the fun times in Paradise. Love, Dottie.'"

I felt myself curse. "Oh, no…"

"I took care of you, Derrick."

"What did you do?"

"It was easy. I wrote a new note."

"Oh, thanks," I sighed. "What did your note say?"

"Where the hell are you, woman?"

"Walter!"

He laughed. We both did. The woman behind the counter looked up from her espresso machine. It was time for me to get down to business.

Walter volunteered to wire two hundred dollars, and pick me up in the morning. I begged another favor and requested that he swing by the office and pick up my passport in my desk drawer.

"No problem. Where do you want to meet?" he asked.

"At the Cash-n-Dash, I guess. It's the only place I know of."

"I'll be there about noon."

"Thanks, Walter."

"Yep. By the way, Derrick, the state police stopped by the paper today. Two of them, actually."

"I figured they'd be along anytime now."

"They wanted to know where you were."

"What did you tell them?"

"Not much. I gave them the slip."

"They'll be back," I said, resigned.

"What are you going to tell them?"

"The truth, I guess." The nice lady behind the counter smiled anxiously. It was time for me to hang up. "Well, most of the truth. I'll see you tomorrow."

Eighteen

At noon the following day, good old Walter showed up at the Cash-n-Dash, just as we had planned.

I wanted to hug him.

He laughed and laughed, knowing full well that I was indebted to him for some serious favors. A paid week's vacation or a gift card for dinner at the nicest restaurant in town wouldn't have been too much.

"Heck, Derrick, I couldn't leave you stranded up here."

"Thanks."

"I would have never heard the end of it around the shop," he snickered.

"You're probably right."

"Now I feel like you owe me one," he said, smiling.

In the time it took to get to customs, I told Walter about what I had done the night before: checked into a cheap hotel, gave the waitress at the wi-fi place a nice tip, and picked up a bite to eat.

We passed through Customs without any trouble at all. I asked him if he called the credit card company.

"Sure did. They said your last purchase was up in Paradise, but you had two cash advances shortly after that."

"What?" I yelled.

"Don't blame me, Derrick," he said. "I'm just relaying the message."

"Where?"

"Bay Mills Casino in Brimley, and the Kewadin Shores Casino in St. Ignace."

"What the hell. How much were they?"

"A thousand each."

I rolled my eyes and sighed angrily. This case was costing me a pile of dough.

After a few miles, Walter asked me, "Who's Dottie?"

"She's a reporter from up by Charlevoix. Nice gal. She saved my life. Why do you ask?"

Walter made a frown with his lips and shrugged slightly. "Why would she be sending you flowers?"

"I know. Seems crazy. Ever meet someone that seems like a nice person and fun to hang around with, but there's something about her that just doesn't set well?"

"You mean like playing with fire?"

"Exactly."

"Of course. It's the black widow effect."

"What's that?"

"The female spider eats the male spider after mating."

"Oh nice. It's a good thing I didn't mate with her."

"But you thought about it."

"Once or twice. She's a beautiful woman and a lot of fun to hang around with. It'd be hard to do that, knowing that I'd have to look Colleen in the eye."

"So, what do you want to do next?" he asked.

"I don't know. I'm just glad to be safe and sound. I don't think I told you about what happened up in Paradise."

Walter shook his head, so I brought him up to speed on everything, including the Garl murders, the reward money, and Becky's theory behind who the killers might have been.

He absorbed everything; the reason why I went to the murder scene, Traverse City, and Paradise. It wasn't until the Rudyard exit, south of Sault Ste Marie, before Walter responded.

"If I were you, I wouldn't be hanging around home. Whoever kidnapped you will come after you again, don't you think?"

"Yeah, I was tied to a bed inside the Luxton cabin, so I have a pretty good idea who it is that would be after me."

"Run away, Derrick. Get your wife and daughter and go somewhere."

"I don't even know where my family is, Walter."

"They're around. I'm sure of it."

"What would I do?"

"Hide out. Rent a cabin somewhere. Go to South Haven, or Holland, heck, go east and stay up in Tawas or Bad Axe."

"What would I do? I'd go nuts. And besides, waiting around isn't really my style, you know that."

"True enough," he said, "but it's better than being tied to a bed post, awaiting your execution."

I sat there in silence, wishing, hoping, begging for my phone. It was my lifeline to the people I love, the information I liked to follow, and the news from the around the world.

Walter stopped for gas in St. Ignace. While he filled his tank, I took his pastie order and scampered next door to a restaurant. The woman ahead of me in line couldn't decide between a traditional pastie and a beef stroganoff pastie. She wanted to know all the bloody details.

Instead of blurting out a terse comment, or sighing rudely, I directed my attention to an abandoned copy of the *Detroit Free Press* sitting on one of the tables. The bottom of the front page caught my attention: "Police still confounded by Garl murders."

As the woman in line finalized her order, the story's lead jumped out at me: *Detectives with the Michigan State Police have released the autopsy results of the Garl murders with hopes that it will stir a new round of tips from the public. Cecil Garl was wearing a St. Christopher medal that hung from a gold chain around his neck. Catholics consider St. Christopher as the patron saint of travelers, but Mr. Garl was an elder in the Lutheran church near his home of Saginaw. Inscribed on the back of the medallion were the words, "Happy trails."*

Strange, the only time I had ever the words "happy trails" was when Genesis said them to me outside the strip joint in Traverse City. Could she have been the person who gave Cecil Garl his medallion?

The thought of him wearing another woman's gift made my stomach churn.

I can't imagine the lie he must have concocted when he showed it to his wife. "I bought it at a pawn shop, what do you think?"

If she didn't buy that fib, he could always say that he bought it at an estate sale; or won it in a game of poker or a round of golf. Of course, the estate sale would be out of town, and the round of golf with phantom customers from a faraway place.

I wondered if he took off the pendant when he rolled on top of her, naked and aroused. Did he let St. Christopher dangle to her lips when they were engaged in passion? Did he close his eyes and imagine Genesis under him when it was his wife he had mounted?

I couldn't wait to ask Genesis if she was the one who gave it to Cecil. It didn't mean that she was the one who murdered him, but it could mean that she was part of his circle of acquaintances.

"I'm not so sure I'd do that if I were you," Walter pleaded.

"Do what?" I asked.

"Go see Genesis. Go if you want to, but I think you're playing with fire. You know that, don't you, Derrick?"

"Maybe it's the black widow effect. I can't just let things go. I have to see Genesis and find out what she knows. I have to get the last word, the best of every situation, the most of every moment."

"Suit yourself, Derrick, but you know where I stand."

Nineteen

The following morning I kissed Colleen on the cheek outside the local rental car business and waved goodbye. She was still a bit upset about what had happened with me smelling like perfume and I couldn't blame her. I didn't' tell her every detail about what happened up north, but I didn't lie, either. My apologies were accepted, but I definitely had to work hard to get in her good graces. The flowers helped, even though Walter's handwritten note, "for the woman of my dreams" on a scrap of Vernor's Ginger Ale box, seemed rather insincere.

I drove east on M-20 from Mt. Pleasant, through Oil City and Midland, and past the overpass where Becky took her plunge. Someone had erected a small cross of plastic flowers and zip tied them to the guardrail on the overpass as a private memento of Becky's last moment of life. Forty minutes later, I was inside Becky Tocca's church in downtown Auburn, a few miles west of Bay City. It was at least a hundred years old and I had to marvel at the architecture with its mile-high ceilings, flying buttresses and ornate statues. It was steeped in tradition, oozed with religion, and had the subtle smell of burnt incense.

I was one of the first people at the service and took a seat way in the back. The altar boys went about their duties: lighting candles, checking the microphones, and making sure the priest would have everything he would need for a smooth service. The organist played a familiar funeral hymn, while a deacon organized the hymnals and collection envelopes in the back of every pew. For obvious reasons, I felt myself opening up to an emotional exercise. It's not much fun confronting death, but it is—after all—part of life.

I felt lost without my phone. In idle times like this, I would check my messages and send out a few of my own.

Instead, I sat there, waiting for the service to begin, watching the visitors enter the sanctuary and dip their fingers in a bowl of holy water. Every one of the people in attendance had a story to tell about Becky. She must have touched them in remarkable ways. What was going through their minds now that she was gone?

My goal was to track down Becky's sister, introduce myself to her, and ask her a few questions about Cecil Garl and Ener-X. Of course, I'd be tactful and pleasant. I'd have to be tactful, if she was surrounded by family and friends. If I got the hunch that she wanted to talk, I might tell her about Becky's last few moments of life on the overpass east of Midland. Either way, I was quite certain that she didn't know that I was inside Becky's storage locker. Heck, without Becky's note, she might not even know it existed.

I couldn't imagine the look on Helen's face when she opened the door to Becky's apartment and realized that everything was gone. "What the…?"

Without the suicide note, she'd have no idea about the storage locker. I'd hate to see Becky's belongings sold at auction at the storage locker, just because I kept the note that was rightfully Helen's. I had to speak to her, no question about it.

As we neared the starting time for the service, more and

more people showed up. Most of them filled the seats toward the front, but gradually, the entire church was almost at capacity. Helen would be one of the folks following the casket, and her seat would be in the very front row.

At last, the funeral directors pushed the casket across the threshold of the sanctuary, a silver-sounding bell rang, and the congregation rose to their feet. In the deafening silence, a baby cried, and several people cleared their throats. The priest called the house to order, but I was distracted by a simple enough inquiry.

"Mind if I sit here?" a woman asked me in a hushed tone.

"Not at all," I whispered. When she squeezed into the pew beside me, I couldn't help but notice the perfume. It was quite familiar and deliciously fascinating.

Instead of looking at the casket or the priest, the woman looked at me.

My jaw dropped.

It was Dottie

"What are you looking at?" she asked me, plain as day.

"Hey, Dottie. Nothing, nothing at all."

"Do I make you uncomfortable, Derrick?"

"Of course not," I lied. "I still owe you for saving my life. Not to mention lunch in Trout Lake."

"Forget about it."

"No, really. I'm going to pay you back. I'd have brought my checkbook today if I had known you'd be here."

"You still get uptight about your debts, don't you, Derrick?"

"I guess."

"Your word was always good with me. It still is now."

The casket and the entourage of family made their way to the front of the church. The priest tossed holy water on the blanket over the coffin as the organist finished playing the funeral dirge.

"I don't have to ask what you're doing here, do I?" I whispered.

"Same thing you are."

"What's that?"

"Paying my respects."

"How did you know Becky?" I asked.

"What makes you think I did?"

I hate it when someone answers a question with a question.

Instead of answering, I let the situation fester.

The more I remembered about Dottie, the less I seemed to trust her. Even though she could carry a decent conversation, and she was kind enough to save my life, I still had my doubts about her intentions, her motivations, and her reasons for being at the funeral.

If she was stalking me, she certainly wasn't the least bit shy about it.

"Why are you here, Derrick?" she asked quietly.

"Why would you ask that?" I gave her a taste of her own medicine.

Dottie shook her head and asked anew, "I thought we were going to work together on this case?"

A lady in the row ahead of us glanced over her shoulder in our direction. I could tell that Dottie and I were too loud.

I reached into the little pocket ahead of our pew, and pulled out a pencil and a blank prayer request card. In bold, capital letters I wrote the words *follow me*. After stuffing the request card back into the pew ahead of me, it occurred to me that maybe the next parishioner would be inspired by the message. *Okay, I'll follow you, Lord.*

The next time the congregation rose to their feet, we did too. Around the back of the pew we went, to the narthex near a pair of wide, wooden doors that must have been nine or ten feet tall.

Almost immediately we got into an argument. I started by tossing a harpoon: "If we're working together, why did you leave me stranded up in Trout Lake?"

"You're so incompetent, Derrick Twitchell. You're an airhead. A dunce."

"Answer me," I demanded, voice raised.

"No, you answer me! I was so vulnerable up there in that bar. I put my heart on the line for you. I thought that maybe you wanted to hook up for old time's sake. You're the one who wanted to make love like a madman." She started welling up. The tears were pooling in her lower eyelids.

I rolled my eyes and let out a sigh. Now I was feeling sorry for her. "Dottie, look, I'm really sorry about that. I didn't mean to stir those feelings. That text was meant for someone else."

The door opened twenty-five feet away and a gush of sunlight poured inside. I couldn't believe my eyes. Two of the three burly amigos from the Upper Peninsula waltzed three steps past the threshold. While they took off their sunglasses and let their eyes adjust to the church's relative darkness, I knew that I had to act fast.

I'm not sure what came over me, but I lunged at Dottie and squeezed her tightly. I felt her hair against my face, her perfume filling my nose. "There, their, they're," I said again, rubbing her back.

Dottie didn't pull away, or resist, which was a good thing. She played the part of a beleaguered next of kin beautifully, even though she was probably wondering if I had lost my mind.

The men didn't think anything of it. They pulled the sleeves of their dress shirts and straightened out their ties. One of them had a dress shirt that looked to be an inch too small around his neck. If ever there was a high-school-athlete-turned-slob, he was it. I believe he was the one I drop-kicked in the package.

"Derrick, what are you doing?" Dottie asked me.

"Don't move, Dottie," I demanded, "we're being watched."

"By whom?" she asked again.

"The thugs who kidnapped me."

"What?" she barked, trying to see what was going on.

I shushed her slightly, and took half a dance step to the right. She looked over my shoulder to the two men but they entered the sanctuary before she could see who they were.

"Are you sure it was them?" she asked.

"Positive."

"What are you going to do, call the police?"

"And tell them what?" I asked politely. "They want to question me for something else. There's a warrant out for my arrest."

"There is?" she asked.

"It's a long story."

"Couldn't you have them arrested?"

"For what? I escaped, remember?" Dottie nodded. "Why don't we figure out who these guys are and who they work for, what do you say?"

I didn't have to ask twice.

"Come on," I said, heading towards a second set of doors.

The bright, June sun almost blinded us. "Keep your eyes peeled for a brown Lincoln. That's all I remember from up in Paradise."

We were on the top stair of the church's front entryway that gave us a relatively decent perspective of the parking lot.

"Why don't we split up?" Dottie gestured. "I'll go left, you go around to the right. Meet you in the back."

"Good call."

Two or three minutes later, we were in the back of the parking lot, standing next to a brownish Lincoln that was tricked out with tan leather interior and a sunroof. I noticed some sort of park sticker in the lower driver's side window. The roof was covered in tiny purple blemishes that must have been the remnants of a mulberry tree or a flock of incontinent starlings.

"Now what?" Dottie asked.

I thought for a several seconds. "First, I'll go get the car. While I'm doing that, why don't you write down the license plate, just in case we need it later. Last, we're going to let the air out of its tires."

"Why do you want to do that?"

"So they can't chase after us."

"Why would they chase you?"

"I don't know. If they kidnapped me, they're capable of just about anything."

Dottie shook her head. I wasn't sure what she was thinking. If she was upset about having to go along with my plan, she didn't say so.

"Derrick, we don't need to write down the license plate number when we have cell phones that take pictures. I'll just friggin email it to you, okay hun?"

"You're so smart," I grimaced. "I have a hunch you're going to win that hundred grand."

I almost skipped back to my little rental car, turned the key in the ignition and drove back to Dottie. She was talking on her cell phone when I arrived, so I jumped out of my car and casually opened my pocket jackknife. It didn't take long to snip the stems of all four tires. They hissed mightily, but gradually lost their nerve as the car bowed to gravity.

It felt relatively good to enact a little more revenge, but I was still confused as to why Dottie was at the funeral. I mean, she didn't know about Becky, her suicide note, or her sister's relationship with Cecil Garl.

"So why are you here, Dottie?" I asked, as she slid inside the car.

"What can I say? I have a nose for trouble."

"What does that mean?"

Dottie chewed on my question for a few seconds but finally said, "Becky Tocca used to work in the bookkeeping department at the Drake Media Group, which is owned by Robert Luxton. Did you know that?"

I nodded.

"You know that Helen Tocca worked for Cecil Garl, too?"

"Yep."

"Well then, you know that Robert Luxton is a person of interest in the Garl family murders, correct?"

"Of course."

"Drake Media handled the printing and the advertising for the magazine."

"The Fatima Society?" I asked.

"Yes, but they also printed Ener-X's brochures and pamphlets. I think Becky knew a lot about Drake and how they spent their money."

"Why didn't you tell me that?"

"You didn't ask."

I was a little bit taken aback with her explanation. It seemed rather dismissive. "Is that how you roll, Dottie, I have to ask for everything you know?"

"I told you that I'm after the hundred thousand."

"What were you going to do, just start asking Mr. Luxton questions?" I asked.

"Of course not. I just wanted to stake out the situation. I want to see who he hangs out with and where he lives."

Her answer seemed to be rather evasive and way too simple, so I jabbed at her again: "So your reporter's instincts told you to come down here?"

"It was just a hunch, but it was a good one, right? It paid off the other day in Paradise."

"I guess so. Is one of the goons inside the church Mr. Luxton?"

Dottie shook her head. "I know what he looks like, and he wasn't one of the two guys there."

"Are you ready to tell me about Shafeek Heanley?"

Her head turned away. "What about him?"

"You said that he did some business with Cecil."

"Well, yeah. Mr. Heanley is the president of Systems Seven."

"What's that?"

"They make car batteries."

"What?" I asked, somewhat surprised.

"Not like the ones that go under your hood, but the big ones," she thought aloud. "You know...the kind it takes to power hybrid cars. They're made in Port Huron."

"Why there?"

"That's where the factory is. Those hybrid batteries are made out of nickel, which arrives by the freighters. They're used in Toyota Prius, Ford Escape and the Saturn Vue. Port Huron has a nice place for the lake freighters to tie up."

"I'm still a little confused about what their relationship might have been," I said.

"I'm not sure of what they did together, but the police think that the two of them were laundering money."

"How?" I asked.

"Mr. Heanley paid Cecil for the ads in his magazine, and in turn, Cecil gave him a kickback."

I felt my eyebrows rise. "How much money was exchanged?"

"Got me, Derrick, but I know that Systems Seven paid the Fatima Society almost fifty grand a month."

"How'd you find that out?" I asked.

"Now, now, Derrick," she urged me, "we have to maintain some borders, don't you think?"

I grimaced. The conversation between us had stalled. We were staked out, behind the church, in the shade of a large oak tree, next to a park where children were having fun in the warm sunshine. The sounds of birds chirping, children playing, and organ music filled the air. It was a pleasant setting, but one filled with potential danger. It seemed that both Dottie and I had come to the funeral for different reasons, but we shared similar goals for an outcome.

"Why are you here?" she asked me.

"The same reason you are. We both want to know more about the Garl murders."

"Is that all?"

"Well, yes," I said, "that, and I want to know what happened to my Impala. I can't keep renting cars forever."

Dottie rolled her eyes and asked me if I got the flowers.

"Yes, I did," I said. "You really shouldn't have done that. If Mrs. Twitchell had found them, I'd have been in hot water."

"Maybe that was my intention," she said, wryly.

"Why would you want to do that? I'm a married man."

Dottie was getting pissed, I could tell. The frown on her face, and the crossed arms said it all. I don't think anyone had ever stood up to her the way I did.

"Happily?" she asked.

I didn't know what to say. She had wedged her way inside arm's length already and I really didn't want her to get any closer. "Happiness is a relative term, Dottie. It's not like peaches and cream all the live-long day. It's a struggle."

Her eyes snapped back to the surroundings, the organ music stopped, and the people gradually filtered out of the church. Aside from a van or two of playground-goers, we were all alone in the rear of the parking lot. The brown Lincoln rested peacefully on its rims, thirty yards away. It was a bait pile of sorts that was sure to get a visitor in the next few minutes.

I felt the adrenalin rise with each passing moment. People were milling about the parking lot. Children ran and played. Their parents demanded that they be careful. A man and a woman in their late fifties ambled towards the car next to us. The husband opened the door for his wife, which seemed like a nice gesture on his part. Chivalry isn't completely dead.

"Looks like everybody's almost gone, Derrick," Dottie mentioned. "Are you sure we're watching the right car?"

"Of course. Have you seen any other brown Lincolns?"

"No, but that doesn't mean that—"

"Just a minute. Who's this?"

I pointed to the back of the church, where a man dug into his trench coat for a set of keys. When he found them, he locked the door and spun our way. There were two men, both in their sixties. One was rather tall, the other, plump as a butterball. They weren't the two amigos we were after, but rather the priest and some sort of associate in a black business suit and a silk red tie.

Dottie said what I was already thinking, "Derrick Twitchell, you are going straight to hell."

I felt terrible. The taller man pulled out his car keys and pressed the buttons. The Lincoln responded with a few blinks of its own.

Dottie slinked in her seat as I started the car. "You really are a dumb ass, aren't you, Derrick?"

"That's not very nice, Dottie. Let's get out of here."

I pulled out of the parking place and casually drifted past the two men. They were scratching their chins and stooping to see what was going on beneath their car.

Dottie's Subaru was at the opposite end of the parking lot. When I pulled closer to her vehicle she hesitated for several seconds.

"What is it?" I asked.

"I don't know," she paused. "I feel bad for those priests, don't you?"

"Of course I do, but I really can't go back there and try to make things right."

"Yes you can, Derrick."

"Please don't, Dottie."

"They didn't do anything to deserve that. They're probably going to be late for the graveside service now…all those people will be waiting."

I rolled my eyes. "Dottie…"

"Bye, Derrick," she said, patting me on the hand. "I'll see you 'round."

She opened the car door, jumped out, and marched towards her vehicle. I watched her climb into her Subaru and felt really, really guilty.

Twenty

Good old Dottie was always a complicated woman. She had an evil side and a wholesome heart, a streak of harshness and an empathetic eye for those in need. One thing was always certain; if she put her mind to something, I had better get out of her way. Instead of leaving the church parking lot, she returned to the two gentlemen and offered to give them a ride to the cemetery. I kind of figured she'd do that, so I waited at the entrance of the park, a hundred yards away from where I dropped her off. The three of them slid past my stakeout, sending me farther and farther down the seat and into the throes of guilt.

Slashing their tires was a foolish thing for me to do, even though I had no idea that they drove the same kind of car as the goons from up north.

For all I knew, it could have been the same car.

I was in a bit of a quandary there. Shame gnawed at my conscience. I could follow Dottie and the priest to the cemetery, or I could clean up my mess with the brown Lincoln.

I chose the latter. Like a shot, I drove back to the parking lot and rolled up my sleeves. The little rental car had a rickety jack in the trunk buried beneath a piece of cheap carpet and a plastic divider.

I pulled the jack from the trunk and propped up the front of the Lincoln, inch by inch. Fortunately for me, the tire iron in the rental had the same size nuts as the Lincoln. With more than a little exertion, the nuts popped loose. They made a nice little pile on the concrete next the car. Five minutes later, I tossed the two flat tires into the trunk of the rental. Two tires down, two to go.

Urgency rushed me along. I had to act fast, if I was to get the tires replaced before the priest made it back to the church. I didn't care what it cost. I didn't care how much trouble I could have gotten into for vandalizing the car; I had to right a wrong that I had created.

It took me ten minutes to pull the front tires from the Lincoln. Sweat engulfed me and I bloodied my knuckles on the pavement trying to set the Lincoln's tires free from the axle. Exhausted, the next problem arose: with only one jack, how was I going to get the rear set of tires off the Lincoln?

I looked to the church. Surely they must have had a cinder block I could borrow. The shadows beneath the shrubs, the back door, and the storage shed at the rear of the parking lot were void of a chunk of concrete, a block of wood, or a five gallon pail. I couldn't find a thing to prop up the car.

Forget it, I thought, *I'll do this in two trips. Get the first set of tires fixed, bring them back and put them on. Then, I'll go back and do it all over again with the rear set.*

I left the jack where it was and raced a few blocks into downtown Auburn. By then I had realized that there was no sense in making two trips. I might as well get the priest a new set of tires for the back of his Lincoln, and I'd keep the old set. They'd be a quick sale on Ebay or Craigslist.

The man at the tire shop was more than happy to

accommodate my unique request: fix the two tires, and buy a second pair complete with the wheels.

Half an hour later, he loaded two tires in the trunk, and two in the back seat. I was thankful for his quick service and the way he loaded them into my vehicle.

"That'll be five-seventy-five-twenty-two, out the door," he said with a snarky smile beneath his unkempt mustache.

I am always confused by the 'out the door' comment. I mean, they were already 'out the door' and resting in my car. Was there a different price for tires 'inside the door'?

Either way, I quickly remembered that I still didn't have my credit card, my checkbook, or a driver's license. Colleen was the one who rented the car I was using. She was the one who would have to pay for the tires, too. I hoped that this latest plea for help wouldn't be the camel that broke Colleen's back, so to speak.

The man behind the counter didn't exactly understand my predicament and was more than just a little concerned that he might not get paid.

"Just a minute," I told the man.

Colleen's cell phone number was on the contract for the rental car company, but when I gave her a call, she didn't answer. The message I left her was a little more than urgent.

This made Mr. Out-the-Door a little perturbed.

Instead of waiting for Colleen to call me back, he marched back out to my rental car and retrieved the tires he had just put in. "Nothing personal," he said. "I just hate to get burned by some low-life loser, know what I mean?"

"Sort of," I grimaced.

He placed the tires inside the shop's front door, and took a picture of my license plate with his phone.

We moved back to the counter, and he fell into his worn leather chair. The longer I stood at the counter of the tire shop, and let his insult metastasize, the more I realized that maybe he was talking about me being a low-life loser.

I should have thought about how I was going to pay for the tires before I jumped into the obligation of fixing them.

I should have had the money in cash, in case the priest or his associate started sniffing around as to who might have put a new set of tires on the car. Without even realizing it, I was leaving a paper trail that the cops would surely have no trouble following.

The man was nice enough to let me keep using his phone. I called my bank, who said they couldn't issue a temporary credit card or give me a loan over the phone. My credit card company was just as uncooperative. They told me that they couldn't issue another card—or authorize more purchases—for forty-eight hours after a card was reported stolen.

"So what do you want to do?" tire-man asked me.

"I guess I want to tell you I'm sorry."

"You guess?"

"Yeah, I apologize."

He rolled his eyes. "You know I can't resell those tires, right?"

I didn't say anything.

"I can't just put them back on the shelf and hope that some other low-life loser has the same kind of car."

I sighed. The 'low-life loser' barb was a little over the top. "Just relax, okay chief?"

"You want *me* to relax?"

"Yes. Let's just calm down, okay? You'll get your money."

"I'm not your chief, got it tough guy?" He stood and puffed his chest. Next thing I know he pulled at the hem of his black rubber gloves. Even though they were the wrong color, they looked like the kind of gloves physicians use before they deal with patients' bodily fluids or the most private of private parts.

Having had my share of scraps up in Paradise, I decided to back down. "I understand perfectly well. There will be no need for violence. You'll get your money."

"Maybe I should call the cops and let them straighten you out?"

He reached for the phone. Before I could get the words, "No, don't" out of my lips, the phone rang.

Amazing how fast he changed his demeanor. As long as it took the voice on the other end to say that she was calling on behalf of Derrick Twitchell, the man smiled and said, "Why yes, Mrs. Twitchell, he's standing right here. We were just discussing his payment options."

He handed me the phone, half grimacing. I walked towards the shop's front door for a little privacy. Colleen wanted to know what was going on, but I really didn't have time to explain. Instead, I talked her into parting with her credit card information. Thankfully, she went along with it and the man behind the counter was momentarily happy.

Relieved, I drove back to the church, where everything appeared to be normal. The Lincoln was still resting on the jack, and the kids were still playing in the park.

I unloaded the front tires and began putting Humpty-Dumpty back together again. The tire rims slid over the bolts, just like I knew they would, but when I searched for the nuts, they were missing.

What the heck, I thought. *I should have taken them with me. Now, I'm really up a creek without a paddle.*

My attention turned to the surroundings. The boys who were practicing their make-believe military battles between the jungle bars and the twisty slide may have seen who stole the nuts. As I started walking their way, they bailed out of their command posts and retreated to the other end of the battlefield.

I didn't yell at them or make a big stink. All I did was climb the stairway to the slide and take a look around.

Sure enough, the boys left the nuts in a pile.

I stuffed them into my suit pockets and returned to the

Lincoln. It had been nearly ninety minutes since Dottie gave the two men a ride to the cemetery. I was mad at myself all over again, but thankful that they hadn't returned. My plan still could work, if I could finish changing the tires quickly.

I almost ran to the Lincoln. The spin wrench spun each nut to the bolt. The hub caps popped into place. I was working quickly, driven by the vision and the good karma of the priest and his associate getting saved by a Good Samaritan.

Just as I placed the jack under the rear axle, my hopes and dreams of a fairy tale ending came crashing back to earth.

It was the priest himself. He stepped out a new Tahoe, ready for battle. "Hey!" he yelled, "what are you doing?"

"Father, wait," I said, hand raised as if I was going to high five him. "I'm here to help,"

The priest kept coming at me. So did his associate who had bolted from the back seat.

"Look," I stood. "I just put a new set on the front. I have a pair of new tires in the back of my car. They're for you."

That confession got their attention.

The driver of the Tahoe stepped outside. She looked to be about fifty years old.

"They're brand new, Father," I said calmly. "I'm into good deeds."

"Let me help you, then," he said.

Next thing I know, he took off his black sport coat, hung it in the back of the Lincoln, and grabbed the spindly jack handle. He spun it like an old pro.

I pulled the new set of tires from the back seat of my car, and rolled them into place.

"What do you do, go around doing random acts of kindness?" he asked.

"Not exactly, Father. I saw the look of disappointment on your face when you came outside and realized that your tires had been slashed."

"Why were you here?" the taller man asked.

"For Becky's funeral," I said, as I picked up the spin wrench. "I'm trying to get a hold of her sister."

"You just found her."

My head snapped to the female voice, above. "Helen?"

"Yes."

I stood. The tires weren't so important any longer.

Helen was rather portly. Short hair. Six or eight earrings. Tattoos. The more I looked at her, the more she looked like the aggressor in the video that was taken in the women's room on Cecil's secret zip drive. "Sorry about your sister."

"Thank you," she said. "We're going to miss her. She was under a lot of stress lately."

"I gathered that. I was the one who was with her on the overpass."

"So, you're the one," she smiled sheepishly.

I extended my hand, "Derrick Twitchell, from Mt. Pleasant."

Our hands clasped for a second before she asked me, "What did she say to you?"

"Not a whole lot," I said. The wheels in my head were spinning. I didn't know where to start. "Obviously, she was very upset, even despondent. Our conversation didn't last that long. I tried to stop her, but she just jumped."

Helen didn't say a thing, so I continued.

"She said that she was under a lot of stress at her job, that she had lost her house, and that her husband had run off with some other woman."

My confession seemed to bend the ear of the priest, who had finished jacking up the Lincoln.

"That about sums it up," Helen said. I noticed the way she looked a lot like her sister, complete with a turned-up nose. "Why were you there?"

"Happenstance. I hit a deer not far from the overpass and climbed the embankment to get away from the traffic."

"Why didn't you talk to the police?"

"The tow truck picked up my vehicle and I had to get my boat to the dealer before they closed."

"The police want to talk to you; you know that, don't you?"

"Yes. I have intentions of going…"

"Was there a note?" she asked.

It was an interesting way she framed the question. "Yes," I responded cautiously.

"Where is it?"

"I don't have it."

"I need that note, Mr. Twitchell. You understand that, don't you?"

"Of course I do."

I had to explain how the note was in my car and the car was stolen. The car I was driving today was a rental.

"What gave you the right to go into her storage locker?"

This woman was three steps ahead of me. "Becky," I lied. "She told me to."

"You're a liar, Mr. Twitchell. She didn't even know you."

I let her accusation dangle, while the priest and the other man spun the nuts firmly into place. "Helen, I'm sorry about your sister. She seemed like a nice person. There's no sense in making yourself upset about things that you can't control."

I looked behind me to the Lincoln. The men had the hubcaps in place. It looked like it was ready to roll. Before she could fire any more insults, I turned to the priest and said, "Father, if it's all right with you, I'll take the old set of tires with me."

"That's not up to me," he said matter-of-factly. "This isn't my car."

"Whose is it?"

"It's his. The deacon." He pointed to the man on the far side of the Lincoln. He was rather tall and skinny and his Adam's apple bulged above his necktie like a Gordian knot.

"I appreciate your generosity, but the rims you bought don't match the front set."

My attention turned to the differences between the set of rims. I noticed that the old set had eight sets of spokes, the new set maybe six. Whatever.

"Why don't you go ahead and keep them," I said, forcing a smile.

"Great idea."

The two men said goodbye to Helen, jumped in the Lincoln, and took off.

I collected the jack and placed it in the trunk of the rental.

Helen didn't back off. She was like a little terrier on my pant leg. "I want that suicide note, Mr. Twitchell."

"I heard you the first time, Helen."

"And I want to know what you stole out of her storage locker."

"How do you know I was even there?"

"Don't deny it, Mr. Twitchell. What did you take?"

I didn't know what to say to her, so I jumped in the car. Before I could slam the driver's side door closed, she grabbed hold of it.

"I'm going to get you for this, Twitchell," she barked. "If you don't get me that note and tell me what you stole from her locker, there's going to be hell to pay."

Twenty-One

Something took hold of me on the drive home from Auburn. Maybe it was divine intervention that stepped in and told me to come clean with the state police. Perhaps it was my own runaway conscience that told me to confess my sins, or quite possibly, Helen's spiteful threats. Whatever it was, I decided to look up the two detectives from the Midland post and tell them everything I knew about Becky Tocca's last few moments of life.

I wouldn't have to lie that much.

She was the one who jumped off the overpass, not me.

It was her own free will that sent her tumbling over the edge; I was just an innocent bystander.

And the note she left behind? It was a run-of-the-mill suicide note, full of sorrowful goodbyes and ink-laden regrets spilled on the paper.

Since Becky wasn't alive, I could tell the cops a lot of things about our conversation. First and foremost, I could tell them that Becky gave me permission to access her locker. They'd have a hard time disputing that statement, because they weren't there to know the difference. Everybody in the interrogation room knew about the police's burden of proof. "Beyond a shadow of a doubt" is a high standard, and I wasn't about to incriminate myself.

And where was the note? It was in the car that was stolen in the Upper Peninsula.

I had everything mapped out in my head as I walked into the state police post in Midland. For some reason I remembered both the detectives names, VanWyk and Nutting. They were pleasant enough and looked rather professional in their short-sleeve dress shirts and slacks. I noticed that they each had a tie clip emblazoned with a miniature state police badge. Their real badge was affixed to a belt loop on their trousers. Nutting had two tiny rubies on his clip, VanWyk only one. I guess that meant that Nutting had more experience.

Make no mistake, they were all business. The badges and firearms on their belts were a constant reminder that they were there to do a job.

My interview didn't exactly get off to a great start. I couldn't produce my driver's license when Nutting asked for it, and when I said that my car was stolen, VanWyk jumped into the fray.

"Why didn't you report it stolen?" he asked me.

"I've been a little busy," I responded. "And besides, I have another vehicle that I can drive."

"Do you own a twenty five caliber?"

"Handgun or rifle?" I asked.

"Either, or," he said.

"No."

"Have you ever been to the Garl family cabin?"

"Yes."

"What did you do?"

"Looked around, took some pictures."

"When?"

"A while ago...after the snow melted."

"Did you take anything?"

"No. I just took a few pictures and left."

"Well, then," VanWyk sighed, "specifically, what did Ms. Tocca tell you before she jumped off the bridge?"

"That I could access her storage locker."

"Really. You're a complete stranger and she said to just go ahead and poke around?"

"Yes."

"Did you go there?"

"Yes."

"Did you take anything?"

"No. Nothing," I lied.

"Why did you look down when you answered that question?"

"I did? Would it help if I looked you in the eye?"

Nutting jumped in. "What else did she tell you?"

"Not a whole lot."

"Like what?" he asked, rubbing his hairy arms.

I stared at his mustache for a second. He was the man who was captured on the camera clock, shortly after the Garls were discovered in their cabin. "That she didn't want the company chasing her any longer."

"Drake Media?"

"I assume so. She didn't say."

Instead of VanWyk and Nutting asking me the questions, I turned the tables on them. "You interviewed Becky about the Garl murders, didn't you?"

"Of course."

"What did she say?"

"Let's not go there. That's confidential."

I nodded. "What about Becky's sister, Helen?"

"What about her?" Nutting responded.

"Have you interviewed her?"

"Sure we did."

"You know that she used to work for Cecil Garl, right?"

"How did you know that?" Nutting leaned on me.

"I'm a reporter, Mr. Nutting, and a thorough one at that."

He sighed.

"There's a lot of money at stake," I mentioned.

"You mean the hundred grand from the newspaper?"

"Yes."

"We're just trying to find out if Ms. Tocca jumped off the bridge or if she was pushed, Mr. Twitchell. We don't care about the reward."

After twenty or thirty minutes of interrogation, I felt like I had finally convinced the two detectives that my story was checking out. As much as I felt like they wanted to hang some sort of charge on me, I managed to wiggle out of every corner in which they tried to paint me.

When they asked why I was in the Upper Peninsula, I told them it was to go trout fishing.

When they asked how long I had stayed up north, I told them just one night.

"Where did you stay?" they asked me.

"On the beach—under the stars—on the edge of Lake Superior."

When asked how I got home, it was easy enough: a co-worker named Walter picked me up and drove me.

They seemed to be focused on Becky's suicide, not the bigger fish to fry: the Garl murders up north. As much as I tried to pry information from them, the more tight-lipped they became. It was a chess game of nerves. I knew that I couldn't give answers that contradicted each other. I knew that I had to tell the truth, but I had plenty to hide. If I didn't convince them of my innocence, the detectives would want me to take a polygraph test, and I didn't want to do that at all.

Both detectives left the little interrogation room. I was all alone with the one-way mirror, my guilty conscience, and my own imagination.

I never would have thought that Dottie would go back to the priest in the parking lot and try to help them out.

I never would have dreamt that Genesis might have given Cecil Garl a gold necklace and a charm, unless they were more than just friends.

Nor, could I imagine ever being thrown into the middle of such a bizarre case in which the victim's perversions were just as lurid as his business dealings. The motive or motives for his demise could have been a combination of perversion and money, guilty pleasure or a business deal gone wrong.

Whatever the case, the two detectives opened the door again, and told me that my trusty old Impala had been found.

"Where?" I asked.

"On federal land in the Upper Peninsula. Way out in the sticks," VanWyk said.

"When?"

"This morning."

"Any damage to it?"

"Not sure about that, but it looks okay." Nutting pulled up a photo on his Blackberry and showed it to me. Sure enough, it was my car all right. It looked like it was parked on a sandy easement, surrounded by forest, way out in the boonies.

"So what do I do?" I asked.

"You have forty eight hours to get it out of there before it gets impounded."

"Thanks. Can you tell me where out in the sticks?"

"Yeah, but it's too hard to describe it to you."

"So how do I find it?"

Nutting pulled out his Blackberry, and was thumbing the tiny button on its face. A second later, he whipped out a note pad and scribbled something on the paper.

"Here's the phone number for central dispatch up there. That'll get you started."

"Thanks."

"Mr. Twitchell?"

"Yes."

"Your next stop is the secretary of state, right?"

"Yes. I will get a replacement driver's license."

Nutting smiled and sent me on my way.

Twenty-Two

The phone number Detective Nutting gave me was for central dispatch in Newberry. When I dialed the number and inquired about my stolen vehicle, I was given the number for the sheriff's office down the street. The nice lady at the office told me to contact the deputy and set up a time and place for a rendezvous the following afternoon. I followed her instructions and arranged to have a meeting, late afternoon the following day.

Instead of convincing a buddy, my wife, or Walter to take me to the Upper Peninsula, I decided to take a Greyhound bus instead. For fifty-seven dollars—and six and a half hours out of my life—it seemed like a pretty fair deal. Instead of concentrating on the road ahead, the bus ride gave me the chance to relax and see the sights I often miss when I'm concentrating on dodging other cars.

I'd spend my time wisely on the bus. There was a story to be written about the Garl murders, even if I wasn't remotely close to solving who might have killed them. Now, I had a replacement credit card, a new driver's license, a new laptop and a stack of currency in a brand new wallet. I remembered to bring a spare key for the Impala and my new cell phone, too. I would need the time to read the phone owner's manual, and learn how to enter my lost contacts.

I made a copy of the zip drive I took from Becky's locker.

By the time we stopped to pick up and drop off passengers in Mackinaw City, I was beginning to get a bad feeling about the deputy up north.

Was this the same clown who tried to throw his weight around at the diner up in Paradise?

Was this the same fellow who was in cahoots with the woman at the hardware store, and the three goons who kidnapped me?

Worry and anxiety rolled across the landscape of my mind like a bank of dense fog across the Dead Sea. Maybe Dead Sea wasn't such a good analogy.

Here I was, all alone, walking foolishly into a trap.

I called Colleen and told her what was running through my mind. She tried to assuage my worries by telling me that it was just a hunch that the deputy had anything to do with the kidnapping. "Besides," she said, "the detectives in Midland sent you up there. There would be too many witnesses for the deputy to do anything crazy."

Her assessment of the situation wasn't quite the explanation I had hoped for, but under the circumstances, perhaps she had the right idea. Instinct and intuition were Colleen's middle names.

Instead of letting the trip unfold without any documentation, I decided to put my new phone to use and take a picture of every stop the bus made. That way, if I was walking into a trap, the producers of *Sixty Minutes* or *Forty-Eight Hours*—if not the authorities who investigate the authorities—would have plenty of clues to my disappearance.

Was I too old or gray to be part of an Amber Alert?

The trap I was waltzing into made me wish I had brought my handgun.

I took a photograph of the bus stop on US-2 on the west side of St. Ignace. It wasn't too far from Clyde's Restaurant and its wonderful cooking.

When we jumped back on I-75, I paid close attention to the railroad grades that might have come from Trout Lake. I spotted a grade, but no tracks. It was painfully clear that there were no tracks when I saw a dirt bike and some four wheelers whipping down the grade without getting their brains rattled from the ties beneath the tracks. The tracks and the ties had been removed. The only thing that remained was the grade itself, which made the perfect corridor for recreational riders in all seasons.

The Greyhound never left I-75 until it reached Sault Ste Marie. I had hoped that we'd go through Trout Lake so I could tell where I went wrong when I jumped aboard the train just a few days previous. If I made it out of Newberry alive, I vowed to pay attention to the train tracks in Trout Lake on my way home.

From Sault Ste Marie, we traveled west on Highway 28, and through the little outposts of Raco and Hulbert Lake. About forty-five minutes later, the bus driver opened the door to let me out at the intersection of Highway 28 and Newberry Avenue. I packed my laptop and my gear, stuffed it all into my backpack and walked north, past the golf course, the flower shop, and the Falls Motel.

The young deputy was waiting for me inside the sheriff's office. "It's about time you made it up here."

"Sorry," I apologized, "I got here as soon as I could. The Greyhound isn't as fleet of foot as she once was."

"Jump in," he said, pointing to the back seat of his patrol car. "Your vehicle isn't too far away."

When I jumped inside, the smell reminded me of authority. Strangely, it had the odor of the principal's office of my youth; leather chairs and cheap cologne, rolled into one. I wasn't in trouble any more, but I could have been. Dear, sweet Mom wasn't available to help bail me out of trouble.

The deputy looked like he had just stepped off the label of a Jiffy Peanut Butter jar, with his red hair and abundant freckles. Instead of listening to the chatter on his police scanner, I tried to hone in on his conversation with central dispatch. They were talking about a search warrant the magistrate had issued for a man who lived in Seney.

Just as we headed out of town, Dottie sent me a text. *Police ask the public for help in finding patients from the State Hospital.*

What about it?

State hospital in Petoskey was closed a week before the Garl murders. All the patients were released to the care of family members, but police say that there are several patients who were turned over to halfway houses. They weren't accounted for at the time of the murders.

What does it mean?

It means that the killer(s) might still be at large.

Well, yeah. Gotta be careful. I sent you a check this morning, on my way out of town. I'm back in the UP again.

You need a wing man?

The deputy and I bounced our way north out of town. We hit an imaginary line that sent my phone into the abyss of no service. After seven or eight miles, he turned on a little two-track that slid east into the forest.

The sandy trail and its loose footing pushed us around. I could feel the deputy's undercarriage getting a good scrubbing from the weeds as we negotiated the rutty, seldom-used trail. When we flew over a small hill or a rise in the trail, I felt the car's shocks bottom out. Ferns and branches, loaded with lush, green leaves whisked past the passenger-side window at what felt like mach speed. If I looked real closely I could see the daintiest of flowers attached to the frail twigs of wild blueberry. I just love the early summer and all the promise that goes along with it.

After two or three miles, the deputy slammed on the brakes. "Your car is up ahead."

I looked through the windshield. The trail dipped into a low spot, where creek water splashed and gurgled over a handful of grapefruit-sized rocks.

"How far up ahead?"

"You'll see it."

"You didn't answer my question."

"That's right."

He put the car in park, jumped out, and opened the back door. I figured that if he was going to shoot me, it would probably be shortly after I jumped out of the car. Instead, he just stood there like a guard at Buckingham Palace.

"How am I going to get out of here?" I asked him.

"You'll drive it out the same way it went in," he chortled.

"How's that?"

"On four wheels, right Mr. Twitchell?"

He made me feel dumb. Perhaps it was his way of making himself feel smart.

"Do you know that deputy from Paradise?"

"I know of him. He's in Chippewa County and I'm in Luce. Seen him a few times at the shooting range over the years, why?"

"I just wondered. I've heard some bad things about him."

He shook his head, but I was still a little unsure if he was at all affiliated with the guy or if he was telling the truth. To make him think twice about whether or not I had arrived in Newberry by myself, I told him: "I have a buddy who came up with me. He's at the Falls Motel getting a room. If I'm not back in half an hour, I told him to tell central dispatch that I've been kidnapped." The deputy looked at me as if I was some sort of mouth breather.

I loaded my backpack and ran down the creek bank, half expecting that I might be shot between the shoulder blades.

No shots pierced the UP air, but I did hear him say, "You're welcome" as he slammed the car door.

He was right; I must have appeared to be an ungrateful down-stater.

When I cleared the rise on the opposite side of the creek, I glanced down the trail from where we had just come from. The deputy was driving backwards down the trail, his arm draped over the bench seat, his head pointed out the rear window.

Now I was all alone, thankful for the lift, and hungry.

In my haste to get to the sheriff's office, I had forgotten all about getting something to eat. Amazing how skinny I feel when my stomach is rumbling empty. Conversely, when I'm really full, I feel like I should get my clothes from Omar the Tent Maker.

I tried not to pay attention to how empty my stomach was.

When I stopped to pour a quarter cup of creek water out of my shoes, the mosquitoes nearly carried me away. They were as hungry as I was, and just as relentless. I hustled away from the clouds of insects, beneath the aspens and the maples that cast mighty shadows on everything beneath.

It was early evening, and the wood thrushes and brown thrashers were serenading the falling sun with their sweet, lonesome songs. If I were to see a bear, a wolf, or a moose, it would be on a night like tonight.

Quickly, I walked farther and farther away from civilization. Twenty minutes of a brisk walk had to be at least a mile. Panic was beginning to set in. If I turned around, it would take me twenty minutes to get back to the creek. Add on forty more, just to get to the blacktop. By then it would be pitch black, and who would want to pick up a hitchhiker at that time of night. At this pace of walking, I wouldn't make it back to Newberry until ten or eleven at night.

I wanted to chew out the deputy for leaving me there in relative peril. Although he didn't have an obligation to give me a ride, he shouldn't have left me where he did.

Now the panic was really starting to ratchet up, which probably made things much worse. Every little oddity in the sandy trail was a track from a hungry bear, a pack of wolves, or a bull moose.

My walk turned into a trot, and the trot to a canter.

The wood thrushes and brown thrashers didn't care. This was their time to sing, regardless if the audience appreciated it.

Five more minutes of jogging and things went from bad to worse.

The trail forked.

One trail went south into a field of young aspen shoots, and the other jutted left into more forest.

I cursed, and cursed, and cursed. The fricking deputy ought to be court marshaled for dereliction of duty.

The longer I stood there, weighing my options, cursing the deputy, vowing to write a career-ending letter to his superiors, the governor, my congressman, the Paradise Chamber of Commerce and every business in the west end of Luce County, the more the mosquitoes used me as a human pin cushion. They were on my neck and in my hair, buzzing mad inside my ears. It seemed like every other swat was rewarded with a smear of blood on my palm.

Through all the adrenalin and sweat, hateful emotions and evil insects, I remembered the photograph of my car that the detective showed me. The Impala wasn't in a clear cut, but rather, the kind of forest whose trail banked to the left.

I dashed left, and sixty yards later my beautiful white Impala was sleeping comfortably on the edge of the trail. My car keys almost leapt from my pocket. A push of the button and the car's lights blinked cheerfully.

This made me smile; the car battery was just fine.

I popped the trunk and looked inside. The spare tire was still beneath my golf clubs and fly fishing equipment. I wondered why they didn't take it.

It just seemed like there had to be something wrong. There always is when Derrick Twitchell is involved.

I checked the tailpipe: no obstructions.

The motor looked as dirty as ever and no sticks of dynamite were taped to the lining of the engine wall.

I dug my mini flashlight from the backpack and looked beneath the seats. No explosives.

Maybe whoever took my car was doing it just to be a jerk, not to kill me.

Last, I backed away from the car and hit the remote start button. The car came to life, and purred confidently in the evening still.

I felt myself smile amongst the cloud of mosquitoes.

In an instant, I threw the backpack inside, rammed the key in the ignition and put the car in gear.

When I looked down to make sure the car was in drive, I noticed a note taped to the gauges and instruments beneath the dashboard. The letters looked like they were cut from a magazine and arranged by a toddler on a plain sheet of paper. My heart sank as I read the words: *if you want to see your family again, leave the zip drive with Phil at the Yukon Inn.*

Twenty-Three

The wording of the note seemed rather profound. Whoever put it together knew that I had been in Becky's locker, and understood that she had produced a zip drive. Becky's suicide note wasn't in the car, and neither were the newspaper clippings. My wallet, car keys and laptop computer were long gone.

I had to get Colleen and my daughter the heck out of Dodge. We'd have to change the locks at home, and while the locksmiths were at it, I might as well install a new security system too. My phone was without service, but my mind was racing a million miles an hour.

I knew where the Yukon Inn was, but who was Phil?

The note said *leave the zip drive with Phil.*

Why would I *leave it with Phil,* and not *talk to Phil?*

I wanted to ring Phil's neck or pound him into oblivion. *How dare you threaten my family. This is between you and me.*

The bastards who stole my car were now threatening my wife and child. They could have whatever information they wanted; just leave my family out of it. Damn it, I was getting mad.

My blood pressure was rising, I was sure of it. The more I pummeled an imaginary Phil with my fists, the more I realized that maybe I should worry about how much gas was in the

Impala. The note taped to the dashboard blocked my view of the gauges, but I didn't dare touch it. There might be fingerprints or DNA buried behind the letters.

I put the Impala in reverse and backed out of the easement. If I went back to where I came from, I'd have to negotiate the creek, then drive back through Newberry. If I went east instead of west, I'd be much closer to Paradise.

Instead of taking chances, I decided to play it safe and go back the way we came in. There was no sense in wandering into uncharted territory with a vehicle that was built for pavement.

My Impala wasn't very good in the sand. It jerked and jolted as we muscled our way towards civilization. Perhaps the deputy was correct in going quite fast. Momentum seemed like an ally as I drew closer and closer to the bedeviled creek bottom.

Even though I pictured the Impala getting stuck in the belly of the creek, and a monsoon washing the vehicle downstream, I was determined to make it past.

The headlights cast a dreamy slice through the woods. The ferns and forest, sand and solitude seemed to swallow me whole.

When I slammed on the brakes at the brow of the creek, a plume of dust and mosquitoes clouded my view. I jumped out of the vehicle and assessed the situation. The reflection of the headlights bounced off the water and onto the hill on the other side.

I looked down at my pant legs, which were still wet from crossing the creek. It looked like the water was as deep as the bottom of the doors. Maybe slightly above the doors. I didn't care. It was time to forge ahead, and throw caution to the wind.

I backed up fifty or sixty yards, revved the engine a couple times for dramatic effect, then stomped on the accelerator. We roared ahead—retracing my steps—over the precipice and into the water. The splash was enormous, but I didn't take time to admire its girth. My Impala's hooves lost her footing in the current and the slippery rocks, but I didn't spare the gas. This was no time to be timid. She collected herself, and we skittered and clawed our way free of the creek's current and the imposing hill on the far side.

Whew, I sighed. *We made it.*

Crossing the creek was a big deal for me. I'm one of those people who go out of their way to avoid confrontation.

As we made our way west, back to the pavement that runs north out of Newberry, it occurred to me that the cops must not have noticed the note taped to the gauges beneath the dashboard. It wasn't a very big note—perhaps the size of an invitation envelope. They were probably paying more attention to the steering column to see if the ignition had been punched.

It made me regret unlocking the Impala when I first arrived. If it was locked it would have meant that the cops wouldn't have had the opportunity to look inside the dashboard. If it was locked then they might have missed the note, or been unable to read it. Since I didn't report the vehicle stolen, they probably didn't make much out of it.

When I arrived at the pavement, I decided to head south into Newberry, instead of north towards the little outpost of Pine Stump Junction and eventually, Paradise. There would be no more risk-taking for me. First things first: call Colleen and tell her to abandon ship and sleep somewhere else. Next, buy a tank of the best gasoline Newberry had to offer. From there, I'd buy a sandwich at Subway, and try to pick up a blank zip drive somewhere in town. Finding one in this small town seemed like a remote possibility, but I was still hopeful. The hardware store in Paradise sold them, seems like there should be an equivalent in Newberry.

When my cell phone regained consciousness, Colleen heeded my warning, but said she wasn't leaving our home.

"Elizabeth is having a sleepover, Derrick," she said. "School was cancelled tomorrow because of a water main break. I have a living-room full of eight year olds. They're eating popcorn and watching a movie."

I understood her reticence, but it made the situation even more stressful.

"What if you installed that trail camera in the bushes by the front door?" I asked.

"What?" she was yelling. "You think that the bad guys are going to come marching in the front door?"

"Heck, I don't know. They have a key."

"Don't worry about us, Derrick. I know where the gun is. The dog will give us ample warning."

The phone went blank for a second.

"Just give them what they want," she said. "Come home, Derrick. Cut your losses on this case, and let it go."

I didn't know what to say, other than it seemed like good advice.

Then again, she wasn't the one looking at a note taped to her dashboard.

She wasn't the one who was handcuffed to a bed and held captive overnight.

If I could just find a blank zip drive and create some sort of phony files, I just might end this thing once and for all.

The woman at Subway said there was a gas station that sold all kinds of knickknacks and trinkets on Highway 28.

"Perfect," I said, paying for a six-inch tuna on wheat, "that's my next stop."

About ten minutes later, I was inside the gas station, which wasn't a typical gas station at all. It was more like a flea market that sold fuel. Yeah, they sold shirts of all sizes with cute saying about the mosquitoes, the moose, the bears in the UP; but they also had a whole aisle dedicated to products related to a car: air fresheners, Turtle wax, phone chargers, fuses, and additives for the fuel tank. Beneath the counter were upscale sunglasses, girly magazines, zip drives, carved antlers and knives. I bought a set of handcuffs, a fair-sized knife, along with a matching sheath that slid over my belt. In the aisle with all the fishing equipment, I found a bat about ten inches long. Burned into the hard, grainy wood were the words, *Fish Bat*. It seemed like the perfect tool for stunning the walleyes into submission once they came aboard my boat. When stuffed into the pocket of my jacket, it could be just the right deterrent to whoever this Phil person might be.

My plan was coming together.

As I roared past the cedar swamplands and hardwood forests between Newberry and the turnoff to Paradise, I fired up the laptop and got down to business. Becky's footage from the board meeting of Ener-X would be the centerpiece of Phil's zip drive. It was an impressive file, with all the yelling and fur flying between the two men. People like to watch fights, even if it's a couple of heavyweights in the business world who never exchange punches.

Instead of cluttering the zip drive with the meat and potatoes of Becky's theory on who killed the Garl family, I decided to leave the rest of the zip drive empty. No sense in giving Phil more than what he asked for.

Phil would have to believe me.

Whoever Phil was.

A short while later I pulled into the parking lot of the Yukon Inn in downtown Paradise. The building was a sight to behold, with its double-decker roof. The original building could have been an outpost for the voyageurs back in the trapping days, because the it looked to be made from logs that were at least two hundred years old. The log building was covered with a second roof that's supported by its own set of four by fours.

The sign that hung a dozen feet above the front door wasn't exactly an inviting beacon, but it did have a woodsy, Alaskan charm. The letters that formed the word "Yukon" were made from cartoonish, birch logs.

When I stepped inside, I noticed a heavy metal grate over a pit that looked to be four or five feet deep. It looked like a little dungeon of sorts. There were hardly any patrons inside the bar. A man and a woman, of nearly forty, were on my left. Their hands were clustered over the tabletop a wine glass for her and a can of beer for him. It looked like I had interrupted a clandestine rendezvous. At almost ten o'clock, I bellied up to the bar and ordered a bottle of O'Doul's from the bartender.

"You want a glass with that?"

"Sure. Is the kitchen still open?"

"Yep," she said. "What do you want?"

"I don't know."

"You decide what you want, and I'll get your beer."

She slid a plastic-coated menu my way. It was covered in greasy, smudged fingerprints.

The six-inch tuna-on-wheat sandwich from Subway had long since been digested. I was after something substantial, something that would fill my belly and satisfy my craving. *When in Rome, do as the Romans.*

"I'll have a Yukon burger."

"Everything on it?" she asked, placing my beer on the countertop.

"Why not."

"Fries or coleslaw."

"Fries."

She disappeared behind the bar and into the kitchen. For all I knew, she could have been the cook, too.

A giant, stuffed whitetail buck looked down at me from above the liquor shelf. The right side of its nose was cracked and weathered from being so close to a lamp above the vodka. On the other side of the bar was a set of moose antlers, which was coated in the same buttery yellow varnish that was used to seal the log walls. Both trophies were illuminated by a string of lights that framed the bar. They were made from shotgun shell casings in several different colors. It was the perfect accent for a friendly, out-of-the-way bar in the UP. This place embraces the ruggedness of the country and the outdoorsy pursuits that it offers.

I looked up at the television. No Tigers. They must have had a day off, been rained out, or been involved in one of those two-hour gems that are highlighted by good pitching and not many hits.

As much as I wanted to be rid of the zip drive in my shirt pocket, I didn't mind the lack of tension. It felt good to order a hot meal and unwind for just a bit.

There were only three people in the bar and none of them looked like a Phil. The couple in back could have been a Bill and Patty, or a Tim and Tammy. The bartender looked like a Billie, a Carmen, or a Jackie. It's fun to guess people's names.

It wasn't my fault that Phil didn't show up.

In the roller coaster of life, however, my calm emotions quickly turned into tension. The bar's door opened, and a couple of rough-looking characters stepped inside. They were taller than me, wider than me, and bristled with testosterone. Maybe it was their leather vests covered with patches of Jolly Rogers, swords and sabers that made me think that I was way out of my league. I didn't dare make eye contact, but felt a bit of solace in the fish bat near my elbow.

The waitress must have known that she had company, because she returned from the kitchen to greet them at the bar, five feet to my right. They both ordered a Budweiser.

She served their beer, pointed in my direction, and said, "Your dinner will be right up."

I smiled.

The man from the back of the seating area ambled up to the bar, twenty dollar bill in hand. I looked past him to the two hairy dudes further down the bar. The man closest to me had a sleeve of tattoos on his left arm and a ring tattoo on his hand. His nose was long and had a nice little slope—a prototype for an Olympic ski jump.

The bartender returned from the kitchen with a plate of food in one hand a tray of condiments in the other.

"Here you are, Love," she smiled, "one Yukon burger, just for you."

I remember saying thank you, just ahead of admiring the food in front of me. It was a hell of a burger—wide and thick—sandwiched between a hefty bun and a slice of Canadian bacon. After a long day of trapping wolverines, panning for gold, or training for the Iditarod in the Klondike, it felt good to sink my teeth into a sizzling hunk of angus.

The bartender took the man's twenty dollar bill and gave him the change. He left two dollars on the bar top and went on his way.

One of the burly fellows stood up and yanked on his blue jeans. He took four or five steps my way. I put down my food, wiped my lips with a napkin, and calmly stuffed my hand into my left jacket pocket.

It was difficult not to flinch.

I watched him in the mirror behind the bar and felt his steps on the hardwood floor. He must have been wearing boots that belonged to Herman Munster. They jarred the floor with every mammoth step. Behind me on the wall, was a jukebox. I turned my head slightly, enough to find him in my peripheral vision. He didn't raise his fist or cock an arm. Mr. Biker Dude kept walking to the jukebox where I heard him wrestle with the change in his pocket. A second or two later, Bob Seger came to life.

I was a little too tall could have used a few pounds.
Tight pants point hardly renowned.
She was a black haired beauty with big dark eyes.
And points all her own, sitting way up high.
Way up firm and high.

It seemed like the perfect song for some night moves of my own. The biker dudes were harmless, it appeared. They were just wetting their whistle in a quaint watering hole at the end of the earth.

The bartender wiped down the bar again, and engaged the

two men with a little small talk, barely out of earshot. I didn't let their chatter interrupt my eating.

The Yukon burger was delicious. The fries, cooked to perfection.

It was summertime. Sweet summertime.

When the bartender asked how was my food, I gave her the thumbs up. She placed the check on the countertop and a salt shaker on top of that. It seemed like my opening to inquire about the man of the hour.

"Any idea where Phil might be?"

She seemed flummoxed. "Who wants to know?"

"Me."

"Who are you?"

"Derrick Twitchell. Know where he is?"

"I'm Phil. My real name is Phyllis." I was surprised and disappointed at the same time. There was no way that I'd beat up a woman. Conversely, she looked like she could handle herself. "Have we met before?"

"I don't think so."

"Well, now that we have the formalities out of the way, what can I do for you Derrick?"

This is the part where things became interesting. She didn't seem to be expecting me, or had any clue about the zip drive.

"What do you know about Cecil Garl?"

"He's dead, right?"

I nodded. "Ever wait on him here?"

"Yeah, a little bit. He used to come in here every now and then. He and Robert Luxton."

"What did he drink?"

"Luxton was a Scotch and water kind of guy. Garl was into hard lemonade and goofy drinks like Tootsie Rolls, Dirty Girl Scout, and Hairy Navel."

"Ever see them argue?"

"Never."

"Did Mr. Garl ever bring a girl up here?"

"What kind of girl?"

"A woman. Blonde and beautiful."

"Yeah," she hesitated, "once in a while. I think they stayed at the Luxton place down on the river."

I dipped the last of my fries into a tiny puddle of ketchup.

"I already gave my statement to the cops some time ago," Phyllis continued.

"You mean after the bodies were found?"

"Yeah, maybe a month after. It was late last summer, right around Blueberry Fest. I can't believe that they haven't made any arrests."

"Me, either. Who do you think did it?" I asked.

"Oh, it had to be Luxton. They had a smug kind of thing going, those two."

Smug didn't seem like the right word.

"What do you mean?"

"The two of them. Luxton ran a media company, and Garl had some kind of magazine that was published up here."

I reached into my wallet and pulled out a twenty.

"Lots of people read it," she said, "but I never did."

"Who is this Luxton fella?"

"I really don't know him, but I've heard some terrible things..."

"Like what?"

"I'd rather not say."

"Why?"

"I don't even know you."

"Am I supposed to give you something?"

"You already did," she smirked.

"Really?" I asked, terribly confused.

She plucked the twenty off the bar top and shook it like it was a balled up sock that belonged to her son or daughter. "You want the change?"

The check came to nine dollars. "Heck yeah, I want the change."

Twenty-Four

Instead of giving "Phil" the zip drive, I went back to my Impala and scribbled my cell phone number on the back of a business card. When two business cards were stacked together, folded in thirds, and taped together, it was about the same size as a zip drive. I stuffed the fake zip drive in an envelope and left it on the bar with a note on the envelope that read, *Do Not Open.*

There was no way I was going to leave my family's fate in the hands of a UP bartender.

My hope was that whoever wanted the zip drive would swing by the Yukon Inn to pick it up. Once there, I'd be able to at least identify that person, if not confront him about who had left the note on my dashboard.

I parked across the street and down the road slightly, which gave me a nice view of the front and back of the bar.

Whoever was behind the threat to harm my family would be along at any moment, I was certain. It didn't take much imagination to picture what might have been taking place inside the four log walls of the Yukon Inn. "Yep, Twitchell was here," Phyllis would say over the telephone, "he left an envelope. Even though he wrote *Do Not Open* on the front, do you think I should open it anyway?"

"No, I'll be right there."

Phil didn't have anything to do with the zip drive, my kidnapping, my stolen car or the threatening note on my dashboard; she was just a middleman between me and the people who concocted the entire plan. The scenario presented an excellent chance for me to flush out whoever was responsible. Since I was flying solo, however, I had to pick my spot when it came to the confrontation.

At eleven fifteen the two bikers left the bar, jumped on their Harleys and roared away. Not far behind them, a group of young people bailed out of an old, Army-green colored school bus and made their way indoors. Seemed odd to be having a pub crawl on a weeknight during the early part of June, but maybe they were having a wedding party of sorts. On second thought, it could have been a group of college kids who were looking to get a jump start on the weekend. Either way they breathed new life into the Inn. Through the cloudy, old windows, I saw the silhouettes of the people who were dancing and twirling and having a good time.

There wasn't much traffic at all that night in the UP. A couple of pickups rumbled past leaving me wondering where they were coming from: a funeral in Ishpeming, the family farm in Rudyard, or a canoe trip down the Fox River? It may not have been anything so adventuresome. Groceries still need getting, and what better place to do that than in Sault Ste Marie.

I was beginning to think that maybe my plan wasn't going to come together when a brown Lincoln eased up Highway 123, and made the left turn towards the rear parking lot of the Inn. This was the man of the hour.

I started the Impala, put it in drive, and slinked out of my hiding spot. Now I was the hunter rather than the hunted, which was odd for an Impala. Doesn't everything on the Serengeti eat Impala? My car jumped on the Lincoln's spoor, just as it drifted off the pavement and into the gravel lot of the Inn.

Instead of following the Lincoln, I pulled into the parking lot of a fishery not far away. I felt like a man possessed when I abandoned the Impala and trotted across the street. The

Lincoln was idling behind the back door of the inn, its headlights beaming a bright reflection off the stainless steel equipment inside. Moths, mosquitoes and mayflies flew crazy eights in the mock sunshine.

For years and years, I've been a spontaneous kind of guy. My friends would say that I don't always think things through. An example of that spontaneity and short sightedness took place as I charged towards the idling Lincoln. At first, I thought I'd jump in the car and drive it back to where they left my Impala, but that wouldn't do much good. This was no time for revenge. Then I thought I'd christen my new fish bat on the first person who crossed the threshold at the back door of the inn, but really, that wouldn't do much good either. Finally, I decided that the best option was to hide in the back seat of the Lincoln and see where it would lead me. After all, whoever was driving it was probably the same fellow who was involved in my kidnapping.

Of course there'd be danger and trouble and potential violence in all three options. I didn't care; the truth about the Garl murders was close at hand.

I hopped in the back of the Lincoln and crouched behind the passenger side seat. There was hardly any room back there, so I reached along the seat's flanks and pushed everything forward. All I needed was an inch or two and I'd be set for quite a while.

My phone was still on, but in silent mode. I sent Colleen a text: *Still in Paradise and on the trail of the bad guys. Don't wait up. Love you.*

It was a relatively risky maneuver on my part. Had the Lincoln's driver reappeared at the instant my phone was still beaming, I would have been busted.

Even though the wait really wasn't that long, I was still startled when the door swung open and someone plopped into the driver's seat. I smelled the scent of bar food and the hint of Old Spice. Whoever was driving put his arm over the seat as the vehicle sped backwards. The hand was five inches above my head, a gold bracelet dangled around a hairy wrist.

That rules out Phyllis, I thought.

The Lincoln lurched from reverse to drive somewhere behind the inn. I could feel the stones and gravel as they peppered the rocker panels.

I didn't have a view of the surroundings but I could feel us negotiating the corner stop sign. Whoever was driving made a right turn and headed south on 123.

"Hell, no, we don't have it," the voice said. His voice was deep and scratchy, like it had been doused in bacon fat, then rolled in peppercorns.

"The bastard left his business card in an envelope and Phil thought it was a zip drive. I'm not sure why we involved her anyway."

Over the bumps we galloped. Frost made the pavement heave every forty feet or so. The shocks on the underside of the Lincoln's carriage were surely getting a workout.

"What would you like me to do?"

He hesitated.

"I realize that Mr. Luxton, but I'm way up here."

More listening.

"Believe me, I'd like nothing more than to….Hello? Hello?"

He cursed and cursed and cursed.

Seemed like the mystery man wasn't exactly satisfied with his job at the moment.

We picked up speed, and the bumps in the road came closer together. I felt like I was on the train again as we banged our way along some desolate track. Just as the lights from town became nonexistent, the car turned right, off the blacktop. I was certain we were headed to the cabin where I spent the night handcuffed to a bed.

My mind flashed to the kayak ride Dottie and I had only a few days ago. If it took us a half hour of constant paddling down the Tahquamenon River, I bet it wouldn't take five minutes of driving to cover that same distance. In my head, I tried to time my next move. As soon as the car began to slow, I figured that we were entering the driveway for the Luxton place.

Twenty seconds later I had my cue. It was probably the last thing the man behind the wheel expected, because my lunge took him totally by surprise. It was relatively easy to subdue him, bat in hand, even though he reached and clawed for my wrists. I had leverage in the back seat, and the bat was the perfect tool for crushing his windpipe.

Oh sure, he put up a fuss and made some gagging sounds at first, but when I whispered that he didn't have to die this way, he kind of saw things my way.

"I want you to slowly reach into your pocket and pull out that piece," I whispered in his ear.

I was half expecting him to gesture that he wasn't carrying a firearm at all, but instead he reached onto his left hip and pulled out a smallish, blunt nosed little handgun. He had the handle pinched between his thumb and forefinger.

"Slowly now," I whispered, "keep reaching back here with it."

He kept reaching, then dropped it over his head. It bounced off my ankle, then my shoe.

I let go of the bat and the man gasped for air.

"How'd you like them apples?"

He couldn't answer. Instead, he slumped over the wheel, choking and gasping for air.

Quickly, I found the gun, opened the action and saw that it was loaded. I didn't know what caliber it was, but something small like a thirty-eight. For all I knew, it could have been the missing twenty-five from the murder scene in Good Hart.

Whatever caliber it was, the safety was still on when I picked it off the floor and waived it in his direction.

"What's your name?" I asked.

He didn't answer.

I looked to our surroundings. We were all alone on a twisty, gravel road in the middle of the bush. The wrought iron gate in the headlights seemed way out of place.

"I asked you a question, didn't I?"

"Lionel Coffee."

Sounds like a train that serves hot beverages, I thought for a second. "All right, Mr. Coffee, you're going to do exactly what I tell you, okay?"

He nodded.

I had never been in that situation before, but I had seen enough of these scenarios in the movies to know that I'd rather be the guy with the gun than the other way around.

"Put the car in reverse and drive out the same way you came in, understand?"

He nodded again.

"What caliber is this?"

"Thirty-two."

"It'd make a hell of a mess of a man at this range, wouldn't it, Mr. Coffee?"

"That's why I carry it."

"Has the upstairs bedroom been fixed?"

"You mean from the mess you made?"

"Yeah."

"Today, in fact. New furniture. New paneling on the ceiling."

"Why did you kidnap me?"

He didn't answer.

"Come on, Mr. Coffee. This is no time to be coy."

He clammed up.

"We can do this the hard way, or the easy way."

As we neared 123 again, I told him to turn left and go back towards Paradise.

Mr. Coffee looked to be my age, maybe a bit younger. Chubby and unkempt. He wasn't the clove smoker, but one of the guys who helped subdue me earlier in the week.

Instead of shooting him, it would have been fun and somewhat rewarding to take him into the woods and handcuff him to a tree. As I toyed with the idea, I pictured him shirtless and without pants, getting eaten alive by a million mosquitoes or a pack of wolves. Perhaps I'd cover him with blueberry syrup and molasses and let every bear in the east end of the Upper Peninsula find out what he tasted like.

A second image passed in my head: handcuffing him to the train tracks in Trout Lake. The tracks down there are curvy enough to keep the engineer from stopping in time. I could get all the satisfaction of having him get eaten alive by the mosquitoes, then have the train do the dirty work of severing his wrist.

Who was I kidding? I didn't have the courage to shoot someone, or leave them for dead in the wilderness.

Colleen says I'm passive aggressive. She's probably right.

Here I had a cooperative victim and I didn't know what do with him. I really didn't want to harm him, but he didn't know that.

As we neared town and the speed limit dropped, the Lincoln sped up.

"What the hell are you doing?" I asked him.

"I'm driving."

"Slow down."

"I don't think so, Vern."

"Who's Vern?" I yelled.

"It's just an expression, duh."

"Slow down, you jackass."

We were going way too fast for conditions. There were driveways and cabins, the library, and the deputy's house. Of all the movies I had seen, none of them involved a hostage driving too fast.

Before I could say "Okay fine, you can have your gun back!" A blinking, flashing light appeared behind us.

"That's just great!" I yelled. "You friggin' jackass, Coffee."

He laughed and laughed. "How do you like them apples now, Twitchell? You're going to jail, dude."

I un-tucked my shirt and wiped down the gun as best I could. As the Lincoln slowly crawled to a stop a quarter mile or so from the inn, I rammed the gun beneath the driver's side seat with my foot.

I didn't know what to say, wasn't sure what to do. My head was swimming in "what ifs" and painful regrets.

This could get really, really ugly.

The cop was on top of us in no time. It was a state trooper, no less.

Coffee rolled down the window and said "Good evening" to the trooper.

"Any idea why I pulled you over?"

"Speed," he said, handing over his papers. "I'm sorry, officer."

"Why were you driving so fast?"

"I just lost track…it was my fault."

The trooper stuck his head inside, glanced in my direction. "Have you been drinking?"

"No sir. Not yet."

"Where are you headed?"

"Up town, we were going to get a bite to eat and a beer."

The cop looked down at the papers in his hand as if they were cards in a game of poker. "I'll be right back."

As soon as the cop returned to his patrol car, the conversation perked up.

"Give me the gun, Twitchell!"

"No! Get it yourself. It's on your side."

Coffee reached between his legs. "I can't reach it."

He moved the seat back, and tried again "Damn it, Twitchell, we still have time. Grab it!"

I don't know what possessed me, but I reached under the seat, pulled out the gun and slid it forward.

Coffee opened the action, dumped the shells in the palm of his hand and stuffed them into his sock. He returned the gun to his hip. It made a "snap" when it locked into place.

Now all of a sudden the tables had been turned. Mr. Coffee had the upper hand, the gun, and the ammunition. If that wasn't bad enough, he had the truth on his side: *Twitchell used a bat to accost me and held me hostage until the cops intervened.*

In the poker game of strategy and bluffs, it appeared as if Coffee held all the aces. He knew it, and I knew it too.

"I'm ready to make a deal, Mr. Coffee."

"I bet you are, Twitchell. What have you got?"

"Here, take it," I said, handing him the zip drive. "I'm done with this case."

"I bet you are."

"Seriously."

"Ten minutes ago, you were ready to blow my head off."

"Worse. I was going to…to…never mind."

"You don't say…"

"It doesn't matter now," I said. "What are you going to tell the cop?"

He laughed.

"Hey, listen, you say one thing about the bat and I'll scream bloody murder about being handcuffed to the bed. Got it?"

Coffee didn't answer. The school bus full of young people drove past, headed in the opposite direction. The heads inside were all pointing our way.

"Mr. Coffee, I have pictures of the bed. I have a witness who will testify."

He fiddled with his phone.

"Answer me, Coffee. Have we got a deal?"

"You never said what you wanted."

"Leave me alone. Leave my family alone."

Coffee was paying more attention to his phone than to me.

"Will you answer me?"

"I can't make any promises."

"Why not?" I asked.

"It's not my call."

"Who is it, Luxton?"

"Of course."

There it was, as large as life. Luxton was behind it all.

"How do I get a hold of him?"

"Mr. Luxton?"

"Yeah."

"You can't."

"What do you mean I can't? You just talked to him on the phone."

"I know that," he said angrily, "but you can't."

"Give me his number. Let me talk to him."

Our conversation was interrupted by the trooper who appeared at the driver's side window again.

"Mr. Coffee, I'm issuing you a citation for excessive speed. Even though you were going eighteen miles over the limit, I only wrote the ticket for ten over."

Coffee took the papers and said "Thank you," as if the cop had done him a favor.

"It saved you two points on your license and an extra hundred fifty dollars in fines."

"Thank you."

I didn't like where this was headed. The cop was about ready to release us. Coffee had the gun and all the ammunition. He had all the control, which was more than just a little disturbing.

I rolled down the passenger side window just as the officer finished his conversation with Coffee. "Can I ask you a question?"

"Sure."

Instead of staying in the car, I jumped out of the passenger side door. "Lionel," I smiled, confidently, "don't worry about hanging around. I'll meet you at the bar."

Coffee didn't hesitate. He put the car in drive and sped away.

The cop wasn't threatened or concerned with what had taken place.

"Where is Pine Stump Junction?"

"That's easy. See the blinking light up ahead?"

I turned my head and nodded.

"Turn left at the light. Go past the falls."

"Got it," I looked to make sure Coffee was still driving away.

"It's a poke-and-a-plum kind of town"

"What does that mean?"

"You've never heard of that saying?"

I shook my head no.

"By the time you poke your head out the window you'll be plum out of town."

Twenty-Five

By the time I fetched my car from downtown Paradise and headed south out of town, I realized that I had dodged a major bullet where Mr. Coffee was concerned. I regretted taking such a foolish risk. Once Robert Luxton heard about it, I was certain there would be major repercussions.

I couldn't do anything about all that was of my control.

What I could control were my actions, thoughts and hopes regarding the Garl family murders.

Even though it was quite late, I still had time to get things done.

Without even thinking about it, I dialed up the strip joint in Traverse City and asked if I could speak to Genesis. Whoever answered the call was less than receptive to the idea, and explained that Genesis was working the floor. The music in the background was overbearing and the conversation was almost as if it were in the back seat of the Impala. Nevertheless, I managed to give them my phone number, and an urgent message that I needed to text or talk to Genesis.

That phone call was the last thing on my mental checklist for the day. All at once I felt exhausted. Driving had become a battle. The road ahead of me became an endless line of pavement. There was no way I'd make it home, let alone to the Mackinaw Bridge. Instead of driving until I couldn't drive any more, I decided to pull over once I arrived in Trout Lake.

The man who answered the bell at the general store didn't seem overly thrilled to see me, shortly before midnight. His bathrobe was old and stained down the front. He had messed up hair and a pair of slippers that could have belonged to Archie Bunker. After I waved a couple twenties under his nose—like smelling salts to a boxer—it brought him out of his sleep-induced stupor.

"I'm going to take you through the store, and then upstairs, okay?"

I nodded affirmatively and took notice of all the items he had on the shelves: the Alpo and beef stew were side by side, so were the scouring pads and non-stick pans. He unlocked a back door that lead up a flight of white-painted steps.

"There's a second set of stairs that goes outside. Use them if there's a fire or when you want to leave in the morning."

"Got it. Thank you."

"You don't really get a key, especially at this hour. Lock the door from inside your room."

"Okay, thanks."

As we neared the top of the stairs, he pointed to the fire escape on the left. My room was on the right. Whoever the man was, he unlocked door number four, took two steps inside and pulled a cotton string beneath a single light bulb.

The room was just what I expected for forty bucks and this far out in the Yooperlands. It was part boarding room, part converted farm house. An ancient comforter atop a tired mattress and a brown, oval throw rug at the foot of the bed looked like they could have been there since Hemmingway wrote the *Two-Hearted River*. The washcloth and towel on top of a rickety chest of drawers made me feel like I was stepping back in time, to when *The Waltons* tried their best to squeeze the most out of every penny.

I thanked him for the hospitality; he mentioned that there was a shared bathroom down the hall.

Oh great, I thought, *I'll have to plan my trips around Mary Ellen, Jim Bob and the other kids in the family.*

I plopped my stuff on the double bed, dug out my toothbrush and toothpaste from the bottom of the backpack, and wandered down the hall. When I returned, I spun the lock on the inside of the door and turned my attention to the closed window. The warm, evening air poured inside over a host of dead flies that were trapped between the window and the screen.

A gentle rain was falling outside and it peppered the tin roof above the fire escape and the pavement down below. With each passing car, I heard the splatter and splash of tires plowing through puddles. Tomorrow the grass would be another shade greener and the forest another layer of lush.

I turned off the harsh, overhead light, and turned on the nightstand lamp. Seemed odd to be crawling into bed without any pajamas on, but that was okay. Every once in a while it's okay to get out of my comfort zone. If I was going to get bitten by bed bugs, I was going to get bitten all over.

In the quiet, dark confines of a faraway boarding room, I texted Colleen to make sure everything was okay.

She didn't respond.

No response seemed to be a recurring theme were Colleen was concerned. I longed for a second or two of the days when we were falling in love. Once upon a time we were carefree and spontaneous as a pair of grade-schoolers.

I turned off the lamp and took notice of the mattress' shoddy posture. Instead of being somewhat flat, the mattress was shaped like an oversized saucer. I felt myself gravitating towards the center; my feet and head elevated.

Just as I was about ready to cash in my chips for the day, my phone blinked.

Instead of Colleen answering, it was Genesis. *What's up?*

Hey, I just wanted to reach out to you and hope we could get together tomorrow.

I get $100 an hour, plus travel, you know.

That's fine.

Where?

My mind was struggling. I didn't know if I wanted to drive too far out of my way. If I drove a half hour west of I-75, and she drove a half hour east of Traverse City, the most logical place for a rendezvous would be Kalkaska. *How about the Trout Town Restaurant in downtown Kalkaska?*

Is one o'clock too early?

Nope, see you then.

Seemed strange to be thinking that one in the afternoon would be too early. I'm used to doing business with people who get things done before nine in the morning. From her perspective, eleven o'clock is early in the morning, but she might not go to sleep before three or four.

Genesis was a business woman, and I appreciated that. She couldn't get a hundred dollars an hour if she didn't ask for it first. I've paid for information before; I'd probably do it again.

My fingers clasped across my chest and thought about the priority for tomorrow morning: stop at a store for some new underwear. From there, the possibilities were endless. I could trout fish the Carp River, or golf at a host of beautiful courses across the Tip of the Mitt.

Just as sleep carried me away, I heard laughter and playful voices outside the open window. One male, one female. As they made the stairs, I heard her yelp in delight "Ouch, quit pinching me."

The voices and giggling came up the stairs, then down the hall.

The walls of the boarding house must have been paper-thin because I heard the woman suggest that he didn't seem very good with his hands. "Can't you find the key hole?"

"I'm doing my best, woman. I got double vision," he slurred.

The room door opened with a squeak and I heard him place the room key on the nightstand. He asked her, "I saw a vending machine outside, you want a nightcap? A bottle of water?"

"Hell no. I want to see what you've got."

"What do you mean?" he asked.

"Come here."

The voices stopped momentarily as I heard her struggle with his belt buckle. It was so quiet I could almost hear his zipper unzip, just before his belt buckle hit the floor and he stepped out of his pants.

You would have thought it was Christmas morning the way she cooed at the sight of his package. I didn't have to imagine what was taking place. She knew just how to make a man feel good.

It made me realize that it had been far too long since I had that feeling.

Twenty-Six

At dawn the following day, I was on a secluded stretch of the Carp River, casting wet flies and streamers to rainbow trout in the rifles above I-75. After two or three hours of flailing the water and landing a few fish, I continued south to Gaylord. Changing clothes in the restroom inside Wal-Mart felt a little weird, but I'm sure it had been done before. A few minutes after noon, I passed the giant brook trout in downtown Kalkaska, then wandered into the Trout Town Restaurant and ordered a corned beef sandwich and a bowl of bean soup.

While I waited for my order, I sent Colleen a text to make sure everything was okay at home. She still hadn't responded from last night's inquiry. On one hand I felt like I was hounding her; on the other hand I was a little worried about what was going on. For a few minutes I beat myself up about taking the time to go fishing instead of taking care of my family.

At a little before one, Genesis pulled her convertible black Lexus in to the parking lot of the restaurant. I watched her fuss with her lipstick and hair in the rearview mirror. She bent out of the seat, like some sort of Barbie doll, and strolled towards the front of the restaurant in high heels and a Daisy Duke outfit.

The men in the restaurant couldn't help themselves. They almost drooled as she floated past the windows. It's not every day that a woman of her looks—and her Lexus—are seen on the streets of Kalkaska.

Instead of waiting for her to find me inside, I greeted her at the door with the warmest smile I could muster. "Have you had anything to eat?" I asked.

"No, not really," she said, "I'm not one for an early breakfast."

"How about lunch? The corned beef sandwiches are excellent?"

"Oh, barf. That would not be good." I pointed towards the booth where I had been sitting and we headed in that direction. The check was still on the table beneath my ten-dollar bill. "I'll just have a salad."

As we sat down at the table, I tried to ease her gently into conversation mode. Weather and traffic are always great topics for breaking the ice.

Genesis would have nothing of it. After ordering an iced tea and a trip to the salad bar, she brought the meeting to order: "Let's get down to business, shall we?"

"Sure," I agreed with her, "you already told me about the hundred bucks an hour."

"Plus fifty for the travel," she said.

"That's fine too. When do you want it, now, or—"

"We can wait till after. Where did you get a room?"

I laughed nervously. "Oh, I didn't get a room."

"You're not one of those freaks that like to do it in public, are you?"

"No, no, no," I smiled. "I think you have me confused."

"You're not a cop are you?"

"No, no Jenna, I'm not."

"Then what's the matter?" she asked, somewhat confused. "Don't you find me attractive?"

"No," I stammered. "I mean yes. You're very attractive."

"What is it then? You're not gay are you?"

I laughed. It was the second time in a week that someone thought I was gay. "I just wanted to ask you some questions."

"You're that friggin' reporter from the other night, aren't you?"

"Yes. That's me, Derrick Twitchell."

"Hell's bells," she sighed, "Cocker shells."

"What?"

"I thought you were somebody else." She rose from the table and took four or five steps the same way she came in.

"Don't leave," I begged her. "I only have a few questions and you're going to get paid."

"Relax, Mr. Twitchell," she cautioned me, "I'm only going to the salad bar."

"Oh," I smiled, "that's cool."

A minute or two later Jenna returned with a plate loaded with a leafy salad, pickled beets and cottage cheese. I whipped out my wallet and slid a fifty and a hundred across the table. She folded them in thirds, then stuffed them somewhere beneath her madras plaid shirt that was knotted above her pierced navel. I wondered for a second or two if it put a smile on the faces of Mr. Franklin and Mr. Grant.

The money seemed to brighten her spirits. "What do you want to know?"

"It's about Mr. Garl. Did you give him a necklace?"

She hesitated for a second, "This is off the record, isn't it?"

"If you want. I'm not writing a story about it."

She seemed to believe me.

"Yeah, I gave him the necklace and a St. Christopher pendant. How'd you guess?"

"I didn't guess. The newspaper had a story about what Mr. Garl was wearing on the day he was murdered."

"How'd you know it was me that gave it to him?" she wondered.

I explained the inscription on the back.

"Guess I'm rather predictable."

"That's not always a bad thing."

"I guess," she sipped her tea.

Our waitress came back to the table with my change. She left another check in its place.

"Why did you give it to him?" I asked.

"I liked the guy," she said, munching on her salad. "He was always really good to me."

"I understand. When did you give it to him?"

"About a year ago, I guess. Wasn't that long before he was murdered."

"Did he ever talk to you about what he told his wife?"

"About the pendant?"

I nodded.

"No. And that's kind of private, don't you think, Mr. Twitchell?"

I raised my eyebrows.

"Lots of powerful men have affairs," she continued. "Success and power have an intoxicating effect on a woman."

I didn't know what to say. She made a good point. Heck, success and power are attractive no matter what your gender.

"Can I mention a few names to you and see if they sound familiar?"

"Sure," she smiled. "I'm on the clock, remember?"

"Lionel Coffee?"

She shook her head no. "Sounds like a train."

"Robert Luxton."

"You asked me that the other night."

"What did you say?"

"I don't remember him. He really didn't introduce me to a lot of his friends or business associates, you know." She nodded her head, "He had a wife and all."

"Does Shafeek Heanley sound familiar?"

She shook her head. "Hang on a second. I'm trying to think…"

I didn't give her long, "How about Dorothy Kalakay?"

"No."

"How about Kelly Mathers?"

"Yeah, I remember her."

"How?"

"She was with the Department of Interior Energy or something or other." Jenna glanced out the window. I think she liked the looks of her car out there, all nice and buff, topless. "Mr. G used to call her his Sugar Momma."

"Why's that?"

"They had a project they were working on."

"At Ener-X?"

"Yeah."

"What was it?"

"Had to do with solar wafers. I think that's the correct terminology."

I was confused. "What's that?"

"Mr. G tried to explain it to me. They capture the sunshine and turn it into electricity."

I nodded.

"If they could make wafers cheaper, it would make solar panels more affordable. The more people want solar panels, the more jobs they would create. The government funded the research and development for making it happen."

"What was in it for Cecil Garl?"

"Fourteen million."

"Really?"

"That I do remember."

"How did it work?"

"Mr. G gathered some of his rich buddies in the business and made a big campaign donation to the president's re-election committee."

"And in turn Ener-X got the contract to do research on the solar wafers."

"Pretty slick, huh?" she asked.

"Yeah, I guess so…"

I watched her take a slug of tea.

"Where was Kelly's office?"

"Down in Detroit somewhere. Maybe one of the suburbs."

"So that was it?"

"Oh I'm sure there was more to the story. There had to be."

"Why do you say that?"

"That's just the kind of guy that Mr. G was. You couldn't just give someone something and not expect something in return. Politics work the same way don't they? 'If you vote for me I'll do X, Y and Z.'"

"So what did you get in return for the Christopher medallion?"

She smiled, and gestured to the parking lot.

I smiled too. "Seems like a pretty good deal for both of you."

"I learned a long time ago to take care of myself, Mr. Twitchell."

"Sounds like it."

While she finished her salad, I started a search for Kelly Mathers on my phone. "Hope you don't think I'm being rude, but I want to find out more about that person, Kelly."

"Take your time. You still have forty minutes."

One-by-one the images popped up on my phone. "Looks like Ms. Mathers is in hot water."

I turned my hand so she could see: *Former Department of Energy boss indicted on charges of bribery.*

"Oh nice."

I clicked on the story. "Looks like she is being charged with accepting free trips and sweetheart deals in exchange for government contracts."

"That sounds about right."

"Mr. G set her up at Treetops Resort in Gaylord a few times. He'd drop her off at one of the condos, pay for all their golf, and then come over to see me. His wife thought he was entertaining clients the whole time."

"The story says that she took a trip to Hawaii, compliments of a Michigan battery company. The batteries are used in hybrid cars."

"I wouldn't doubt it," she lamented. "You don't think there are any free lunches, do you?"

I shook my head.

"What was the name of the battery company?" she asked.

I scrolled down the page, scanning the words for anything relevant. "Doesn't say."

"I've been thinking. That Shafeek guy you mentioned... I've heard that name before, but I can't figure out why."

Jenna's eyebrows had crinkled into a trimmed little line beneath her forehead. With that kind of intensity, she could have passed for a banker, a stock broker, or a future's analyst in the financial district of Chicago. Instead, she was a stripper, and an upscale prostitute, stretching the limits of her memory.

I didn't notice any needle marks in her arms, nor the telltale symptoms of a meth addict. She may have been new to the entertainment business, or an old veteran, but one thing was for certain: she knew how to take care of herself.

"Systems Seven," she blurted out. "That's it."

"That's what?" I asked, somewhat confused.

"The name of Shafeek Heanley's company."

"What about it?" I smiled.

"He and Mr. G did business together. Heanley was one of Mr. G's people who donated to the president."

"Are you sure?"

"Yes, I'm sure. Systems Seven is a company that makes the giant batteries for hybrid cars. I think they're downstate somewhere."

"What does that have to do with the solar panels at Ener-X?"

"Nothing."

"Nothing?" I asked, somewhat surprised.

"Mr. G used to laugh about it. They all got a piece of the government pie."

"What's that?"

"The fourteen million, silly," she smiled. "Mr. Garl and the rest of his buddies each put money towards the president, who in turn gave companies no-bid contracts."

"Didn't they have to show the government what they got for their money?"

Jenna looked at me like I was crazy. "Heck, no. He had it all set up so that his buddies got paid on their investment. I think Mr. Heanley put in fifty thousand dollars but when the government passed out the fourteen million, Mr. G gave him a million-five in return."

I shook my head.

"I think Mr. G told me that Heanley bought a big yacht and kept it up north somewhere."

"You don't say..."

Twenty-Seven

By the time I stopped at Jay's Sporting Goods in Clare and a giant hardware store in Houghton Lake, it was almost five in the afternoon when I finally reached home. Everything seemed honky-dory when I pulled in the driveway and the dog trotted out to greet me, tail wagging like a little egg beater. After cautiously opening the front door and having a quick look around, my enthusiasm for a kindred family reunion was dashed when I read Colleen's note on the counter: *Gone to Mom's.*

On one hand I was happy that my wife and daughter were okay; on the other hand it seemed like a blunt way to say "so long." Communicating with me must have been the last thing on her mind, right after making sure that she had packed her toothpaste and toenail clippers. My feelings were hurt, but then again, isn't marriage about surviving the body blows of unintended punches? After ten years of matrimony, I knew I was no longer at the center of Colleen's universe, but I didn't expect to be pushed into the stratosphere of her priorities, either.

I dashed any thoughts of mentioning my hurt feelings, because I knew that I wasn't exactly the model spouse.

It wasn't like Colleen to ignore my texts, so I gave her a call. She said that her parents needed help on the family farm back in Wisconsin. In the coming weeks, they were putting it up for sale and having an auction for all the equipment. She had no interest in the Garl case, and quickly passed the phone to our daughter, who was happy to speak to me. She babbled on and on about the fun she had the night before with her friends at the sleepover.

I was all alone, but not necessarily lonely. There were jobs to do around the house, which I had neglected since the case took hold of me several days ago. The grass needed mowing and I wanted to change the door locks. When I looked up at the eavestroughs, they were sprouting tiny, healthy maple shoots. *I could open a nursery or clean them out*, I thought to myself.

Even though Colleen didn't like my plan about the trail camera near the front door, I figured that it wouldn't be a bad idea. If it was good enough for Cecil Garl to put in his bedroom up at the cabin, it'd be good enough for me, too.

That would make two, I thought to myself: *one by the front door and the new one by the end of the driveway. Thank you, Jay's Sporting Goods.*

A holly bush near the front door concealed the first camera. The one at end of the driveway was attached to a white pine, and placed in such a way that I might catch the faces inside a vehicle on the way in and their license plate on the way out. My old trail camera by the front door held seven hundred images, while the new one from Jay's at the end of the driveway, a thousand. I knew that there would be plenty of images of me and the family, but that was okay; it might give the cops damning evidence in the event that something happened out of the norm.

What was really gnawing at me though, was the light that Genesis cast on Kelly Mathers. It seemed unlikely that someone could be so corrupt as to take bribes in exchange for the government contracts. I mean, *wouldn't you expect to get caught if you did something so blatant?*

Even though Detroit was a long way to go, I could justify the trip in my head if I got a story out of it. I didn't have any boss to contend with; nobody at home would wonder where I was.

My plan was hatched in the time it took me to fetch the ladder out of the rafters in the garage. By the time I cleaned out the gutters and mowed the grass, I had already decided to pack my camera bags and head down to the "D" for the Mathers' hearing Monday morning.

After installing new locks on the doors, I took my dog to a gigantic mowed field in the neighborhood where he pointed robins and almost caught a ground squirrel. When we returned to the house, and I started packing, he looked at me with hopeful eyes like we were headed on a grand hunting trip. "Hardly, my friend. You have an important job to do and that's to keep an eye on the house."

Early Sunday morning, I woke up and headed into the office where I signed a few checks and picked up the important mail and the phone messages from the last few days. My plan was to return the phone calls I could while driving to Detroit by way of Port Huron. I was pleased to see that the insurance adjuster had called and said that the boat payment had been approved and the Suburban was a total loss. It'd be nice to get into a new, used truck in case I ever had time for another fishing trip. From there, I went online and had a mixed bouquet sent to the in-laws' farm in Friendship, Wisconsin. As much as I wanted to come up with something warm and sociable for the message, it turned out rather cheesy: *Heartfelt words to my favorite curds...Love, Derrick.*

I was sure Colleen would roll her eyes when she read that one. Elizabeth would want to know what was a curd. And my in-laws? They probably smiled politely and reserved judgment just like they always do. "If you don't have something nice to say, keep your words to yourself."

The jaunt to Port Huron was more of a wild goose chase than anything else. I knew that System Seven would be closed, but I wanted to take a few photos of the plant in case I needed them at a later date.

The drive from Flint to Port Huron, across the heart of Michigan's thumb, isn't all that bad. The countryside is littered with ponds and forests, farm fields and fencerows that vary in thickness and wildlife attraction. Seeing the land fifty years ago would have been great, when pheasants had many more places to live and the farmers weren't so hell bent on cultivating every square inch of land.

By the time I made it to downtown Port Huron and crossed the smiling drawbridge over the river, I was hungry. Breakfast sounded great, but it was close to lunch time. I saw a sign for the Raven Café and flew into the parking place as if I had called ahead with reservations.

Not every spur-of-the-moment decision I make turns out well, I had to remind myself. A lot of times they turn into disasters.

The Raven Café was a good decision. As soon as I opened the door I was swept off my feet with the ambiance and eccentric qualities. The place was more like a museum to Edgar Allen Poe and the middle 1800s than a place to eat. Someone had spent a lot of time—and a small fortune—collecting the antique books and artifacts that adorned the walls, shelves, and circular staircase. There, I was stepping back in time and shaking hands with a creepy author dude who embraced the dreary side of life back in the 1800s.

The bacon, eggs, hash browns, and toast were nothing new. The classics never go out of style.

As I sat there, reading the paper, munching on my breakfast, and taking in the ambiance, the manager or the owner of the restaurant stopped by to ask how was my meal.

I affirmed what he already knew; it was excellent.

The chitchat continued for several sentences, before I asked where the Systems Seven plant might be. He gave me directions and then gently floated an inquiry as to why I might need it.

"I keep hearing about their owner, Shafeek Heanley," I said.

The manager didn't hesitate, "He's a great guy and a regular here in the restaurant."

"What do you mean, 'a great guy'?"

"He does all kinds of charity work, volunteers for the sports boosters, and sponsors little league baseball teams. We're in the same league."

"That's nice to know."

"Want to see a picture of him?"

"Sure."

The man put down his sandwich board, whipped out his cell phone and pecked at its screen. I read what was written on the face of the board: *Today's Brunch Special—whitefish pate, creamed asparagus on rye toast, honeydew melon, $7.99.* It sounded perfectly wonderful and a meal that Mr. Poe would be proud to serve.

If Cecil Garl were still alive, I'm sure that he would have loved this place too.

"Here it is," the man finally piped up. "He's the one on the far left side of the picture. That's his team, the Battery Packs."

I looked down at the screen but couldn't quite make out his face. There were lots of young faces on the little screen, shadowed by the brim of their baseball caps.

"Can you enlarge it?"

"Sure."

When he did, the image became more grainy, but there was no mistaking what I saw: Shafeek Heanley was the man who fired the clove cigarette into my Impala.

"That's him, huh?"

"Yep. That's his wife, Emily, by his side. Their son, Hunter is on the team." Emily looked to be quite tall, blonde, and natural in a baseball cap.

"Does he happen to smoke?"

"Yeah, I think he does. They're weird though. Not your normal cigarettes."

"Do they smell like cloves?"

"Yep. I think he said they were from Jakarta or maybe Indonesia."

"Where does he live?"

"Out of town a few miles. His wife runs a bed and breakfast in an old Victorian. It's called the Manhattan Manor. You can probably Google it. He's not in any trouble is he?"

"Not at all."

"Are you with the government?"

"No."

"What's your story then?"

"Just passing through. Thanks again for breakfast."

I stuffed some cash in the check holder and left. The manager waved, as I pulled away from the curb and headed south to the Manhattan Manor.

Twenty-Eight

The doorbell for the Manor wasn't really a doorbell at all, but rather a gargoyle's cement tongue. Thankfully, Emily, or maybe it was Shafeek, taped a small sign on his tongue that read "push." When I depressed its metal tongue, the bells inside made a gong-like noise that reminded me of the chimes on a church.

Through the wavy stained glass, I saw the figure of a woman approaching the door. She wiped her hands on a towel, then stuffed the it into the drawstring on her apron.

"May I help you?" she asked.

"I'd like a room."

"Come in. Come in," she gestured. "Mr…"

Without hesitating I said, "Ong. James Ong."

"You sound like Double O Seven, Mr. Ong."

"Maybe I am," I said, winking facetiously.

"I like you already. Won't you come in?"

She opened the enormous front door; its hinges creaked and groaned from the stress. I followed her a dozen steps to an antique piece of furniture that could have passed for an oversized podium. "What brings you to town, Mr. Ong?"

"I'm a writer, actually. And I'm on assignment for *Michigan Living* magazine."

"Really? All my friends read it." She blinked the blinks of incredulousness. I detected a bit of skepticism in her Danish-looking eyes.

"Hope you don't mind, but they sent me here to do a story about you and the Manor."

"Hmm."

"My editors suggested that I come here unannounced to make sure that I wouldn't get any special treatment."

"Well then," she sighed. "I suggest you take the Wordsworth Lair."

"Why's that?"

"It's our nicest room and has a Jacuzzi, too."

"That would be fine," I smiled.

"Unless you'd rather have the Tennyson Space."

"No, that's okay. The Wordsworth would be fine."

She smiled halfheartedly. "All our rooms are named after famous Victorian poets. We're rather nuts about the romantic period."

"I see that."

Emily opened her guest book, and asked me to sign in. She handed me a pen, and I scrolled the list of names and cities on the page. That momentary distraction is all it took to take me off guard. Instead of writing a "J" for James, I used a "D" for Derrick.

You dumb ass, I thought to myself. *Change the D to a J.*

Emily didn't pick up on my blunder, thank goodness. When she handed me the registration form, I gave her an address and phone number, both of which were bogus.

"May I?" I asked, lifting a plastic lid off a plate of cookies.

"Absolutely. I just made them last night."

"Sugar, I assume?"

"No, they're almond palmiers."

"Interesting. They're Victorian too, correct?"

"Yes."

"The editors are going to eat that up."

"Figuratively speaking, right Mr. Ong?"

I forced a smile. "Of course."

"Will you be paying with a credit card?"

"Is cash okay?"

"Absolutely, it'll be one ninety-five."

"Fair enough."

"That's not too high, is it?"

"Not really, you have a nice place here."

I forked over the cash. She handed me a receipt and we were on our way for the nickel tour.

"This is the parlor, of course," she said, as she pointed to a collection of perfectly uncomfortable-looking chairs and love-seats. It was just as stiff and old looking as the dining room, and of course, the "sitting room," where I couldn't imagine sitting longer than two minutes. There wasn't a television in sight, not a lazy chair to sit on. No wonder Mr. Heanley liked to spend so much time on his yacht.

It was easy to act like a writer. The name James Ong came from a psychologist in Mt. Pleasant who bilked me out of twenty-five thousand. I could have used a thousand different names; all I wanted to do was shield my identity to keep her husband off balance.

Up the stairs we went. I noticed Emily's hosiery and the way it cast a faint, black line from the bottom of her dress to a pair of clunky high heels that laced in the front of her feet. I looked up at the blouse on her back. Above the neatly tied bow of her apron were the tell-tale signs of a corset. *This woman is taking the Victorian business way too seriously.*

"You're the only guest I have registered tonight," she smiled. "What time would you like breakfast?"

"Oh, heck, let's make it nine," I smiled. "No sense in hurting ourselves."

"You're my kind of man, Mr. Ong."

We made it to the top of the stairs and Emily was slightly out of breath.

"Why am I your kind of man?" I asked rather innocently.

"Well, you seem to have an interest in sleeping in and having a leisurely breakfast."

"I see."

"Your husband isn't the type?"

She shook her head. "He's always on the go. Work, work, work."

"I understand," I smiled. "He must be an important man."

"Well..." she hesitated long enough to look away. That little delay gave her the opening to go back to the topic at hand. "You'll be staying here, in the Wordsworth."

The door opened like some gigantic red curtain on Let's Make a Deal.

I smiled. "This is marvelous. Just marvelous."

Emily smiled back. This was her crowning moment, I could tell.

"Would you mind if I took your picture?"

"Not at all," she said, beaming. "Where do you want me?"

"Right there," I said, pointing to the doorway. She coifed her hair as I dug out a flash from my vest.

Next thing I know, she's struck a glamour pose in the entryway. I captured her from the hallway, the Jacuzzi tub and the colossal bed in the same frame.

"Marvelous," I egged her on. The flash must have sparked something inside Emily, because she struck another pose, with her hand beneath her blonde curls.

"The editors are going to love it."

She giggled and pirouetted to the bed. "Couple more?"

"Sure. This is fun," I lied.

Emily grabbed hold of the bed post and let herself dangle my way. "Fill your paper," she said, hand over her chest, "with the breathings of your heart."

"That sounds familiar," I said, as I took another photo.

"Wordsworth, Mr. Ong. Wordsworth."

Just as Emily was starting to let herself go, her phone rang. She reached into her apron and pulled it out of a laced pocket. I was half expecting it to be a miniature version of one of those old-fashioned phones that Alexander Graham Bell might have designed. Instead, it looked like the latest and greatest in its own pink case.

I pretended not to listen, but I could tell that our informal interview was just about over.

"I'm sorry, Mr. Ong, but I have to pick up my son from baseball practice." Her body language said it all: she was disappointed. Gone were the fantasies of a Victorian photo shoot. I felt like we were starting to get to know each other when we were interrupted.

"I'll only be an hour or so, Mr. Ong. We could finish our interview then, but what I really want to know is if you'd stay for dinner."

"I'd be honored."

"Very well. My husband will be happy to meet you."

"He's in town?" I asked, a slight lump in my throat.

"He should be later today. He's up north with his boat."

"Whereabouts?"

"Beaver Island. Is that a problem?"

"Not at all," I tried to act casual.

Emily pointed to the towels on the dresser. They were soft and fluffy and matched the washcloth. It was a far cry from the boarding house in Trout Lake.

"I think he said he had to be in Detroit in the morning."

My heart sank.

"I'll get you a key." She stormed out the bedroom door and down the hardwood steps. "We lock the front door at eleven."

"Fair enough. What's your son's name?" I asked.

"Hunter."

"And the little dog outside?"

"Dash. She's a King Charles spaniel."

"Interesting."

"They're known for their exquisite nose. Some people call them 'carpet spaniels' because they're built so close to the ground. Queen Victoria had one when she was a little girl, and I guess I always wanted one, too."

Emily grabbed a key for me and her purse from beneath the podium-desk.

"She's a good little watchdog and will bite strangers."

Emily Heanley tromped down the hallway, through the dining room, and towards the kitchen, I assumed.

"Why don't you get settled in," she said with a smile. I watched her walk away. "There's lemonade in the fridge. Have some more cookies. Make yourself at home, Mr. Ong," she said, over the shoulder.

I stood at the front desk, wondering what the heck she meant by that. The sitting room looked uncomfortable; the parlor like an ancient wing on a funeral home. Artifacts and dead people's portraits stared back at me from the walls that were coated in monotonous, textured paper. It was creepy, stiff and unwelcoming.

Make myself at home? I thought to myself. *I don't think so. When the cat is away, the mice shall play.*

Twenty-Nine

I was half expecting Emily to stroll down the Manor's driveway in a horse-drawn carriage, powdering her nose with makeup from Queen Victoria's secret stash. Instead, she peeled away in shiny, new BMW complete with a magnetic sign "Manhattan Manor" stuck to its flanks. A wide-brimmed summer hat completed her Victorian image.

This was my chance to make things happen. Ticking clocks were the only sound I heard as I made my way through the kitchen and into the Heanley's private residence in back of the Manor. It looked like the kitchen served both sides of the building. When guests were afoot, she served meals on the Manor's side; when she fed her family it was on the private side. Emily kept the house just as neat and tidy as the Manor, but the family side was much more homey.

I almost stepped on their little dog, Dash. She looked like a white and red little mop with an upturned snoot. I couldn't help but snicker at her stink eye and a growling, cleft smile. "It's okay, Miss. Dash." She ignored my gentle words and growled something vulgar under her breath.

A pack of Djarum cigarettes were on the counter, next to the stash of balsamic vinegar and olive oil. Seemed like a bizarre, exotic combination.

My phone had been completely silent until it blinked a little whistle. Dottie was on the hunt again: *What are you doing?*

I probably should have ignored her, but I didn't. *Nothing good.*

What are you doing was a clever way to draw me in to her ultimate goal, *Wanna have dinner?* Had she opened the dialogue with that request, she knew I would have ignored her. Since she started with an open-ended question, I took the bait.

That's when I ignored her.

The Heanley's living room was a little more my style. It was comfortable and cozy, appointed with a nice television, book shelves stuffed with hundreds of hardbacks, CDs and an occasional surround-sound speaker. Against the far wall was a small desk; its computer screen drew me in like a moth to a mercury light. The images on the screen cast a familial image: Hunter in his baseball outfit, Emily and Shafeek in their wedding attire, Grandma and Grandpa, I assumed. One by one, the pictures appeared then drifted away on a time-lapse computer program.

I pulled a zip drive from my pocket and jammed it in into the little port on the front of the computer.

It wasn't like I was trying to find something in particular; I thought of it as an electronic fishing expedition. If I cast enough lures in the water, sooner or later I was going to get a bite.

Then again, if the Heanley's had their computer equipped with a password, I might be out of luck.

I clicked the mouse and the screen came to life.

Password appeared.

Damn, I thought. *Now what?*

Dottie just couldn't let me go: *I'm going to be in your neck of the woods.*

That girl is unyielding, I thought to myself. *She won't take no for an answer.*

I thought about what the Heanley's would have for a password.

Their name plus a number afterward seemed likely. When that didn't work, I tried their son's name, plus his age. After that failed, I tried their son's name minus a year, then two, three, and four.

For some reason the dog barked. It sent me scrambling around the corner of the living room, through the swinging wooden door and into the kitchen.

Breathless, I looked out the kitchen window and across the expansive yard of the Manor. No sign of the BMW or Shafeek's brown Lincoln. Pots of lush geraniums framed the closed garage doors, their leaves quaking from the afternoon breeze. Hunter's whiffle ball caught the gentle wind too, and it drifted across the concrete until it bumped into the lawn on the near side of the driveway. The fruit trees had lost their blossoms, and now all that remained were the bulbs of apple, pear or peach, I assumed. Beneath the trees, a robin was evicting a nightcrawler from its hole, little by little.

When I walked past the dog, she snapped at me.

What the hell, I thought to myself. *Shafeek must have said something bad about me.*

Back to the computer I went.

I entered the dog's name, plus the year. Of course, that failed. I added 69, 17 and 50—all my favorite lucky numbers—and they were rejected as well.

I looked beneath the desktop calendar. Leaflets and fliers from church. A page from a boating catalog, and a circle around a pair of boat shoes written with a ball point pen. A menu from the Raven Cafe. A fifty-week-old Father's Day card and a gift certificate from Starbucks. No damn password.

"It has to be here, Dash," I said out loud.

My back was to the kitchen.

She could have been a foot behind me or around the corner, sleeping in her oval office; I didn't look.

When I crouched beneath the desk and took a look at the undercarriage, I found a stack of files on the floor tucked against the back wall. The files were manila, and their tabs encrypted with handwritten topics.

I got down on my hands and knees for a closer inspection. The top file was labeled *Boat.* The one beneath that was *Manor,* then *Personal, Baseball, Investments,* and finally *Systems Seven.*

I grabbed the file from the bottom of the stack at about the same time I heard the door to the garage slam shut.

Oh crap, I winced to myself.

The dog barked like mad.

"*Tattletale,*" I yelled silently.

I crouched behind the desk chair and felt my heart pounding against my ribs.

My watch said that she shouldn't be home for another twenty-five minutes.

If it was Shafeek, he'd kill me.

Everybody talks to their dog when they get home, even if they've only been gone a few minutes.

Say something, I cried to myself.

The dog kept barking: "He's-under-the-desk, he's-under-the-desk. This way! This way!"

I wanted to ring her little yapping neck, but instead, I pulled my secret weapon from around my wrist.

Little Dash was about five feet away, and when the rubber band whacked her in the butt, she let out a mighty yip and went yelping back to the kitchen.

Nobody said a thing.

What the hell, I thought to myself. *I might wiggle out of this without getting caught.*

I waited for someone to pass by the dining room, to wander up the stairs, and for the love of God, to say something to the dog. Nothing.

Ms. Dash had abandoned her barking and her vigil for justice where I was concerned. By the looks of her posture—and the way she stared aimlessly at the back door—it appeared as if nobody was home.

Just to be sure, I waited another two or three minutes.

The dog returned to the corner of the kitchen, made several miniature circles then plopped down in her throne. She heaved a sigh of relief, and I knew that the coast was clear.

Whoever it was that slammed the door must have picked something up inside, then went on their merry way.

It couldn't have worked out better.

Thirty

Four hours later, Emily and I were seated on the front porch of the Manor, a glass of Pinot Gris for her, and lemonade for me. The neighbor kid was mowing the grass, sending a wholesome, summertime plume of scent our way. Traffic roared by, but it didn't keep her from telling me about the Manor, her husband, and his business. I tried to strike a mild balance between being interested in the Manor's history and the underpinnings of her husband's private life. The more she drank, the more she wanted to tell me about how important Shafeek was and what a great provider he had become.

I nodded politely and absorbed anything I could.

She made a veiled reference to the Garl family and their horrible demise.

Although I didn't come right out and ask, I had to find out if the police had interviewed her husband.

Emily saw right through my query. "Of course they did, Mr. Ong but we had nothing to hide."

I smiled, unabashed.

"It doesn't hurt when you have a hell of an alibi."

"Oh?" I floated an air bubble.

"We were boating…" she hesitated, "at least Shafeek was."

"Where?"

"On Lake Huron. He was up at Mackinaw City. He had paid for the nights he kept his boat in the slip. The folks at the IGA near I-75 gave him a receipt for the provisions he bought there."

I didn't react. Mackinaw City isn't that far from the Devil's Elbow.

"Do you like lamb chops, Mr. Ong?"

"They're not baaaad," I joked.

Emily laughed. "Dinner should be ready in ten minutes or so. I have them in the oven now, braised in a balsamic reduction sauce."

Some people really get into cooking. Others think of food as a necessary evil.

Me? I'm someplace in between.

The food didn't really matter all that much to me. What was important was the introduction to Emily's husband.

I came prepared. Inside my overnight bag, I had packed a portable document scanner. Between the time I snared the file, and our little get together on the front porch, I had scanned every page and saved it to my laptop. Every ten pages was its own little electronic folder, and I emailed it to myself.

This Shafeek fella wasn't going to get the better of me. He may have had the upper hand in the Upper Peninsula, but I wasn't going to go quietly now that I was on his turf.

"Why don't you get washed up for dinner, Mr. Ong, and I'll meet you at the formal dining room table in twenty minutes?"

"Sounds great," I smiled, even though it felt a little weird to be told what to do.

She disappeared inside.

I checked my phone. Dottie had sent me a photo. It was a plate of oysters, with a stack of crackers and of course, her rum and Coke on the side.

You're sick, I typed. *You know I hate those things.*

You're still a wimp, she responded.

I assume you're at Tom's, for old time's sake?

Something like that. I might be with a source, too. Gotta save my receipts.

Her response was somewhat vague, so I let the electronic conversation stall. This was no time for frivolity.

My Impala was parked at a bank, across the street and three doors away. All my belongings were packed in the car. There was no way I'd spend the night, not after confronting Shafeek. By the time they realized that I had snared the secret file on his business dealings, I would have been long gone. There's no telling how long it might take them to find the file stuffed between the mattresses inside Lord Tennyson's room.

Just to be on the safe side, I had packed my little handgun. It was on my right hip—in its own little holster—beneath an extra baggy golf shirt.

Casually, I moved to the dining room, and found a seat where my back would be against the wall. That way, Shafeek wouldn't be able to sneak up on me. On my left, a screened door lead to the wraparound porch where Emily and I were sitting only a few minutes ago.

The stage was set. Now all I needed were the players.

I heard Emily's voice in the kitchen. She wasn't crabbing at anyone, but it sounded like she was explaining something important. There was no laughter in her voice, no joy in her expression.

The smell of food penetrated the wooden door of the kitchen. It was well seasoned. Perhaps Middle Eastern. Maybe it was Shafeek's favorite. I didn't care. The late breakfast I ate had long since been digested.

The kitchen door burst open and the young man Hunter dropped off a tray full of quart-sized bowls: cottage cheese, chickpeas, and lentils mixed with tomatoes. He carefully placed each bowl on the table complete with a spoon tucked inside. We were having Middle Eastern cuisine.

A minute later, he reappeared with three glasses of ice water and milk for himself. I didn't try to engage him, which was fine. He didn't seem like the talkative type.

About the same time, Emily backed her way into the dining room carrying a round, ceramic platter loaded with chops.

She was followed by her husband, Shafeek, who was carrying a breadbasket. Inside the basket was a linen napkin.

"Mr. Ong, this is my husband," she said matter-of-fact.

I stood up from my chair and extended my hand.

He was paralyzed with the quandary, terrorized by uncertainty. An intense, stiff posture engulfed him.

It took him forever to set down the breadbasket.

My hand still stretched across the table.

"Shake his hand for goodness sake," Emily said.

Instead of reaching my way and eagerly clasping hands, it was all he could do to extend his arm.

When his hand was close to mine, I seized it tighter than a fifty-dollar bill.

Shafeek winced when I really put the clamps to him.

"Nice to meet you," I said, teeth clenched.

He didn't reciprocate.

We stood there like dueling bucks in a late October meadow, sizing each other up, waiting for the other to make the first move. He didn't look like he was packing, but then again neither did I. If ever there was an element of surprise, this was the time. He didn't expect any trouble; I had counted on it.

"Have a seat, you two."

Slowly and steadily, we both sat down.

"Are you hungry, Mr. Ong?"

"Yes, I am. Everything looks fantastic. Thank you for having me."

Instead of saying a blessing, everyone dove into their dinner. I kept one eye on the food as it made its way around the table, the other eye on my adversary.

"Mr. Ong is writing a story about the Manor for *Michigan Magazine*," Emily said, June Cleaver style. "Isn't that terrific, honey?"

Shafeek didn't say a word. He kept his fork upside down in his left hand, the knife in his right. I watched him saw a chunk of lamb, push some lentils on top with his knife, then stuff it in his mouth. He never switched hands with his utensils, like most people I know. He made me think that he wasn't from around these parts.

He chewed from side to side methodically, like a camel or a dairy cow in a green pasture.

Emily must have been used to being ignored, because she tried to explain her way out of her question by saying, "I think it's great."

Hunter didn't say a thing. He was ramming his face with French fries dipped in ketchup and a cheeseburger that came from a Burger King wrapper. The kid didn't know what he was missing. The chops were fantastic and the lentils, wonderful.

"It has to be good for business," Emily said.

"I'm sure it'll make your phone ring, Emily," I said. "Lots of people read it."

Shafeek didn't say a word. I'm sure he was planning my demise with every gnashing bite of flesh.

"I spent a little time up at Robert Luxton's place in Paradise and read a whole bunch of back issues," I said, matter-of-fact.

"You know the Luxtons?" Emily asked.

"Not really. I just spent the night there."

Emily piled lentils on her plate. "They're the nicest people, aren't they, darling?"

Shafeek kept his vigil, but wiped his face with a cloth napkin.

Now that I was fed, it was time to turn up the heat. "Seems like you and Mr. Luxton did some business together..."

Emily took the bait. "We went to a fundraiser for the president in Grosse Pointe. Do you know where that is, Mr. Ong?"

"Of course. Was it twenty-five or thirty grand a plate?"

Shafeek sighed.

Emily kept blabbing, wonderfully. "I never asked what it cost, but I know it was at the yacht club. We took the boat down the St. Clair River the night before, and spent the night in Anchor Bay."

"Is that where you met the Luxtons and the Garls?"

Hunter had finished most of his dinner, and was busy with his handheld device. Every minute or two, it uttered an authentic rendition of Godzilla's haunting roar.

"No, we've known them for quite some time," she said. "I don't remember where we were. Actually, I think it was at…"

"Emily, please," Shafeek finally spoke.

She bowed her head as if she had been shot in the rump roast with a rubber band.

"This man is an imposter. His name isn't James Ong, or whatever you want to call him. He is Derrick Twitchell and he's a reporter."

Emily looked in my direction with a hurtful look on her face. The silence was broken by the silverware clanging against the china.

I didn't answer.

"What have you told this man?" he demanded, loudly.

"Mom, I'm finished," Hunter nagged.

"Go!" she said, rather abruptly. For a second, I wasn't sure if she was talking to me or her child. Hunter pushed himself away from the table and disappeared into the kitchen.

"Maybe you could bring your husband lamb chops when he's in Jackson State Penitentiary," I said. "Think they'll allow that, Shafeek?"

"Get out of my house," he said, angrily.

"What's the matter, have I struck a nerve?"

Shafeek stood.

So did I.

"I thought we could go outside for a clove cigarette."

Shafeek didn't appreciate my sarcasm.

I backed away, towards the screen door.

"You're going to jail, Shafeek. The cops are on to you. So am I."

He stepped my way, but I kept my distance.

"You're not going to mess with me any longer," I warned him. "I know where you live, where you work, and who you associate with."

"Get out of here!" Emily cried.

"You're not going to mess with me any longer!"

Thirty-One

The next morning, I was elbowing my way through traffic on westbound I-94 from Port Huron towards Detroit. I found myself sitting a little more erect in my seat, following a little closer to the person in front of me than where I come from. No need for a blinker; just nose your way between the other race cars.

It's quite a challenge to keep up with the others while sipping on a coffee and chatting on the phone. Of course, the texts and emails kept coming at me, including one from Dottie, who was blunt as ever: *I'm headed for Detroit.*

I didn't have to wonder what she was doing in Detroit. We were headed for the same destination.

Instead of answering her text, I had to pay attention to the traffic in the outer suburbs of Detroit. I needed to be doing eighty miles an hour in the left lane, or I would have been trampled by the other, more important people. We all seem to be chasing, skating, and fighting for an imaginary puck on the ice rink of life.

It broke my heart to stop for a coffee and a pit stop because I had worked so hard at getting ahead of the pack.

As I approached Detroit and sliced through the abandoned neighborhoods south of Grosse Pointe, I couldn't help but notice the boarded-up windows and the filthy conditions above the grassy easement to the freeway. Now all that lay before me was the hub of commerce in the heart of a giant city with a checkered reputation.

The federal courthouse is planted amongst the skyscrapers, the pigeons, and foul-smelling odor of metropolis. The windows in the Impala were rolled up, but when I approached a traffic light not far from the courthouse, a black woman in a red fleece vest stepped off the sidewalk and tapped on my window: "Please help me," she cried, "my son has sickle-cell anemia and he needs help."

Her request took me off guard.

I was thinking *Does he need a ride to the hospital?*

Some pamphlets about the disease?

A blood transfusion?

How about a bone marrow transplant?

She danced at the window, waiting, begging, and hoping impatiently that I'd do something. I didn't know what I could do, but she was making me incredibly anxious.

Finally she yelled through the closed window, "Give me some money, Cracker!"

I looked at the traffic light; it changed from red to green.

The guy behind me laid on his horn, so I punched the accelerator and this cracker was off like a bag of Cheez-its dropped from the top row of a vending machine.

My heart was racing, although I'm not sure why.

It was okay that I ignored her.

She probably gets turned down all the time.

The justification for rejection started to kick in. I doubted that her son—if she even had a son—had sickle cell anemia or any other disease. It was just a ruse designed to elicit pity, when she most likely needed money for a drug addiction.

The mad beggar stayed in my head for several seconds. It was a unique and novel angle she was working. We don't see a lot of panhandlers in mid-Michigan. Heck, the only time I see them is when we travel to Detroit to watch the Tigers play baseball.

My attention quickly turned to finding a place to park.

Instead of parking in a garage, I whipped into a vacant lot behind a church. The attendant took one step outside his booth, took my twenty dollar bill, and slid a red receipt under my windshield wiper. He pointed to another fellow, sixty yards away, who was waving a shredded checkered flag as if I was the first to cross the finish line at the racetrack in Brooklyn.

I thanked them for helping me, although I'm not really sure they did me any favors.

Ten minutes later, I skipped past television trucks for Channel 7 and 4, up the stairs of the federal courthouse, and slid past the metal detectors. I caught my breath in the elevator, and wished that I was allowed to have a bottle of water inside the courtroom. A group of six or seven people was huddled in the hallway outside the elevator door, undoubtedly listening to their attorney give advice on what was to take place once they were inside. None of them looked to be Kelly Mathers.

The courtroom was deadly still. A dozen or more souls were glued to the wooden benches, fiddling with their phones, reading the newspaper, and waiting the good wait. When I walked between the rows of bench seats, I glanced down at an artist's rendition of the courtroom setting. He had the boxy, wooden frame of the judge's throne in the foreground and a weight scale in the background. I got the feeling that all he had to do was sketch a face on top of the partially finished black robe and his work would be done for the day.

The reporter didn't have it so easy. She was sifting through a stash of index cards and partially memorizing the script for her report.

A pair of pigeons on the window ledge was dancing the dance of courtship, oblivious to the feces they were standing in. Rapping on the window would have spoiled their frolic and fun.

Instead, I sat down amongst the other people inside the courthouse and waited for the proceedings to begin.

The bailiff opened the door to the judge's chambers, stepped inside the courtroom and flipped through the pages on a clipboard.

I looked down at my phone. Dottie had sent me a text. *You're not in Detroit, are you?*

Yes, why?

I just had my car-jacked.

What?

Yeah. :(

Where are you?

Downtown.

I know, but where?

Inside Lafayette Coney Island.

I'll be right there.

I flew out of the courtroom doors to the guard post near the entrance of the courthouse. The men behind the metal detector gave me directions to the Coney Island, which was only a block east. As I skipped along the sidewalk, listening to the honks and beeps of cab drivers, and the wail of sirens in the distance, it occurred to me that maybe I should have told Dottie to come to the courthouse instead. That way, we wouldn't have missed the start of the Mathers proceedings. Then again, if she was as upset as I was, maybe she wanted the company.

I didn't need to search for Dottie when I plowed through the restaurant door. She was seated near the grill, a cup of coffee between her hands.

For some reason, I wanted to give her a hug. Instead, I just put my arm around her.

"Are you okay?"

She smiled, slightly, then dabbed a tissue to her nose. "I guess so."

"Was it the woman with the red vest that car-jacked you?"

"No, why?"

"I'll tell you later."

I ordered a coffee. Dottie summarized the car-jacking in seven or eight sentences. Bottom line: "He just came out of nowhere and threw me out of my car."

"That's awful," I lamented. "What did you have in your car?"

"All my camera equipment. An overnight bag, a laptop, and my purse."

"I'm sorry."

"What did the cops say?"

"Not much. It took them about a half hour to get here."

The coffee hit the spot, so I ordered breakfast, too. Dottie followed my lead, and in no time at all, the man behind the counter had our eggs and hash browns sizzling on the griddle.

"Why didn't you tell me you were coming down here?" I asked.

"I did, remember the photo of the oysters?"

"Well, yeah, I remember." I stuttered. "I should have written back to you."

"It would have been nice."

"I was right in the middle of something. Can we talk about the case for a minute?"

"Of course. What about it?"

"Is Kelly Mathers a suspect in the Garl murders?" I asked.

"She was. Once the feds started looking into the way she handed out government contracts."

"It seems like she'd have the motive once it started getting warm in the kitchen."

Our chef looked over his shoulder and wiped the sweat from the end of his nose. He missed a drop, and it fell to the griddle, where it sizzled next to Dottie's blueberry pancakes.

"Remember that time we went to that Mongolian barbecue in downtown Grand Rapids?" she asked.

Her question made me pause for an instant. We kept veering off course. "Sure…and the chef had that little accident?"

"It was more than just an accident, wouldn't you say, Derrick?"

"Well, yeah," I grimaced.

"Anytime you lose part of your finger, that's a pretty big accident."

Dottie glanced at her watch. "Where did we go kayaking that weekend?"

"I think it was down the Rabbit River…maybe the Kalamazoo. It was definitely one of those rivers that dumps into Lake Michigan."

"That was fun."

"It was."

Dottie sipped her coffee, and I couldn't help remember the picnic we had on a secluded stretch of the river. I put a lot of thought into trying to impress her, so I packed a blanket and a picnic basket loaded with supplies. It was one of those days that was easy to recall, because of the nice weather, the fine scenery, and the way Dottie cast her wetsuit aside once the picnic was nearly through.

"Did you ever replace the wetsuit you ripped up north?" I asked.

"Not yet. I figured that I'd try to get it done while I was down here. Not much of a chance now."

"Why's that?"

"Because I just had my purse stolen. I have no credit cards. Nothing to my name."

Her plea tugged at my heartstrings. "Don't worry about it, Dottie. I'll take care of you. It's the least I can do."

"Really?"

"Heck, yeah," I said confidently. "You saved my life up

north. We just have to figure out what we're going to do about the Mathers situation."

"There's not much to do," she said, looking at her watch again. "They've probably already read the indictment against her."

"We'll get there in time. You'll see."

The cook must have known we were anxious for our breakfast. He slid the blueberry pancakes off the griddle and placed them on a plate next to a pair of butter pats. Dottie placed a napkin on her lap and picked up her knife. The butter was no match for the pancakes. It left a wake of goodness as she pushed it around the pancake plenty.

The hash browns, eggs and bacon weren't far behind.

"Don't you just wonder where all this food comes from?" I asked.

Dottie looked at me like I was weird. Of course, there's no denying that.

"I mean, where was this pig living before he was turned into bacon?"

"Derrick, would you mind passing me the cream, or is that too ethereal for you?" She was laughing.

"Don't you want to know?"

"Not really. I want to find out who killed the Garl family."

"Really?"

"Well yeah. That's part of the reason why I'm here."

"What if it was Shafeek Heanley?" I asked.

"You're crazy, Derrick."

"I am?"

"Yes, Shafeek wouldn't do that."

"How do you know?" I demanded.

"Cause I work for him. I've known him for years."

I sprinkled salt and pepper on my plate of eggs, then dipped my toast into the yolk. "How well do you know him?" I asked.

"Pretty well, I'd say."

I chose my words not-so-carefully. "He's a chump."

"Derrick, why would you say that?"

"He's one of the guys who kidnapped me."

"Seriously? Up in Paradise?"

I nodded definitively. "Absolutely!"

Dottie took a sip of coffee and I felt her stare at me. "Why do I get the feeling that you're really not telling me the whole story?"

"Why do you ask that?"

"It just doesn't add up."

"What doesn't add up?"

"There's no reason why they would kidnap you, unless they knew you had something that would incriminate them," she said.

Now it was my turn to come clean. "There is something I need to tell you."

"What is it?"

It took the remainder of breakfast to tell her about hitting the deer east of Midland, meeting Becky Tocca, what she said, where she worked and the contents of the zip drive in her storage locker.

"What was on the zip drive?" she asked.

"It was devastating, I'm sure."

"Why do you say that?"

"Becky told me that the people at Drake Media were after her."

"I know, but what's on the zip drive?" There was no getting around Dottie. She was a good interrogator.

"There was a lot. The confrontation at the board meeting between Luxton and Garl. The financial records from Drake Media…"

"What about them?"

"It looked to me like Garl and Luxton were laundering money somehow."

"How?" she asked.

"That's the thing. I'm not exactly sure how it all went down, but I know that Luxton printed Garl's magazines."

"Derrick, you've had her zip drive for more than a week. Why don't you know?"

Dottie shook her head just like she used to do when we were dating and I had let her down. I could tell she wanted to lecture me on time management, but instead she mentioned that the benefactors of government contracts are exempt from federal antitrust laws. "No competent CPA can understand it all. Their bookkeeping methods and write-offs are designed to be confusing, because they don't want the public knowing what's really going on. You'd probably fall off your chair if you knew how they operated."

"How do you know all this?"

"I've written stories about it on other cases."

"Up north?"

"Yes. The nuclear plant in Charlevoix. It was called Big Rock back in the day, remember that? They got boat loads of government money. Heck, it cost almost four hundred million just to close the plant back in the late nineties."

I shook my head. It seemed remotely familiar.

"So why haven't you got into the zip drive yet?"

"I've been a little busy."

"I understand, but if Shafeek and Luxton wanted to know what was on the zip drive you bet there would have been something damning on there, don't you think?"

I didn't let breakfast get in the way of the conversation. It was delicious.

"Of course, but what I can't figure out is how Shafeek and Luxton knew that I was the one who had Becky Tocca's zip drive."

I had her stumped.

We sat there, eating our breakfast and sipping our coffee.

I told her about the man at the storage facility, but she shook her head. "He wouldn't know anything."

"I know, but he called the cops and told them that I was the one in Becky's storage locker."

"That was the end of the line, though. The cops wouldn't have told anyone else."

"Well then, why did they kidnap me?"

Dottie made a funny face. "Derrick, we already know why they kidnapped you: to get the zip drive. What we don't know is how they knew it was you who had it."

Dottie swung herself around on the swivel chair as if she was a little girl. The other patrons looked up from their newspapers and their cups of coffee with mild amusement. They must not have seen anything so uninhibited in quite some time.

"I don't know what to tell you about the kidnapping, Derrick, but I think we should still find out more about Kelly Mathers."

I picked up the check and looked at the amount due.

"Everything okay?" she asked.

"Yep, but I insist on paying," I said with a smile.

Dottie made a horribly contorted face as if she was holding back an f-bomb. Finally, she said, with a resigned look on her face: "I can pay you back, Derrick."

"Forget about it," I said with a smile. "Let's go check in on the Mathers situation."

"She might be the key to figuring out this whole case."

I peeled a twenty out of my wallet, and laid it on the counter, next to the check.

"Here, I'll take that," she said, picking up the hand-written check. "Don't let a receipt go to waste."

Thirty-Two

Five minutes later, we were at the courthouse steps, looking up at the swarm of reporters as they took photos and barked questions to the lead defense attorney in the Mathers case. Dottie and I elbowed our way to the rear of the pack. Whoever the attorney was, she stood shoulder to shoulder next to her client, who was dressed in an angelic, blue sweater. If ever there was an attempt to look innocent, Kelly Mathers had mastered it.

All at once, the defense counsel brought the house to order: "Ladies and gentlemen, please," she said, raising her palms to the masses, "I will answer your questions after I read my prepared remarks."

"What's her name?" I asked Dottie.

The timing of my question seemed crazy-perfect.

"My name is Fern Lazopoulos. That's L-a-z-o-p-o-u-l-o-s."

I pulled out my camera from my vest and began taking pictures. Dottie asked for a scratchpad and some sort of writing utensil. We were in business.

Ms. Lazopoulos' statement lasted for three or four minutes, most of which was boilerplate denials and suggestions of prosecutorial misconduct. Her client had every right to award the contracts that she did and she reimbursed everyone for the trips she had taken.

"We categorically deny the charges," she suggested, "besides, these were no-bid contracts. Ms. Mathers had all the discretion, and we'll prove that once the trial begins."

She went on for a minute or two about the pre-trial motions she'd be filing, and that she'd need more time for preparation. There would be no shortage of witnesses, either.

Ms. Lazopoulos tugged at her thin, silk scarf, then the lapels of her cream dress suit. With a little imagination, this Greek dynamo could have been on the top stairs of the some ancient ruin.

"Who has questions?" she asked.

Her announcement served as a battle cry for the story hounds in her midst. They barked and bayed as if a raccoon toddled past the kennel door.

"One at a time," she demanded, "you, sir, in the red sweater."

Dottie's hand was feverishly scratching notes on her pad of paper. I flanked the masses and clicked shot after shot of a sad-faced Mathers and her attorney as she wagged her index finger, Bill Clinton style.

Dottie and I might have missed the actual reading of the indictment, but we could get a copy of that as soon as the fireworks had ended. Most of the newsworthy activity was going on right here, right now. The reading of the charges draws people in; the statements from the defense team gives a voice to the human interest side of every trial.

All the reporters' questions seemed to deal with the amount of the bond, the penalties, and the charges against Ms. Mathers; none of them seemed to see the big picture as it related to the dead family up north.

I raised my hand politely, as courteous as a boy scout. The lawyer seemed to appreciate my thoughtfulness and pointed in my direction.

"Derrick Twitchell, *Gratiot County Recorder*, here." The other reporters didn't introduce themselves before they asked a question. When I did, a couple of them uttered a sarcastic groan, as if they should be impressed. "Has your client been questioned in the Garl family murders up north?"

"Next question."

"Wasn't Cecil Garl known as a campaign 'bundler' for the president's re-election campaign?"

"Couldn't tell you. Next question."

"What is your client's relationship with Shafeek Heanley?"

"Next question. Please, somebody else." The attorney pointed to a woman in the crowd with a spare pencil tucked behind her ear.

"How many other clients of yours have had Judge Kipler?"

"A dozen or so. Maybe more. She's been fair, but tough. I'm convinced that she'll give us a fair trial."

The press conference lasted for another four or five minutes, before Mathers and her attorney stomped down the granite stairs. It could have been their husbands, or interns, who were waiting for them curbside. Either way, the two women hugged for a second or two before opening their respective car doors and zooming away.

That hug—and the brief hand holding—were the images that would sell thousands of newspapers across the state.

Just as I glanced at the camera's viewfinder, a voice came at me from the crowd. "What the hell are you thinking, Twitchell?"

I looked up to find a young, geeky looking person standing in front of me.

"What do you mean by that?"

"Your line of questioning..."

"Whatever, dude. Get out of my grill."

He heeded my warning and took a step backward, but the questions kept coming at me. "Who the hell is Shafeek Heanley?"

"Never mind."

I tromped down the stairs to where Dottie was waiting. "All set?" I asked her.

"Sure."

"Hey Twitchell," the voice kept badgering me, "what is it with you and the Garl murders?"

"Listen," I turned in his direction. He was a step above me, so I climbed two stairs. Daddy always taught me to take the high ground, whether it was in a fist fight or a moral argument. In this instant, his advice worked beautifully. The geek's head was at shoulder level for me. "I don't know who the hell you are, or what your problem is, but I want you to leave me alone. Got it?"

"I just want to know…"

"Leave me alone. Leave *us* alone."

Shaking this guy seemed impossible. Is everybody in Detroit an in-your-face kind of character? I turned to Dottie and asked her if she wanted to see if the indictment was filed, while I fetched the car.

She didn't have any money, I was certain, so I whipped out a twenty dollar bill in case there was a fee for the copying service. Most courts charge a dollar a page, and I couldn't imagine the indictment being more than twenty pages in length.

"This ought to cover it," I said. "If it's not enough, come back out, and I'll give you more."

Dottie gave me the thumbs up. "You want the receipt? Because if you don't, I'll take it."

"You haven't changed a bit," I told her, "still trying to fleece the system."

Thirty-Three

Dottie and I really didn't have anyplace to go, but we did have stories to write and deadlines to meet. Instead of leaving the city, we decided to hang out in Greektown until the police finished their report about Dottie's stolen car. We could take turns using my laptop and get our stories in to our respective newsrooms in time for the afternoon deadline.

It seemed like a good idea at the time.

Deep down, I think she thought that her car would show up on a street corner; the thieves abandoning it after a brief joy ride.

I didn't have the heart to tell her that it was probably being chopped to smithereens; its parts sold to the highest bidders like an ivory tusk from an African bull elephant.

We were inside the Parthenon Restaurant with a view of the foot traffic outside. Businessmen walked past; so did the delivery men, dressed in their company uniforms. It was in between breakfast and lunch. I wasn't really hungry, but I was in the mood for a little more coffee.

Dottie didn't have to tell me what she was going to write about: it was as obvious as the nose on her face. *A government employee and former business associate of slain CEO Cecil Garl was indicted today on eleven counts of bribery in federal district court.*

Since she was writing for the paper where the murder happened, she could tailor her story to the residents' familiarity to the Garl situation. My article could be a lot more general because most of the readers were not acquainted with what had taken place up in

Good Hart. It was newsworthy to report a government employee taking bribes; how it related to an unsolved murder mystery cast a glorious spotlight across the pages of the newspaper.

The second cup of coffee—and the jolt of caffeine it delivered—had my skin crawling so I decided to leave a five-dollar bill on the table and wander across the street to the Greektown casino. Dottie had to finish her story, and she probably would appreciate the time alone without any distractions. I never thought anything of leaving my laptop with her, even though it had everything on there from Becky's storage locker. Dottie had scaled the walls of privacy I keep between myself and the outside world.

A busload of senior citizens had been dropped off at the casino lobby, and the place was teeming with wheelchairs and walkers, blue-haired folks with bingo, Keno, and penny slots on their minds. It seemed like the perfect field trip for a Monday morning; a close second might be the zoo, the art museum, or Cabela's in Dundee.

I'm not sure why I was there. Casinos really aren't my cup of tea. Nevertheless, I stuffed a ten-dollar bill in a slot machine, and began pulling the arm like it was going out of style. Eleven pulls later, I was out of credits and my ten dollars were long gone. No thrill in that.

The dollar machines were too rich for my blood, so I tried my luck at the quarter machines a few aisles away. My ten dollars racked up forty credits, which seemed like a lot better bang for my buck. Instead of pulling the arm on the side of the machine, I pushed the button that sent the wheels tumbling inside. Two seconds later, a cherry, an orange and a lemon appeared. My credits dropped to thirty nine. Losing seemed to be contagious.

I watched one of the staff empty ashtrays that were wedged in between the machines. She dumped the butts into a small garbage can and wiped the trays with a dingy cloth.

The place was dinging and buzzing with the monotonous whizzes and bells of slot machines. It was hard to hear myself think.

"Would you care for a nutty berry?" I looked up at the waitress who was holding a tray of highball cocktail glasses, which were filled with tomato juice and a stalk of celery.

It took me a second or two to figure out that she didn't say 'nutty berry' but rather *Bloody Mary.*

"No, thanks."

"Can I bring you something else?"

"Yes…some good luck."

She smiled pleasantly. "I'll work on that."

I pushed the button again and the wheels inside the machine spun like mad. This time I racked up three peaches, which sent the device into a minor seizure of blinking lights and whirly bells. The credits climbed to ninety-nine, which meant that I was ahead of the gambling game.

Instead of pushing my luck, I decided to cash out. Quarter after quarter dumped into the metal tray beneath the machine. What a nice little pile.

I stuffed all ninety-nine quarters into my pockets and got out of dodge. On the way outside, I dropped three or four coins into a panhandler's metal cup. He didn't have time to tell me about his time in Viet Nam, his crippled mom, or his son with sickle cell anemia. I barely heard him say "Bless you."

Just as I crossed the street, I saw Dottie leave the restaurant, but she wasn't alone. Shafeek Heanley had her by the elbow, and was marching her down the sidewalk at a quick pace. As much as I wanted to scream, I put a clamp on it. The element of surprise was my ally. Instead, my attention turned to the briefcase in Shafeek's hand. It was mine, and I'm sure my laptop was inside along with the indictment.

Now I really had to act fast. I dashed between businessmen and delivery people, wheeling dollies loaded with alcohol, sliced lamb, cheese and olives. I nudged the sidearm on my belt and thought for an instant that I'd finally get to use it.

They were stealing my property.

Dottie might be in trouble.

Should I call the police or take matters into my own hands?

Just before the intersection of Monroe and Antoine Streets, they turned the corner behind a storefront. I ran as fast as I could, mindful of the trap that might have been set, but oblivious to the busyness around me. Fifty steps later, I rounded the corner at the same time that a hobo pushing a shopping cart full of belongings undercut my footing. I flew ass over teakettle onto the concrete sidewalk and a metal sign post.

Three or four seconds of gasping later, I caught my breath. When I raised my knees, the quarters in my pockets poured onto the sidewalk as if I was a two-legged slot machine.

The hobo came to my aid, sort of. He kept asking me if I was all right while at the same time picking up the bounty, coin by coin. I looked into his toothless, whiskered grill and thought that there was no way he was going to give me mouth to mouth resuscitation.

I took a flying leap when I rounded the corner of the building. My back must have nailed the post and knocked the wind out of me.

I lay there, taking an inventory of my senses. All ten toes wiggled, which was a relief. When I rolled on my side, more coins plinked out of my pockets. The hobo uttered an exaggerated "ohhhh" as if I had just stepped into his Thanksgiving dining room with a platter loaded with a sliced butterball.

The instant I put my hand on the sidewalk, I knew something was wrong. The pain was excruciating. I tugged at my sleeve, which revealed a peculiar bump about half way between my hand and my elbow.

"Your wrist is broke," the hobo said.

"Broken, dude," I managed to correct him.

"Whatever. Give me your phone. I'll call an am-bul-ance?"

"No," I groaned. "I'll be okay."

At that point I remembered why I had been running. *Where are you Dottie?* I thought to myself. *I'm going to save the day, heroically.*

The traffic on Antoine rushed by. Same for Monroe. I heard honks and beeps and a distant siren. A flock of pigeons took flight from atop the storefront, and distracted my attention for an instant. Dottie was gone. So was my laptop.

My camera's neck strap served as a makeshift sling, as I held my wrist to my chest. Thankfully, my car keys weren't hard to dig out of my pocket. The church parking lot was barely a block away. Both men in the little booth looked at me with mild concern and gave me directions to the nearest clinic.

I pulled out of the parking lot, went around the block, and eventually made my way to eastbound Jefferson Avenue. The clinic was only a stone's throw from downtown, but it was close enough to the ghetto that I wondered if the old Impala would be there after the plaster cast was dry.

When I yanked open the front door, I was greeted by the receptionist who was seated behind a bulletproof window. I had to put my driver's license and health card on the same kind of miniature lazy Susan that party stores use to dispense of 40 ounce malt liquor.

"Here," she said, stuffing a clipboard and a pen into the Susan. "Fill this out and bring it back. We'll be witchoo shortly."

I smiled cordially, and stepped into the waiting room. The faces looked up at me as if I was a skunk at a picnic. There wasn't a white person in the crowd. It was just me and Jerry Springer instigating his guests on the television.

Drives me nuts when I have to fill out the doctor's paperwork. I mean, it's not like we're dating or anything. All I needed was my broken arm fixed. They didn't need to know if I buckled my seatbelt or if I had ever been incarcerated. As much as I wanted to storm out of there, and go someplace else, I knew that I'd have to do paperwork wherever I went. It took forever to scribble down my answers left-handed, but that was okay; I had nowhere else to go, nobody else to meet. Dottie's rescue would have to wait.

A nurse opened the door at the far end of the waiting room and blurted out "Shashika Jones." A little girl of five or six, with beads in her hair, grabbed hold of her mother's hand and they both went inside. What a goofy name.

One down, fifteen to go.

I might see the doctor sometime this afternoon.

After finishing the paperwork, I responded to a few texts and emails. Colleen was never far from my mind, but I wasn't quite sure that the reverse was true. I felt like she was slipping away from me; like we were drifting apart. Perhaps I should have listened to her and let the case go. It might be fun to go with her to the family farm in Wisconsin and help with the auction.

Are you okay, darling? I typed. *I miss you like the heavens miss the rain, like there's no tomorrow, like you're my salt and I'm your pepper.* As much as I hoped to spice things up between us, it seemed to be a one-way street where she was concerned.

Where did I go wrong, what I could have done differently, or if she was growing tired of having me in her life?

About an hour later, I was lead into one of the examination rooms. I took a seat on the bench and examined my surroundings. The walls were covered in posters detailing the skeletal system, the nervous system and muscles. Above the sink was the supply cabinet, which was locked with the same metal rod I might find in the electronics department at Wal-Mart. No sense in rummaging through the supply cabinet, filling my pockets with tongue depressors and gauze; I'd have to go to the store and buy them just like everybody else.

The doctor was a really nice man. Barely thirty, he took his time explaining what might be going on with my wrist. In no time at all, I was on my way to the x-ray machine. Twenty minutes after that, he informed me that I didn't need surgery. My wrist was something that could be taken care of in house. He gave me a Valium and let me stew for twenty minutes so the drug could take effect.

When he rapped on the door and appeared with four nurses, I knew I was in trouble. They were ganging up on me. One nurse cinched my legs to the bench and grabbed my thighs. Another nurse pressed my left arm to the bench. The third nurse backed her fanny up to my ear and grabbed hold of my right bicep. If her fanny was a giant sea conch, I could have been listening for the sounds of the ocean. The biggest and meanest looking nurse looked a little like baseball slugger David Ortiz the way he stands in the batter's box, spits in his gloves, and grabs the bat. I had a grisly feeling what this job entailed.

"Are we ready, people?" the doctor asked.

They all nodded.

"On three," he said. "One. Two. Three."

I was startled by the commotion. They all tried to pin me down, except for the slugger at the far end of my wrist who was tugging on my arm as if was an uncooperative steer in the 4-H ring. When the doctor mashed the bones back in place, it hurt so bad that I yelled at the top of my lungs. I don't know who might have heard me, but I really didn't care. It was excruciating and thankfully, over quite quickly.

"We're done," the doctor said. "That's it."

Breathless, I thanked him, although I'm not sure why.

"In no time at all, you'll be running down bad guys."

I chuckled halfheartedly. They were never in any danger.

"All we have to do is make a cast."

Three of the nurses left. The fourth unlocked the medicine cabinet and removed the supplies they'd need for the cloth sleeve and plaster cast. They worked well together, and in the course of their doctoring, asked who was picking me up.

"My wife," I lied. "She's on the way."

"That's good," the doctor smiled. "We can't let you drive or operate heavy equipment while you're under the influence."

It was nearly two in the afternoon by the time I buckled my seatbelt and pulled away from the curb. Yes, I could feel the numbing effects of the drug, but it wasn't like I couldn't control my limbs. The traffic lights still had color, and the lines painted on the street were plain as day.

When I approached the church parking lot again, the two men were more than receptive to the idea of me parking there anew. I promised them that I'd only be there for a few minutes. "No worries, sir, your permit is good for all day." They smiled and laughed when they saw the cast. One of them volunteered to autograph my cast with the name of one of the Detroit Lions' players.

I skipped around the corner to the Parthenon Restaurant, and asked the manager if someone had left behind a computer case and laptop. He shook his head no. Shafeek had stolen it and kidnapped Dottie at the same time.

From there, I walked to police headquarters a few blocks away. Up the stairs I went to a shabby elevator; its insides coated in a quilted material like I might find in a padded cell. It was old and clammy and incredibly dirty.

When the elevator door opened, I walked down the hall to a cluttered room with a long countertop near the door. The officer behind the counter asked me to spell Dorothy's last name. A spare pen and a pad of paper made it real handy, although trying to grasp a pen with my hand in a cast made it rather cumbersome.

She typed the letters into her keyboard, fiddled with the mouse for a few seconds, and then shook her head.

"I'm sorry, sir, but we don't have a report for Kalakay."

"How about a stolen vehicle?" I asked.

"Oh we get those all the time."

"Just not this morning, and not for Kalakay."

"That's right."

"What are the odds that the officer who took the report hasn't finished it yet?"

"Not very good. The officers are required to finish their reports before they log out for the day. We already into the afternoon shift now. I'm sorry, sir, but there just ain't a report."

"Thanks."

Thirty-Four

I was in a terrible quandary after I left the police station. Was Dottie's vehicle really stolen, or was she playing me for a fool the whole time? If her car was car-jacked, why didn't the police have any record of it?

My mind was working overtime as to what my next move should be. I couldn't just call her and ask, "Were you pulling my leg when you said that your vehicle was car-jacked?" Worse yet, "Was Shafeek dragging you out of the restaurant, or was it your plan all along to ditch me?" It would be unwise of me to ask when she could have been sitting next to him in the car.

And what about my laptop? Did she steal it, or was it collateral damage when Shafeek whisked her down the street? I just had to get it back; my whole life was on that computer, including the entire Garl investigation. With each step away from the police station, I became more and more angry.

If they were in cahoots together, surely he told her about me being inside the bed and breakfast. Undoubtedly, Dottie had some stories to tell about me from our distant past and our time together in the last few days.

If she and Shafeek were truly engaged in some sort of conspiracy, why did she drive to the Luxton cabin to save me? It made no sense. I wanted to trust her, because I'm a trusting kind of guy.

I pulled my cell phone out of my pocket and thumbed through my contacts until I reached her number. She wouldn't answer a call from me, but she might be tempted if the call came from a number she didn't recognize. What would I say to her?

A pay phone in the heart of Greektown was calling my name. I dialed her number and stuffed seven quarters into the machine. That meant I still had forty-three in my pocket. On about the fifth ring she picked up. "Hello, Dorothy Kalakay."

I let her voice dangle for a second or two before I hung up.

She was okay.

The two of them had to be involved with each other somehow. I bet they had opened up my computer and found the file titled, "Systems Seven." It was right there, plain as day, on my desktop.

About a block away from the parking lot, I ran into the bum who had clipped me with his shopping cart. "Careful, now," he said, laughing.

"All right," I said, "I'll be real careful."

He glanced at my cast about the same time I looked into his shopping cart. A couple giant bottles of Milwaukee's Best were riding shotgun on top of a blue, ratty parka. Somehow I think the quarters that spilled out of my pocket contributed to his happy hour.

I continued to the parking lot where the two attendants gave me directions to the nearest public library. Since it was only a few blocks away, I decided to walk there instead of driving.

After skipping up the stairs of the library and opening the massive front door, I found a vacant computer. My email was waiting for me, and the papers related to Shafeek Heanley's business were laid out in spades.

It looked like Systems Seven had been started eight years ago, according to the articles of incorporation. The members of the company were Mr. Heanley himself, Cecil Garl, Robert Luxton, and three other people I had never heard of. Five of the six gentlemen had contributed fifteen thousand dollars for the company's creation. Mr. Heanley, forty-five, so that's why he was the majority share holder. Any profits the company made would be divvied up according to the number of shares.

The company's purpose couldn't have been any clearer: to produce, manufacture, and market hybrid car batteries.

At least once a year, they were supposed to have a shareholder's meeting at a time and place to be determined.

I skipped ahead to the individual shares of stock, the papers related to the creation of a checkbook, and the tax identification number. It looked like Emily Heanley was the secretary on record. For the first several years, the bank statements were all paper, then they switched to electronic. The company had several accountants, I assumed to keep the others honest.

The lease for the business' building looked to be straightforward. Rent was thirty-five hundred a month. All utilities, premises upgrades, and environmental cleanup would be paid for by the company. After three years, the lease would be renegotiated with the understanding that the rent would not increase more than fifteen percent.

Next came the buy-sell arrangement. The shares of stock were not transferrable, but they were valuable if the company became successful. Each member bought a life insurance policy on themselves with a face amount of a hundred thousand dollars. The beneficiary was the corporation, which would use the proceeds to pay off the decedent's heirs. That arrangement—of buying a share in the company for fifteen thousand, and if they died it's worth a hundred thousand—seemed like it could have been a motive for murder. Then again, who would kill someone for a hundred thousand? Not this group of investors.

Fifteen or twenty pages into the file, I found spreadsheets for the company's profits and losses. Its revenue increased steadily over the years, while the expenses stayed in check. Shafeek was at the helm of a vibrant, up-and-coming business, with annual sales of ten million.

I scratched my head when I turned the page in the file. Shafeek had written reams of details about Cecil Garl: his address, his wife's name, the three kids. He wrote where the kids went to school, what were their teacher's names were. I don't know why it was relevant, but he wrote how often they went to the cabin, and where they played tennis. The details kept getting more and more weird. Shafeek had written the times of the Garl's flights when they went on vacation, who their family doctors were, and what was in their curbside recycling bin.

I don't know how he obtained it, but Shafeek had all kinds of information about Cecil's bank accounts, the log in passwords, and retirement fund balances.

There were photocopies of photographs of Cecil Garl. He was heading into the office, into the dentist office, his CPA, into church, into Déjà Vous in Saginaw. Each image was mounted on a piece of paper; the date and time written beneath the caption. Shafeek must have had close to a hundred pictures in his file. Whoever took the photos did so with a long lens. The foreground was a bit blurry, but there was no mistaking Cecil's face as he went about his daily life. Photo captions never mentioned Cecil by name, but referred to him as the "subject."

Shafeek had to hire a private investigator to do his dirty work. Whoever took the pictures had done so over an extended period of time. All four seasons were captured.

There were some familiar faces in Shafeek's gallery: Genesis, of course; Fischer's Happy Hour Tavern, Cecil's wife and kids; and the woman of the hour, Kelly Mathers. She was in quite a few pictures: at Treetops Resort in Gaylord, tipping the attendants in front of the clubhouse at Oakland Hills, and boarding a Mackinac Island ferry. Her husband seemed to be enjoying the ride too. He was smiling in every one of the photos.

The library was relatively quiet until a group of middle schoolers plopped their backpacks on the table behind me. They jumped online and commenced with fake farting sounds, giggling and laughing. The chief librarian glared in our direction, but she ignored my unspoken pleas for help.

Next came the emails in Shafeek's folder. There were scores of them, in varying degrees of relevance. I found myself scanning the subject line and if it didn't grab my attention I kept flipping the pages. The company distributed ninety thousand dollars to each member three years ago. That number jumped to one forty-five the year after that, and one seventy-five the year Cecil was murdered. I assumed that the increase in profits had something to do with the gush of money that Kelly Mathers provided. It looked like some serious cash flow.

When "minutes" became the subject line, I figured that it had to do with the annual board meeting. I was correct; the board meeting was held in the heart of summertime at the Grand Traverse resort. Golfing and vacationing were part of that trap. Cecil Garl was mentioned under "new business." His reason: making Systems Seven part of a group of contributors to the president's reelection campaign. The minutes of that meeting recorded a brief discussion, but the motion to contribute two hundred thousand dollars to Mr. Garl's political action committee was passed on a unanimous vote.

It seemed simple enough. Instead of splitting up the two hundred thousand amongst the corporate members, they agreed to hand it over to Cecil with the hopes that he could turn it into an even bigger payoff. Most companies invest in research & development, bricks, mortar and new employees. Not Systems Seven. They realized that the government was a fertile place to invest their hard-earned money. They weren't the first company to do this and they wouldn't be the last.

The papers in Shafeek's file were out of chronological order, but generally, the more recent documents were closer to the back. As much as I tried to rearrange the documents, the task became very frustrating. I guess it really didn't matter what the order was; the papers provided insight into what Shafeek's business was all about.

It was a rather sickening arrangement they had. Cecil Garl and Robert Luxton were part of Shafeek's business. Luxton had a hand in Ener-X and the printing of Cecil's magazine for the Fatima Society. There were layers and layers of connections, arrangements, and money changing hands. They all spent a lot of time together, which was rather odd for independent businessmen. I've always thought of them as too busy to do much of anything but stay on top of the tidal wave of activity around the office. It's no wonder that the police had so much difficulty pinning the murder on the perpetrators; there were so many angles to investigate.

Just when I thought I had seen everything relevant in Shafeek's folder, I noticed a handwritten note at the bottom of a piece of paper: "per Lionel: office snitch Becky Tocca." They had an interesting choice of words. "Snitch?"

Who was she tattling on?

Why was she tattling?

It was rather odd, but certainly worth checking out.

The one person who knew Becky better than anyone else was her sister. I had to get a hold of her, but I didn't know how. Heck, I didn't know her last name, where she lived, or where she worked. The wheels in my head were spinning again. The flier from Becky's funeral might have Helen's last name, same for the funeral director. I got on the phone and called the church. The woman who answered said that the priest was off today and that she really couldn't give me Helen's last name or her phone number. What she could do was take down my information and reach out to Helen as soon as possible.

As soon as I finished saying the last syllable in "Twitchell" the nice lady on the phone recognized my name as the person who slashed the deacon's tires. Dottie must have told the priest.

I hemmed and hawed, stumbled and stammered. "Well, I, ah…"

"Don't even think about saying you're sorry, Mr. Twitchell. Confession is tomorrow morning from nine to eleven, and for an hour before mass this weekend."

I chuckled under my breath.

The woman was being totally serious, "Or by appointment."

Thirty-Five

It didn't take Helen long to receive the church's electronic correspondence and get back to me via email. Her blunt style of communicating was the same on the phone as it was in person: *What do you want?*

It's about your sister.

What about her?

Can we get together?

If you'd like.

When? I typed.

After work.

Where?

Crossbow Inn. Grand Blanc. Six thirty.

I looked at my watch. Ten after four. The timing couldn't have been better. An easy drive up 75 would get me there on schedule. *Sounds good.* I gave her my cell phone number in case she was running late. She didn't reciprocate.

Quickly, I printed a copy of Becky's suicide note and her letter to the *Free Press*. If Helen wanted information about her sister, I would be happy to hand it over to her. I might even use it as a bargaining chip during my discussion with her.

On my way up north, I called Colleen. Before her voice mail said to leave a message, I decided to hang up. There was no sense in leaving a sappy message about missing her, or loving her, or the fact that I couldn't wait to see her again. She had a lot going on in her life and so did I. We were both busy people with careers and commitments and a blur of responsibility.

It seemed like I had to wow her somehow. The flowers were a nice idea and a kind thought, but they really didn't have the impact I had hoped for. My heart, my thoughts, my mind was in Wisconsin—on the family farm, with the people I cared about most.

I hated the notion of losing her, or at the very least, letting her down. Between the exit for Rochester and the Palace of Auburn Hills, I weighed my options carefully. The car dealerships along the edge of the road tempted me with a new ride for her. A grand vacation to a far away destination sounded wonderful, too. Who was I kidding; everybody knows that diamonds are a girl's best friend. All I had to decide was if they'd hang around her neck, dangle from her ears, or be the centerpiece of a new ring. By the time I had reached the exit for the restaurant, I had decided on something sparkly.

The Crossbow Inn had a really cool home page when I pulled it up on the internet. With knights in armor promising "great food and wet goods," I couldn't help but think that maybe an episode of *Game of Thrones* might have been shot inside the castle walls. When I pulled into the parking lot shortly after six-fifteen, however, it was anything but a castle or a manor or a fiefdom fit for a king; it looked like any other corner bar.

Helen didn't exactly wave me over to her table, but she did cut to the chase: "What did you want to see me about?"

"Your sister," I said, taking off my jacket.

"What about her?" she asked.

"I just wanted to know what she said to you about her time at Drake Media."

Helen swished the cubes in her drink. I would have thought that the Crossbow Inn would serve their drinks in metal goblets. "That's what everyone wants to know."

"Like who?"

"The police have talked to me. The Department of Energy,"

"Really?"

"Yes. A couple of detectives talked to me on the day she died, and the lead person at the department is in trouble," she said, flailing her hand south, towards Detroit. "Kelly something or other."

I tried to lead her slightly. "Is it because of the time you spent at Ener-X?"

The waitress interrupted our discussion and took my drink order. Helen said she'd have another.

"Not exactly, but I will say that Cecil Garl was a real jerk. I'm not surprised he ended up with a bullet in his head."

"What made you think it was his head?"

"It wasn't?" she acted surprised.

"No. Two in the chest."

My revelation seemed to buckle her knees, but I wasn't here to make her feel worse than she already did. All I wanted to do was glean information. "That reminds me, Helen. The note that Becky left you, I have a copy of it right here." I pulled the note from my back pocket. It was a hard copy of a photo that Colleen had taken with her camera. Before I could unfold it, Helen nearly ripped it from my hands.

"I'll take that," she said, eyes teeming with curiosity.

The waitress emptied her tray on our table: tonic water for me and a screwdriver for the lady. While Helen's eyes darted back and forth across the page, I slipped the waitress a twenty and said that I'd be paying for all our drinks.

Helen grunted slightly and shook her head. The note was tugging at her emotions, I could tell. She reached into her purse and pulled out a slightly worn tissue. A second later, she dabbed it to her bottom eyelid.

A couple of regulars at the bar caught my attention. They were laughing and backslapping about something important. It couldn't have been the golf channel or the weather on the two televisions.

"Oh, man, you don't know how bad I wanted to read this," Helen said.

"I can only imagine."

"You should have turned it over to the police on the day she died."

"I know," I said, "that was my biggest mistake."

"Well, why didn't you?"

"I don't have a good excuse, other than I had broken down on the side of the road and my ride was there to pick me up. The traffic was terrible that day and I would have had to cross it on foot in order to get to the cops."

"Why didn't you give it to me on the day of her funeral?" she asked.

"I didn't have it then."

Helen frowned. "Why do I get the feeling that you're not telling me the whole story?"

"Because of what's on page two."

"There's more?"

"Yes. Much more."

"Well, give it to me!"

"I will, Helen, I just have to know more about Cecil Garl."

Helen took a sip of her drink. "What is it? I only worked there a short while."

"I heard he was a leg man."

"No doubt about it. We couldn't wear pants. The women had to wear dresses."

"Did you ever see a man named Shafeek Heanley around the office?"

She nodded, affirmatively. "Not a whole lot, but I remember the name."

"What did he do there?"

"I don't know if that's a really good question."

"Why's that?"

"Well," she said, sipping her drink, "it's not like he worked there in an official capacity."

"So, in other words, he didn't draw a paycheck."

"That's right, but I saw him in there quite often."

"What about Robert Luxton?"

"Yeah, he was there, too, probably more than Shafeek. I don't know what else to tell you about my time at Ener-X. They were crooks. Them and the government both."

I could tell that she didn't want to talk, or at the very least, didn't want to talk to me about her time with Cecil. That was fine. The more I looked at her, the more I thought she was the aggressor in the secret bathroom scene on Cecil's secret zip drive. I guess it didn't matter now.

"Are you going to show me page two?"

"Of course," I said, reaching into my other pocket.

"I don't know why you have to keep me in suspense like that. It was my sister who died, you know. How about a little compassion?"

I acknowledged her complaint with a nod of my head. She was right; I should have been a little more understanding.

As she read the second page and twisted her studded earrings, I took a sip of my drink.

"What the hell," she said angrily. "I suppose you're going to try and shake me down for more information before you tell me what the letter to the *Free Press* was all about."

"No, I have that right here."

I felt a little like Monte Hall when he used to tempt the guests with what was behind door number one, two or three. In this case, the letter to the *Free Press* was in my shirt pocket.

Of course, it took Helen more than a minute to digest everything.

"Where's the zip drive?"

"I have it at home."

"Wouldn't the police like to see it?"

"I'm sure."

"Why don't you give it to them?"

"I need the reward money just as much as everybody else."

"What the hell, Mr. Twitchell, I need the money too."

My face made a contorted smile. "Helen, you're not eligible for the winnings, I'm afraid. I checked the rules on the *Free Press'* website, and since Becky is the one who wrote the letter, she's the one who has to collect."

"That figures," she sighed.

"What about her comment in the letter about the company hassling her?"

"That's true. You wouldn't believe how bad it was."

"Please, Helen. I want to hear about it."

She took a deep breath, held it for a second, then let it go. "Where do I start?"

Instead of interrupting her, I let her sort everything out inside her head.

"About ten years ago, things started going south, I'd say. The company hired a security analyst who changed how things were done around Drake Media. They started monitoring the employees' computers and eavesdropping on their emails. They even installed a jamming device on campus that made it impossible to use cell phones inside the company buildings."

"How did that work?"

"I don't know how it worked, but it's the same technology that makes your phone useless when you go into a concert hall."

"I never noticed."

"Ever been to a concert or a performance at the Soaring Eagle or Little River?"

"Of course."

"It just kills your cell phone inside."

"What else?"

"Oh, they made the employees sign confidentiality notices,"

"What's wrong with that?"

"Nothing, I guess, but that practice was right out of the blue. Becky thought it was the about the time they started doing things that were a little sideways with the law."

"Like what?"

"I think Drake Media realized they could get more money if they tried to elect people who were sympathetic to the green energy cause. Cecil Garl was the ring-leader. He's the one who saw the value in having elected officials in his back pocket."

"There's nothing wrong with making campaign donations, right?"

"You're right, but these guys took it too far. They took the government people on trips and junkets, but they also directed business to the husband of the woman at the department."

I scratched my chin. "What kind of business did he have?"

"They made their own granite. Synthetic granite. Countertops, flooring, all that."

I almost tossed my cookies. Granite seemed to be everywhere: in the restroom at Ener-X, inside the Devil's Elbow, and at the Manhattan Manor. If I put some thought on it, I'm sure I could come up with some other places, too. Shafeek, Cecil Garl, and Robert Luxton couldn't just bribe Kelly Mathers herself; they had to pad the pockets of her husband, as well. These guys were serious.

"That granite business really didn't have anything to do with your sister, did it?"

"No, until they started tapping her phones."

"What do you mean?" I asked.

"Becky became so suspicious of what was going on, that she hired a private investigator."

"Seriously?"

"Heck, yeah. It was a crazy time in her life."

"What were the results?"

Helen slugged her drink. "He found a transmitting device in her phone at home, and one of those cameras that you can bury in a potted plant or a box of tissue."

"You don't say..."

"And he knew someone at the National Security Agency who said her texts were being monitored."

"Why?"

"The PI was very vague about that. All he would say is *suspicious activity*."

"Did he have a report, or did Becky just tell you about it?"

"Oh, he put together a big report. It was huge. Becky kept it in her file cabinet. I saw it in there several times."

"How did Becky feel when she realized that the government might be spying on her?"

"She was distraught, obviously. I know that she had poured her heart and soul into that company, but the company really turned on her. I don't know what I would do if I were in her shoes."

Helen seemed to pluck a distant memory from the fog of time, "Like I said, it was a crazy time in her life."

"Are you talking about her husband?"

"Yes. The bastard was cheating on her."

"I remember Becky said that. She said he was messing around with some floozy."

"You got it. Becky put the PI on him for a few days."

"Wasn't that expensive?"

"She told me that the investigator had a five-day minimum. He only used up three days with the phone tapping and the NSA, so she decided to put a tail on her hubby and the other woman."

I nodded. "That was smart."

"He caught them doing a little kayaking down the Jordan River up north."

"Together-together?"

"Complete with a picnic," she nodded. "He caught them having a candlelight, whitefish dinner up at Terry's Place Restaurant in Charlevoix, too."

"That stinks."

She shook her head, "No, whitefish is very mild. It doesn't stink."

"That's not what I meant…"

"I know what you meant—that her husband was cheating on her."

"That's right. Who was it?"

"Who was what, Derrick?"

"Who was the floozy?" I raised my voice.

Helen dipped an index finger in her drink and gave the cubes a swirl. They sounded like marbles. "I don't know. Becky said she was a reporter of some kind. At least she worked at a paper up there."

"Really…" My heart jumped into high gear. I felt it pounding to revelation's delight.

"She couldn't have been too successful if she worked as a reporter. Aren't most reporters poor, money grubbers who will sell their souls just to cover a story?"

"That's what I've heard," I said, grimacing.

Helen kept her cool so I asked her another question: "Do you think the reporter's name could have been Dorothy…Dorothy Kalakay?"

"I think so," she said, pulling on the last of her drink, "I think you're right about that."

"Lovely. Simply lovely."

Thirty-Six

At nearly seven thirty, Helen and I had finished our business, so I decided to head for home. It had been a long, but exciting day. My broken wrist had started to ache, and I figured that it was because I didn't take the doctor's advice and have it elevated. As I tooled along I-75 with my wrist resting upright on the console, past the exits for Flint, Birch Run, and Bridgeport, I kicked myself for not asking more questions about her interview with Detectives VanWyk and Nutting. I just hate getting sidetracked.

The miles clipped along. My head was on a swivel as I took in the view. When I passed over the Zilwaukee Bridge, I couldn't help but look north, into the marshy, flooded breeding grounds for mallards, wood ducks and Canada geese. If they weren't already hatched, there must have been a thousand waterfowl eggs being incubated beneath their mother's downy fluff at that very instant. Further north, near the exit for Bay Road, I noticed red-winged blackbirds sparring for their own parcel of cattails. They must have had some territorial battles to dispute, because they chased and scuffled with each other as if their lives depended on it. In the big picture of life, I'm no different from the ducks in the marsh, or the blackbirds in the cattails: pick out a mate, stake your claim, raise your young, and make a living as best you can.

Instead of turning west on US-10—towards home—I made an impulsive decision and turned east in the direction of Becky's storage locker. There was a good chance that VanWyk and Nutting wouldn't know about the private investigator or his report in Becky's possession. If they had taken an inventory of her belongings, they might not have seen it. At the very least they might have dismissed it as irrelevant. It was just a hunch that I was playing, but since I was in the neighborhood, I might as well make a stop.

When I pulled into the compound, the place was nearly abandoned. A tawny cat with a fluffy tail scrambled across the gravel path ahead of me, hopped the chain-link fence, and disappeared into the woods on the other side. The cat's presence must have upset the chipmunks in the woods because I heard them chirp and squeal as I hopped out of the car and approached Becky's storage bin. There was hardly anybody around, so I left the windows rolled down and the keys in the ignition. It never occurred to me that I should use rubber gloves when I grabbed hold of the lock and gave the tumblers a twirl. Heck, rubber gloves probably wouldn't have fit over my cast anyway.

After two or three attempts at the lock, it snapped open. A sigh of relief poured from my lips as I placed the lock on the trunk of the Impala. A glance to the left, another to the right, and the coast was clear.

I grabbed hold of the door handle and gave it a mighty heave. When I did, the door skittered up its tracks, revealing an ungodly vision.

Four steps inside was a body, wedged alongside a dresser, next to a coffee table, and covered in a drop cloth.

"Holy hell," I said to myself.

Covering my mouth when I see something awful is almost second nature to me. The trouble with that reaction is that my right hand had a cast on it. Instead of covering my mouth—aghast with shock—I bopped myself in the lips and nearly broke my nose, too. The pain stung badly as I tasted the salty warmth of my own blood. I didn't want to spit—for fear of leaving my DNA—but I hated the taste just the same.

It's hard to be a professional in every occasion, but I try my best.

I took another look around to see if anyone was watching. The enclave was all mine.

"Sir?" I asked of the corpse.

It didn't move.

His shoes were leather, newer, and looked like they could have been some kind of Topsider, size ten or eleven. Closer I stepped—like a deer hunter to a fallen buck—with caution and concern. I was afraid that he might jump up and run away.

"Pardon me," I said, stepping closer.

Of course, he didn't answer. A pair of khaki pants were above his shoes; the hems sporting cuffs as thick as ribeye steaks. Where the trousers met a belt buckle, the drop cloth started. It covered his chest and head in a wrinkled, disheveled heap. Near the top, a stain of blood had soaked through the cloth. It made a bizarre pattern that looked like it had been poured from a cup.

Who could this be? I thought to myself. *One of the detectives? The storage facility's caretaker? Or was it just an enormous hoax?*

"Hey," I said, tapping him on the heel. "Are you okay, sir?"

The body never moved, or flinched, or lifted a tentative finger. The drop cloth didn't swell or drop with his faltering breaths.

I grabbed hold of the coffee table and pushed it towards the file cabinet. Now all that lay before me was the drop cloth and the body.

Slowly, I pulled the cloth away. The man's shirt was long sleeve, white cotton. The cuffs weren't cuffs at all, but rather hemmed cotton. It was a long sleeved tee-shirt.

Higher and higher I lifted the cloth. The emblem on the left breast, Ducks Unlimited. On the right—just below the clavicle—a pinky-sized hole and a nasty blot of spilt blood.

Smelling the odor of rotting bodily fluids brought to mind the stench I had witnessed up at the Devil's Elbow. My left hand slowly pulled away the cloth; my right partially shielded the view. His neck and Adam's apple were clean shaven; his mouth slightly open.

Opening the door to the locker must have been like ringing the dinner bell to the neighborhood flies. There were swarms of them now, and the buzz of their wings seemed to reverberate inside the facility's makeshift chuck wagon. They climbed inside his mouth and blotted the blood with their tongues that had trickled to his ears.

I pulled away the cloth. It looked like his forehead had been hit with the same sized bullet that had penetrated his chest. I wondered if this person saw the bullet coming at him; after all, his eyes were still beaming straight ahead. They had lost the glossy hue of life; now they looked like they had been wrapped in wax paper.

No need to search for a pulse. He was deader than a doornail.

The mystery man wasn't either one of the detectives, the caretaker, or even Shafeek Heanley. I recognized the curve of his face, the pointed, distinct hairline. It was Robert Luxton, himself.

"Damn," I said under my breath.

The scene almost took my breath away, but it was second nature to whip out my camera and start taking photos. I took a close up of his face, then his torso, and last, his whole body. As I checked each photo and lamented about the phone's dying battery, I stepped backwards toward the open door. The coast was still clear.

I'm no forensic expert, but it appeared as if he wasn't shot inside the locker. No blood spattered on the sheets behind him. Nothing on the wall, either. I wasn't sure where the bullets ended up, but I guess it really didn't matter now. It only took a minute to come up with a theory about how the murder took place. He was probably shot somewhere else, wrapped in a sheet, and his body dumped inside the locker.

If only Luxton could talk. Did he beg for mercy or did he defy the shooters until the very end? Was it his business relationship with Shafeek that caused his murder, or was it some other reason that caused his demise?

I touched his front pants pockets. They were cold and lifeless, but it appeared as if he had a set of keys and a few coins inside. I straddled him, then grabbed hold of his belt buckle. With all my might, I pulled up. When I did, Mr. Luxton uttered a slow, guttural sigh. It was if I had chased the remaining air from his lungs.

Undaunted, I was able to fish his wallet out of his rear pocket.

Inside the wallet was five hundred fifteen dollars, a Visa, Discover, and a Shell credit card, a stack of assorted business cards, his driver's license, a boat registration, a concealed carry permit for a twenty-five caliber, a family photo, and some handwritten information about his children. I'm one of those people who can't remember their kids' date of birth and social security numbers; it appeared as if Mr. Luxton needed a little cheat sheet as well.

On the flip side of the paper were more notes. They looked like passwords for his on-line accounts: Edward Jones, PNC Bank, Amazon, and Ticketmaster. At the bottom of the sheet of paper were three numbers, 12-22-06, which could have been another person's date of birth or a combination to a safe or padlock.

I wasn't sure what to make of it, so I switched gears and took a closer look at the business cards. Most of them seemed to be related to Drake Media and his personal life: a trucking company from Holland, another from Webberville; a snow plow service up in Paradise; paper mills from Traverse City, Ada, and Munising; and an ink wholesaler from Portage. I was half expecting that maybe I'd see a card from Kelly Mathers, but the closest thing I got to any government employee was for Detective VanWyk. It was the freshest card in the bunch, and it made me wonder how long it had been in his possession.

I tucked everything but two hundred dollars back inside his leather wallet and set it on the concrete floor next to his hip.

His other rear pocket didn't have a phone, which kind of bummed me out. It could have revealed the most about his life and who he kept in contact with. One thing was for certain: Robert Luxton would never be confessing to the murder of the Garl family up north. Dead men tell no tales.

Who murdered the Garl family?

Better yet, who killed Robert Luxton?

This gruesome discovery had me worried. I couldn't get caught here. I couldn't be found tampering with the evidence. VanWyk and Nutting would kill me if they knew I was contaminating a murder scene. The prosecutor's case would be crumbling with the way I had picked apart the information in his wallet and meddled with his body.

My mind was a blur of details, theories and hypotheses. It was just about that time that I realized that another vehicle was on the gravel drive and headed in my direction.

What the hell, I yelled inside my head.

In an instant, I reached up to the overhead door and slammed it shut. It was dark and humid inside the tin-and-concrete box, but I figured it was my best play under the circumstances. My thinking was that the car would pass; I'd casually reopen the door and go about my business like everything was hunky-dory. I listened carefully as the car noise came closer and closer. Instead of passing the Impala, however, it stopped just short.

Damn, I screamed silently.

I listened to its engine purr, and the subtle click from the air conditioner's condenser as it dripped water onto the rocky drive. It was warm outdoors, even warmer inside the sardine-can borders.

At last, I heard the car door open, and the sounds of feet shuffling on gravel.

I kept waiting for the footsteps to engage the lock on the neighbor's vault, but they didn't. At any second, the door on my left, across the gangway, or down the block would be rifling up its tracks, I was hoping.

For a second or two I regretted being inside the storage locker, instead of outside. It was dark, and warm, and buzzing with flies. I should have ducked beneath the door and talked my way out of whatever trouble awaited.

Too late.

When the lock snapped shut on the outside of the door, it sounded like the locks shutting on the vault at Fort Knox. It was loud and cloaked in authority.

"No!" I screamed, but it didn't do any good.

When I yanked on the door, it was stuck.

"Who are you?" I yelled, banging on the door. "Why did you do this?"

Whoever it was on the other side ignored me, just like I knew they would. Their car backed down the drive, out of sight, out of earshot and out of my grasp.

Now I was alone and trapped inside a little jail cell full of antiques and a dead body.

I tried to imagine who might have been on the other side. The first person who came to mind was Helen. I had just given her the suicide note. Perhaps she wanted to find out for herself what was inside her sister's locker. When she saw the door closing, she might have guessed that it was being robbed. It made sense that she trapped whoever was inside. My Impala had no relevance to her and could have thought I was an intruder.

If that was the case, the police would be along at any moment. It's not every day that a Good Samaritan traps a thief inside a storage locker. For all I knew, she could have been idling fifty yards down the gravel driveway waiting for the sirens and the patrolman to show up.

When I pulled out my phone and tapped the screen, it illuminated my little jail cell. The setting was creepy and desperate all at the same time. I don't know how much longer my phone might last, but it didn't look like long.

Without hesitation, I texted Colleen: *If you happen to be in the Bay City area, I could really use your help.*

Instead of lamenting my bad luck, I used the phone's remaining life to scurry through the folders in the filing cabinet. Becky had tons of files related to her income taxes, her home assessments and the foreclosure, a kitchen remodeling project, and photographs of her family. Behind the folder for "Attorney", I found what I was after: the file from "The Kaatz Group." It was made out of thick cardstock, and on the front was a picture of a magnifying glass resting on a pair of gentleman's leather gloves. In small writing beneath the graphic were the words, *private investigation & security consultants.*

I tucked the file under the back of my shirt, and looked around for a sledgehammer, a spade,, or a crowbar. Nothing.

Jim Rockford would never have been caught in this predicament. He would shut the door behind him—not in front of him—and wiggle out of trouble with a silver tongue and the smoothest of moves. At the end of the day, I guess I'm no Jim Rockford.

The only light inside the chamber were the slivers that penetrated from the edge of the door, which would be fading fast with the setting sun. I wasn't sure about my next move: try to escape or serve my time in solitary confinement?

The longer I looked up at the ceiling and remembered what the outside of the building looked like, the more I realized that there were probably two-by-four rafters over my head. A sloped roof must have been supported by wood trusses. The metal ceiling inside the locker had to have been screwed to the joists that separate each partition.

My mind started working again the way it always does when the chips are down and desperation is at hand. Instead of smashing the door down, I decided to go up, through the ceiling and amongst the rafters and the inner workings of the building. The office was at the far end; and if I could make my way there safely, freedom awaited.

Instead of searching for a hammer, I grabbed an old fashioned dairy jug that looked like an overgrown fire extinguisher. I hopped on a kitchen table and put the coffee table on top of that. My left hand provided the muscle; my right the direction. The first blow dented the ceiling, while the second ripped the overhead screw from its mooring. I heard it plink on the metal ceiling plate, then roll down the slope.

Six or eight breathless bashes later, I wiggled into the attic, which was cloaked in spider webs and the stagnant grit of concrete dust.

The office was maybe fifty, or a hundred, feet away. Its light glimmered a ray of hope. All I had to do was hop down, unlock the door, and be on my merry way.

The rafters were wood all right, and they were spaced perfectly for a rapid getaway. I felt a little like Tarzan the way he swung through the jungle vines in perfect rhythm.

When I approached the office, I realized that it was command central for the compound's security system. In fact, a camera was mounted in the corner, pointing down—through a small hole in the false ceiling—and into the office itself.

After several seconds of thought, I decided to unscrew the cable from the back of the camera, and remove one of the panels from the ceiling.

The camera was mounted on a rather elaborate frame that was wedged between two joists. Its lens was long and skinny and about the size of a pencil eraser. I unscrewed the cord from the back of the camera, and the little red light turned off.

Three minutes later I had dropped from the ceiling into the office and was busy checking out the monitors related to the security system. There appeared to be four cameras on the premises—one near the entrance, two pointed down each aisle, and a fourth that was blank. Each view was depicted on a monitor the size of a computer screen. I assumed that the blank quadrant was for the camera that I had dismantled.

It was rather weird to see my Impala resting comfortably in the aisle, oblivious to the massacre that was lurking behind the metal door. I felt the need to rescue it.

The mystery car was nowhere to be seen. Whoever locked me inside the locker was long gone, unless they were waiting for the cops outside of the camera's view.

The gravity of the situation suddenly hit me. I was in deep trouble even though I really hadn't done much wrong. It wasn't me who killed Robert Luxton or the Garl family. The only thing I did wrong was a little malicious destruction of property, but I could see that a judge or a jury would be sympathetic once I explained what had taken place. A reasonable person would want to get out of that locker; the course of action I took was quite rational under the circumstances.

On the other hand, I was dying to know who might have trapped me inside. The images on the television screen would tell the entire story.

Trouble was, I didn't know where the images were being captured. The cable from the back of the monitor snaked its way to a black box on top of a dusty computer tower beneath the rickety wooden desk. It was covered in coffee cup rings in varying degrees of decay. I grabbed hold of the computer mouse, cleared away the papers, and gave it a swish. The desktop icons popped into view; almost covering the entire screen.

Quite a few of the icons were taken by the security system itself. I clicked on one and without hesitation, a video jumped to life. The date and time were indicated in the lower left and lower right corners. In between, I noticed the word "Equa-Vision," which must have been the name of the company that patented the system.

The screen was split into four quadrants, just like it was now. I watched as a car pulled in the front gate, then turned down one of the driveways. A second car followed the same path as the first several seconds later. Just as the woman climbed out of her car and unlocked the door to her locker, the second vehicle roared to a stop. Three men jumped out of the second car and approached the woman. They looked like they were up to no good, the way they tried to surround her. As they moved in for the kill, the woman pulled a handgun from under a baggy blouse and pointed it at one of the men. His hands immediately went in the air, and I could almost hear him say, "Whoa, whoa, whoa."

The guys jumped back in their car and sped off. The whole scene only took one or two minutes, but it was important enough for the owner of the storage facility to save it.

All the videos had something to do with Equa-Vision. After several pensive seconds, I found an Equa-Vision icon on the desktop.

Thankfully, it wasn't password protected, so I gave it a click.

I glanced up at the monitor. The resident cat had reappeared. It trotted along the edge of the chain link fence, carrying what looked like a chipmunk in its jowls.

Accessing a strange computer program was a little out of

my realm of expertise, but I tried my best. The computer's motor sounded as if it was powered by gerbils on a treadmill. It grunted and groaned free of inertia.

I wanted to get out of that office in the worst way, while at the same time, I was dying to know who had trapped me inside.

Gradually, the Equa-Vision program came to life. It interrupted the silence with an ominous, three-tone gong as if it was signaling judgment day. Maybe it was.

I clicked the tab for "real time" and the computer screen was a match to the monitor. A tiny arrow at the bottom right of the screen let me know where I was in the timeline. When I pulled the arrow several inches to the left, it gave me a date of three days prior. As soon as I let go of the cursor, it played what was being recorded at that specific instant. Really nifty stuff. With the tiniest of moves on the timeline, I was able to decipher what was going on at that moment in time.

I kept thinking to myself that this was going to be easy as pie. All I had to do was back the device up to the precise time, and let the images on the screen solve a couple of mysteries.

For a second or two, I couldn't decide which felony I should solve first: Luxton's murder or my entrapment.

Go for the easiest one first, I thought to myself.

I clicked on the timeline, maybe a quarter inch away from the far right side. The time on the monitor was 2 a.m. A smidgen more to the right and the images jumped eight hours.

"Come on," I said to myself.

My third move to the right lopped off three hours more. There must have been a better way to do this, but under the circumstances, I didn't have time to mess with it. Finally, I managed to queue the right time. It seemed weird to see myself driving into the premises, my cast hand working the phone.

As I jumped out of the car and nervously glanced right and left, I looked like I could have been escaping Alcatraz.

When I whacked myself in the chops, it sent my head reeling backwards in a fit of surprise and pain. I shook my head again and felt the scab on my upper lip.

Minutes passed.

I relived the horror inside the locker walls and smelled the smell of death all over again.

Finally, I saw myself poke my head outside.

The mystery person would be along at any second.

I held my breath and waited. A drum roll or climatic music should have been heard.

It was Dottie.

What the hell is she doing here?

She was as cool as a block of ice the way she rolled into the compound, sunglasses pressed to her face.

I watched her make the gentle turn from camera number one onto camera two. It was hard to see the locker's door close, but from Dottie's perspective she must have seen what was going on. Her Subaru coasted to a stop behind my Impala. While I was sweating bullets behind the door, Dottie casually exited her car, grabbed the lock from my trunk, and snapped it to the bracket. She did it with the same casual nonchalance as if she was checking the mail. Without an ounce of remorse, she slid into her car and backed down the drive.

There was no way she could deny knowing that it was me.

She knows what kind of car I drive and had to have known that it was me she had trapped.

How could she be so cruel?

How could she be so mean?

As she drove away on camera one, I couldn't help but start to add everything up where she was concerned. There were lies upon lies, half truths, and outright deceptions.

Her car wasn't stolen. Heck, she drove it to the compound.

She was sleeping with Becky's husband. I had the proof in the Kaatz' report.

Instead of rescuing me, she trapped me inside.

My goodness, this woman was nothing but bad news.

I'm glad I didn't sleep with her.

What was I thinking?

Somebody had to stop this person, and quick. That somebody was me.

Thirty-Seven

At nearly midnight that evening, my headlights finally plowed a hole through the shadows on the darkened driveway of home. My trusty dog trotted out of the garage, wagging his tail spastically and barking the barks of "Welcome, welcome, welcome." He was such a good boy for not chewing up the shoes and boots that were lying beside the back door, or running away from home out of sheer boredom. I patted him on the head, spoke to him lovingly, and made sure his collar for the underground fence wasn't too tight. Maybe I'm an evil person for keeping things from a loved one, but I didn't have the heart to tell him that the electric fence had been shut off months ago.

The key for the back door was still at the bottom of the empty popsicle box inside the upright freezer. Together, Jacque and I went inside. The neighbor kid had put the mail on the kitchen counter just as I had instructed. He had found the fifty dollar bill I left for him, too.

House and home seemed fine until I turned the corner, and saw that the front door was missing part of its jamb. A twelve-inch chunk of wood trim was lying on the hardwood floor, cracked and splintered.

Who did this?

The first person to come to mind was the youngster from next door. *Wait a second,* I thought, *why would he do that when he knew the key was in the popsicle box?*

I turned on the porch light, opened the front door, and had a look around. The secret camera was still hidden in the holly bush, pointing up in my direction. When I took one step off the threshold, the motion light tucked under the soffit illuminated the area.

Where the front door lock met the jamb, someone had wedged the pointy end of a crowbar into the crack. They must have given the bar a mighty heave because the indentation on the jamb was almost a half an inch deep.

Casually, I walked to the back of my car and popped the glovebox open. A second later, the cartridge clicked into place and I worked the action so that a bullet was in the chamber. If someone was still inside the house, they'd have a heck of a wakeup call.

It can't be the neighbor kid, I thought to myself. *He wouldn't have done that in a million years.*

I tiptoed back inside. The family room was clear. So was the kitchen. When I poked my nose inside the den, however, the place was a mess. Someone had rifled through our possessions. There were envelopes, tax returns, bank statements, and stamps strewn all over the floor. The cords and wires for the computer tower were lying on the carpet, unscrewed and abandoned.

Jacque put his nose down and was sniffing the carpet as if there was a pheasant somewhere under the padding. I was thankful he was okay, and that my family was still out of town. Part of me wished that Jacque could speak, and that he'd tell me who had done all this terrible damage.

It was an awful feeling, but in an indescribable way, poetic justice for the way I had broken into so many places myself.

This was no time to let my guard down; however, the computer under the desk was gone. The checkbooks and zip drives I kept in the top, middle drawer were missing, too. I gripped the gun a little tighter. My left hand was wringing wet, and I noticed the way the barrel had a bit of a tremor.

As I climbed the stairs, thoughts were swirling that the intruder might still afoot. I wasn't sure if I should announce my presence or try to sneak up on him and hold him at bay until the cops arrived. Part of me wanted to be a hero, but on the other hand, I wasn't sure if I had the testicular fortitude to make it happen.

Step by step I climbed. Just as I reached the top of the stairs, Mr. Jacque trotted past me and into the bedroom, wagging his tail profusely.

So much for a sneak attack.

Had there been someone in the bedroom, I'm sure he would have barked or growled.

Thank goodness for man's best friend.

Our bedroom was just as bad as the den. Both nightstands had been disemboweled. The massage oil, lotions, matches, and candles had been strewn all over the floor. *Fifty Shades of Gray* looked like it had been used and abused; its cover laid spread eagle on the floor. The reading lamps were lying broken, helter-skelter. Colleen's beloved Amish comforter was a mess.

There were socks and underwear, tee-shirts and blue jeans everywhere.

Whoever had done this was looking for something. Apparently, I wasn't their size.

Reality hit me. I told Dottie that I had hidden Becky's zip drive in my sock drawer. Was she the one who had done this? Good heavens, this woman was mad.

Colleen's jewelry box was still intact. Most of the goodies were still inside.

After a short while of picking things up and putting them back together, it occurred to me that maybe I was destroying the evidence that had been left behind. There may have been fingerprints the cops could have used.

"What the heck, Jacque?"

Of course, he didn't answer. He stood in the piles of clothing as if they were round bales of hay in his very own barnyard. The confusion and clutter didn't bother him a bit. He looked up at me like a miniature Hereford bull; white face and curly chest hair and all. All he had to do was jam his tongue in a nostril and the imitation would have been complete.

I thought about calling the cops, but really didn't want to. It took two or three hours to give my statement to them in Bay City and I was emotionally drained from the experience. VanWyk and Nutting could be a little overbearing.

I had been inside the storage facility's office for quite a little while, figuring out how to operate the security system. My goal was to record two tracks: Mr. Luxton's body dump, and the part about Dottie locking me inside. Both instances would help keep me out of trouble and the cops' attention on somebody else. After turning off the computer, then turning it back on, I figured out that all I had to do was click and drag part of the timeline. Most of the action was saved on my zip drive, which was still in my pocket.

I had called the two detectives to the storage locker's office, and together with the manager of the facility we scrolled through the video surveillance system. It was high drama there for a while. All four of us huddled around the monitor as if it was the final afternoon of the Masters golf tournament.

The first part we watched was my arrival at the storage locker. My nervous mannerisms told everyone in the room that I had no business being there.

When I opened the door and bopped myself in the face with my cast, everyone laughed.

"That's why my lip is all busted up," I told them. "It's not every day you see a dead body."

Instead of bolting to the storage facility, VanWyk and Nutting stayed with the images on the screen. Together, we watched the whole situation unfold.

I didn't feel the slightest bit shy about ratting out Dottie.

When her Subaru pulled into view on camera number one, I pointed to the screen and almost shouted, "That's Dorothy Kalakay."

Nutting was scribbling notes on a piece of paper. VanWyk had an IPad.

The tension was cut by the manager: "I know who you are. You're Becky's neighbor, aren't you?"

The two detectives looked up from the monitor momentarily.

I felt the blood rush to my face.

"You're the one who paid her security deposit," he chimed in again. "It was a little better than a week ago."

"That was me." My head was reeling in what my next statement should be. Deflection is always my biggest helper: "Watch this now," I pointed to the screen. "I'm inside bin two-twenty-four and I just closed the door."

The detectives' attention went back to the screen just as Dottie got out of her car and stepped toward the back of the Impala.

"Ms. Kalakay just locked me inside."

Everyone was silent.

"I had no way of getting out, so that's why I had to bust through the ceiling."

"Did you have to unscrew the camera for the office?" the manager asked.

VanWyk and Nutting didn't care about the camera in the corner of the office ceiling. All they cared about was the body of Robert Luxton.

"You say there's a dead body inside that locker?" one of the detectives asked.

"Yes, I saw it with my own eyes. It's Robert Luxton."

"Are you certain?" they asked in unison.

"Yes I'm certain. Don't you want to see how he got inside?" VanWyk and Nutting looked back to the computer screen. "I do too, but I didn't have time to watch it all."

The manager floated a rhetorical question, "How far back do you want to go?"

"Give it a week," I said.

"How about a day?" Nutting suggested. "And if that doesn't work, we'll go back another twenty-four hours."

"You're the boss," the man said, clicking one of the tabs along the edge of the image. "This is exactly twenty four hours ago."

We watched an individual unload some boxes from a rather large trailer into a storage locker three bays north of Becky's.

"Can you hit fast forward?" Nutting asked.

"Sure can," the man said, clicking another tab. "This is ten times as fast, so a twenty-four hour day will take twenty-four minutes."

All of a sudden, the man with the boxes on the screen went into warp speed. The boxes flew off the trailer, and when it was empty, the man sped off as if he had rocket fuel in his Avalanche.

There wasn't much activity on Sunday night. The tawny cat made an appearance. It lounged in the next aisle over from Becky's for quite some time.

"Forget this," Nutting said. "If there's a body in that locker, I want to see it." He stood up from the chair and yanked up his trousers.

VanWyk took the cue and chimed in, "I'll get the yellow tape. We have to secure the area."

Nutting came back with a question for the manager: "Didn't I tell you to put your own lock on the unit when I was here the other day?"

The manager hemmed and hawed, "Yeah, but I've been busy. My aunt died this week."

I was standing in the office, amongst the weed eaters and lawn mowers, chemicals and hand tools, trying my hardest to blend into the surroundings. Nutting popped a piece of chewing gum into his mouth and mashed it angrily between his teeth. After ten or fifteen seconds of silence, he said, "Twitchell, you're coming with me."

Thirty-Eight

To my embarrassment, and shock, Mr. Luxton's body was no longer inside Becky Tocca's locker.

VanWyk and Nutting glared at me like I had just lost my mind. After a minute of listening to my description of what Luxton had looked like, where he had been shot, and the sheet he had been wrapped in, they started hammering me with questions about what color was the shirt, his pants, the sheet, and so on. Our conversation was much louder than it had to be; everyone involved was amped up from the gravity of the situation. At one point, VanWyk put his hand on my upper arm and gave it a squeeze. I got the feeling he was trying to get even with me for dragging him to Bay City when he was probably missing his kid's baseball game. "I don't know what kind of game you're playing here, but this is serious business, Twitchell."

I yanked my arm free and somehow managed to keep my cool. There was no need for intimidation or coercion. "You're going to get the truth, detective," I said, forcefully, "I don't have anything to hide."

After twenty-five questions it occurred to me that I had the greatest proof of all: pictures of the body on my cell phone.

Unfortunately, my camera-phone was dead.

I had seen the look of incredulity before—from Colleen when told her that I didn't give the suicide note to the cops, from Dottie just before she called me a dunce, from the bum on the streets of Greektown when I was lying on the concrete sidewalk, and now from the detectives from the state police. Maybe I am a little off kilter and bend the rules on occasion, but that doesn't make me a cheat, or for heaven's sake, a murderer.

VanWyk and Nutting needed to be reminded that I was the one who called the cops.

They didn't initiate contact, I did.

They let me charge my phone, but insisted that we go back to the office and review everything on the tape. I was thankful for the opportunity to see what took place. After all, it was my credibility on the line.

So, while my phone charged in the Impala, all four of us went back to the office and watched more tape from the previous days' events.

The urgency of the situation came to the fore.

We had to find out who dropped the body and more importantly, who picked it up from under our noses.

The manager took his place at the control panel, and we all watched him play with the knobs and buttons. The trouble was, just about the time he started clicking the buttons on the computer, it occurred to us that I had inadvertently shut off the machine's recording feature.

"What did you do?" the manager yelled at me as if I was a referee in a high school basketball game and I had made a bad call.

There was no way I'd wiggle out of this. "Nothing. It was just right there. Me and my zip drive."

"How did you stop recording?"

"I didn't."

Nutting and VanWyk were getting angry. I could see it in their eyes and sense it in the way they mashed their teeth. They made me feel like a petulant child. Maybe deep down I am.

"I don't believe this," the manager blurted out. "How could you be so stupid?"

"Hey watch it, tough guy," I said. "We wouldn't be in this mess if you had secured the area with your own padlock."

"You think this is my fault?"

"Gentlemen, please," VanWyk interrupted us. "Knock it off, will you? It's not helping at all." It's probably a good thing the cops were there, because I was really getting sick and tired of the manager's mouth. "Forget about tonight," VanWyk said, "just take us back another twenty-four hours, will you?"

The manager went back to the keyboard. With one stroke of the mouse, we were transported back in time, to the previous day. He clicked another tab and the image on the screen went into warp speed.

Twenty-four minutes later, the manager clicked again, and he had lopped off another date on the calendar. That made it two days.

I was starting to get a little antsy. We all were. The feeling was the same as first-time dads in the maternity ward of the hospital. At any second the nurse would deliver a glorious bundle of joy.

Shortly into the second twenty-four hour period, VanWyk cried, "Right there!"

We all huddled around the computer screen as the manager backed up the time, then adjusted the playback so it proceeded at normal speed. Instead of starting when the car pulled up to locker two-twenty-four, the manager hit reverse until the vehicle had entered the compound.

"Who is that guy?" Nutting asked.

I stared intently at the screen. The glare off the lens was rather strong and the man behind the wheel of the car had on a pair of sunglasses. It was difficult to see what kind of car it was, let alone the identity of the driver. When the car made the turn from camera one to camera two, there was no denying the brand: Lincoln.

"See if you can zoom in on the license," Nutting said.

The manager followed directions, but the plate was too blurry. The excuses rained from the sky: "I didn't have time to clean off the lens. We have an old system here..."

I didn't need any prompting. "I'm pretty sure that Mr. Luxton had a Lincoln."

"How do you know that?"

"I just do."

"What color?"

"Brown."

Nutting raised his eyebrows. "Are you sure?"

"Of course, I'm sure. Who do you think I am? Looks like it could be a brown Lincoln on the screen doesn't it, detective?"

He nodded slightly.

We watched the car pull up to the locker and the man jump out of the driver's side door.

There was no mistaking the beard, the long, wiry posture: it was Shafeek Heanley himself.

"That's your man, right there," I said aloud.

"Who is he?"

"Shafeek Heanley."

"How do you know?"

The detectives had become a burr under my saddle. They weren't dealing with some kind of amateur. I was anything but inexperienced and far from a rookie when it came to investigating a murder. "I know all these things. Have you forgotten that I've been investigating this case for a week now?"

Although I didn't necessarily mean to, my question served as the greatest insult imaginable. After all; they had been working the case for almost a year and didn't know that Robert Luxton drove a Lincoln?

"So why would this Shafeek fella be driving Luxton's car?"

"Got me," I said. "Why would he do anything of this sort when he knew that there were cameras on them?"

The questions, theories and conjecture kept floating from

our lips like dialog bubbles in the Sunday funnies. VanWyk and Nutting did the most. I kept my mouth shut and became a giant sponge. It was easy to figure out what they knew. Not a whole lot.

Metaphorically speaking, the *Free Press*' reward money was the carrot that was dangling just out of reach. As much as the detectives would have loved to collect it, they were ineligible. Dottie seemed to be my biggest competition for the reward, and now, she had become a nemesis too.

Shafeek looked to be as cool as a block of ice as he engaged the padlock on the front of the door. He sent the door up its tracks with hardly any effort.

We knew what to expect when he clicked the button to unlock the trunk.

"Here we go, boys," Nutting said.

Instead of a body wrapped in a sheet, Heanley pulled out a rolled up piece of carpet, maybe six feet long. We all surmised that whatever was rolled up in the carpet was quite heavy. Heanley seemed to grunt and groan when he yanked it out of the car.

"What the heck," Nutting wondered. "What's he got in there?"

Heanley disappeared into the locker. Five minutes later he reappeared, still carrying the carpet. Judging by his body language, there was something just as heavy wrapped up inside.

"Are you sure you saw a body in there, Twitchell?"

I shook my head. "Of course, I'm sure."

"Go get your camera."

The guys were demanding, but under the circumstances, I could see why. All of us were being mentally yanked around by Heanley, Dottie, and the remains of Robert Luxton.

I trotted out to my car, pulled it around to the office, and brought the phone inside. As I brought the camera feature to life, I figured that with my luck the images of Luxton's corpse would have magically been deleted.

They were not.

Each shot filled the tiny screen with pale, macabre images. It was Luxton all right, stiff and dead, and caked with blood. VanWyk and Nutting asked me if I'd email the photos to them. I wasn't about to turn them down. My integrity and innocence were on the line.

Nutting suggested that they get the state police's crime lab on the scene. They mentioned that they would look for sheet fibers and DNA on the floor of the locker. After that, they debated about how they were going to notify the next of kin. Since there wasn't a body, or confirmation of a body, they hemmed and hawed about calling their commanding officer just to make sure everything was on the up-n-up.

This was the opening I was after.

"If it's all right with you, fellas, I'm going to head for the hills."

Nutting and VanWyk didn't object. They also said not to go out of town without checking in with them first. What an enormous mess.

I drove from Bay City, west on US-10, past Auburn and the site of Becky's funeral. When I zoomed under the overpass where Becky took her fateful plunge, I never thought that nine days later I would be so involved in the mystery of who killed the Garl family and now Robert Luxton.

It had been a long day. A really long day.

My encounter with the cops in Bay City was emotionally draining. I didn't want to call them about the break in at my house. There would be time to file a second report, if I really wanted to. It was after midnight, and I was exhausted. The burglars may have obtained a handful of zip drives containing blueprints for my mom's new kitchen, and the photos from a family vacation, but they weren't going to get what they were after: the zip drive Becky created was hidden in a shoebox above the washer and dryer.

Besides, I'd find out soon enough who broke into my house when the remote cameras were purged.

Thirty-Nine

At nearly twelve thirty, Jacque was eager to go outside again, even though he couldn't technically follow me down the long driveway. Brittanys—especially male Brittanys—have an independent, mischievous streak that prevents them from getting bored when their masters leave them for a day. They don't sulk or carry on in fits of melancholy, but rather fill the hours with faraway dreams laced with great adventure.

After grabbing the camera at the end of the driveway, I found Jacque staring into the darkened treetops, seemingly waiting for a raccoon or an owl to bring him a pheasant to play with.

With that little bob-tailed dog, anything's possible. His imagination is as wild as his master's.

Since the computer had been stolen inside the house, and Dottie had made off with my laptop, I really didn't have many options for accessing the hidden camera's contents. Both cameras would tell me who had broken into the house, I was sure of it.

I put away my sidearm, locked the house, grabbed Becky's infamous zip drive, and let Jacque ride in the backseat. Together we made our way to Wal-Mart at the south end of Mt. Pleasant. As much as he wanted to venture inside the store with me, he could not. For a half second, I pictured him hosing down the end-caps full of Chinese-made tube socks or sniffing hello to the guests who were there in the middle of the night. Every time I go in that place, I look for the people who are dressed in drag, in pink thongs, or jeans that are way too tight. In other words, I keep my eyes peeled for the folks who eventually end up on ghastly emails that float around the internet. Maybe it's just me, but everyone in Michigan seems normal. It's the other states that have a monopoly on the weird people.

It didn't really matter which camera I viewed first, so I decided to dive into the one that was hidden at the end of the driveway. After removing the chip from the back of the unit and loading it into the machine, its images started popping up in the opposite order from which they were taken. In other words, my face was the first image on the screen. The second image was my face behind the wheel of the Impala. The third image was the back end of Dottie's Subaru and the fourth was my former lover herself entering the driveway.

She had pulled in the driveway about two hours before I did. That means she could have dumped Luxton's body in a number of places and had time enough to go to the car wash, too. She would know enough to clean the car so thoroughly that the forensics team at the state police crime lab would have a hard time finding anything that didn't belong. Hard to believe that my former lover was now part of a murder and cover up. This girl was possessed.

She was always a little different, but she was never devious. Could she be a criminal? No way.

Her family seemed normal, and she had plenty of friends. Of course, she loved to drink, but lots of people do. It didn't bother me that she didn't need an excuse to throw a few back. Drinking was her way of enjoying life.

As the photo machine loaded the images, I thought about the pills she used to take: Xanax and Zoloft. The Xanax was for panic disorders, the Zoloft for depression. When she first revealed her conditions to me, she joked that occasionally she'd panic about her depression.

In my wildest dreams, I never would have imagined that she could be so calloused as to lock me inside the locker, or steal Luxton's body from under my nose. Here she was, doing all those terrible things, and breaking into my house, too. I printed the pictures of her and her car at the end of my driveway, then set my sights on the camera from the front door.

The photos were unveiled in the same backwards scenario as the other camera: first it was me standing on the front porch, and then it was Dottie holding an enormous screwdriver. That girl had a lot of guts.

And thanks to the magic of crude photography, she was in a world of trouble.

I didn't stop the inquisition there.

Becky's zip drive and all its folders had a total of one-hundred-fifty-nine pages. I printed them all, twice. One copy would go home with me, the other copy I stuffed in a giant envelope, from the office-supply aisle. The front desk sold me some stamps, and I addressed the envelope to Walter Claety at the office. I marked it "Personal & Confidential" so nobody at the front desk would open it.

I paid for everything and went home, thankful that Colleen and Elizabeth were out of town. It would have been awful if they had been there when Dottie showed up at the door. If Dottie was capable of murdering someone, then breaking into my house, there's no telling what she would have done to my wife and child.

The question remained, however, what should I do now?

Dottie could have been waiting for me somewhere at home, in the garage, or in the front closet. If she had broken into my house once, she could a second time as well.

When I returned to my car and jumped inside, Jacque was happy to see me. He always is.

"What do you think, Jacque?"

Of course, he didn't answer, but I didn't think that he would. Dogs love the sound of their master's voice.

"Should we run for cover or try to get to the bottom of things?"

The little dog with the big heart went spastic. A rhetorical question with an upturned inflection was akin to asking about a long walk or a pheasant hunt.

One thing was for certain; I didn't want to spend the night at home. There'd be nothing worse than to die in my sleep at the hands of a lunatic like Dottie. On second thought, maybe there would be something worse: Dottie stuffing a twelve-gauge down my throat as I wake up from a deep slumber.

Since I am a spur-of-the-moment kind of guy, I decided to re-pack my bags and head north, to Clare. The Doherty Hotel was only fifteen minutes away but I knew that I'd be safe there. Jacque could go with me, and spend the night in the backseat of the car if I couldn't bring him inside.

I didn't care about spending the money; it was all about being safe. Besides, I was playing with "house money." Robert Luxton's hundreds were still in my wallet.

Dottie was no person to mess with. She knew how to use a firearm, could handle herself in a wrestling match, and had plenty of guts, too. After what I had seen on the monitor at the storage facility, it seemed as if she had lost her marbles.

Even though I asked Jacque about paying Dottie a visit, I really didn't have any intention of it. What was I going to say, "Why did you lock me in the storage locker?" Or how about, "Where did you dump Luxton's body?" No, it seemed as if my best course of action was to lay low for a while.

All I wanted to do was collect the hundred grand. Surely, Dottie didn't have anything to do with the Garl murders, did she?

Maybe she did.

As I packed my bags, tidied up the house, and tossed Jacque's provisions into the front seat of my Impala, I realized that I had three items to read before I called it a day. The first were the documents in Becky's zip drive. The second was the private investigator's report from Becky's locker. The third was the Mathers' indictment from earlier in the day.

"Earlier in the day" felt like a lifetime ago. I had spent the previous night south of Port Huron, and then traveled to Detroit, Grand Blanc and Bay City. The miles, the memories, the mayhem in the storage facility had taken their toll.

There was no way I'd get through all that information before I had to sleep.

Even with a cup of coffee and a warm shower, I'd be lucky to make it to Clare.

Strange, though, how adrenalin and motivation can take hold of a person. By the time I roared past Rosebush, I was flying high with paranoia. Every headlight in the rearview mirror was a Subaru, every clump of trees along the side of the road held a suicidal deer that was ready to leap in front of my car. I was the one having the panic attacks; maybe I needed medication.

The woman at the front counter of the Doherty was more than happy to accommodate me, despite the late hour. I paid an extra ten dollars for the pet fee, which seemed more than fair. It was early summer, and Jacque had a tendency to shed.

What the Doherty didn't know is that I would have paid twice as much on that particular night to have Jacque with me. For some reason, I craved companionship, even if it came in the form of a freckle-faced Brittany.

At one-fifteen, Jacque and I were in bed, watching television, and flipping through the piles of paperwork. My mind was already thinking about tomorrow morning's breakfast and whether or not the Doherty would have a waffle machine at the ready. I pictured them covered in whipped cream and sugared, fresh strawberries. The hot coffee, the morning paper, the easy-going ambiance would be just what the doctor ordered after such a hectic pace I had been carrying. I could get used to laying low for a while.

Everything changed, however, when my phone sounded the subtle notice that I had received a text. I was hoping for an electronic goodnight kiss from Colleen or Elizabeth; what I got was an angry notice from Jenna: *Thanks a lot,* she texted. *That witch Dottie just got booted out of the club.*

Oh, no, I replied.

I thought we were speaking off the record the other day?

We were, I responded.

She knows about the fourteen million.

Oh no. A frowned face accompanied my text.

This woman is possessed.

I'm sorry.....what can I do to help?

Jenna never responded.

Hello? I typed, impatiently.

It was too late. She was lost.

Forty

A little before eight the next morning, I took Jacque for a spin around Shamrock Park, just north of the Doherty. It was fun to let him off his leash and watch him torch the afterburners. He was running at mach speed all right, until he came upon a family of Canada geese, who were having a picnic on the lush, green grass twenty yards from the water's edge.

Of course, Jacque only weighs about thirty pounds. He had to look up to see the gander, hissing vile warnings in his direction.

I had to give Jacque credit, though. Even though he was outnumbered, outweighed (by the parents anyway) and outmatched on the geese's home turf, he still gave them a run for their money. He tried pointing, barking, ambushing, and stalking the geese before they finally plopped into the water and paddled away, scot-free.

Maybe that's why the signs in the park read that dogs have to be on a leash.

In a lot of ways, Jacque had the same determination as Dottie. I don't know what Dottie was up to up in Traverse City, but she sure had a lot going on when it came to Robert Luxton, Cecil Garl, and Shafeek Heanley. Two of the three men were dead. Shafeek Heanley was in a world of trouble, and Dottie was up a creek without a paddle. I beat myself up for trusting her the way I did. It seemed foolish on my part, and very naïve.

Before driving back to the Doherty for breakfast, I was overwhelmed with guilt. I felt horrible that Jenna had to deal with Dottie. It was my mess, my disaster that had to be taken care of. Mom always told me to clean up after myself. This was one of those times where I couldn't just ignore the situation. Dottie probably muscled her way inside the strip club and foisted herself upon Jenna. Lord only knows if a cat-fight broke out, or why the bouncer had to throw Dottie out of the establishment.

It made me mad to realize that Dottie had gone up there and wrecked a relationship I had cultivated with Jenna. I take pride in protecting my sources and I'd like to think that my word is golden.

Over a toasted bagel, a Styrofoam bowl of cereal, and a cup of coffee, I thought about driving up north again. At a little after nine I had taken a shower, packed my bags, and tossed everything in the front seat of the Impala. Jacque took up his position in the back seat, and we were off.

Jacque wouldn't mind the road trip; in fact, he probably welcomed the change of pace and the chance to spend a little quality time with the big guy. I had my golf clubs, the fly rod and waders in the trunk. What more could a man need for a spur-of-the-moment kind of adventure to northern Michigan?

If I struck out where Jenna was concerned, I could always hit the links or try to do a little trout fishing.

Jenna might be a hard one to track down. All I knew is that she lived at the Arbors Apartments in Traverse City. When I pulled up the Arbors on the internet, there were hundreds of units at the complex. There may have been a ton of people who lived there, but I bet there was only one convertible Lexus in the whole manor.

It was worth a shot to drive up there. With any luck, I might be able to interview Dottie after she had been picked up by the police. And what the heck, I wanted to get my laptop from her. The darn thing was only a few days old.

By the time we made the sweeping left turn from 27 on to US-10, Jacque had balled himself up in the backseat and had started to snore. I noticed that he smelled a little gamey, and I had written it off as the remnants of his dip in Shamrock Lake. I made a mental note to buy an air freshener the next time I stopped for gas.

It was a perfect June day—sunny and warm—as we charged across the west edge of Clare County. The Impala roared along merrily until I noticed a drake mallard standing on the very edge of the concrete. His mate had just been hit by a car, I assumed, and he stood there, quacking the quacks of sorrow: "Get up, get up, get up." Her brown, drab feathers were blown into the shoulder's grass like the brittle leaves of fall. I was sad to think about his plight, all alone, and her nest full of eggs—forever orphaned.

I don't know how long the mallard situation stayed with me, but it was at least until I left the freeway and started motoring northwest up 115.

A few miles up the road, I spotted a state trooper who had backed his cruiser onto a sandy easement on state land near the Muskegon River. His nose was sticking out of the dense copse of aspens mixed with the thorny canes of blackberry. I held my breath and looked down at the speedometer: sixty-six. There was no reason in the world to be driving eleven miles over the limit, so I stomped on the brake. That was probably a dumb move on my part, but the trooper stayed frozen in his leafy lair.

For the remainder of the trip up north I set the cruise for sixty-four, nine miles over the limit. No sense in tempting fate.

Jacque and I made a pit stop in Cadillac, then continued north on 131—past the turnoff for Manton, and through the sleepy little town of Kingsley.

When we rolled into the apartment complex for the Arbors in Traverse City, I had peeled the wrapper completely off the air freshener we had bought an hour before. Jacque's condition was festering in the sunshine and warm temperatures.

After fifteen minutes of patrolling the apartment complex, I found Jenna's black Lexus sleeping beneath a covered parking structure. 58B was spray painted through a stencil on the wall in front of her vehicle, so I knew exactly where she lived.

I found a shady spot for the Impala, rolled down the windows about two inches, and gave Jacque a pat on the head. He smeared nose prints on the window as I made my way up the stairs to Jenna's apartment. Her door had a giant, brass knocker on it. When I raised the knocker and slammed it into the metal plate, the door clicked slightly open.

"Jenna…" I said.

She didn't answer.

"Jenna!" I said, slightly louder.

A crumpled voice drew me inside. My neck seemed to grow three or four inches as I peered around the cracked, open door. No sign of life in the living room. I recognized the print from Jack Vettriano above her leather sofa. It was a man and a woman dressed in a tux and a long, white gown. They were embraced in a dancer's stance, ready to spin and swirl and engage in musical courtship. Adjacent to the print, a pair of leafy, tall houseplants near the television and the end table gave the room a cozy, jungle effect.

A calico cat trotted down the hallway, then laid down casually on the carpet. The very end of its tail curled slightly, as if it had a nervous tick.

"Jenna…it's Derrick Twitchell. Can I come in?"

More muffled voices.

I stepped inside. Her kitchen was decked out in granite countertops and cherry-wood cabinetry. The cat's bowls were resting on the kitchen tiles. Five straight-backed chairs surrounded her modest kitchen table. It seemed like an odd number.

Slowly, I made my way down the hallway.

"Jenna…" I said again.

Nobody answered.

The wood beneath the carpet creaked slightly as I slid past the bathroom door. I wondered if the bathtub had overflowed in the past, and the water warped the plywood.

"Jenna," I said confidently, "it's Derrick Twitchell. Are you okay?"

Two more steps and I was at her bedroom door.

I looked inside and found Jenna tied to one of the kitchen chairs, a piece of duct tape stretched across each cheek and her mouth.

"Oh, Jenna…" I cried, urgently. "Are you okay?"

Jenna didn't move much until I ripped the tape from her face. She yanked her head in the opposite direction as if to quicken the torture. A white tube sock was stuffed in her mouth. It felt warm and moist when I pulled it out and tossed it on the floor.

Jenna heaved.

"Are you okay?" I asked.

She huffed the unfiltered air. "Yes…"

I reached for the rope behind her. "Let me help you." It was tied fifteen ways to Sunday—around her midriff, her waist and ankles, to the bed, back to the chair. It looked like whoever tied her up used a half hitch around her wrists, which were raw.

"Hurry," Jenna pleaded.

Instead of untying it, I decided to slice it with the knife in my pocket.

"Oh my God," Jenna cried. "Thank you."

I slit the rope from her ankles and she fell to the floor, exhausted.

She laid there for a minute or two while I gathered the rope and cleared away the chair.

Her bedroom was a mess. The mattress was askew and the nightstands tipped over. Her clothes were strewn about, and the dresser drawers open.

I looked down at Jenna, and noticed her pink, silky pajamas. They were summer weight, shorts, and short sleeves. Whoever did this to her waited until Jenna came home and changed her clothes. It had to have been one of her "gentleman" clients.

Not even close.

"That bitch friend of yours."

My heart sank. "Oh, no. What happened?"

Jenna rose to her feet, stiffly, then paraded across the hall to the bathroom. She closed the door behind her.

I figured that Jenna would want some privacy, so I walked back to the living room and locked the front door. If Dottie was on her way back to murder Jenna, she'd have to get past the deadbolt, the chain across the door jamb, and me.

A few minutes later, Jenna had finished her business in the bathroom and made her way to the kitchen. She had found the matching mini-robe for her pajamas, and it was cinched at her tiny waist. I watched her open the refrigerator door and pull out a bottle of water.

"Oh my," she said, somewhat breathlessly, "this tastes so good."

Instead of asking her again about what happened, I let her relish in her recovery.

She rubbed her wrists and placed a leg on the rung of a chair. Her ankles looked like they had been scraped with a rasp.

"Looks painful. Can I get some medicine for you? Maybe some salve or cream?"

She shook her head. "That's okay. I'll get it."

"I'm glad you're okay," I said as sympathetically as I could.

"Me, too. That girl caught me off guard."

"How?"

"She was waiting for me, here."

"So, you went to work dressed like that?"

"Well, not exactly. I came home, changed my clothes, and there she was on the couch, pointing a gun at me."

"How did she get inside?"

"I don't know. She was just there."

"What did she want?"

"Cecil and his fourteen million."

"Cecil's dead, and the fourteen million is ancient history, right?"

"Apparently she didn't get the memo," she said between gulps.

"What did you tell her?"

"Not a whole lot, and only after she tied me up and threatened me with that tube sock."

I shook my head. "I'm so sorry. That must have been terrible. "

"It was…" she lamented. "But it's over now. Time to move on."

"That's a good way to look at it," I said, noticing the red stripe on her face from where the tape ripped her skin. "No sense in dwelling on the past."

She didn't acknowledge my redundancy, and I probably made it worse when I said, "Glad you're okay."

It was almost like she had to get something off her chest when she piped up and remarked, "Cecil ran all that fourteen million through his company in Antigua."

"Why do you say that?"

"Because that's what he did."

"He did?"

"Yeah. He ran all his money through there. That's where he and his family were going the day after they were murdered."

"Why?"

"He called it 'round tripping.' The government paid Ener-X for the green energy contracts, but the checks were never deposited."

"Where did they go?"

"To Antigua."

"I'm confused. What do you mean by 'round tripping'?"

"Instead of running the checks through the books, he made deposits in an offshore account in the Caribbean. The money was then wired to a law firm."

"Why a law firm?" I urged her.

"Because the money coming into a firm is confidential, and the money going out can be distributed as a trust, or proceeds from a legal matter."

"Anything else?" I asked.

"They set it up so that the money was used for a retainer. Since no legal work was ever done, the fees were returned it to Cecil, tax free. No social security tax, no Medicare tax, nothing."

"So why did he call it 'round tripping'?"

"Because the money went down and back on the same day or in the same week. He thought it was the greatest scam ever."

"Who's firm was it?"

"Cecil's dad. He's the one who came up with the idea. He was a lawyer."

"How did you find out all those things?"

"I just listened," she sighed. "Never did ask a lot of questions."

"So what did you tell Dottie about Cecil and the fourteen million?"

"Not much."

"She just charged in here and tied you up?"

"I'm telling you, that woman is possessed."

"Want me to call the police?" I asked her. "You could file a report and press charges."

"No, no, that's okay. I don't want anything to do with her or the police. They'll just stir up trouble."

I shrugged my shoulders. There really wasn't much else I could do for her.

Jenna skated from the kitchen to the living room and sat down on the leather sofa. Her cat hopped on the couch, too, and together they seemed to be having an unanticipated rendezvous. "Come here, Coochie," Jenna purred.

What a cute name for a cat whose owner was a stripper.

"I should tell you one more thing about Cecil's dad," Jenna said, almost under her breath.

"What's that?"

"He died about ten years ago."

"Who's been doing the firm's dirty work?"

"Cecil's mom. They believed in keeping it all in the family."

Forty-One

Saying goodbye to Jenna took a lot longer than I had hoped. She wanted to meet Jacque and take him for a walk around the property, which we did. It gave him the chance to hose down some unfamiliar shrubbery and make feint charges at the complex's fox squirrels and rabbits. I felt a little weird, hanging out with an upscale prostitute, but at the end of the day, she was a really nice person who made her living just like everybody else: from the gifts she was born with. There's nothing wrong with that.

Until that morning, our conversations had always been more of an inquiry than anything else. I was the one to ask her questions and she did the answering. As we walked along the trails outside her apartment, Jenna turned the tables on me.

She was the one who was asking questions about the case.

I didn't mind answering. It helped sort all the facts.

There was plenty to go over. The most pressing issue at the moment was where Dottie was headed next. I asked.

"She never told me," Jenna said. "Where do you think?"

I expressed my thoughts: to her home in Charlevoix, to the

newspaper, to work at the bar, to Mr. Heanley's boat on Beaver Island.

"I love Beaver Island," she perked. "Take me with you. I don't have anything going on until Thursday night."

"No way. Might be dangerous."

"Sounds exciting. Come on. I've got a reason to track her down, too, you know. She has my last night's tips, not to mention your laptop."

"How did she get your tips?"

"I left 'em on the kitchen counter when I walked in the apartment. They were gone when you rescued me."

"Listen, I fly solo when it comes to these things. When I track down Dottie, I'll get your money back. How much was it?"

"About three hundred."

"You got it."

When we returned to the parking lot, I gave her a hug goodbye. We had a harmless little friendship brewing.

"Good luck," she said. "Maybe I'll see you up there."

I laughed, nervously. She was bluffing.

Jacque jumped in the back seat, and I removed his leash. Less than an hour later, we had cruised up the Lake Michigan coastline to the sheriff's office in downtown Charlevoix. The woman behind the counter with the crooked neck and half-moon eyeglasses wouldn't say where the sheriff was, nor would she release the police report on the Garl matter. For two or three seconds, I wondered if I had a dishonest face, or if she was trained to protect one of her own from the whims of an out-of-towner. I was striking out.

A deputy with short, black hair and fading acne was sitting inside his idling patrol car, sorting out the stacks of traffic citations he had written. When I asked him where I might find Sheriff Jackson, he shrugged his shoulders and said that he didn't know. He was just as evasive when it came to my questions about Dorothy Kalakay.

From there, I went back to the Town House Bar. The front door was locked, and I assumed that it didn't open until at least four. The lights inside were off, so I went around to the back door with hopes of catching the owner, or a manager, in their office.

What I found was the beer delivery person, who had a key to the walk-in refrigerator. Even though he was hustling cases of suds inside the cooler, he still had time to deny knowing anything about the bartender, Dottie, or her work schedule.

Frustrated, I walked down to the harbor and looked for Shafeek Heanley's boat. The *Fortitude* wasn't in its spot, but rather, a sailboat at least fifty feet long.

I was starting to run out of options as to where Dottie might be. The treasurer's office inside the county building gave me her home address, and someone on the parking enforcement team gave me directions on how to get there.

Her house wasn't that far out of town. It was a mile or two down a gravel road that was lined with hardwoods and the occasional balsam. When I made the right turn onto her driveway, I couldn't help but think she must not have trimmed the brush in months, maybe years. A UPS truck would have a hard time plowing through the understory. A thin strip of meager grass had grown between the tracks, and there was enough gravel to disguise any tire tracks. If Dottie had been there recently, I certainly couldn't tell.

No sign of her Subaru. No hint of a barking dog, a cat in the window, or a notice from the police taped to the front of her door. I checked her mailbox, which had eight or ten pieces of mail inside. The postmark on her electric bill was from three days previous. A statement from her car insurance carrier was postmarked the day before. The other items inside were fliers and mass mail that had no relevance.

The vacant house, a quiet setting, and an unsolved mystery felt like the calm before the storm.

Instead of waiting around for Dottie to show up, I called the newspaper to see if she was at work today. She wasn't. They didn't even know what her work schedule was, but mentioned that I wasn't the first person to ask.

The longer I thought about where Dottie might have been, the more I realized that she must have been on Beaver Island. I called the harbor master and asked if the *Fortitude* was still there.

It was.

I've followed a lot of hunches in my day. Some of them paid off; a lot of them didn't. Going to Beaver Island seemed like a winner. The cops surely wouldn't know the name of Shafeek's boat, or have a clue where it was. If it wasn't for Shafeek's wife telling me where the boat was located, I wouldn't have known. Michigan is a big state with lots of water. Even a yacht the size of Shafeek's could be hidden in a variety of ports on either side of Michigan's mitten.

Of course, that left dear Jacque out in the cold. My sidekick had become a ball and chain.

There were plenty of kennels in my phone's version of the yellow pages. Some of them called themselves "doggie spas," which was a step up from the regular kennels where Jacque was accustomed to staying. My pooch needed a place to stay and a bath, too.

A few minutes later, I was at one of the doggie spas on the outskirts of town. It was more like a finished garage, with six-foot wooden fencing. The women who checked Jacque in would never need to know that he was prone to swimming in lakes strewn with goose droppings, eating cow pies when he could, and rolling on the carcasses of dead possums if given the opportunity. All that was important was that he needed a bath, and he might be an overnight guest. Jacque was eager to be taken care of. He hardly looked over his shoulder as the friendly staff led him away.

Half an hour later, I was seated in an eight-passenger airplane, as we roared along the bumpy runway at the Charlevoix Airport. As much as I hated to fly, I despised the notion of getting beat by Dottie. I had a funny feeling that she'd be on Shafeek's boat, and if I had the chance to confront her, it would make my flight to the island worthwhile.

The other passengers on board were mostly quiet as the little plane's wheels finally cleared the runway. I held my breath and tried to have pleasant thoughts as the nose tipped up and the engine responded to the pilot's demands. Almost at once, we were pushed around by the breeze. It was rather scary, but the pilot seemed to take it all in stride. When we cleared the tree line, and everyone else looked at the scenery, my attention turned to the Devil's Elbow and the burned hole in the earth. I kept thinking, thinking, thinking who might have killed the Garl family?

Becky's theories had holes in it.

Everyone's did.

I certainly couldn't prove motive, but neither could the police.

When we were over the heart of Lake Michigan, I glanced north to where the big lake shook hands with the Upper Peninsula. Seemed like a lifetime ago when I spent the night above the general store in Trout Lake, then fished for rainbows in the Carp River. *What was I doing getting involved in a mystery like this?*

Why didn't I listen to Colleen and bail out when I had the chance?

I was no closer to solving the mystery than the professional detectives on the government payroll.

On the descent into the airstrip on Beaver Island, I noticed that the pilot had a tall order in front of him. The airstrip was perpendicular to the wind, which presented a challenging landing. I felt him wrestling with the joystick, the throttle, and the pedals, all in an effort to keep us safe. He kept the nose into the wind, while the air gusts pushed the tail section off line. It wasn't the smoothest of landings, but a few of the passengers appreciated his command of the mechanics. They applauded casually.

After taxiing to the modest block structure that served as a terminal, someone on the tarmac opened the door to the plane and we all piled down the portable steps. A couple of the folks began their reunion as soon as their feet hit the ground. People were hugging and smiling, and urging their loved ones with pleas of "Come on. I've got margarita mix chilling and bratwurst for the grill."

They were laughing and ambling towards the parking lot, a brand new Suburban waiting as if it were a horsedrawn carriage.

Of course, nobody was waiting for me.

It had been forever since I felt the hug of a loved one, the wholesome warmth of a kind greeting. My skin craved affection from the silky goodness of the woman I love.

Someday, I kept thinking to myself, *it'll happen. For now, just keep your mind on the task at hand, and your nose to the wind.*

I caught a bus from the airstrip to downtown.

Upon arrival, I wasn't exactly sure how to tackle the whole Dottie situation. I couldn't just go barging up to her; then again, I couldn't let her get away with murder, either.

The shops along the main street offered plenty of opportunity to change my appearance. A pair of sunglasses and a large, straw hat helped to conceal my identity. I may have looked like a flamboyant cross-dresser, but at least I could hide behind my façade in the event I had to dodge Shafeek Heanley or Dottie.

At almost five o'clock, I made my way down the boardwalk, amongst the boats and seagulls, and the whipping wind that had the halyards thumping mad. The scent of suntan oil and barbecued beef galloped past me, and it made me realize that I hadn't had lunch. Hunger, adrenalin, and the urge to confront Dottie lead me farther and farther down the boardwalk.

There were boats of all sizes in the marina, which wasn't all that large. Shafeek's boat should have stuck out like a sore thumb.

After twenty minutes of searching, I approached the young men tending the gas pumps.

"Yeah, we seen the *Fortitude,*" they said. "It was here about an hour ago. They bought eighty-five gallons."

"Who's they?"

"A man and a woman."

Their description fit Shafeek and Dottie to a tee. When I whipped out my cell phone and showed the young men a picture, they said it was them.

"Did they say where they were going?" I asked.

"No, they didn't," the young men said sheepishly, "and we're not supposed to ask."

Heartbroken, I turned to the sea of freshwater beyond the breakwall. It seemed ruefully ironic that they would escape in a body of water known as Paradise Bay.

I was bumming. The gamble I had taken didn't pay off. Shafeek and Dottie had slipped through my fingers.

Chartering a plane seemed like a viable option at that moment. I'd like to see where they might be headed. The *Fortitude* could be spotted from five hundred feet in the air, no doubt about it.

The car ferry blew its horn, which sent the seagulls into a tizzy. My ride home was pulling away from the dock, thanks to an oversized diesel motor that was billowing black smoke into the bluster. The flight I had taken to the island was the last flight of the day back to the mainland. In other words, I was stuck.

Even though it was the start of the tourist season, I wasn't worried about finding a place to stay. It was a Tuesday in June and a host of mom-and-pop-style motels would have vacancies, I was sure of it.

The first order of business was a bite to eat, and what better place than at the Shamrock Bar, just off Main Street.

I sauntered inside, slipped past the tables, and sat at the bar. The waitress asked me if I wanted a Guinness, which sounded downright tempting.

"No, thanks," I said in the most masculine voice I could muster, "A Shirley Temple and a menu would be great."

"Coming right up," she said, smiling.

The Shamrock was like a lot of other establishments I had been to in the past week. This one, of course, had an Irish theme—complete with shamrocks, four-leaf clovers, and leprechauns.

Just as I pulled out my phone and started fiddling with the keys, I heard a familiar voice, "Well, well, if it isn't my knight in shining armor."

It was Jenna.

I smiled, "At your service."

"I told you, you should have taken me over here," she smirked.

"What the heck are you doing here?" I asked.

"Same thing you're doing: tracking down the murderers."

Jenna had lost her glamorous facade. She wore hardly any makeup. A flannel lumberjack shirt was tied above her navel. Blue jeans. Tennis shoes. An orange baseball cap embroidered with the little polo rider hid most of her hair. The remainder stuck out the back in ponytail fashion.

"When did you get here?" I asked.

"On the ferry," she dodged the question.

"Did you try to find Dottie?"

"Sure did, but I really didn't know where to start. She wasn't on the ferry. I didn't know anything about their boat until it pulled out of the harbor and headed north."

She raised her hand and flagged down the bartender. "I'll have another Absolute 'n tonic, if you get the chance."

The bartender nodded.

"Are you here alone, Derrick?" she asked.

"Yep."

"Why don't you join us? We're sitting right over there."

I looked over my shoulder. Three tables away was the redhead from the strip club. She raised her glass and waved her fingers.

Her proposition was innocent enough. The companionship of two beautiful women sure beat the pants off the electronic distraction of my phone. "That would be great," I said.

"Grab your cocktail. You're gonna love Sheila."

I followed Jenna to the table, and after a few pleasantries with Sheila, the conversation started flowing. Of course, her dancing career was front and center on my mind.

"Aren't you the one who's stage name was Climax?" I asked.

Sheila nodded, "That's me."

"How did you come up with that?"

"That's my hometown; just outside of Kalamazoo," she said wryly. "Not too original, I know."

We chuckled, slightly.

I ordered a whitefish dinner and my companions, appetizers.

"How'd you end up in Traverse City?" I asked.

"I fell in love."

"With the city…"

"A truck driver named Bill."

"Okay."

"That was before my dancing career. Have a son now and the truck driver's hit the road. I had to keep food on the table, so I started dancing."

"You got-a-do, what you got-a-do."

"That's right."

Sheila took a slug of her cocktail. Jenna did, too. I felt like making a toast, "To the great chase."

Our glasses chinked over the salt 'n pepper shakers and the single-sided menus covered in plastic.

"So, what about the boat?" I asked Jenna. "Are you certain it was the *Fortitude* you saw?"

"Yeah, I'm sure. We spoke to the guys at the fuel dock."

"What do you want to do?" I asked.

"What can we do?"

"I don't know," I said with a sigh. "I thought about chartering a plane, but it's probably too late for that."

The waitress brought drinks and the girls' appetizers. "Your fish will be right here," she said with a smile.

I nodded.

"Why don't we charter a boat?" Sheila wondered.

Her idea seemed to capture our attention.

"Think there's a place on the island?" Jenna asked.

"There has to be."

Both dancers pulled out their phones and dove into cyberspace. The waitress brought my plate of whitefish, potatoes, and veggies. It was as pretty as a Pure Michigan ad, and oh-so-apropos since we were in the heart of Lake Michigan.

Eating broiled whitefish isn't like rolling up your sleeves and plowing through a feed of battered perch. Each forkful has to be gently pulled away from the skin. Every bite is a dainty mix of mild flavor and subtle texture. It's like eating edible flower petals.

Jenna and Sheila struck out on the boat rental issue.

A moment later they realized that there was no other way off the island.

Out of the bar's bustling chatter and clinking plates came the most painful of realizations: How do we stop Shafeek and Dottie?

"Can't we just call the police?" Sheila asked.

"Already did that," I said. "I'm sure they've filed warrants already."

"Why don't we call Shafeek and Dottie?" Jenna asked.

"And say what?" I asked.

"I don't know," Jenna frowned.

Sheila piped up: "Tell them that you're from the marina and they forgot to sign the credit card slip."

I nodded. "That's not a bad idea but they probably don't have to sign…"

"What would work?" Sheila asked.

Jenna: "Maybe they left something on the dock?"

"No," I said, "let's say that they got some bad gas and they're supposed to return to port."

Sheila and Jenna both nodded. "That would work."

We let the idea simmer. Their morel and garlic brochette hardened on the plate.

"Are you going to call them on the phone or use a ship-to-shore radio?" Jenna asked.

It was the first time all night that she asked an intelligent question.

My head was swimming in details and possibilities. "We can't really call them on the phone, can we?" I asked. "The two young men at the gas dock wouldn't know Dottie's phone number."

I took the last bite of fish and washed it down with a slug of Shirley Temple.

"Ladies," I said, "we're going to need a diversion to get those two young men out of the gas pump station."

"Why's that?"

"So I can get on the ship-to-shore radio and hail Shafeek and Dottie."

I glanced at Jenna. She had more curves than a racetrack, more charm than a Pandora bracelet. Her compatriot was just as alluring, with her red, white and blue bikini top, brimming with patriotic goodness. They didn't need a brass pole and funky music to capture the attention of the opposite sex; sensuality oozed from their pores.

"Oh, we'll think of something," Sheila said, a devilishly glib smile piercing both cheeks. "We know just how to get them riled up."

Forty-Two

The following morning, I caught the bus from one of the motels downtown to the airport on Beaver Island. The ten-minute flight back to the mainland was as smooth as the lake's surface, which was most comforting.

Jenna and Sheila put on a masterful performance outside the gas pump station the evening before, and Shafeek seemed to buy my story about having to idle into port before blowing up the yacht's motors. I told him I was the owner of the gas distribution company and that I deeply regretted the inconvenience. "I'm terribly sorry to inform you, but we delivered a load of bad gas. It's contaminated with water."

It never hurts to have a battery of accents and bizarre dialects to hide your identity. In this case, I tried to sound like a southern gentleman and said "We will pay for everything: the pump out and the re-fill of eighty-five gallons."

I probably could have talked to Shafeek for ten or fifteen minutes on the ship-to-shore radio with the diversion Jenna and Sheila had concocted. The two of them got into a fake argument, which eventually lead to Jenna pushing Sheila off the boardwalk and into the crystalline waters of the harbor. Jenna, of course, was remorseful a second after it happened and screamed for help from the two young men inside the pump station. They abandoned their post and left the little building high and dry.

One of the young men grabbed a life ring and flung it at Sheila, who struggled to grab hold. When they finally towed her to the ladder, Jenna asked if Sheila might have hypothermia, which was the codeword for her experiencing a grand mal seizure.

It was Jenna's job to make sure the boys didn't call the cops.

It was my job to find out where Shafeek might be going.

Eventually, Shafeek came around: "We'll be in Ludington for the evening."

"Excellent choice," I commended him. "They' have everything you need. I'll be there at noon and we'll pay for it all."

I waited a second or two for Shafeek to change his mind.

He didn't.

The radio was silent until a fisherman out of Petoskey wanted to know if there were any fishing nets in Little Traverse Bay.

When I left the pump station and rushed to help Sheila and Jenna, the two young men looked a little disappointed that they didn't get to perform CPR or mouth-to-mouth resuscitation.

Sheila snapped out of her unconsciousness, and hugged each young man as if they had saved her life.

The boys lapped up the gratitude like a dog to water on a steamy northern Michigan afternoon.

It's not every day that a couple of gorgeous women throw themselves at you.

Jenna couldn't believe that Shafeek and Dottie were headed south, not north.

"Maybe they went north to fake us out," she said, after we returned to the Shamrock.

"Sounds like it worked."

"They might have told you Ludington, but that was just a lie."

"I guess we'll find out soon enough."

Of course the "we" part of that sentence was used loosely. I didn't want Jenna and Sheila to tag along with me. They had no reason to be there. Besides, I was certain they couldn't answer the bell first thing in the morning. They stayed up late and partied. I found a motel and went to bed a little before twelve.

It was just as well that they didn't go to Ludington.

Colleen texted me and said that she and Elizabeth were planning on taking the afternoon ferry from Manitowoc to Ludington.

Her timing was impeccable.

Want to have dinner? I texted her. *I'm headed there now.*

Sounds great.

What about a place to stay? We could watch the sunset and head home in the morning.

After an agonizing ten or fifteen seconds she finally responded, *I'm game if you are.*

It had been quite a while since Colleen was open to doing something fun. It was a welcome prospect because I felt like I had let her down by continuing the chase for the Garl family murderers.

We' have some catching up to do, I typed with a smile. *And it's all good.*

At a little before nine, I picked Jacque up from the spa. His coat was bright and shiny and he pranced around the parking lot of the spa like a miniature Lipizzaner stallion. I was proud of that little dog and the pompous way he carried himself. He knew that he looked good and wasn't afraid to show off.

He jumped in the back seat and together we drove south on 31, along the Lake Michigan coastline. It was the second time in a week that I had made the trip, only this time I did it with the windows down and the music blaring.

In my head, I was already ninety miles south of Traverse City in Ludington. There was more than one marina there and the *Fortitude* could have been in any one of them.

It might have taken a little boot leather to find them, but that was okay. Hustling, scratching and clawing are my cup of tea.

I'd start in the Municipal Marina, which isn't far from the boat launch and the big lake just outside the piers. If I had to bet, Dottie and Shafeek would be there, waiting for the man who sounded like he was from Oklahoma.

When I arrived in Ludington a little before noon, I found a shady spot a block away from the marina. All was quiet in the early part of summer on the gold coast of Michigan. A landscaping crew was tending to the grass along the edge of the concrete, and boat owners were hosing down their crafts from the spigots at the corner of every slip. Purple martins had returned to the North Country and filled the air with their nonsensical babble and whimsical flight paths.

I stood on the hill above the marina and looked down on the labyrinth of boardwalks and watercraft. The *Fortitude* wasn't there, and the harbormaster said it hadn't come ashore last evening.

Back to the Impala I went, and eventually to the east end of Pere Marquette Lake. There were plenty of boats moored in their slips, but not Shafeek's monstrosity.

I was getting a little bummed out.

The third and fourth marinas were filled with pleasure boats and fishing vessels.

Nobody was at the marina offices.

An hour later, reality was starting to sink in. Shafeek had given me the slip.

The Ludington ploy was a desperate move on my part, but I don't regret taking the chance driving all the way down here. Had Dottie and Shafeek been in Ludington, I might have become a hero. Since he didn't take the bait, I had become a zero.

Instead of giving up all hope, I engaged a rather distinguished looking gentleman sipping on an iced tea in the cockpit of his cruiser. A set of downriggers stuck out the stern of the boat, which prompted the most obvious of questions: "How's the fishing?"

He claimed that he had a good spring for brown trout, but the salmon were scattered throughout the big lake. We both surmised that it was a typical season in that regard. After ten minutes of conversation, I asked if I could borrow his ship-to-shore radio. The man bought my story about meeting an old friend who was overdue for a rendezvous. He put his iced tea down and played with the knobs until the radio squelched to life.

"*Fortitude, Fortitude, Fortitude*," I said, as plain as possible, "this is the schooner Colleen calling. Come in *Fortitude*."

No response.

"Do you read me, *Fortitude*?"

The radio was silent. Deathly silent.

"Sounds like your pal made other plans," the fishermen stated.

"I guess so."

Flummoxed, I walked back to the Impala, then drove downtown for a banana split at House of Flavors. It was delicious.

From there, Jacque and I went for a long walk down the north pier. He wasn't real keen on the splashing waves, nor the tail-flopping salmon that had just been caught by a lucky angler. It was fun to let him work off a little pent up aggression, just the same.

I thought about going to the driving range and hitting a bucket of golf balls, or digging out my fly rod and waders from the trunk and doing a little trout fishing on the Pere Marquette River. Instead, I put Jacque back in the car and ambled down

Main Street to do a little shopping. I found a family-owned jewelry store, which had a big poster in the window announcing a sale on watches. After engaging the man behind the counter with a little small talk about the weather, and the perch fishing in Lake Michigan, we got down to business. I wanted to wow Colleen with something glittery. The man had watches of all sorts that ranged in price between twenty-five and five-hundred dollars. I split the difference and settled on a gold plated beauty designed by Coach.

I wasn't quite done shopping. A men's shop several doors down the street had the perfect shirt and tie for me, a prefabricated, black bow tie for Jacque. A soulful family reunion was important to me. Ludington, and the *SS Badger*, held a special spot in my heart. The *Badger* was, after all, the scene of my wedding to Colleen.

It was going to be fun, I just knew it.

For the next half hour, I cruised around Ludington, looking for just the right motel. A heated pool and plenty of coin operated video machines were at the top of my priority list. Elizabeth would want to go for a swim, I was certain of it, and I couldn't wait to drive the streets of Monte Carlo in a simulated driving machine, even if it was with one hand in a cast. Without consulting Colleen, I made reservations at Scotty's restaurant on the outskirts of town. There, the three of us would have a nice meal in a cozy, friendly atmosphere.

Who could resist a block of family time like that?

The ferry was scheduled to arrive in Ludington at five. At a quarter to, I swung by a flower shop and picked up a dozen red roses.

Colleen would be impressed, and Elizabeth would be sure to take notes: this is how you treat a lady.

Was it guilt that had brought this fruit to bear, or was it the loneliness stirring in my heart?

I hadn't been a model husband, but I hadn't strayed, either.

Either way, I was ready to put the week's events behind me and relax with my family if only for an evening.

I made it to the ferry's loading dock just as the big boat slid through the piers. Instead of waiting in my car, Jacque and I ambled through the rope line to where the ship's guests pour out of the giant stern.

I felt a little foolish waiting there with a dozen roses and a birddog wearing a bow tie, but I swallowed my self consciousness and patiently waited for my family to arrive. The scene reminded me of the strangers' reunion at the airport on Beaver Island.

When my girls arrived, I couldn't help but scoop them tightly in the biggest bear hug I could muster. Even Jacque joined the fray, nearly tripping us with his leash.

They both wanted to know what happened to my wrist. I told them that it was a long story that would have to wait until dinner.

"Hope you're hungry," I egged them on. "I made reservations down the street, and you're going to love the place where we'll stay."

Elizabeth was smiling ear to ear. "We got you a surprise, Daddy."

"Oh, boy!" I cried, cheerily. "I love surprises."

It was a bustling scene. Car after car backed out of the ship's bowels to the staging area a couple hundred yards up the driveway. The valets of those cars ran back to the ship to grab another vehicle. There were honking horns, and people pointing at the vehicles zooming past as if it were their luggage at an airport baggage carousel.

Colleen was thankful for the flowers and was quite impressed with the threads I was wearing.

"What can I say, Colleen? This is a special place for me. I married my best friend on the deck of that boat, somewhere between the states of Michigan and Wisconsin."

Forty-Three

The conversation over a perch dinner was all about what had taken place in Wisconsin. There seemed to be a little tension about the family farm and its ultimate disposition. Colleen's family wasn't prone to outbreaks of drama, but this situation seemed to stir the souls of the entire clan.

Of course, Dad's developing dementia wasn't helping matters. Colleen said that Dad kept calling Elizabeth by the wrong name, and that Mom had to hide the car keys. He still liked to drive, but he had become an accident waiting to happen. The police gave him a ticket for going the wrong way on a one-way street. Before that, he went to town for fuel in the pickup but he never made it. Instead, he went forty miles past town, where he eventually ran out of gas. His condition seemed to worsen every day, and it broke everyone's hearts to watch him slide into a state of confused oblivion.

After dinner, we went to the motel, changed into our bathing suits, and headed down to the pool. I poured Colleen a plastic cup of white Zinfandel, on the rocks.

While Elizabeth swam and splashed, Colleen wanted to know what really happened to my wrist.

"It's kind of a long story," I warned her.

"That's okay," she said, sipping her wine, "we have all night."

I really didn't know where to start, because I couldn't remember where we had left off. There were some things I wanted to tell her, and there were a few details that probably should have been deleted. As I hit the rewind button in my head, and panned through the events of the last week, I couldn't help but realize that trying to solve a cold-case murder was a fool's errand.

Of course, Colleen wouldn't remind me of that fact. She did a lot of listening as I waded through the details of the Mathers' indictment.

"I'm kind of surprised that they didn't look into her as a suspect in the Garl murders," she wondered. "Seems like if he was going to testify against her in the criminal proceedings, she might have the motive to have him killed."

I nodded. "There are lots of people who might want him dead. Cecil had two business partners and a money laundering scheme in the Caribbean."

Colleen shook her head.

I kept the story going, "He had a mistress up in Traverse City. A stripper if you can believe that. He paid for her apartment and her new Lexus."

Colleen huffed incredulously. "What about Becky's theory about the Luxton fella?"

I shrugged my shoulders. "It couldn't be proven, and Luxton was murdered."

"Murdered?"

"I saw the body myself. He was shot twice, once in the chest and once in the head.

"That's awful," she frowned, "You mean all this happened while I was gone?"

"Yep, the first six days in June."

"I'm glad you're done with this case."

I smiled.

"You are done, aren't you Derrick?" she asked sternly.

"I think so. This seems like a good place to stop."

"Don't you think that the cops will eventually find out who killed those people?"

"Eventually, yes. Probably," I shrugged my shoulders, "who knows."

"I think you're smart to let the cops do their job."

"What about the reward money from the *Free Press*?"

"Somebody else can get it. We don't need it that bad. I'm just glad you're okay."

We both breathed a sigh, then turned our attention to the pool, where Elizabeth was working on her dead man's float.

"That glass of wine was so good I think I'm going to have another. A warm shower sounds wonderful. Why don't you spend some quality time with your daughter?"

I smiled. "Of course."

In no time at all, I was on the edge of the pool with Elizabeth, giving her pointers as to where she might find buried treasure on the bottom. She didn't realize that the buried treasure came from the coins in my pocket. We were having fun; great fun in a daddy-daughter kind of way.

Twenty minutes later we were giggling and snorting while at the helm of the pinball machines and video games. I kept stuffing the quarters in the machines as if they were going out of style. Elizabeth kept prodding me, "Come on, Daddy, let's play."

I don't know how many dollars worth of quarters I dropped that night, but I knew it was a bunch.

When we made it up to the room, Colleen was already in bed, reading.

"Mommy, Mommy look at the buried treasure we found!" Elizabeth said, extending her palm loaded with coins.

"Oh wow, aren't you lucky," Colleen said, looking over the tops of her reading glasses. "When we get home you'll have to put it in your piggy bank."

Elizabeth smiled, and then suggested it was time for my supplies.

"What supplies?" I asked, somewhat confused.

"Dad…I said 'surprise," not 'supplies.'"

Everyone laughed but me.

Colleen whispered that it was in her suitcase, near the door.

Whatever the surprise was, it fit in a plastic bag. "It's a little early for Father's Day, but that's okay," Elizabeth said.

She handed me the bag, and I pulled out a red sweatshirt, emblazoned with a Wisconsin badger on the front. It was thick and warm and fit like a glove.

"Thank you," I told them both. "I love it. Why don't I check on the dog and leave this in the car."

They both wanted a kiss, so that's what I gave them. It warmed my heart to have those feelings.

I had plenty of feelings at that instant. In my head, I was through with Cecil Garl, Robert Luxton, Shafeek Heanley, and the mess with Drake Media, Ener-X, and the Fatima Society. The ghosts of lover's past almost came back to bite me when Dottie promised a tempting, yet naughty glimmer into what might have been. I enjoyed my time with Jenna, even though she had an aloof, independent personality.

As I passed the front desk of the motel and wandered through the parking lot, I thought about VanWyk and Nutting, and where they might have been at that very instant. Were they interrogating Dottie and Shafeek, or was the *Fortitude* still missing? For a half second, I pictured Dottie and Shafeek anchored behind some rocky peninsula in the Les Cheneaux Islands, east of the Mackinac Bridge. Then again, they could have gone west into Wisconsin waters or north to the Upper Peninsula. Maybe they were having a last supper together in the

Fortitude's galley, or had already abandoned ship. It wouldn't be the first time that someone had discarded their boat in a Great Lake and faked their disappearance.

Outside the front entryway to the motel, the air was heavy with the fragrant aroma of lilacs. Early June is such a wonderful time to be in Michigan. Northern Michigan is my favorite place in the world.

Good old Jacque was waiting for me in the backseat of the car. Instead of letting him out and risking tiny white hairs on my brand new sweatshirt, I decided to throw the bag in the trunk.

The Impala's lights blinked twice and I heard the trunk's lock pop.

In the warm, muggy air—pursed with the light of a small city on the edge of a huge lake—I lifted the trunk and couldn't believe what I saw.

Or what I smelled.

It was an immediate reminder that this Garl matter was far from over. The cast of characters would haunt me for months and months to come.

All the fun we were having would go for naught. All the joy in my life had been squashed in one horrific, grisly image.

In the midst of the golf clubs and putters, fishing rods, waders and my vest stuffed with insect repellent and tippet, was the body of Robert Luxton.

The vision, the sight, the putrid smell nearly took my breath away.

I found myself backing away, as if Luxton was some sort of zombie and at any second he might pop out of the trunk, wielding a five iron.

"What the hell," I yelled to myself. "This is sick!"

I looked to the surroundings. Sprinklers cast a rainy pall on the setting. Cars and trucks were sleeping, peacefully in the parking lot. There wasn't a soul in sight.

The longer the trunk stayed open, the more the smell escaped. It would draw attention, I was sure of it.

After fifteen or twenty seconds, the initial shock was beginning to wear off.

I had to come up with a plan.

Think fast, I thought to myself.

As much as my heart was banging holes through my chest, I knew that I couldn't go back to the room and get a good night's sleep. The whole time I'd be thinking about the rotting corpse in my trunk.

Damn that Dottie! She's the one who left the body in my trunk!

Jacque started barking, *let me out! Let me out!*

I slammed the trunk shut, tossed the sweatshirt on the front seat, and let Jacque out of the back.

As he trotted to the rear of the parking lot, and began his search for the men's room amongst the flower beds and shrubbery, I weighed my options carefully. There were acres and acres of state land east of Ludington and most of it was interspersed with trails cut through the forest. If my Impala could handle the paths cut through the bush north of Newberry, it could certainly handle the two tracks south of the Mackinac Bridge.

Meijer in Ludington sold shovels and pick axes. It wouldn't take that long to dig a grave in the sandy earth and bury Luxton amongst the scrub oak and sweet fern.

That was a dumb idea.

A better idea was to drive back to Charlevoix and dump the body on Dottie's front porch.

That was an even dumber idea.

I could buy a lock cutter from the hardware store, snip the cables to the storage facility's camera system, and break into Becky's storage locker in Bay City. The cops would discover Luxton's body eventually and they'd find him exactly where I did.

The cops had to get involved.

This case was way over my head, way out of my league.

I probably made the situation worse, not better, when I became involved.

Instead of putting Jacque back in the car, I pulled off my leather belt and turned it into a leash. Together, we walked back to the Impala, where I grabbed Colleen's watch, still in its fancy box. Jacque and I scampered up the back stairs of the motel, found our room, and stepped inside.

Elizabeth and Colleen were both reading books, in their own queen bed. It was a quiet setting until Jacque jumped on Elizabeth's bed and nosed his way under the covers. She yelped in delight.

While my daughter and dog continued their happy reunion, I sat on the edge of Colleen's bed and put my hand on her shoulder.

"I have a supplies for you, too," I said with a sarcastic wink.

"What's that, Derrick?" she asked, just as sarcastically, "a hearing aid."

I placed the watch box between the pages of her open book. She smiled wonderfully, and said that I shouldn't have done it.

"I know," I said, blushing. "You mean the world to me, and I wanted to give you something special."

Maybe I felt guilty for walking the tightrope of infidelity.

She untied the bow and opened the case. The gold and sparkle hit her right between the eyes. She fussed with delight. "I love it. Thank you."

"You're welcome, Colleen. I've had a lot of great memories of Ludington."

"Why the gift?"

"I don't know. I just wanted to make sure you know that I haven't quit loving you."

"That's nice." She put the watch on her wrist and held it up to the lamp light. It twinkled and sparkled so much that it caught Elizabeth's attention.

"That's pretty, Mom" she said.

"Colleen," I asked sincerely, "can I ask you a favor?"

"Sure, what is it?"

"Can you take Jacque home with you?"

"Of course…when?"

"When you leave tomorrow."

Colleen hesitated. "Sure…I guess. Why can't you?" she asked, somewhat confused.

In the quietness of that family setting, my hand cupped the side of her face. Without an ounce of remorse, I looked her in the eye and said, "I gotta run."